Praise for **DOUG RICHARDSON**'s
previous novel

DARK HORSE

"Ingeniously plotted . . . riveting and crisp . . .
impossible to put down . . .
a pedal-to-the-metal thriller."

Steve Martini

"An edge-of-the-seat novel that is both
realistic and compelling."

Houston Tribune

"Doug Richardson gives us two of the great
things a storyteller has to offer: a compelling
glimpse into the conflicted human soul and a
heroic, two-fisted nail-biter of a thriller."

Detroit News

"Terrifying . . . a riveting tale."

Booklist

"Top-notch."

Fort Worth Star-Telegram

"Imagine Stephen King collaborating with
Bob Woodward, and the result might be *Dark Horse*."

St. Louis Post-Dispatch

Also by Doug Richardson

DARK HORSE

DOUG RICHARDSON

TRUE
BELIEVERS

HarperTorch
An Imprint of HarperCollinsPublishers

❦

HARPERTORCH
An Imprint of HarperCollins *Publishers*
10 East 53rd Street
New York, New York 10022-5299

Copyright © 1999 by Doug Richardson
Cover illustration by Hal Just
ISBN: 0-380-78771-7

First HarperTorch paperback printing: December 2000
First Avon Books hardcover printing: June 1999

HarperCollins ®, HarperTorch™, and ❦™ are trademarks of HarperCollins Publishers Inc.

Printed in the United States of America

Visit HarperTorch on the World Wide Web at www.harpercollins.com

10 9 8 7 6 5 4 3 2 1

for Henry

Acknowledgments

Special thanks to those whose assistance and counsel are so valuable and welcome: Lou Aronica, Martha David, Carrie Feron, Robert Gottlieb, Dennis Harmon, Alisa Herring, L.S. Kim, Mary Loving, Laurie Paredes, Karen Richardson, and Lauren Sheftel.

PART | ONE

Ten Years Ago

"Oh, Jesus!" she cried. "I'm alive!"

Isadora wanted to be dead. Like all the others, she'd expected to be sleeping in the sweet afterglow. But she'd screwed up. She must've. But how? Sorting through the buzzing in her head, she hadn't a screaming notion. The narcotic mixture hadn't yet worn itself out. It left her half-paralyzed, in the same fetal shape in which she'd chosen to end her broken life.

No, Izzy. You aren't dreaming.

Heaven couldn't look like this. Izzy's eyes flickered open to a disturbing vision. It was daylight still. Sometime after five. Four stories up, the late afternoon sun busted through the hanging dust of the abandoned movie soundstage. Thirdhand mattresses had long ago been tacked to the walls for cheap soundproofing. Forty feet high of used Orthos, Sealy Posturepedics, and Simmons Beautyrests. The mattresses were riveted and rippled, torn and bleeding stuffing of yellowed feathers and polyurethane foam. The dying sun cast the mattresses in yellows and oranges, an unearthly texture. The gargantuan space resembled a massive padded cell more than a former movie soundstage.

Before Izzy lay all her brothers and sisters. A hundred dead. She knew because she'd counted. Her eyes scanned madly, clicking off the bodies and adding the numbers. Each one lay on a cardboard mat, naked and dead, just as she should have been. But the peaceful sea of death had been broken by a single ripple. *Izzy was alive*. And though her body remained nearly as fixed as the dead, her mind was cramping with questions. Why me? All the mixtures were the same, albeit a bit more narcotic was added for the men. Two parts Seconal, one part barbital, ten milligrams of Valium, a quarter-cup of strawberry-flavored Jell-O, and a tablespoon of sour cream. That was the recipe. She'd happily taken hers with all the others.

But I'm alive! God, no, I'm alive!

She reasoned it must've been all the drugs. It had to be. A lifetime of experimentation had bolstered her tightly muscled body into a narcotic-resistant vessel, immune to some of the hardest dope cocktails. She'd always been able to out-drink, out-snort, and out-shoot the men in her life. All but her beloved Dean. And now *he* was dead and gone with the rest of them.

A shudder of loneliness overcame Izzy. She lay there, motionless, eyes shutting out the horror that lay before her. They'd left without her. Brothers and sisters. Left their bodies, left the earth, and crossed over into the mysteriously wonderful beyond. The ultimate trip. The afterglow.

Fuck!

"Fuck!" retched a voice. A man's voice, sounding more like a guttural howl than a curse at the heavens. There was no echo. The sound waves shattered and died when they crashed into the mattresses. Once again, Izzy's eyes burst open, scanning the room for her brother. Any brother. The one who cried out. Yet she saw nothing. Just death. A mass of bodies lying in their final state. Then she heard sobbing. A woman's cry. A sister, somewhere to her right. Slowly, Izzy pushed herself up onto her hands, arched her back, and scanned the dead for some kind of movement. Something to tell her the drugs weren't playing tricks. Otherwise, it could just be a dream. The feared shitty ride that might come before death.

"I'm alive!" she called out. Her voice ached before being sucked into the mattress fiber. "I'm awake!"

"So am I," said a sister. Izzy recognized the sound of little Starr. But where was she? Where had she laid herself down to die?

More sobs rose up from among the dead. Some bitter. Others doleful. Far across the space, Izzy saw Clem sitting up and rubbing his face. Then Sheila. And Markus. Izzy struggled, found her feet, at once happy that she was not alone, yet afraid that she'd made some terrible, horrible mistake.

She shouted at the heavens as if looking for an answer, "I'M ALIVE!"

"Yes, you are. Arise and come sit at my feet," said a voice in soft and familiar phrasing. Izzy wheeled and saw him, his translucent, unblemished skin glowing. Pale, thin, and naked but for a bedsheet wrapped about his waist, the familiar blue tattoo of a medieval sword stretching like an inverted crucifix from his navel to the top of his breastbone. His arms beckoned wide, spread open with an alien grace.

Come to me.

Dean stood at the rail just outside the upstairs offices. The abandoned loft. That's where Dean slept. And that's where he'd chosen to die. She'd watched him herself. He was the first to have swallowed the poison. After which he had demonstrated to the others how they were to lie down and wait for death to come and sweep their souls away. Izzy had cried tears of joy at his bravery. Then, as per his wishes, passed out Baskin-Robbins cups filled with the magic Jell-O to the others. Each waxed container was indelibly marked with a name. That was Dean's idea. His final, most personal gift to his family.

"Come," he repeated to the resurrected.

Twelve naked bodies rose from the dead. Empty souls, ready to be fitted with a new message. One by one, they climbed. As Dean embraced each one, he recalled the shattered people that they once were.

First was the slight and gentle Starr with her flaming red hair and sugar-green eyes. Used, abused, and cut off from her family, she'd turned her first trick at fourteen.

Clem, with his dead-blue eyes, rotting teeth, and bleached dreadlocks, had suffered through more foster families than there were eggs in a carton.

And Sheila, always regal inside her Latina-brown skin. And Madison, another prostitute he'd served up then later saved from the street. There were the twins, Timothy and Jack, heads always shaved to a domed shine; they were the unwanted children of a long-past incestuous liaison. Then came Asia, and Markus with his permanently retarded grin and bulging gray eyes. Arletta and Kris and Jane.

Finally, there was Izzy. The youngest of them all. Barely nineteen with straw hair and the face of an angel. Her wings had been broken since birth. Fatherless, motherless, and fending for herself in a traveling carny brigade that landed one weekend in Pasadena. Izzy had run off to Hollywood and somehow found her way directly into Dean's growing covenant. She was the very last up the stairs, still sobbing. She was oh-so-very-special to him. And Dean kissed her tears.

"Be happy," he said. "For your new life has dawned."

"But the others," she said, pointing her chin back over her shoulder at all the frozen bodies below.

"They weren't chosen," he said. "But *you* were. Now come. Hear what I have dreamed. Can you do that, my child?"

Yes, she nodded. He took her into his arms and held her for what seemed like forever.

The abandoned office was merely an upstairs loft floored with cracked linoleum. Chairs stacked against the wall were unfolded and arranged in a semi-circle. The half-wakened twelve shook off their goose bumps and obediently sat.

"We died. You. Me. All of us," said Dean, with a balletic gesture to the dead that lay below. "And now we have been reborn. We are new souls, returned to do the work the others could not."

They all listened, semi-doped and transfixed by their master.

"God foretold to me who I am, who you are, and what is to happen. The Quickening has begun and we have been resurrected to make way for the end. The human pollution that have poisoned the universe are to be returned to the dust from which they came. Blooded without mercy."

Blooded? Izzy looked at Clem. He was staring dead ahead, eyes locked on Dean.

"God said that for the death of our brethren I am to be tried in an earthly court, found guilty, and then sacrificed to the state."

"No!" cried Izzy. "Not again!"

"I am already dead, my love," said Dean. "And so are you. You've been resurrected to *begin* the work. The end is upon us. And you are the messengers." His eyes squeezed shut as if in sudden pain. "One of you will betray me."

It was as if an electrical charge was set off within each of the twelve. Who would it be? Who *could* it be? Dean's disciples rumbled with disbelief. The biblical parallel of it all.

And with that, Wesley Dean Theroux stood, straightened, his arms held waist high, his palms facing forward and bleeding from fresh razor cuts. Blood spilled onto the floor.

"We came together in *abstinence* and *heavenly love* and as a *family*," said Dean. "And we left this world as one. So we must stop trying to remember who we were. Those are the thoughts of the dead. We must live on with a new purpose."

"But what is our purpose?" asked Starr. Her eyes were black, smeared with tear-streaked mascara.

"Our purpose? We are the chosen. We are to usher in the apocalypse. Put the world as we know it out of its misery. And with every ounce of blood you spill in *my* name, the message will spread that much further. God is angry. God wants his experiment on earth to end. And God wants a martyr. I am the beast to carry that burden. And yours is the privilege of delivering his final wrath."

"You spoke to God?" asked Clem, rubbing at his stubbled face.

"God *spoke* to me," said Dean.

"And he wants us to kill?"

"Yes," said Dean.

"Who and when?"

"You will find out soon enough," said Dean. "Remember. We are all *new* souls. But our hearts are as old as mankind itself. God will tell us who is to live and who is to die. All we need to do is look. With our eyes. With our heads and hearts. You will know what to do. Of that, I promise. Just look. And then act swiftly. Look to me. For I am *always* guiding you."

"Why?" cried Izzy. She didn't understand. She was alive. But her soul was dead? A new one, installed like a transistor in a radio? One that would kill for him?

"YOURS IS NOT TO ASK WHY!" boomed Dean. "YOURS IS TO DELIVER MY MESSAGE!"

1

Present Day

The pregnancy test was negative.

It was one of those do-it-yourself kits found in a small cardboard box, strategically placed in the supermarket aisle between the tampons and condoms. Totally disposable. Pee on the plastic stick, wait three minutes, and see if the dot turns blue.

For Gwen, those three minutes might as well have been three hours. She'd been late again that September. And with the lateness came hope. And with the hope came a prayer and another failed pregnancy test. Her cycle was a viscous beast. Hard to pin down. And unlike the woman herself, never on time.

If only the harsh feelings had been disposable, too.

Gwen sat on the toilet seat in the master bathroom for a good ten minutes, surrounded by the beauty of antique-glazed tiles and imported porcelain installed at the turn of the century, but stared only at that damn plastic stick. *Willing* it to turn blue. Then finally cursing it for remaining the same, negative white. Tears followed the brief rage. But they always did, cracking the cool and savvy veneer Gwen had cultivated for over the last twenty years.

Gwen Corbett-Sullivan. A name with a ring and a sterling reputation. Good breeding, her father used to say, was in the heart and not the wallet. But Daddy'd never said good breeding hurt so damn much.

She dumped the failed test into a wastebasket under the sink. The aging housekeeper, Geneva, would see to it that it was emptied by the time she returned from her office. So by bedtime, Gwen would wipe away the day's makeup and lipstick with a sterile cotton ball and toss it into an *empty* receptacle, cleansed of any reminder from that horrid morning.

Such had been the ritual for nearly three years now. Every month, when she'd take that test only to find no blue dot or plus sign or double vertical lines developing in that damned little window, it killed her that much more. She'd sit in the bathroom and cry, eventually showering off the feelings that she was defective in a hot spray, dress in something crisply Armani, touch up her delicate face with a little blush and powder, stuff the leftover emotions in her empty womb, and head off to the office.

With her maternal duty complete for another twenty-eight days, happiness would have to wait. Fulfillment, somewhere down the road. She speed-dialed her husband's private line in Washington D.C. from her Ford Explorer. After it rang three times, she was certain she'd get shuttled off to voice mail. Instead, Will Sullivan picked up.

"This is Will," he answered.

"It's me," said Gwen. Her voice was slightly choked, but she covered it well. "Betcha thought it was Sully."

"When it rang, yeah," said Will. "But then I heard it was a car phone—"

"Dead giveaway."

"Where are you?"

"Just pulling out of the driveway. The leaves are turning. You should see 'em."

"I'll be up for the weekend, so save some for me."

"I'll see what I can do. But me and Mother Nature haven't exactly been getting along."

Will knew what she meant. On first hearing her voice he

had thought he'd get back to her once she reached her office. He was already behind with his daily staff meeting. But another negative pregnancy test was a priority. "I'm sorry."

There was a dull moment of cellular static between the couple. The tension was real. Then Will, always with the solution, served up some encouragement. "So we go back to Dallas. You give me the date, I'll book that old suite at the Melrose."

"I'd rather not talk about it," she said, her voice cracking. Or was it the cellular? "Not now. So . . . I saw you on *Nightline*."

"What'd you think?"

Her voice was bolstered by the change in subject. "I thought you were really strong on the committee's overall goals. But I don't think Koppel believed you when you said that Justice was on board with the committee's investigation."

"He asked and I answered," he said a bit tersely. Practically his entire key staff was in his office, eyes on him, waiting for the personal call to come to a close. "I'll let the Ladies Justice speak for themselves. They had the opportunity to go on air with me and they bugged out at the last minute."

Both the attorney general, Margie Van Hough, and her right arm, FBI Director Lois Freehold, had been engaged in a proprietary war against Will Sullivan and his committee hell-bent on oversight of the scandal-ridden Food and Drug Administration. In twenty-four hours, at 2 P.M. Eastern time, Will would chair the first round of live televised hearings, embarking on what was certain to be a trophied moment in his young career. In Will's opinion, the FBI had bungled *their* two-year investigation of the FDA, leaving the agency ripe for the political picking.

"I can't believe they put on that prick of a shill Bob Jamison instead," said Gwen. "And I really think you let him off the hook when it came to all that money he took from the drug companies."

"Purely tactical. I need him on my side for SB245."

"Was that a spot decision or did someone twist your arm?"

"No arm-twisting. Koppel clued me to the questions during the break, so I made the deal with Jamison right there in the studio. If I choose, I can come back and hammer him anytime I want if he doesn't go my way when it comes to the floor vote."

"That's fine and dandy, sweetie. But what works on the Hill doesn't necessarily work for TV," she reminded him, sounding every bit as patronizing as she could muster. "Ma and Pa America don't know your deals from their local Wal-Mart. You get hit, you hit back. Nobody gets off the hook unless they deserve it." He was *her* husband, *her* partner, and *her* political prodigy. And hell if she'd ever let him forget it.

Will switched back to the subject of progeny in an attempt to close out the conversation. "I'm thinking the sooner the better, hon. I say we pick ourselves up and get back into the saddle, so to speak."

"I'm the horse, remember?" said Gwen. "I need to be the one to say when I get back in the stirrups."

Will knew to dump the subject. She'd rebound in her own quick time. "Okay, fine. What else?"

"I can tell you're in a crew call," said Gwen.

"What was your first hint?" he asked. "My precious staff get so little of me as it is." With that, Will gave a wink to his silent clan, spread out on the chairs and the sofa while the boss held court from behind his desk.

Gwen could picture them. Levinthal, Will's legislative director. Sandra Corwin, director of communications. Four ferrets—Gwen's description of either legislative assistants or legislative correspondents. Two different jobs, but both requiring the same masochistic attributes of youth, character, and an unmitigated willingness to stay up the ass of an issue.

"Give my regards to La Roy. I'll betcha he's on the sofa, boots on the coffee table, halfway through something called Samoan java."

Will Sullivan let his gaze swivel across his Senate office

to his chief of staff, Wild Bill La Roy. Half-Seminole Indian, half-Haitian, and one hundred percent American, whose dress de rigueur was pressed jeans and a white, open-collared shirt hugging a small potbelly bulging over a silver rodeo belt buckle. Then there were those trademark lizard-skin cowboy boots—La Roy was rumored to carry a small, semiauto handgun inside the right boot. If asked, he would always grin and deny that he ever packed heat. La Roy's look was capped off by a gold Rolex and a thin platinum neck chain, all in stark contrast to the darkest, most chocolate-brown skin a black man had ever been blessed with.

"She's got your number, Bill," Will said to La Roy.

"Tell the Boston Ballbuster that one, she's making *my* meeting go way too fuckin' long," answered La Roy. "And two, that if she keeps you on the phone any longer, a black man's gonna start making policy in the name of her husband's lily-white uppity fuckin' state."

Gwen heard La Roy over the car speaker. "Okay, you gotta go. So do I."

They said their good-byes and Will hung up, catching a wide grin from La Roy and a line that drew titters from the crew. "What, y'all forget to say 'I love you'?"

"After twelve years, we don't need to say it," said Will, returning to the docket. He had to hurry up and cut through the chaff of the daily legislative agenda so he could get on with the ten-minute underground walk over to the Dirksen Building for his last and final prep-day before the FDA hearings. Tomorrow was his big show. And the star wasn't about to go on without a full dress rehearsal.

"Earnest is as Earnest says. Is that it?" teased La Roy, hooking Will simply for the sheer amusement of the staff. He loved calling Will by his own pet nickname, *Earnest*. It came from Will's uncanny ability to stare a constituent in the eye and, no matter how great the gulf between them, or how deep the bullshit, seem just that. Earnest in every way. As for the marriage part? La Roy had seen better. He'd also seen worse. Two of them his own.

"Wasting my time," said La Roy. "Let's move."

"Wasting *your* time?" mocked the senator. "Okay. Moving on. Who's chasing the Speaker on the proposed AFDC cutbacks?"

"I'm on it, Senator," said one of the ferrets, seemingly out of breath before she'd gotten her first words out.

"You're not *on* it," barked La Roy. "You *own* it. The job's about accountability, kiddo."

Will's Amtel beeped with a scrolling message:

COMMITTEE READY FOR YOU IN TEN.

Will double-checked the Amtel against his watch. "Finish up without me." He let his arms stretch out over an oak desk formerly belonging to Huey Long, then shook them as if he was an Olympic swimmer about to dive head-first into a piranha-infested two-hundred-meter medley. He stood, swung on his off-the-rack, navy, forty-two regular—the same exact size he'd worn since graduating prep school—and stepped into a private bathroom to check his hair and tie.

With a simple thumb-gesture La Roy successfully shooed out the rest of the staff, half of whom never got to their own agendas, dockets, or questions.

"I betcha Mrs. Sullivan's got you a closet fulla Italian threads back up in you-know-where."

"In my uppity house in my uppity state?" asked Will.

"Versace?"

"I might have had a couple."

"But would you ever wear one?"

"Let's just say I mothballed the fleet at the same time I sold the Porsche." The flashy car, the suits, the attitude—all gone when Will finished the booze.

La Roy smiled. Will Sullivan was hardly a man of the people, but boy, he was sure trying. Will was convinced that's what had got him elected to the House, then four years later, the U.S. Senate. Man-of-the-people talk. Man-of-the-people walk. That, and he was the first politician to come out of an alcoholic's closet on TV. Fox's popular *Overnight with Buddy Prince*. On the nationally syndicated program, the reformed boozer made the kind of statement reserved only for Alcoholics Anonymous meetings:

My name is Will Sullivan, and I am an alcoholic.

Will had ridden his public sobriety wave into office with help from his friend and sponsor, Bill La Roy, a wife who believed in him, and a couple of well-fitting department-store suits.

"You know Versace wasn't really killed by that spree-killer-guy?" said La Roy. "I read it was the Italian mob. He was up to his eyelashes in their confederate cash, but wasn't paying the vig."

The Amtel beeped again.

LUNCH?

Leaning over his desk, Will punched up a one-key, pre-programmed response.

COME IN, PLEASE.

Exactly three seconds later, that oft-polished plank of a door opened and shut. Myriam stood on her mark, just inside the threshold, medium-sized, medium-aged, medium looks, with medium-brown hair. And that's just the way she liked it. Anonymous and totally accommodating. Just what a U.S. senator needed in a personal secretary.

"I've got you down for Ray Hensel with the Lobby Reform Institute. Billy's Green Room, one-thirty."

"Move him," said Will. "See what he has next month. Cocktails. And make sure it's pushed up against some kind of sit-down, black-tie event so I have an excuse to leave early."

"See what I can do. And in his stead?"

"I'm taking Senator Akira to lunch. Let his office pick. Just as long as it's not that far off campus."

"What if he wants the CDR?"

The Congressional Dining Room. Will was actually fond of the in-house eatery. But only for breakfast. At the beginning of a new session, he'd regularly show up early, just when the doors opened. There he'd always find a freshman congressman or youngish senator. He'd invite himself to sit, he'd shake their hand, then respectfully introduce himself as if they'd never met, setting himself up to have his own ear bent. "Give 'em a platform and let 'em talk," ol' Sully used to say. "Politics is a pair of good ears and never fogettin' to fix them potholes."

That was from back when Will used to listen to his father.

La Roy had a different take on it. Politics is power. Power is addictive. And recovering alcoholics *need* a vice. Most end up as chain-smokers. Will quit smoking the same day he quit booze. La Roy, himself a former fall-down drunkard, hooked up with hourly doses of gourmet coffee, single white women, and conspiracy theories—the more outlandish the better.

"Akira won't want the CDR," said Will. "My esteemed cochair from Hawaii wants to grind me one last time before tomorrow. He won't want to shake that many hands while he's trying to sell me softballs. Where's Allison?"

"On her way," Myriam said, straightening out Will's tie. "In her case, probably at a dead run."

"And don't you like to see them young white things on the move?" said La Roy in a not-so-subtle attempt at getting under Myriam's leathery skin.

Myriam fired him an ugly sideways glare. The man reeked of impropriety and, in her opinion, did not belong in the building, let alone the office of a United States senator. She'd made a deal with Will that over her resignation would she take an order or instruction from Bill La Roy.

In her lime-green Hush Puppies, Allison Flannery skidded around a marbled corner, meeting up with Will and La Roy just before the doors of the Russell Building's private elevator closed. She was twenty-five, freckled from head to toe, with a frizz of radiant red hair. Flushed and panting from sprinting down the entire length of Pennsylvania Avenue, she swung off her backpack and shucked her mohair sweater. The backpack contained so many files it shook the elevator when she dumped it onto the floor.

Allison looked right at La Roy and made sure she used his standard. "I *own* this speech."

"Good girl," he said proudly. The smart ones learned fast. Allison was displaying promise.

"You showed it to Bregman?" asked Will, referring to the White House's unofficial liaison to the FDA hearings.

"Showed it to him," she said. "And I swear, sir, as I'm standing right here, Bregman walked me across the street and straight into the Oval Office."

Without missing a beat, La Roy turned instantly abrasive. "That sorry Southern sack of shit! He's worse than a barn-yard dog!"

"Bregman?" asked a stunned Allison.

"Not Bregman," riffed La Roy. "The president. Did he ask you to do the Dance of the Seven Fucking Veils?"

Allison was lost, shocked, and too mystified to respond. That, and she was locked in La Roy's surly gaze. Will cut in, righting the subject. "You showed the speech to the president?"

"Actually, sir," said Allison, regaining focus, "it was more in the manner of performance art."

"Ah-hah!" shouted La Roy.

Will ignored La Roy and allowed his interest to pique. He'd known for some time that the White House had an acute eye on him. And hell if he didn't like basking in the glow of the presidency.

"Did he give you any notes?" asked Will.

"Other than ask me to read it again?" Allison shook her head and sneaked a glance at La Roy, who was rolling his eyes. Allison was such a muffin. Will could see La Roy cat-aloguing every drop of her young sweat into his sub-sexual cortex. Just as President Addison most likely had.

"Well done. Leave the speech with Myriam and she'll set aside thirty minutes this afternoon for us to lock it." Will gave Allison a confident wink. His opening speech was the first big piece that Allison had outlined, run down the dog on, and *owned*. Finally, Will had given her an hour of dic-tated notes and the go-ahead to write the all-important opener. Eleven drafts, twenty hours of lost sleep, and six pints of Rum Raisin later, she'd delivered a spirited little masterpiece.

They'd been walking the connecting tunnel between the Russell and Dirksen Buildings, when La Roy made a scheduled pit stop into the nearest men's room. Will had a mind to join him, when Allison tugged at his arm.

"Senator? I don't mean to be a bother. But I have to ask. I don't think Mr. La Roy likes me very much."

Will read the pain on her face. La Roy was her superior—and a man who sometimes appeared out of control.

"It's an act," said Will.

"Excuse me, Senator?"

"All the bluster. Bill La Roy's a puppy dog in wolf's clothing. That, and he doesn't care much for our commander in chief. It's a Florida thing."

"The president and Mr. La Roy?"

"They go way back," said Will. "Plus the last time La Roy saw the inside of the Oval Office was at a NAACP luncheon with Jimmy Carter."

"Oh, gawd. I feel so young." She blushed. "I think I was about only eight years old back then."

"There!" said Will, hands up and framing her face in his fingers. "That's your secret, Allison. Stay young. And as long as people underestimate you, you'll retain the element of surprise."

Allison beamed and almost followed him into the men's room, but caught herself short of the threshold. She took a deep breath. She couldn't believe she was there. In Washington. Making policy. Working for *him*. "He is *soooo* amazing," she sighed to herself. Then she spun a one-eighty just to make sure nobody had heard her.

2

North Carolina, Kentucky, Tennessee, Arkansas. Izzy had crossed four state lines, stolen two cars, changed the registration tags and plates on each, slept all of eleven hours in less than four days, and put eight hundred and twenty-seven miles between herself and a seaside motel room where she'd killed a man. His name was Charlie Hunt. A lumbering drunk reporter for the *Charlotte Observer* and wannabe true-crime writer who'd been shopping an updated Theroux cult manuscript to New York publishers. Dean had instructed her to take care of Charlie Hunt in the usual way. And that's what she'd done. Just as she'd done so many times before.

It was 1:43 A.M. She'd used the deserted two-lane before. Twenty-some miles ahead, it would cross the state line into sleepy Paris, Texas. Quiet. The occasional pair of headlights crossed her path. Some too lazy, sotted, or rude to turn off their high beams. But she wouldn't think of flashing them back. It was her practice not to attract the *wrong* kind of attention.

It was the numbers game that kept her going. That's how

she kept track of the hours, days, and years. Twenty-nine years. That big number was still looming in her head. Big-time. Just a little more than two months until the big three-oh. Seventy-one days and counting. The numbers played on and on through her head as the miles clicked on the stolen Mazda's odometer. Twenty-three thousand, nine hundred, fifty-five and four-tenths miles.

Twenty-three thousand . . . twenty-three . . . Now that was a good number to ponder.

Kurt Cobain was born in 1967 and died in 1994. The number 1-9-6-7 and 1-9-9-4 both added up to twenty-three.

It took twenty-three seconds for blood to circulate through the entire human body.

There were twenty-three letters in the name William Jefferson Clinton.

Twenty-three was the first prime number where both digits were prime unto themselves, and both adding up to another prime number, five.

There were twenty-three vitamins and minerals in a Centrum Silver tablet.

Twenty-three was the limit of members in an America Online chat room.

Ooh. When the numbers were right, Izzy'd get an adrenaline charge out of it good for another two or more hours of drive time. It was almost as good as an amphetamine. She'd be in California in four days. Back home. Maybe she'd head south, down San Diego way to Black's Beach just below the cliffs at Torrey Pines. It was the only legal nude beach south of Santa Barbara. She could lie out for a few days and let her skin eat up some sun. Turn her golden once again. Then, maybe, she'd send the scanned pictures to Dean and, for once in a long time, he'd *approve*.

Headlights fast approached in her rearview mirror. Closing a hundred-yard gap. It had to be a cop, she thought. Otherwise, the car would up and pass. She checked her speedometer. Fifty-three miles per hour. Legal as hell. In the glare she could make out the squared features of the cruiser and the mounted shotgun bisecting the front windshield. One driver. Highway Patrol, most likely. Or some countymountie bored out of his skull. Sure as shit he was calling up the tags. And no way would they be coming up on the computer. She'd stolen the Mazda from an airport car park. She'd watched the owner take his bags from the trunk, check in at the ticket counter, walk to the gate, and get on the aircraft.

Ten minutes later, once she'd sparked the car's ignition, all she had to do was say she'd lost her parking stub and pay the maximum. Only the cashier thought she was cute enough to cut her some slack on the price, taking her word for it that she'd parked the car for less than twenty-four hours.

No way would those tags come up stolen. Not yet.

But the lights went on anyway in a blaze of cop car glory. They loved to do that, she thought. Flashing those red lights got 'em all hot and hard in the pants.

Dumb fucker.

Carefully, she eased the car over to the shoulder, checking forward, then back. She could see a good three hundred yards of road in either direction. Plenty of warning were an unsuspecting car to round the bend. In a practiced move, she kicked off her panties and hiked up her skirt to just above mid-thigh. She put her hands at the ten and two o'clock positions on the steering wheel, just where cops liked to see 'em when they approached. She'd do her best to be a *good* customer. Question was, would he be a *good* cop?

With her right hand in clear view of the oncoming officer, she so-very-obviously switched on the overhead dome-light and adjusted the rearview mirror to face herself. Out came the lipstick. At twenty-nine, Izzy was afraid of the day she'd lose her precious looks. Ten years of running had turned that angelic teenager's face into a visage sculpted from make-believe granite. And it killed her to so much as glance at it through her rearview mirror. What looks she had left, she knew were mostly compliments of Maybelline or Revlon, smeared over cosmetically improved cheekbones and collagen-injected lips. Hell, she thought. Her breasts weren't even hers anymore.

But who was she tonight? The Darvon prescription she'd

dipped out of an old woman's purse made it a bit fuzzy and hard to remember.

Ten years.

One town after the other, city upon city, state lines crossed a hundred thousand times. Or so it seemed.

"And my name's Dorothea Jean Haskell," she said aloud, suddenly remembering, to the mirror. Just to make sure, she checked her wallet and current driver's license to see if she'd passed the little quiz. There was her name, Dorothea Jean Haskell of Memphis, right next to a younger version of the same face, under a brassy wig. The license lied that she was only twenty-five. At least the picture passed for twenty-five. The dim lighting and rearview mirror said otherwise. Twenty-nine going on forty. A stone's throw from premature middle age. After that, it would all be about wiles and wit. Turning heads from across a room might be too much to ask for. From then on, *she* would have to do the inviting.

Deputy Duwayne Burnap was bored out of his skull. The graveyard shift in McCallister County had a way of doing that to a fellah. Was a time, he remembered, when the late shift was buoyed by the old buddy system. Partners in a car, cruising the backwoods' two-lane, answering domestic violence calls, outpacing drunk drivers, and jabbering about local and national sports through the night. That was before the county started with the cutbacks. More welfare. Fewer cops. Smart, thought Duwayne. Real fuckin' smart.

The department still had plenty of cars. Just not the cops to fill them. The younger guys had to either move out of state or take lower-paying security jobs that didn't have any benefits. As for Duwayne, he was right on the seniority bubble. Had he come out of training a couple of months later, who knows? He might be working the graveyard watch at some Little Rock construction site.

No thank you, ma'am.

Instead, it was single-man duty from then on, day and night. Nobody to talk to and lonely as hell. Creeping up on the Mazda, Duwayne could make out the shine of a woman's honey-blonde hair behind the wheel. She'd been right at the speed limit, but who was there to tell him he had no probable cause to pull her over?

Absolutely nobody.

Duwayne could pull the governor over if he damn well pleased. White, black, Ford, or Cadillac, he would say to himself. It didn't matter. Just as long as the driver spoke English and politely showed him his license and registration.

It was procedure to call in the tags of the car before the approach. Suspicious cars with suspicious plates. But the only thing suspicious about the blonde in the Mazda was that she was headed for Texas somewhere close to two in the morning. That wasn't quite enough to radio the dispatcher for a routine tag check.

The deputy stepped from his cruiser, adjusting his Stetson. Flashlight in his left hand, right thumb hooked inside his belt and close to his gun. It was all standard. For appearances mostly. After all, Duwayne was a professional. He wanted to impress the lady.

She had both hands on the wheel, waiting for him to tap the flashlight against the windshield.

"Wanna roll down yer window, ma'am?"

She smiled, nodded stupidly as if she should have already done it. "I'm sorry," she said. "Cops make me nervous."

"Why?" asked Duwayne. "Were you doing anything illegal?"

"I might've been weaving. It's late and I'm kinda tired."

"Where you goin'?"

"Paris."

"But you're from—"

"Tennessee."

"Can I see your license and registration, please?"

"Oh, sure." She had it planned that way. Waiting for him to ask the license and registration question. So when she reached over to the glove box, her left hip would turn up, revealing a slight bit of bare rump. He'd be sure to look. Any man would. They really were that predictable. She handed him the registration, already having memorized it. "As you can tell, it's not my car."

"Whose is it?"

"My brother's."

"And what's wrong with your car?"

"Nothin's wrong with it. I just don't have one."

"Driver's license, please."

Seemingly embarrassed again, she dove to her right into her faux Chanel bag, pulling out her faux Chanel wallet and giving Duwayne another peek at her ass. She showed him her license.

"Take it out of the wallet, please."

"Sorry." She slid the driver's license out of the wallet and handed it over.

The picture was definitely her. The name identified her as Dorothea Jean Haskell from Memphis.

"Brother's car, but he lives in Little Rock. You're from Tennessee, but headed to Texas," surmised Duwayne. "Am I missin' somethin'?"

"The asshole I *divorced* is in Tennessee," she said with a slight huff. As if she was put upon. "I'm living in Little Rock with my brother. But I don't got a car on account that the *asshole* got drunk and rolled it into a ditch. He's okay, but the Toyota's totaled. Don't ask me if I wish it was the other way around. Anyway, my brother? He's a local rep for Michelob, so he had to go outta town on business, so I'm going to Paris to see our mother." She batted her eyes and smiled. End of story.

Duwayne gave her a dirty-dog grin that she'd seen too many times before. "And you don't wear no underwear. Now, what's your momma gonna think?"

Bingo. That's when she knew she had him.

"You noticed that?" She tried to blush. "Stick your arm in here. Go on. You feel around? Floor heater's broke. Turned all the way up and I got a little . . . well . . . you know. Anyway, you ain't met my momma." She giggled.

"Oh, it's all beginnin' to add up." Duwayne was pleased he hadn't called into the dispatcher.

"Well, ain't you an ol' dog on the prowl." Her voice was getting stickier and Southern-infected. He didn't seem to notice the change. "Step back and lemme get a look at ya."

Duwayne sucked in his beer gut and took two steps back. In his most charming move, he aimed that flashlight on his pudgy face.

Dumb with a gun. Isn't this precious?

She swung her door open and swiveled ninety degrees, leading with her left leg. She followed with her right, but never imagined bringing her knees together. With that flashlight, Duwayne decided to inspect the merchandise, that beam crawling up her inside thigh . . .

"Uh-uh," she said, bringing her knees together. "Turn it off and come here."

Obediently, he switched off the flashlight and holstered it. Before approaching, he looked both ways, up and down the road. No cars. No headlights coming. It was dead out there. That time of night, that stretch of two-lane was *always* dead.

Duwayne stepped up to her. "What you got in mind, *Dorothea?*"

"Just call me Dotty." She unzipped his pants, reaching inside for him with her right hand. He knew what was coming. A dream. A cop's midnight fantasy. A lonely perk of the single-man graveyard shift. He arched his back, hands on his hips, eyes flashing left and right once again for any sign of oncoming headlights.

In her left hand, Izzy found something hard. The plastic butt of Duwayne's Glock 19. She knew the gun well enough. All the bumpkin cops were carrying the Glock. The plastic grip molded well to just about any-sized hand. The nineteen-round clip enabled cops with the worst aim to put a hail of hot lead into the air as quickly as they could pull the trigger. Cops felt safe with the gun.

"C'mon, sister. Pull it out." But Duwayne wasn't thinking about the Glock. She had it cleared of the holster and stuck underneath his jaw before he realized the ploy. After that, everything went black. She popped off the first round, cutting his motors and dropping him to the pavement like a wet sack of seed. Quickly, she switched hands and finished him off, squeezing two more rounds into Duwayne's head.

Pop pop!

She stepped over the body and, in her bare feet, strode back to the cruiser. Careful not to touch anything, she reached inside and switched off the headlights with the Glock's muzzle, then leveled the semiauto on the squawking police radio.

Pop pop!

The radio sparked, dead as Duwayne. She was back in the Mazda inside ten seconds and roaring down the highway. At the first bridge, she tossed the gun out the passenger window into a creek. And by 2:10 A.M., she'd crossed the state line into Paris, Texas, where she left the car in the courthouse parking lot and walked to a nearby motel. There, Dorothea Jean Haskell checked in under another assumed name. Cathy Brewer.

And though McCallister County had cut back on manpower, they hadn't cut back on those fancy Glock 9 mills or an even newer invention that guaranteed more coverage on prime time. Four of the department's radio cars had been outfitted with a video surveillance system called Vid-Safe. Deputy Duwayne Burnap's had been one of them, with a fiber-optic eye posted just above the rearview mirror and aimed at twelve o'clock through the cruiser's windshield. From it a mini-cable snaked to the trunk where the unit was still recording in black and white digital bytes.

3

10:00 A.M., EDT. The Dirksen Building.
"Good morning," said Will, addressing the four hundred-plus, standing-room-only crowd of would-be witnesses, attorneys, and media. He was flanked by twelve other U.S. senators, six to his left, six to his right. Each of them backed up by their own staff members, ready with a factoid or written rebuttal to hand off. And though by his youthful looks Chairman Will Sullivan was clearly the junior statesman on the committee, he took command of the room with all the authority of a future commander in chief. It didn't hurt that all the lights and the TV cameras gave him an adrenaline rush more powerful than a night of tequila-induced sex.

"This committee's purpose and proxy is in oversight of external and internal actions involving the United States Food and Drug Administration. Therefore, as cochair, I open this forum with a public promise. It is that this committee believes that high-ranking officials in the FDA have been involved in the obstruction of commerce and free trade by favoring certain pharmaceutical companies over others.

"This committee believes that certain pharmaceutical companies have engaged in fraud, extortion, and payoffs to certain high-ranking officials in the FDA through gifts, low-interest home loans, and even special favored lease agreements on the luxury cars they drive."

Still cameras popped relentlessly while TV cameras broadcast live as Will Sullivan personally took the helm of his Beltway destroyer. All TVs from Congress to the White House were tuned to the event. And the pundits wondered: Would Will Sullivan succeed in his public peeling of the FDA's corrupted layers? Or would the behemoth agency eat him alive as it had so many young scientists and corporate competitors?

On Will's immediate right, waiting his turn to speak, was his cochair, the aging and cautious senator from Hawaii, Philip Akira, chosen to appease the loyal profiteers of the status quo. Next to Will's exuberant posture and camera-ready attitude, the old senator looked positively embalmed.

Bundled behind Will, cluttering the pool camera's frame, were the senior members of his committee staff along with a rarely-suited Bill La Roy, Allison Flannery, and former FBI agent turned private investigator Benjamin Yao. As committee chair, Will had made a controversial choice in foregoing FBI investigators in exchange for the high-profile services of Benny Yao. The *Washington Post* had jumped on the story, leading the way with a fistful of queries about the rift between Will Sullivan and the Ladies Justice. Why wasn't the FBI investigating for the committee? Sources surfaced, revealing Will Sullivan's personal distrust of the feds. After all, hadn't the FBI been investigating the FDA for years without a single indictment?

So began the war of words between Camp Sullivan and the Department of Justice.

It was two months of strike and counterstrike, with the FBI accusing the Massachusetts senator of political opportunism while Will staunchly defended his committee's power of oversight on the Sunday talk shows. Meanwhile, on ABC's *Politically Incorrect,* the colorful Bill La Roy publicly began a gender war, renaming both the attorney general and the FBI director the Slammer Sisters. He'd said the two women had set feminism back a decade in their preternatural zeal to "clean the House on Capitol Hill," and that instead of carrying a stick, "the attorney general carries a broom and dustpan."

La Roy was referring to Margaret Van Hough's feat of successfully putting two senators, four congressman, and a cabinet head behind bars for various indiscretions since her installment as attorney general. More indictments were on the way. It seemed that all of Washington was running scared from the Slammer Sisters.

Everybody, that was, except Will Sullivan and, apparently, the FDA. Will's popularity was high, he had the ear of President Addison, and, in the opinion of many, a slam dunk in his FDA investigation. Heads were ready to roll and scalps were about to be hung on Will Sullivan's political totem.

As Senator Akira began his opening statement—political pablum with a dash of caution added just to stay on the good side of Madame Attorney General—Will turned to face Benny Yao. "Give me the witness list."

Benny shuffled some papers and came up with a Xerox. As Akira droned on, Will perused the names and the order in which they were to appear. Halfway down the page, Will stopped on a familiar name. Mo Gaffney. He underlined it, then passed the list back to Benny. "Think we can move him up a few notches? If this soap opera starts to get dull, I think this guy could give it a little ratings push."

"See what I can do," said Benny.

Mo Gaffney had begun his quasi-legendary career selling used cars in a dirt lot next to a strip joint in Worcester, Massachusetts. The lease on the South Main lot was largely financed by the nightly renting of some back-row product to the dancing ladies and their after-show *customers*. The code for a come-on in the club was something like "You wanna go next door for a test-drive?" Being that there was no state law against charging prospective auto buyers for test-driving a used Lincoln or Cadillac, business was brisk, most of the cash went unreported, and the rent on the lot was always paid on time. Whether a single car ever rolled off the lot was moot. Mo was in the car business.

Two years later he went legit with a second lot in Framingham, after which he bought out a failing Ford dealership across the state line in Rhode Island. Word on the street was that Mo Gaffney had set himself up with a Providence crime family who wanted to wash cash and stolen auto parts. As a gesture of their new partnership, the crime family even bought a new road sign for the dealership, complete with a twenty-by-eighteen-foot likeness of smiling Irish Mo, gapped teeth and all.

Fifteen years and multiple Lincoln-Mercury, Nissan, and Lexus dealerships later, Mo's gap-toothed grin was pretty damned famous. And so was Mo.

"So what? You're here to kiss my ring or my ass?" bullied Daniel "Sully" Sullivan from the comfort of a worn, antique leather chair that he claimed once belonged to Joseph Kennedy.

Across from Sully sat Mo Gaffney himself. Barely five foot six, round as a wine barrel, wearing a long overcoat to slenderize the puffy frame that pedestaled his famous cartooned face.

"You mind turning the TV down?" asked Mo. "I got only one good ear to hear with."

With a remote, Sully turned down the twenty-five-inch Zenith perched above the corner liquor cabinet. It was tuned to CNN's live coverage of Will's FDA hearings. "If you're here to listen, lemme give you a quick tip. My boy Willy plays it like he's Joe-the-boss-of-his-own-destiny. If he wants you up before that committee of his, hell if I'll be the one to tell him otherwise."

"Aw, Sully. I got nothin' to do with this FDA scam. The only reason your boy wants me up there is cuzza my name goes a long way with the local constituents." With his thick Worcester accent, Mo couldn't mouth *constituents* without fouling the word into something worthy of Mike Tyson.

"Because you're famous?"

"Somethin' like that," said Mo.

"You're sorta famous, yeah. And you're also under a federal subpoena to testify in front of my boy's committee." Sully was shaking his head. "I can see right through it, Mo. So can any other son-of-a-wise-guy. You think if you can twist my arm hard enough, my boy might hear you all the way down on the Beltway."

"If I go up in front of that committee," said Mo, "my chances at public office go straight to zero."

"You?" asked Sully. "A public servant?"

"Nothin' big. Just some statehouse gig. That way, I figure, I can get a little respect."

"Respect."

"Yeah. And why not me? I got name I.D. from here to New York. I'd play the party line just as long as nobody crossed me."

Amused, Sully swiveled left in that big Joe Kennedy chair. He gestured toward his rogues' gallery. Black-and-white photos of himself arm-in-arm with a who's who of American politics. Jack Kennedy. Robert. Teddy. Nixon. Reagan. Carter. Clinton. Just about every dignitary, presidential candidate, winner, and loser had come to Boston's Southy to shake Sully's hand. He was the local crown whose ring required kissing before that certain block of poor Irish Democrats would pull a voting lever.

"Look at 'em," said Sully. "You think you measure up to any of 'em? Every one of them fat bastards was right where you're standing. That very spot. Every one of them to pay their respect to—"

"Okay," said Mo. "So in your eyes I'm just a car salesman. And here's my best pitch. I give big to the party. They ask. Mo gives. But I swear, if I'm forced to go up in front of that committee, no Democrat's ever gonna get another dime outta Mo Gaffney."

"I could give a crap about the party," said Sully, ready to count off on his fingers. "I got two causes in my life. South Boston. And my one and only son, U.S. Senator William Daniel Sullivan. And so help me God, he's gonna be the next president of the United States. Bank on it."

Mo pointed at the TV. "I don't wanna be no part of your

little Willy's TV circus. I just need you to tell me what it's gonna take."

Sully snatched a price out of thin air. "How many car dealerships you up to?"

"Eleven."

"Then may I suggest you build number twelve in old Southy," said Sully. "Create some jobs. Buy some sewer line. Hell. I'll bet with a little rummaging down around city hall, I could find you some Expressway-friendly lease space with a grandfathered property tax assessment—"

Mo laughed. "Folks don't buy cars in Southy. They fuckin' steal 'em."

"You asked me what it would cost—"

"Be reasonable. Mo Gaffney sells luxury cars. Caddy's and shit, you know? Who in Southy's gonna buy a fifty-thousand-dollar Lexus?"

"It's called *access,* Mo!" said Sully. "And my boy doesn't break the surface for a feeding unless his daddy says it's time for supper."

"I thought you said he was Joe-the-boss-of-his-own-whatever. Destiny?"

"He is," said Sully. "But I'm still his old man. And there's only three ways to get to him. His wife. His chief of staff. And me."

"You're an asshole." Mo's face was the color of a filet mignon cooked rare and beaded with a million points of sweat. He was half-clown, half-connected guy with the Providence mob. It was no wonder he was getting yanked in front of Will's committee. He'd be a peripheral witness at best, but a guaranteed boon in the New England ratings. Famous Mo. Gap-toothed. Meat-faced and grilled by a coterie of senators dying for a taste of televised blood.

"You know, how about we start with somethin' kinda social?" offered Mo. "Like dinner. Me and my wife. You and your missus. Will. That honey of a wife of his. What's her name. Ginny? Gwenny? You pick. Some joint down here in Southy. Like McCarthy's. Yeah. Your turf. We can talk. Your little Willy can share a bottle of wine. See that this whole

FDA thing is a mistake. Then maybe you and I can talk business. Maybe I'll throw some money into a restaurant—"

Sully rose, showing his six-plus feet over the chipped oak desk. "The only thing you share with '*my little Willy*' is when your feet are flat on the floor, you *both* look up to me!"

Mo didn't want to take any more shit. "You sit there in Joe Kennedy's big chair, thinking you're just like the man himself. Makin' as if you and your connections are gonna make your little boy the next Irish president. Well, I got some words for ya, Sully. You ain't no Joe Kennedy. Most you ever did was carry the water."

"I carried the sword," said Sully. "And lemme tell you, it was an *honor*."

"Well, you can go ahead and pull that sword out of your ass," said Mo. " 'Cuz it's been stuck there for as long as I've known you!"

The parting words from Mo Gaffney left Sully turning up the volume on his TV so loud he hoped the sound of his son's ongoing FDA hearings would be the Kryptonite that chased Mo and his boys out of the building. Sully sat, pulled open his desk drawer, and muscled the childproof cap off a bottle of Cozaar, a valve stabilizer for his double-bypassed heart.

"I can't believe Sully tried to sell Mo Gaffney *access* to me," said Will.

"He just thinks the apple doesn't fall far from the tree," said Gwen.

"What's that supposed to mean?"

"It means that he's your *father*," said Gwen. "And that's how fathers think. It's in the wiring. You screw up? You're a no-good son of your mother. You succeed, it's the old man who takes all the credit."

They were in the backseat of a government Town Car on their way to a state dinner at the White House. It was the first time they'd actually seen each other in weeks. Strangely, they'd been holding hands ever since he'd picked her up at the airport. As if a constant connection was required to re-juice their marital batteries. The deeper each had gotten into their careers, the more shallow their marriage had become. As much as their bones ached for the other, politics was a certain wedge.

"I love him, but he's a fossil," said Will. "A relic of the way it was and will *never* be again."

"All those back rooms and bare knuckles." Gwen gave Will a gentle elbow. "You gotta give some credit to the old school. It was simpler then."

"Yeah. Back when the only women in politics were in the president's bed." Will finally cracked a smile, catching a glimpse from the Marine Corps driver and making a mental note not to let the conversation stray too far off the public record.

Gwen opened the window to get some cooler air. It was a rare night for her in the government seat. A city she preferred to keep at arm's length. And the longer the arm, the better. Boston was sedate, civilized, and only a phone call away. If Will ever made it to the White House, she just might have to lobby to play the part of First Lady from New England.

"I want our child to know his grandparents," said Gwen. Both her parents were dead. So Will's had stood in for the past twelve years. They weren't perfect, but in the absence of a mother and father . . .

"It's a blessing," added Gwen. "Even if ol' Gramps turns out to be such a cantankerous—"

"Old prick?" finished Will. "We're agreed."

"I think Sully'd make a fine granddaddy."

"I thought we weren't going to talk about *it*," said Will.

"We weren't talking about *it*. We were talking about Sully."

"Oh. Him again?"

Sure. She was trying just a bit to rattle Will. It was part of their little game. And Will's father was the only sure-fire red-button issue. Only Gwen would invariably lose the game. That's because Will Sullivan *did not actually rattle*. Not anymore. The most he'd get was slightly hot under the collar. Getting rattled equaled a return to the bottle and Will had long ago vowed that he would never drink again. And Gwen, taking his promise to heart, had vowed that should he return to that unhappy, unhealthy, and unsavory pastime, she'd be gone before he'd knocked back his first fifth of Stoli.

"Maybe he should retire," said Will. "He'll live longer."

"You believe that?"

"No," laughed Will. They were both pros, understanding that the only thing more annoying than a permanently entrenched politician was a *retired* one. They tended to grow tumors on their overgrown egos from all the calls that never got returned.

"And I think your mum would make a fine grandmother," said Gwen.

"There you go again. And I didn't bring *it* up. You did," warned Will, his voice still sounding *somewhat* collected. They were getting a little too personal in front of the Marine driver.

Gwen pulled her shawl over her bare shoulders. Her Vera Wang dress was black, shorter than the White House Protocol Office would have preferred, and left over from a busy summer. She'd bought it on a lunch-hour whim at a resale boutique, chewing thirty percent off the price before she walked out the door with it. Will reminded her that she could've afforded to buy the dress new. But that wasn't Gwen. The pride she'd taken in her staunchly middle-class upbringing had a retroactive effect. Whenever she found herself writing a check for more than two hundred dollars, her knuckles would turn bone-white. As for the dress, she hadn't had a chance to wear it until that night. The protocol officer be damned. She'd make President Del Addison look twice. Or three or four times if he was lucky.

Finally, Will spoke. "Maybe we should slow *it* down."

"Can't take the pressure?" she teased.

"I was thinking of you."

"I'm not getting any younger."

"Thirty-six is *not* old."

"I've *decided* I don't want to slow down. I don't want to ease up. If we do, it won't happen, okay? That much I'm sure of."

"Just a month, for God's sake."

Ah, the blood pressure was finally rising. And Will's pulse heading north of fifty.

"You got some other plans?" asked Gwen.

Will pulled at his bow tie. His shirt collar was getting hot and the damned dry cleaners had starched it so crisp it could cut birthday cake.

"I talked to Dr. Bertrand." She retreated, letting Will off the hook. She'd seen a little bit of steam. Enough to satisfy her. He was human again. "Dr. Bertrand says it's time he took us to the next step."

"Which is?"

"More drugs. Up my antibodies," she said. "He was also thinking of switching from the synthetic progesterone to a natural by-product. There's some extract they get out of the rain forest."

Jesus, thought Will. *They're chopping down the rain forest so wealthy, infertile, white Americans could have babies of their own.*

"I know what you're worried about," she said. "Senator Willy wants to know how many more times he has to wank into a plastic cup."

Right in front of the driver. Will could see the Marine smirking in the rearview mirror. So he decided to make a joke at his own expense.

"It's not masturbating into a plastic cup that scares me. It's having to fly all the way to Texas to do it." Will saw the driver's eyes smile. "Look. We could still go the adoption—"

"I want a *baby* of my own!" she said, hushed but full of force.

"And you think I don't?" asked Will, already feeling somewhat shut out of the parenting process. "Since when do you have the market cornered on parental ambition?"

"It's different," said Gwen. "To have a little life inside you—"

"Fine, fine," said Will. He'd heard the argument before. She wanted a baby. Hers. From the womb to the tomb.

"Adopting's too cynical. And you agreed. A man who wants to run for president doesn't need his baby's picture on TV and the opposition looking for a five-second sound bite saying that we adopted the precious thing simply to court the family values vote."

"I don't think anybody's low enough to do that."

"You want names? And they're not all Republicans, sweetie-cakes." As with most of her repartee, Gwen's use of the endearment had a sting to it. It's what had attracted him when they'd meet at Damiano's, a small Italian restaurant in west Washington, D.C. They were at separate tables, each celebrating their birthday with a few close friends. The waiters decided on a two-for-one aria, singing "Mia Bambino Caro" to Will and Gwen at the same time. Later, both guests of honor shared a private toast. Gwen knew a fair bit about the young congressman, but he'd only *heard* of her. Will was at an instant disadvantage and Gwen appeared to have the makings of a superior challenge.

The driver braked the Town Car, making a right turn off Executive Drive through the East Visitors' Gate. He dropped the senator and his wife at the East Portico, where they were greeted by an honor guard and a wooden young lady from the Social Office staff. The Sullivans were checked off the list, then escorted by two Secret Service agents through a metal detector. They were finally left on their own to join the parade of guests walking down the East Colonnade and by the C-SPAN camera crew.

As they were about to enter the palatial residence, Will whispered to Gwen. "How about we talk to the owners and make an offer on the property?"

"I heard they weren't selling for another five years."

"Escrow might take that long," said Will. "But you gotta admit, it's *some* house. It might be worth the wait."

Gwen giggled, then self-consciously tugged her dress down a notch. She was clearly wearing the shortest dress at the event. A real heart-stopper. She'd wanted to wear it because it showed off what she thought was her best asset. Her legs. But could a future First Lady afford to come off like a gam-queen?

Cocktails were served to more than a hundred and forty people crowded in the East Room. Guests were dressed to their personal nines, bejeweled and bedazzling the competition with political chitchat and gossip.

In no time at all Will and Gwen split up, forging their own headings in a room full of handshakes and insincerity. Senator Akira blindsided Will mid-sentence while he was chatting up National Security Advisor Vernon Schmidt. Akira led Will by the elbow, a quarter-click across the room for an informal face-off with Attorney General Margaret Van Hough. This was Akira's idea of détente. The attorney general was tiny. A girlish fifty, attractive, and wearing a size two designer gown. No matter how many times he'd met up with Margie Van Hough, Will was always taken aback at just how petite America's top cop appeared in person.

"Round one of your hearings, Senator," said Margaret, "and so far you haven't unearthed a single FDA skeleton."

"Well, if you trip over any skeletons lying around the DOJ," said Will, "do me a favor and send them over my way. I'll be sure to give them a good shake on TV."

"If I were you, Senator," said the attorney general, "I'd worry about your own skeletons."

"You keeping a file on me, Margie?" asked Will, undaunted by her not-so-subtle threat.

"Excuse me, Senator. I see my husband. And he appears in desperate need for me to put the correct words in his mouth." The attorney general smiled and turned away.

Will was quick to take Phil Akira to task. "Nice try, Phil. But next time you want to play diplomat, might I suggest Norway?"

Cocktails wore on and Will quickly found himself cornered by the Irish ambassador, Cap Rennet, and the undersecretary of commerce, Frank Zozovicz. Both were already half-lit, and laying out the same cards they'd played earlier in the week at a public hearing on the renegotiation of GATT. Their mistake was in assuming that Will gave a shit. Instead, they were simply taking advantage of his practiced ear. Senator Sullivan could look fully interested—arms crossed, head slightly tilted forward as if teetering on every word—but still be a million miles away. In this case, he was keeping an eye on a blonde knockout named Vanessa Curran, the former evening anchor for the Boston CBS affiliate, recently kicked up to the network's Washington bureau. She was in a long, sparkling evening gown with a dangerous slit up the side, nuzzling very close to Gwen. Vanessa was rumored to switch-hit. Will wondered if Gwen was interested or playing the same silly game he was with Cap and Zozo. Hearing but not listening.

"So are you still trying?" Vanessa asked Gwen. She was a full eight inches taller, so she had to stoop a bit. No worry. It showed off her cleavage.

"What? Is *everybody* talking?" asked Gwen.

"I'm sorry. Is it a secret?"

"I guess not anymore," said Gwen, painting on a smile. "Of course, Will's old man thinks there's no such thing as bad publicity for Will. He'd leak my Pap smears to the *Boston Globe* if he thought they'd print them."

"And if it does happen?" asked Vanessa. "The baby, I mean. It could put a helluva hitch in your velocity."

"Don't think so," said Gwen. "I've got a pretty good machine working for me. Once I find a good nanny, I don't see any reason why I can't hit the ground running after a month or so. My mom did it. So can I."

Vanessa squirmed. The idea of being pregnant made her queasy. "You really want this?"

"I really want it."

"A little Willy in the family."

"Or a Wilhemina," said Gwen. "I don't care. All I know is that it's now or never. That, and if we decide to make a run for this place . . ."

"A baby *and* First Lady. Well, I think that's as ambitious as it gets."

"What do you think of my *velocity* now?"

"Warp speed, sister."

"Well, if the truth be known, *I'll* take the baby and *he* can have the White House."

"You wouldn't want to live here?" asked Vanessa, looking around the incredible East Room and sounding far more foolish than friendly.

Gwen was profoundly ambivalent. Who wouldn't want their change of address cards to read 1600 Pennsylvania Avenue? On the other hand, the property came with so much baggage.

"Think about it," joked Gwen. "You win. You move. It's a minimum four-year gig. If you're good at it—which we would be—then it's eight years. You get zero privacy. Out-of-town guests every night. And you can't redecorate without an act of Congress."

Vanessa laughed. Then, as if returning from a commercial and reading the TelePrompTered copy from a news story, she turned serious again. "But it's what Will wants, right?"

"And *I* want a baby. It's a good deal. If only it weren't for that silly part about conception." Gwen pointedly snapped her fingers as if she'd missed something.

"You want me to make some calls for you?" There was a certain swing of sex in the way Vanessa made the offer. Her voice dropped half an octave with a bit of a purr at the end. Gwen caught it, but didn't let it throw her. She'd been hit on by women before. For a while, it was happening so often that she'd let her hair grow out to shoulder length. But that hadn't stopped the offers from coming. She was a tough woman and to a free-wheeling bisexual, an attractive package.

"I really like this clinic in Dallas," said Gwen. "It's small and very discreet. When we walk through the door, we're just Will and Gwen from Beantown."

"So next time I'm in Boston, what about lunch?"

"I work most lunches. I got races in California to watch over and there's the time difference."

"Dinner, then?" asked Vanessa.

Gwen was pressed. She didn't like to say no to someone she didn't *have* to say no to. "Call my office. We'll make a date."

"Great." Vanessa smiled. And that's when she kissed Gwen right on the lips. Right there in the East Room of the White House.

"Ladies and gentlemen," announced the White House's chief social officer. "The president and First Lady of the United States."

As if applause signs had lit up on all four East Room walls, the gathering turned toward the center staircase to greet President Addison and his wife, Agnes. A receiving line instantly formed with the president and the First Lady standing alongside their honored guests, President Mubarak of Egypt and his wife, Susanne.

"She kissed you," said Will, gripping Gwen's hand and pulling her down the line. "I saw it."

"You and who else?" Gwen wondered aloud. Then she kind of lied. "She was just trying to be nice."

"She wants to fuck you," whispered Will.

"So what if she does? You jealous?"

"Of her?"

"She's beautiful."

"I noticed."

"Maybe she wants to fuck *me* to get to *you*."

There was a sudden silence. Gwen gripped his hand that much tighter as they approached the president and First Lady.

"You wanna fuck her?" whispered Gwen. "Or did you already?"

Will ignored the question, sticking out his hand and putting it into the president's. "Mr. President."

"Senator," acknowledged President Addison. He towered over Will. Six foot five with a Mount Rushmore face under a shock of black Grecian Formula hair. The President was sixty years old and commanding. He turned at once to Will's wife. "Love the dress, Gwen. I'll bet that little number added some gray hairs on our friendly protocol officer."

"Mr. President?" cooed Gwen. "I misunderstood my husband. I thought you'd invited us to a *steak* dinner."

"Steak dinner!" roared the president. Then the commander in chief bent forward to his favorite senator's ear. "Will? How about this for fun? After dinner, we go bowling in the White House rec room. You and your missus against me and mine."

Will could see it now. Gwen in that short evening dress, rolling a twelve-pound ball down a private White House bowling lane. Addison's eyes up her ass. If there ever was going to be a declaration of war between the president and his First Lady, Gwen's dress could be the start.

But who was Will Sullivan to refuse his president? The ultimate father figure short of God. And Will and God hadn't been on speaking terms since his last confession at age fifteen.

4

The fax arrived in the basement storage closet of the converted Beacon Hill brownstone. Sophie, the youngest and newest of the interns, was a practical politics major at Wellesley. She carefully collated the eight pages, stapled them as she'd been told, then hurried past the other moles working in the basement apartment, up the stairs, through the lobby, then up three more flights of stairs until she reached the top floor of Gwen Corbett Consulting. G.C.C. Aptly referred to by many as Girls' Club Consulting, since Gwen was reluctant to hire men. It was her own fight to keep what was left of affirmative action.

Sophie huffed at the top the stairs, handing off the stapled fax to Yvonne, Gwen's fifty-year-old, bronze-skinned assistant.

"You'll get used to it."

"What?"

"The stairs," said Yvonne. "You know, Gwen coulda put an elevator in here a long time ago. But she said no thanks. Know why?"

"Why?"

"One. Because she's thrifty. Two. Because she thinks shapely butts make for better business."

Sophie laughed, then coughed. She still hadn't caught her breath.

"I'm not kidding."

"No way."

"Way, girl." Yvonne was telling the truth. In her master's thesis at Columbia, Gwen had addressed the virtues of sexuality in American politics and the necessity of an attractive candidate in an ever-growing mass-media market. The *fuckability factor* as Gwen worded it in private. Will Sullivan had been one of her first, prime examples. She hadn't been wrong since.

"Who's this from?" asked Yvonne about the fax.

"Harvey Bertrand Reproductive Clinic," answered Sophie, semi-embarrassed. She didn't know much about Gwen and Will's scientific adventure.

"I'll see that Gwen gets it."

"Can I give it to her?"

"The document's private."

"I didn't read it . . . Really, I didn't."

Yvonne believed her, but didn't let on. She had her arms crossed. This was a test.

"Okay," Sophie admitted. "I just haven't met her yet."

"You'll meet her when you meet her. Now, scurry back downstairs and join the rest of the moles. What are they working on today?"

"Phones and stuff."

"For who?"

"D'Angelo," answered Sophie, catching on to the quiz. "New York City mayoral race."

"Polling subject?"

"Racial preference versus performance preference."

"When the numbers are in, I'll see you get to hand-deliver them to the boss. Good enough?"

Good enough.

Gwen's office occupied nearly the entire top floor of the brownstone. Large windows overlooked the Charles River.

The room was flanked by down-stuffed, sea-foam corduroy sofas. The rest of the furniture was all custom-made from honey-stained pine. There were fresh flowers and embroidered pillows. And where most political consultants plastered their walls with photos of their winning candidates like hunting trophies, Gwen adorned hers with pastel prints and hand-tinted still-life photographs.

A circular wrought-iron staircase led to a private sundeck. On warm days, Gwen and Yvonne would sit up there and roll calls while counting the strollers they'd spy along the river's bike path. Mothers and nannies pushing their babies were a sight for Gwen's aching eyes.

Yvonne dropped the fax on Gwen's desk. "From Dr. Harvey B."

Gwen nodded while listening to the caller on her headset. She smiled and motioned for Yvonne to wait.

"Wally," said Gwen, "listen to me."

But Wally clearly wouldn't listen. Gwen's lacquered nails impatiently tapped the glass desk protector.

"Wally? It's only twenty grand," she said, when a word got in edgewise. "To the Democratic National Committee, that's who." Gwen rolled her eyes at Yvonne. "How do I know your candidate will get the money? One? Because I say he will. And two? Because someday in the very near future and out of the earshot of the F.E.C., your candidate will stick his hand in yours and say, 'Thank you, Wally Mayfield. I wouldn't have made it to Congress without *you*.' "

While Wally continued to litigate his position, Gwen began perusing the fax. One page after another of numbers, blood tests, progesterone levels, blah blah blah. The amazing thing was, Gwen could read the data and listen to Wally's whining without missing a lick of either. "Wally . . . Wally! Can you hang on a second?" Gwen handed the fax back to Yvonne. "Make a copy and FedEx it to my husband, please."

"Want to put a note on it?"

"Yeah. Tell him it's getting to be that time of the month."

Yvonne quietly excused herself and closed the door. She could hear Gwen drumming the same line to Wally Mayfield about the money, the committee, the candidate. Yvonne wished she could've gotten on the line and just told the moron that he could save his breath. Gwen would get the cash out of him one way or another. She always did. That's why she was in such demand. Gwen was the best spin doctor in the game. She could spin for you or against you. Spin you into running for office, or staying the hell out of a race. She could also spin money out of the tightest pockets. It was a gift.

"Drivin' slow enough for ya, Senator?"

"Doing fine, LBJ."

Will was reading his FedEx'd copy of Dr. Bertrand's fax while being driven back from the Washington press corps dinner to his rented Georgetown condo. The Lincoln Town Car had built-in halogen reading lights in the rear. His favorite driver, Levon Byron Johnson, was doing his level best to keep the ride smooth and steady, knowing the senator was prone to motion sickness.

"Lotsa talkin' tonight?"

"What's that?"

"You know. How's it you always say? Everybody in politics must be from Babylonia or somethin'?"

"That's Babylon."

LBJ laughed. "That's right. Cuzza they babble on and on and on and on. And then you all just stand there and, like, listen."

"That's the job."

Will welcomed the break from his reading. His eyes were tired and his head was buzzing from inhaling all the secondhand smoke. The damn Press Corps. Not only did the rattlesnakes booze like lab rats, but while they gladly carried the banner against the evil tobacco industry, they all seemed to belch more cigarette smoke than you'd see at an Alcoholics Anonymous meeting.

Will's eyes drifted to the seat cushion next to him. Tucked into the crease was a decade-old hardcover, the five-by-seven color photo on the rear jacket staring back at him. The man pictured was awfully familiar-looking, approximately the same age as Will, arms crossed in an authoritative pose, and dressed in a natty double-breasted Hugo Boss suit. Every bit the man in his prime.

Where do I know this man?

Turning over the book, Will was at first surprised. If asked to venture a guess, Will would've thought the author to be some former White House counsel or someone of that ilk. Instead, it proved to be none other than Vance Allatore.

How could I forget.

Vance Allatore, the brilliant Los Angeles prosecutor who, at the book's publishing date, was undefeated in a courtroom. He'd capped his career with the nationally televised trial of mass killer W. D. Theroux. The book Will held in his hand was the best-selling tell-all tome that followed.

TRUE BELIEVERS
The Killer Cult of W. D. Theroux

The jacket looked aged and cheesy. A yellow background with the title spelled out in spatter of spilled red ink. Vance Allatore's name was boldly featured across the bottom. His fifty-and-zero courtroom record touted as a kicker to his famed name.

On the inside flap were enough reminders of the case. The killer. His cult's supposed suicide turned into a sensational conviction on Court TV. Followed by the brutal single-night slayings of ten key trial members. Two defense lawyers. The judge. Six jurors. The bailiff.

Will flipped the book over and gave Vance Allatore another once-over. "Whatever happened to you?"

"What's that, Senator?"

"Good reading?" Will held up the book so LBJ could see it in his rearview mirror.

"Not my book."

"Not mine," said Will.

"Sorry, Senator," said LBJ. "Didn't see it. Musta been left over by the last driver."

The Cecil Place condo was a rental and otherwise nondescript. After his first year in the House, Will had cut loose from the frat-house atmosphere of the Kramer Building, Capitol-convenient but about as private as the center of a city newsroom. Instead, Will chose to forego convenience in exchange for a thirty-minute commute to and from cozy Georgetown. The condo-cum-senatorial-flophouse had two stories, a Potomac view, security, basic furnishings, a kitchen freezer stocked with frozen dinners and gourmet ice cream, and provided a home for Will's ever-growing collection of Civil War memorabilia. The senator had begun the hobby within the first week of joining AA. At La Roy's suggestion, he'd begun supplanting his alcohol addiction with another. Collecting. It started with a coffee table book that had been a Christmas gift. In it were photos of famous Civil War battlefields. La Roy had packed a bag for Will and they were off, beginning at Arlington and finishing at Gettysburg. They returned to Washington two weeks later with a trunkload of memorabilia.

The new addiction turned out to be as sticky as day-old bubble gum.

Since then, Will had practically gone mad with the hobby. He'd buy books and antiquities by the case. Swords, uniforms, muskets, pistols, belt buckles, canteens, percussion cartridges, buttons, caps, flags, even currency. Confederate. Union. It made no difference. A Confederate officer's coat adorned a seamstress's mannequin near the condo's front door. Cavalry sabers were mounted on walls or stacked in corners. Union flags, draped over the sofa. The rest of Will's five-year harvest was still in boxes which had to be stepped over just to get to the stairwell. Then there were the gifts. When it became public knowledge that the senator was a collector, the gifts and letters never seemed to stop coming.

There were two bedrooms upstairs. One was a home office, shelved with legislative briefs and leftover law books, borrowed during his days in the House and never returned. On the desk was a laptop computer for outlining speeches and receiving and sending e-mail.

The other bedroom? That was for sleeping. Smaller, it was adorned with little more than a TV permanently tuned to CNN and a paisley comforter stretched over a king-sized bed. There was a sliding glass door leading to a small balcony that overlooked the Whitehurst Freeway, with the river to the south and the sleepy lights of Georgetown University to the north.

From the phone at his bedside, Will discussed Dr. Bertrand's fax with Gwen. "These numbers are gibberish to me."

"Maybe you should have one of your staff read up on fertilization and translate for you."

"I'm not laughing."

"Did I say it was funny?"

"I'm tired, Gwen. All I wanna know is what this means in practical terms."

"It means I'm ripe," she said, overflowing with a renewed optimism. "The blood numbers say with another try or two, it should take."

"I'm worried about what this stuff is doing to your system."

"Whatever it's doing, it's doing it to me. Not the baby. So are you up for this or what?"

"No pun intended?"

"All you gotta do is—"

"Jerk off into a plastic cup. I know."

"Doesn't sound very presidential, does it?" Suddenly Gwen broke into a silly rendition of "Hail to the Chief." *"Dah-dum-dah-dumdum, dahdum dahdum, dah-dum-dum . . ."*

"I'd laugh, but I'm too tired."

"So, do we have a date?"

Will's chest heaved. He looked at the clock. It was half past eleven. "Sure. Have Yvonne set it up with Myriam."

"I'm feeling lucky."

"Then so am I," said Will. They bade each other a perfunctory good night and hung up. Will waited. Looked over to the empty side of the bed where he'd left a pile of dull legislative memorandums. He'd even set his reading glasses on top of the stack as a poignant reminder. God, he wanted a drink. The temptation always proved the strongest when he was alone. His guard was down. Nobody was there to look to him as some kind of role model for public sobriety.

He twisted back to the phone and dialed an all-too-familiar number. And when a woman's smoky voice answered, he spoke in an equally easy timbre. "Hey, it's me. I'm a little lonely. What about you?"

"Me too."

"So what are we gonna do about it?" asked Will.

"We're gonna talk."

"You first."

"Okay. What are you wearing?"

Will laughed. "Black knee socks. Boxers. T-shirt."

"Ooh. Sounds sexy. I think I'm getting horny."

"You?"

"Flannel nightgown. Courtesy of Ton-Ton the tent-maker."

Will laughed. "I'm getting a very flattering picture."

"Do you know how to make love to a fat woman?"

"No."

"Roll her in flour and look for the wet spot."

"Oh, my God," groaned Will. "Thanks for sharing, Lane."

"Okay. Change of subject," said the congresswoman from Santa Fe. "Any booze in the house?"

"Not a drop. You?"

"Me too. Not even NyQuil."

"So we're safe," confirmed Will.

"I know an all-night liquor store. And they deliver."

"You got the number?"

"I burned it," she said. "Then I burned the phone book."

"Too bad you can't kill the girl from Directory Assistance."

"You forget," she said. "I'm on the CIA Oversight Subcommittee. I *know* people."

"You're a dangerous woman."

"Only when I'm on top."

"Good night, Lane."

"One day at a time, brother."

"One day at a time, sister."

5

Holed up in a Galveston Island motel, Izzy stepped from the shower, buck-naked except for the towel wrapped around her hair. On the back of her neck was a tattoo—a valentine heart roped in the words:

Second Chance

She bore three tattoos in all. The second was two inches of Latin text that scrolled horizontally across the small of her back. And the third tattoo was accented by a silver ring piercing her navel. It was a miniature version of the inverted sword which graced Dean's chest.

Izzy plugged her laptop into the motel phone line, expertly configuring the automated dialer to recognize the number nine as the first digit, pause for a brief second, then finish off the tone sequence when the modem picked up the outside line.

She checked the clock. It was five to midnight. Time enough to check her e-mail before logging into a private chat room where he'd be waiting for her. While the modem whined, she pulled on a T-shirt and underwear. It took another ten seconds to lock into the Internet provider and another five for Microsoft Explorer to fill the screen with blazing color. She punched up the e-mail icon. She had three pieces of mail. One from Starr. Another from Jack. And surprise, a rare note from Clem who, in the past ten years, had been the last of the clan to accept the computer as the primary means of communication. Clem would have much preferred a thousand-mile bus trip with a face-to-face talk over a beer rather than let his fingers do the talking over the Internet. If he had something he wanted to say to Dean, he'd tell Izzy. She'd tell Dean. And vice versa. Nonetheless, Clem had typed her an e-mail.

To: sistersuperior@silversprings.com
From: leatherneck@zippedeedooda.org

Dear sis,

How many lawyers does it take to screw in a lightbulb?

neck

Thirty days since she'd heard directly from Clem and that's what he sends her? A riddle? A joke? Izzy thought to respond, but her eyes caught the clock in the corner of her computer screen. Midnight straight up. In an upper-left hand box she typed the complicated URL from memory. Pressed ENTER, then waited for the answer:

ARE YOU THERE?
    i'm here.
GOOD EVENING, MY LOVE
    i love you.
ARE YOU WELL?
    just got out of the shower. need sleep.
AND YOU WILL DREAM OF ME?
    every night.
BEAUTIFUL. AND WHAT NEWS DO YOU BRING ME?
    used a knife on the <u>hunt</u>.

ANOTHER CHAPTER ENDED?
>   yes.
WHAT ELSE?
>   had to slaughter a pig.
WHERE?
>   283 by 655.

There was a brief pause on screen. Then an answer.

YES, I KNOW THAT PLACE. ARE YOU FRIGHTENED?
>   i am not.
DESCRIBE FOR ME YOUR ROOM.
>   it is a motel. like all the others. I have two queen beds.
>   i am sleeping in the one nearest the bathroom and far-
>   thest from the window. the cable on the tv is poor. all the
>   pictures are fuzzy. the walls are cream and the room
>   smells of disinfectant.
A CHEAP PAINTING ABOVE THE HEADBOARD?
>   a seascape.
WHEN WE ARE FINISHED HERE, YOU MUST TURN OUT YOUR
LIGHT AND REST. SET THE ALARM FOR SUNRISE AND DRIVE INTO
THE WEST. YOU MUST FIND A PLACE TO REST. FINALLY, I AM
PREPARING TO PLANT MY SEED. AND I WILL NEED YOU TO TEND
TO IT ONCE IT HAS BLOSSOMED.
>   have you picked a fertile place?
I HAVE. AND AS YOU ONCE DID, <u>SHE</u> HAS CAUGHT MY EYE.
>   i remember that day so well.
THAT IS YOUR OLD SOUL REMEMBERING. IT IS NO LONGER WHO
YOU ARE. DO YOU REMEMBER WHO YOU ARE?
>   i am the messenger.
GOOD. NOW SLEEP UNTIL I WAKE YOU.
>   i'll dream of you.
I KNOW.
>   i love you.
I LOVE YOU, TOO.

She touched the screen, letting her fingers drift back and
forth across his final words. But he was gone. The screen
blanked, spitting her back into reality. The stuffy motel. The

lousy bed with the concave mattress. She unplugged the computer and pulled the sheets off the bed, making a place for herself on the floor. It took her back to the days when they *all* slept on the floor. Her. Dean. The rest of them. Old souls or not—they were still a comfort.

I'm a dead man.

Essentially, Will was scared of nobody but Gwen, but while she was waiting for him in a Dallas hotel room, he was stuck on a soggy San Francisco tarmac with Bill La Roy and two hundred other pissed-off passengers. The phones on the aircraft were not operational while grounded and the use of cell phones was strictly forbidden.

"America's number-one power couple, healthy as Uncle Joe's hogs, and you wanna go fussin' up with ol' Momma Nature just so you can say the child's your own."

"You know I'd do anything for Gwen. It matters to her," said Will.

The senator and his chief of staff were traveling business class, waiting on the side of a runway for well over an hour for some nickel-sized silicon chip to be reinstalled in the cockpit. All the gates were occupied by other aircraft, so the poor passengers had to wait it out in stifling, recycled air. The flight attendants hustled to buy the passengers' patience with free liquor and, to Will's keen eye, were discreetly sucking back some of the hard stuff themselves. Who knew *what* the pilots were drinking?

"Anything for Gwen. Blah blah blah. You're still makin' deals with your marriage. And that's why they don't work no more. Ever since Marilyn Monroe and Joe DiMaggio."

"You telling me *that* was a deal?"

"Joltin' Joe couldn't buy an endorsement deal until he married into Hollywood. And she wanted an *entree* to the Kennedys."

"I thought Frank Sinatra introduced her to the Kennedys," posed Will, gamely playing along. "Or was it Peter Lawford?"

"It was DiMaggio," said La Roy. "The Italian connection. DiMaggio, Sinatra, and Sam Giancana. You know, Gian-

cana used to fix games in his last years so Joe could keep
his lifetime average above three-twenty. Just so an Italian
could beat out a black man like Jackie Robinson."

Bill La Roy. Southern-fried, bacon-spattered political
strategist by day. Conspiracy theorist by night. The stuff La
Roy would read and repeat was a constant source of
amusement for his ambitious boss. And it wasn't that La
Roy believed a word of it. Outlandish conspiracies were
possibly the only pure entertainment La Roy allowed himself. Everything else was as serious as a heart attack. Politics was serious. Sports were serious. Babies were serious.
The universe was really serious. No sense in making fun of
the real world when there was so little time to change it.

"What time is it?" asked Will.

"Two forty-two."

"Four-forty in Dallas."

"She'll wait for you. If you're worth it . . ."

"Can't exactly do it without me." Will's eyebrows rose up
and down, knowing that Gwen would have every right to
turn into a raging demon if he blew the appointment.

"How many babies out there you think could use a pair of
good parents like yourselves?"

"White babies? We'd have to stand in line unless I was
willing to pull rank. Black babies, well . . ."

"Don't talk about takin' no black babies from their black
mommas."

"Couldn't if we wanted to. Uppity white parents can't
adopt black babies in uppity Massachusetts."

"An enlightened state. I like that. But the cookin's still for
shit."

During the scheduled break in the FDA hearings, Will
and La Roy had flown west, completing a three-day tour of
the delegate-treasured state of California. Will was already
making inroads there in both Hollywood and Sacramento.
The trek had gone swimmingly with a luncheon with the
governor, speeches in San Francisco and Newport Beach,
and a thousand-dollar-a-plate movie-star-infested dinner in
Beverly Hills where Senator Will Sullivan was the State Democratic Committee's guest of honor.

La Roy couldn't believe the female attendees. The glamorous and the glitterati. He'd bragged to Will that there was a high probability he'd get laid that night. After the meal, while La Roy was plying his act upon a willing female TV actress, Will had himself taxied down to Culver City for an eleven o'clock Alcoholics Anonymous meeting. Once safely ensconced inside the grade school auditorium, he dumped his jacket and tie, rolled up his shirtsleeves, and took to the podium like a reborn revival minister. It was Will's personal tent show. No matter what city he was visiting or which political kingmaker he'd just supped with, Will always made a point to attend an AA meeting.

He would quietly arrive, wait his turn, then stand before his fellow addicts without the aid of speechwriters or note cards or rehearsal. As La Roy had once coined, speaking at AA meetings was as natural for Will as a baby suckling at his own mother's breast. All from the gut. No bullshit. No politics. Just some old-fashioned spiritual tonic delivered to an ever-thirsting choir.

Confession, forgiveness, release.

La Roy swirled his coffee with his index finger then sucked it clean. "You know, Earnest? If you and Gwen go the adoption route, you could have a smiley-cute, toddler-sized kid by the time you take on New Hampshire and Iowa. Might even be walkin' and talkin' by then. Precinct by precious little precinct."

"Gwen wants a baby. Her baby. Bun in oven, natural childbirth. The whole ball of wax."

"Betcha she draws that line when it comes time for an epidural," said La Roy. "Women say they like the pain, but it's all a buncha feminist bullshit. Like that whole Anita Hill thing . . . It's a known fact that Clarence Thomas had a jones for white women. And from what I gathered, a particular white woman who was married to a major stockholder in AT&T. That whole harassment crock-o-bull was a vendetta disguised as a—"

La Roy stopped himself as he caught a glimpse of Louisiana congressman Dodge Heebler separating the curtain between first class and business. Heebler was the seventy-one-year-old house minority whip and resident rabble-rouser. A thirty-two-year vet of the Beltway, complete with a gin-blossomed nose and a bellyful of pork rinds hanging over his belt.

"I thought I heard me some familiar voices," said Heebler with a smile as transparent as Saran Wrap.

"Ugh," whispered Will to La Roy. "Heebler actually thinks he'll be the next to redecorate Ye Olde Queen Anne on Observatory Hill."

"Dodge Heebler? The VP slot?" asked La Roy.

"Just watch."

And watch he did. Will was so damn fast at sizing up the enemy, La Roy constantly marveled at his instincts. Will had the personalities that ran both houses mapped out like a Rand McNally road atlas. He'd done it with governors and state representatives, too. The media, local and national. Forget the lobbyists and special interest groups was Will's credo. They controlled the lion's share of the campaign money, but it was Congress who spent it. Then the only thing left between policy and law was the president of the United States and five affirming Supreme Court justices.

Uncanny, thought La Roy. Dodge Heebler was ambling up the aisle and Will already knew the old fart's agenda.

"If it ain't ol' Wild Billy La Roy," started Heebler. "How's it goin', son?"

The *son* part pissed La Roy off. It was kissin' cousin to *boy*. La Roy simply returned a wide, bullshit smile and said, "First class, Congressman? Who's buyin' this week? Big tobacco? Or the Double-A-R-P?"

"Frequent flyer," said Heebler. "Got my stickers to prove it. Wanna see?"

Before it got ugly, Will stood, stuck out his hand, and greeted the old gomer as if he was a long-lost uncle. "Good to see you, Congressman." He gripped Heebler's hand tight and respectfully, knowing the exact words that were about to come out of the rep's mouth.

"Your little FDA show?" said Heebler. "It might make for some snappy TV. But if you think it's gonna be some kinda launchpad that puts you in the VP seat, well, you got yerself a surprise comin'."

"Actually," spun Will. "I heard you were at the top of that shortlist."

"The president and myself go *waaayy* back," said Heebler. "No secret that he likes y'all. But it's only a father-son kinda affection, know what I mean? Seen it a few times before. Young, ambitious senator hooks his wagon to a wise old commander in chief."

"And that must make you . . . lemme guess," said Will. "My wise old Uncle Dodge?"

"I like the way that sounds." The congressman winked. He leaned in over Will. The stink of recycled gin made Will want to shove a plug in the old man's mouth. "So here's my advice, Little Will. Do your tap dance on the grave of the FDA and make a name for yourself. But leave the coattails to those of us who've earned the ride."

Or what? was the obvious question. But Will knew the answer to the unveiled threat. The next time Will brought a piece of legislation to the House, Heebler would do his damnedest to bury it deeper than toxic waste.

"The president *owes* me," said Heebler. "Are we understood?"

"I gotcha," said Will with a wink and a nod. He felt a little sorry for the aging representative. Threats and intimidation were all the old guard had left. With constituencies as safe as seat belts, old congressmen roamed the Beltway, often playing fast and loose with what power they'd accumulated over their endless careers. They lorded over youth and practiced the art of political gridlock.

"Y'all have a good flight." Heebler grinned and withdrew without saying another word to La Roy. He disappeared into the lavatory.

"Why is it that racist old cocksuckers never die young?"

"What time is it?" asked Will.

"Two fifty-eight. Four fifty-eight, Texas time."

"I'm so sorry, Gwen," Will whispered.

"Fuck him," said Gwen. She'd said it to herself over and over again in the hotel room. She'd said it in the cab. She'd said it in the clinic's lobby and now in Dr. Bertrand's mauve-wallpapered examining room.

Fuck him.

That morning she'd awoken her husband in his Fairmont Hotel guest suite.

"Happy birthday, sweetheart," she'd begun.

"Is that what it is?" asked Will. He'd gone to bed wearing his watch, but he could only read the time. 4:00 A.M. The date was not illuminated. The best he could summon was "Well, happy birthday to you, too."

"You know what I want for our *birthday?" asked Gwen.*

"A seat on the Supreme Court?"

"I want you and your fast swimmers in Dallas. This afternoon. You, me, and a turkey baster."

Will waited for lucidity to rise. "I thought the window wasn't for another five days."

Gwen was sweet, but on point. "What can I say? I'm early. The biological barometer says today."

She had administered the ovulation test, come up with a positive imprint, and dialed Will to give him his marching orders. Dallas. Six o'clock.

With Will semiconscious and on the phone, she'd made sure he'd confirmed the time and place by writing it down on the notepad next to the bed. He promised to cancel his afternoon and evening appointments and meet her at the Dallas Melrose. That was the last time they'd spoken.

And Will hadn't so much as shown his face, let alone lent his semen. He hadn't even had the courtesy to call to say he'd be late.

"We can do it without him."

"Without Will?" asked Gwen. She was already in the disposable paper gown, IV needle stuck in her arm, sitting erect at the edge of the examination table, being attended to by Dr. Bertrand's nurse, Elena. It was her fifth attempt at the procedure. Her first without Will present.

"I'm sure Dr. Bertrand still has some of your husband's sperm frozen as a specimen sample from your original visit," said the nurse, a brown-skinned, thirty-eight-year-old former beauty turned possible spinster. The gold band Elena wore on her right ring finger was an antique. Her hair, pulled tight into a ponytail, seemed to smooth her aging skin.

"You're kidding me," said Gwen. It'd been over a year since their first visit.

"Dr. Bertrand freezes what he doesn't use," she said. "Just in case."

"In case of what?"

"Circumstances arise." The answer was veiled. Gwen hated when people weren't straight-on with her.

"Circumstances such as . . ." prompted Gwen.

"Such as, God forbid, your husband should die. There'd still be some of his sperm left. Frozen in a nitrogen-oxide cylinder." There. She had said it, even though it was policy for her not to bring up such occurrences, especially when patients were in such a vulnerable state.

But there wasn't much vulnerability in Gwen Sullivan. Even in the hospital gown she looked devastating, yet hard as nails. Impenetrable. Dark hair. Dark eyes. Luscious lips that formed words faster than most people could think. Gwen was a total package. She came off secure, as if she didn't need men *or* women. And didn't let many people in. Will was the exception, she'd sometimes say. Only because he was exceptional.

Until now.

"He isn't dead," said Gwen, certain Will was only delayed. Her main concern was *delayed by what* . . .

. . . or whom . . . and what the hell did she look like?

Her mind shot back to Will's boozing days and the women she'd found him with. He'd get so drunk, discretion was often forgotten in the simple tilt of that fourth or fifth vodka martini. And though Will hadn't resumed the binge-drinking, she'd never quite forgiven him the infidelities or regained her trust in him.

"I'm sure he's just fine," said Elena. "Let me talk to Dr. Bertrand."

Elena left the room, leaving Gwen alone with her speedy imagination. Here she was. As vulnerable as she would ever let herself be, ready to take to the stirrups and be impregnated in the most unromantic of circumstances. And Will? He could be anywhere. Fact was, he was anywhere but where he was supposed to be. Which was right there, next to her, holding her hand, then leaving the room to jerk off into a plastic cup when Dr. Bertrand gave him the green goddamned light.

Recovering alcoholic or recovering asshole?

"Hello, Gwen," said Dr. Harvey Bertrand. "Don't you look lovely this month." He was halfway through the door, chart in hand, giving his greeting without so much as looking up at her. The first thing he noticed was that Will wasn't in the room.

"Your husband in the washroom?" he asked.

"He's not here," answered Gwen with as much dignity as she could muster.

"He's not here *yet*," corrected Dr. Bertrand, wanting to give Will the benefit of the doubt. For an OB, a man whose business was dealing with women, he was very much from the old Southern school. The husband *always* came first in matters of respect and consequence.

Harvey Bertrand was nearly sixty by most accounts. He was of medium height with a cask-shaped body and a whisky voice. He preferred baby-blue lab coats over the sterile white, and clip-on bow ties over the hassle of anything that required more than a square knot.

"Will isn't here," said Gwen. "I don't know if he's coming. And I don't care."

"Well, that makes for a bit of a problem, don't you think?"

"Elena said you might have one of his samples," she said. "Some of his sperm. You know. Frozen."

Dr. Bertrand rubbed at his beard. "I do. Yes. But I'm not exactly a sperm bank. And it's not really my practice to do procedures without the husband present and accounted for."

"That's very polite of you. But I'm here. He's not. So why not make the exception?"

"Could we call him?"

"I've tried. None of his offices have the faintest where he is."

He was tugging harder at the beard. "I think we should wait. Perhaps another month?"

Gwen brought her hands up to her face. She was shaking her head. She didn't want to lose it. Not now. She never liked to cry in front of anyone. Not even when she was in therapy. It showed weakness to a world that only looked up to strength.

But the tears came anyway.

"Gwen. I was only thinking of the *two* of you." Dr. Bertrand was there at her side, his hand on top of her head, stroking her hair ever-so-gently. "The husband sometimes has a proprietary need to be here at the time of fertilization. I know what I'm talking about."

"And I know Will Sullivan!" snapped Gwen. "He promised me he'd be here. And he's not, okay?" More tears came. "We had a deal!"

"That's between you and him."

"But if I said to go ahead anyway?"

Dr. Bertrand would clearly have preferred not to answer. Not even to have been asked the question.

"Then I would go ahead with the procedure," he relented. "If you insisted."

"I'm insisting," said Gwen without a second thought. She'd made up her mind a long time ago—with or without Will Sullivan, she was going to have a baby. It was her goddamned right as a woman. She could not be denied by her husband, God, or Mother Fucking Nature. "Do it!"

"I'll have Elena prepare Will's original sample." Dr. Bertrand stroked her hair once again, gave her a fatherly pat on the back, and left the room.

Alone again, Gwen braced herself against the counter. The tears evaporated and she washed her face at the stainless steel basin, blotted it dry with a paper towel, and then stared back at herself in the mirrored finish of the towel dispenser. Her storm-gray eyes were barely streaked with the telltale broken capillaries from crying. Her olive skin—a gift from her mother's Italian side—was unblemished and rarely in need of makeup. No white pallor here. The fear wasn't showing. Nor was her weakened stomach.

There, she said to herself. *I'm me again.*

Fourteen months earlier, Gwen and Will had held hands in Dr. Bertrand's small, diploma-plaqued office on the fourth floor of the Liberty Bank Building in the heart of Dallas. They'd chosen Dr. Bertrand for two primary reasons—his recent success rate and the privacy he guaranteed his patients. Larger clinics wanted to publish their results in exchange for more research dollars. Dr. Bertrand seemed only to find satisfaction in making his patients happy.

Palms sweating and trying so hard to look the responsible and well-to-do couple, Gwen and Will appeared to have everything, denied only the privilege of bearing children and the happiness such an event would bring. Gwen wore a simple ankle-length print dress and Will was also casual, dressed in chinos, chocolate bucks, and a hand-knit sweater. He had wanted to wear his trademark suit and tie. The uniform, as Gwen liked to call it. But she'd won out, making her case for a softer image. Perfect packaging was one of Gwen's trademarks. Will knew better than to argue.

"You are very good candidates for *the procedure,*" the doctor had reassured them, having carefully studied both Gwen's and Will's medical histories and blood work.

The procedure, as he would always refer to it, was complicated science but seemed so simple after his gentle explanation. Dr. Bertrand loved leaning back in that big leather chair of his, venetian-covered window behind him, giving the speech that had yet to wow the medical establishment, but had made for some very happy couples.

"You look at each other and see the differences. Man and woman. Male, female. Husband and wife. But in the eyes of nature? She sees you are more *alike* than *unlike.* With the exceptions of a few organs that make up your reproductive systems, you may as well be the same sex.

"Nature, though," continued Dr. Bertrand, "sometimes she sees that a man and woman are *too* alike. For example, a brother and a sister."

Will quickly bristled. "We're not even remotely related."

"Exactly. But if we were all so different, there would be no such thing as kidney or heart transplants. Bone marrow treatments. You see my meaning?"

"You mean, our problem is that we are too much alike?" asked Gwen. "That's why I can't get pregnant?"

"Well, here's where the road forks between the medical establishment and those of us in the reproductive sciences." Dr. Bertrand leaned forward on both elbows, his chin slung in his laced fingers. "Without getting too complicated, the reproductive research we do here focuses primarily on couples in your situation. First with the RSAs, or recurrent spontaneous abortions. In your case, Gwen's four miscarriages. After that, no pregnancy whatsoever. Your cycle goes haywire. It's as if your body's trying *not* to get pregnant at all.

"To be even more precise—and all this is in the literature, by the way—it's all about this thing called HLA-DR and HLA-DQ antigen sharing and the woman's fertile controls. In many cases, there's a decreased level of something else called the maternal alloantibodies. Simply put, these are the woman's reproductive functions that recognize the new life inside her as something altogether its own. A new being." And then, with a warming glance to Gwen. "A baby."

"So if a couple are too much alike?" asked Will. "At a DNA level, too closely related—"

"Nature," answered Dr. Bertrand. "Or call it the woman's reproductive system. *It* chooses to *abort,* then after further attempts, refuses to get pregnant at all. But we are *here* to *make* babies. And that begins with a series of immunizations with lymphocytes until your anti-paternal antibodies are adequate. It's mixed with small doses of heparin and prednisone. After which, the work begins. And this much you've already been through. You come on the day on which you ovulate. We fertilize in the lab to avoid any anti-paternal antibodies we haven't been able to neutralize." Dr. Bertrand then shrugged and grinned at Will. "Then we wait and see. If it takes, then we break out the champagne. But only for you and me, Senator. At that point your wife will be pregnant and no longer drinking any alcohol."

"And if it doesn't take?" said Gwen, steering the discussion back on course. If there was to be cold water, she wanted all of it tossed out in one big bucket.

"We continue treatment until it *does* work—mostly with increased levels of immunization." The doctor turned his confident grin to Gwen. "So far, I've been very successful."

"So you say," said Will. "But why is it you and the medical establishment don't see eye-to-eye?"

"Sadly and simply," said Dr. Bertrand, "to be recognized requires clinical, double-blind testing. That means treating some couples with a placebo while others get the real thing." Bertrand was shaking his head. "It would break too many hearts. By the time couples come in here or other clinics, they've been through the whole gamut, medically *and* emotionally."

Gwen squeezed Will's hand. There was genuine feeling in her touch. Hope. Love. A future.

6

8:31 P.M. Texas time.
Will's flight eventually touched down at DFW International. The appointment with Dr. Bertrand had obviously been blown. The window was most likely slammed shut for another month. To make matters worse, when the jet had finally become airborne, its phones had been out due to electrical storms passing underneath the crucial satellite linkups. Will hadn't been able to reach Gwen all damn day.

And though the phones were working in the terminal at DFW, Will decided calling Gwen at that point would do little good. The apology would have to be made in person. He could only pray she hadn't been so steamed that she'd hopped on a flight back to Logan.

But a key was waiting at the Melrose's front desk. Yes, Mrs. Sullivan was still registered. And no, she hadn't checked out or changed rooms.

Will palmed the concierge a hundred-dollar bill to get him a dozen yellow roses—Gwen's favorite color. And while he waited for the flowers, he ordered a tiramisu from the restaurant next door. It was the same dessert they'd shared thirteen years prior on that special birthday evening. The night they'd first met at Damiano's. After their respective friends had said their good nights, Will and Gwen had doubled back to meet up in the bar. They'd shared a bottle of Cristal, a tiramisu, and Will's bed, and in doing so had started the longest ongoing debate of their marriage. Just who'd seduced who? From that sleepless dawn of the morning after, Will had steadfastly maintained that he'd invited her up to his Surrey Place apartment, kissed her on the first landing, then ravished her on his mother's Persian rug to the strains of a Steve Miller Band compact disc.

Gwen lauded his version for the romance novel quality of the tale, but insisted to a fault that he was falling-down drunk, could barely get his pants off without her help, and that he hadn't a prayer from the first moment she'd seen him. From when she'd put him in her sights, he was as good as laid. Her plan went south when she'd fallen asleep in his arms. When she awoke short of sunrise, she'd discovered an odd feeling of safety in his embrace. Cozy. Warm. Something fit.

When the Melrose Hotel concierge delivered Will the roses and tiramisu, he took the elevator up to the ninth-floor suite. He knocked at the door. "Room service," he said. But he wasn't fooling Gwen. He heard the chain unhook, the door unlock, then the soft sound of her stocking feet heading back to the bedroom.

This is going to be harder than you thought, Willy.

He entered with the flowers and dessert, swinging the door closed with his foot. The suite was just as he remembered it. Heavy furniture, navy print curtains pulled back with a sash. Subtle wallpaper. A couch, a love seat, a TV mounted in an armoire so it could swing both ways, either into the lounge or the bedroom. He turned the corner into the bedroom, sculpting a warm smile on his face, yet equally prepared to dodge some flying object. Gwen's aim was notoriously dead-on.

"I hope you're not expecting anyone else," Gwen said, back propped up against the headboard, feet crossed and looking at the TV.

"Just you and me," said Will, flashing the flowers as if she hadn't yet noticed.

"Yellow roses in Texas," she said. "How appropriate."

"I thought you'd like them," said Will, his voice sounding apologetic already. Then from behind his back he revealed the tiramisu.

"Thanks, but I've already eaten," she said.

"It's our birthday, sweetheart."

"Ask me if I care."

"Would you rather I ordered a bottle of Cristal?"

"I'm not drinking. Ask me why."

"Why?"

"Because I'm pregnant."

Pregnant?

The word repeated in Will's head like a stuck record.

"Surprised you, didn't I?" asked Gwen, smug grin firmly in place.

"Look," he began. "I wasn't there. And I'm sorry—"

"So am I," she said, keeping a grip on her righteous anger. "No matter. We did it anyway."

"Without me?"

"Dr. Bertrand had a frozen sample of your semen. We used it instead of the real thing."

"The plane was late—"

"Please, Will. Don't spin me."

"I couldn't call—"

"Did you hear what I said? I don't *care*."

"You don't care?" Will stuffed the flowers into an empty ice bucket and slid the tiramisu on top of the bureau.

"Not really," she said, swigging from her bottle of Evian. "When it comes down to it, it really doesn't matter to me one bit. I don't care if you're lying or not. I don't care if you were fucking some Hollywood actress."

"I said I was sorry."

"Moot point. I'm pregnant. I can feel it."

"You've felt it before."

"Not like this!"

Will began pacing. He looked like a duck in a carnival shooting gallery. Left-face then right-face. A clear sign that the unshakable Will Sullivan was getting rattled. "You're messing with me just because I wasn't there. Nothing *happened.*"

"Oh, your poor little ego. Couldn't bear the fact that when his wife got preggers, he wasn't there."

"And you couldn't wait?"

"For you? Wait for *you?*" she said. "Hell could freeze over if I waited for you."

"I'm not that bad."

"You're *never* there. Not when I *need* you. Not when I *really really* need you." Then she stuck the knife deep into his psyche. "And don't ask me if I expect you to be there when the baby's born, or when he's five, or when he's—"

"You know, Gwen? You can be a real bitch."

"That's why we're meant for each other. The bitch and the self-absorbed asshole. We're the perfect political couple."

Will threw up his arms, left the room and headed right for the mini-bar. His room key fitted in the lock, and the little door swung open to reveal a potpourri of tiny hard-liquor bottles and premixed cocktails. When a knock came at the door, he accepted the distraction, opening it for the bellman and tipping the young man ten dollars in exchange for his luggage.

"Thank you, Senator," said the bellman with a respectful touch to his cap.

"Hang on a sec," said Will, who moved back to the bar, and swept all the booze into a wastepaper basket. The glass clattered loudly. Will crossed back to the door and handed the wastebasket to the bellman. "Get rid of this, will ya?"

"Very good, sir."

Will thanked him, shut the door, then leaned against it with his arms wrapped tightly around himself. It wasn't his habit to clean out every hotel mini-bar. Only when he was rattled. It was a *secondary* impulse. The first was to twist off the caps and knock back a couple of those little vodka ampoules before taking so much as a breath. So he'd dumped the bar before his subconscious reached full, uncontrollable throttle.

When his nerves eased, he found his way back into the bedroom. But Gwen had already turned off the light, pulled herself under the covers, and curled into a fetal ball. It was her *don't-even-think-of-touching-me* pose.

So Will retired to the couch in the sitting room. He kicked off his shoes, flipped on the TV, and soaked up the darkness until sleep came somewhere during a taped segment of CNBC's *Rivera Live*. He slept hard, waking from a nightmare sometime after daylight had broken. Someone was knocking on the door.

"Housekeeping," called out a woman's voice.

Dammit, he thought. He hadn't put out the DO NOT DISTURB sign before curling up for the night. And wouldn't you know there'd be a knock around seven-thirty, followed by a voice from somewhere south of the Panama Canal.

Housekeeping.

He wasn't quick enough to answer. He heard the key in the door and pulled himself upright just in time to see a large Bolivian woman in a hotel uniform enter, a housekeeping cart in tow. She stopped when she saw the rumpled senator on the couch. "Oh, I'm so sorry."

"Please come back later," groaned Will.

"I come back later."

"Right." Will forced a smile and a courteous wave as the woman exited the way she entered. The door latched closed behind her.

Between the mothballs on his brain and the landscape of the suite, his memory came rushing back. The night before. The fight with Gwen. Dumping the bar. The couch.

What a mess.

The door to the bedroom was closed. Time to make up. Suck up to the missus. Be contrite. Give her the words of wonder and encouragement he'd left out the night before. Gwen *thought* she was pregnant. And maybe she was. It wasn't the first time and, if history was a teacher, this one might not be a keeper either. All that mattered right now was that he needed to be there for her.

He stood, bumping a shin against the coffee table. And though it hurt like hell, he didn't cry out because he didn't want to wake Gwen. It was a rare day when she got to sleep in. Maybe he'd order some breakfast in bed. Eggs Benedict was her favorite. A decadent room-service meal. As he recalled, the Melrose did them quite well.

Bleary-eyed, he found the room-service button on the phone and whispered the order. Eggs Benedict for her. Coffee and a blueberry muffin for him. Then, stripping himself down to his boxers, he crept up to the bedroom door, quietly twisting the knob. It barely made a sound and the hinges, praise be, didn't squeak. All he had to do was ease into bed, cozy up next to her, slide his knees in behind hers, close his arms about her body, and bury his face in her hair. Then it would once again be the way that it was meant to be. The two of them in peaceful sleep until breakfast arrived.

Only Gwen wasn't in the bed.

Nor was she in the bathroom. She was gone. Clothes. Toilet kit. Overnight bag. All vanished while Will was sound asleep.

Crossing the threshold back into the living area, Will heard the slight scraping of an envelope being slipped underneath the door. Then footsteps.

Gwen!

He rushed to the door, thinking he'd caught her. His mind kicked through the rough logic. She must have gone downstairs moments before he'd been awakened by the housekeeper, only to regret not leaving him *some* kind of note. Tossing open the door, Will stepped into the hall, only to find it empty save for the shape of a man hurrying away from him.

Will called out, "Excuse me!"

But if anything, his voice made the little man speed up. Any faster and he'd be running.

"I said excuse me!"

The man didn't stop, nor did he even pause a beat to acknowledge the raised voice calling after him. And before the man turned the corner, all Will could make out was a tired gray rain jacket and a black watchman's cap. Hardly a hotel uniform.

Realizing that he was standing in the ninth-floor corridor wearing nothing but a pair of boxer shorts, Will retreated into his room where he picked up the envelope. His name was written neatly in blue ink. Tearing at the seal, Will extracted what seemed to be a blank card. He needed his glasses. Pillaging the inside pockets of his jacket which was draped over the armchair, he came up with his prescription frames—a pair of horn-rims he'd never worn in public. He stuck the glasses onto his face and sighed, preparing to read some more vitriol, this time from Gwen's own hand. Instead, the note was typed, the words centered in the middle of the card:

> But so much the more malign and wild does the ground become with bad seed and untilled, as it has the more of good earthly vigor.

A chill chased up Will's spine from his tailbone to the base of his skull. This wasn't Gwen's sort of wit. Hell, it wasn't witty at all. The chill repeated, hammering his lower cortex in what was the clear beginning of a skull-splitting stress headache. That, and the damn phone was ringing. How long, Will hadn't really noticed. He'd been so absorbed staring at the note, wondering who was responsible for the twisted prank, it must have taken five or six rings before he even thought to answer.

"Hello?" he croaked, his eyes still stuck on the words on the note card.

"How's the view?" asked the voice.

"What?"

"From the doghouse?" The phone was at Will's ear and he could tell La Roy was calling from a crackling cell phone.

"Where are you?"

"I'm at the stew's place."

"The one from the flight."

"What is it about white girls and that oral sex Watusi?"

"I have no idea what you're talking about. And I don't think I wanna know. Why are you on a cell phone?"

"I swear, Earnest. She came to me like a Holyfield over-hand right. I got worried she was workin' for somebody else's DTT. Phone could be bugged."

DTT. Beltway lingo for *dirty tricks team*. Will thought La Roy was on the paranoid side of sane. But that's part of what he was paid for. "You don't think it's a little early in the game for that kind of stuff?"

"Wild Bill's rule number one. Never too early to mess with the opposition. We're talkin' about the future leader of the free world and all them powers that wanna be. Oh, you're in it, Earnest. Dodge Heebler knows it. And plenty of the bad guys know you're in it."

"But which bad guys?" asked Will, staring again at the words on the note.

"You mean *our* bad guys or *their* bad guys?"

"I know," said Will. "La Roy's rule number two. They're *all* bad guys."

"You'll make a president yet, son."

"You ever read the Bible?" asked Will. "You're half Seminole. So there's a Catholic thing going on there, yes?"

"My daddy was a Seminole and it was a *culture* thing. My momma? She's *still* a Southern Baptist."

Will took off his glasses and rubbed his face. "I got this note under the hotel room door. My name on the envelope. Inside's this note with a verse that, frankly speaking, gives me the creeps. I'm wondering if it's biblical. See if it sounds familiar."

"Give it a rip."

" *'But so much the more malign and wild does the ground become with bad seed and untilled, as it has the more of good earthly vigor.'* "

"Uh-uh. I don't think it's the Bible," said La Roy. "Literary, maybe. Anybody put their name on it?"

"Unsigned," said Will.

"Bother you?"

"What do you think? Bad seed? I know we get the crank stuff at the office all the time. But I'm in Dallas."

"You're a public figure. And the shit sticks to you everywhere you go. I heard Pig Pen was a politician."

"I need coffee," segued Will. "Do me a favor. Get Myriam to book us an earlier flight and send a car."

"For two or for three?"

"Two. Gwen is . . ." Will thought about it, then decided not to finish the sentence. "Just two. You and me."

Vance Allatore, former famed prosector, drove with the heat on full blast, the fan whining in the rental wreck, a rosary hanging from the rearview mirror. The old Mazda 626 was a cheap deal for a man who used to favor expensive suits and the roar of a Mercedes-Benz. After dropping the note at the Melrose and nearly being caught by the addressee, Allatore had driven straight for the suburbs, looking for a gas station with the least expensive gasoline. After filling the tank at a Sunoco in Denton, he headed north to Interstate 40. When the car eventually warmed, he shrugged his way out of the gray jacket, tossed the knit watchman's cap into the backseat, and settled in for the long drive ahead.

By 10 P.M., he'd reached western New Mexico and a Motel 6. He didn't check in, though. He found a well-lit parking space, curled up behind the wheel, and fell asleep saying his prayers while he expertly worked over the rosary.

Hail Mary, full of grace . . .

As usual, he dreamed in color. That night, a vivid replay of his days of wine and glory. Of Los Angeles, sunny and sweltering. When he was an undefeated prosecutor, with a wife, a beautiful little girl, and the case of a lifetime . . .

A record heat had swarmed Southern California's San Fernando Valley along with four days of first-stage smog alerts. Children were asked to play inside and commuters to keep their windows up and air-conditioning on high. It was only May 11 and Southern California was already cooking under a Santa Ana siege.

Then on the fifth day, in the north valley city of Chatsworth, the residents began to report a revolting stench. A stink that the Santa Ana winds swept off the mountains across five square miles. Some claimed to have passed out from the fumes. Paramedics were put on alert. Geologists from Caltech in Pasadena scrambled in search of possible new seismic cracks that might have cut loose a lethal mixture of natural gas and sulfur. Residents, fearing some kind of secret, toxic poisoning, fled for the Los Angeles basin and the nearby beaches.

The mystery of the foul smell was solved when an off-duty homicide detective, driving the 118 Freeway to his home in Simi Valley, instantly recognized the odor as that of rotting flesh. But how much flesh to create such a massive and overwhelming stench? A call to his duty officer prompted a call to a captain, then the chief of police, who called the mayor. A CDC team in chemical suits was helicoptered in from UCLA. By nightfall, they narrowed the search down to a single block of abandoned movie soundstages at the end of a potholed cul-de-sac. Protected by cyclone fencing and razor wire, the property had been condemned since an earthquake some two years earlier. The owner was still toying with the idea of bankruptcy. And not many residents knew or cared that the site had been temporarily annexed by a commune of former hookers, porno actors, drug addicts, and runaways. Not even the Valley cops, who'd heard the reports of trespassing, had cared enough to check up on the cult. After all, they didn't seem to be bothering anybody.

But on that fifth day, they were bothering the entire city.

The first reports were unbelievable. A mass suicide in Chatsworth. LAPD cops from the Van Nuys division were either sobbing or hunched over and puking. Live video was patched through to the satellites and broadcast nationwide. A chemical-suited camera crew followed the CDC team inside the main soundstage, catching scattershot glimpses of naked bodies peaceful yet decomposing. Each had his eyes closed. Each held or lay next to his own personalized Baskin-Robbins ice cream cup.

By dawn the next day, the nation was either scorning, mourning, or questioning why. Who were these lost souls? What would lead to such mass self-destruction?

By ten that same morning, the Baskin-Robbins corporation delivered its first press release, claiming their product had nothing to do with the deaths of the poor suicide victims.

By eleven, the mass suicide had turned into a murder investigation. All counted, there were eighty-eight bodies. Men and women. All between the ages of nineteen and twenty-seven. But the LAPD detectives had found one hundred and one used ice cream cups, allowing for the possibility of thirteen survivors.

A team of diligent LAPD investigators assigned from Parker Center went about the painstaking task of matching the eighty-eight naked bodies with the names on the personalized Baskin-Robbins cups. It took a bit more than eleven weeks. And when it was over, there were thirteen Baskin-Robbins cups with thirteen sets of unclaimed fingerprints. The cups were labeled:

Markus
Isadora
Jane
Asia
Starr
Clem
Dean
Kris
Madison
Arletta
Sheila
Timothy
Jack

Two weeks later an FBI fingerprint analysis delivered positive IDs on six out of the thirteen. The one name that keyed the LAPD's interest was that of Wesley Dean Theroux. According to detectives in the Hollywood Vice Unit, the former pimp-cum-actor-cum-street-hustler had moved off the streets of Hollywood to start his own tax-sheltered religion called The Lifeforce. The police had gladly left him alone as, one by one, he'd culled his flock from the delinquents and addicts who crowded the sidewalks of Sunset and Hollywood Boulevards. To the police, Wesley Dean Theroux was simply performing a public service and at no cost to the taxpayers at that.

The FBI also assisted in testing the contents of each of the one hundred and one Baskin-Robbins cups left at the death scene.

LAPD Special Crimes Investigator Daryl O'Rourke delivered his evidence to top L.A. County Deputy District Attorney and resident bulldog Vance Allatore at the downtown Criminal Courts Building.

"Here's what we got," said O'Rourke. "Eighty-eight cups come up positive for strawberry-flavored Jell-O mixed with lethal doses of Seconal, phenobarbital, and Valium."

"Got it," said Vance Allatore, scratching notes on a yellow legal pad with his silver Montblanc, a gift from the governor. "A nice little suicide solution I could recommend to my mother-in-law. But I'm looking to prove a homicide here."

"It gets better," said O'Rourke. "Twelve of the cups, notcoincidentally matching the names of those who weren't amongst the dead . . . The lab came up with a nonlethal mixture of strawberry Jell-O, Seconal, and heavy dosing of a drug called—get this—Chlorpromachol."

"Chlorproma-what?"

"That's what I asked the guys at the FBI lab," said O'Rourke. "They turned me over to some Pentagon pharmacologist. Turns out this Chlorpromachol is what's called a hypno-narcotic. Used by Eastern bloc governments. Creates, and I quote, 'a hallucinogenic suggestibility.' "

"In other words, a brainwashing drug," confirmed Allatore, his fountain pen never leaving the legal pad.

"For lack of a better description, yeah."

"And these twelve didn't die."

"Let's not forget the *thirteenth cup*," said O'Rourke. "One we've matched up with this loser named W. D. Theroux."

"The leader of the happy clan."

"That's him. And guess what we found in his little cup?"

"You got me."

"Strawberry fuckin' Jell-O."

"Nothing else?"

"Swear to God."

Vance Allatore put down his fountain pen and tilted backwards. The county-issued chair squeaked. His prematurely balding head was in sharp contrast against the black vinyl. But his dress was impeccable for a city salary. When Vance Allatore walked into a courtroom, he refused to be outdressed by the competition. The same went for the make and model of car he parked in the courthouse lot.

"Theory?" asked Allatore.

"We found some bank receipts in a dumpster near the crime scene," said O'Rourke. "But the accounts were cashed out on the day of the suicide—"

"Murder," corrected Allatore.

"Murder, fine," said O'Rourke. "I'd say Theroux first built his little 'love me' cult, then bilked his followers out of whatever savings they had, then killed 'em for the cash."

"How much we talking about?"

"More or less," said O'Rourke, "could be two hundred and fifty Gs."

"That doesn't explain those twelve unidentified Jell-O cups."

"That part's got me scratchin' my head. Maybe he brainwashed 'em into thinkin' their money went to support the Dalai Lama in fuckin' China."

"Okay. I got enough motive," said Allatore, sounding as cocksure as his forty-nine-and-zip courtroom record. "You guys pick him up? I'll burn him at the stake."

Sixteen days later, following a trail of murder that began with the bloody butchering of a Spokane lumber industrialist, and ended in Heber, Utah, shortly after a college professor and his family were torched in their own home, Markus Arquette was arrested. One of Theroux's twelve resurrected souls, Markus was remarkably quick to give up his master's whereabouts before hanging himself in a Flagstaff holding cell. The next day, Wesley Dean Theroux was arrested in a Mojave, California, motel. Upon his extradition to Los Angeles and a face-to-face meeting with

Vance Allatore, Daryl O'Rourke, and two more Special Crimes investigators, Theroux looked the prosecutor straight in the eye and spoke.

"I would like to request a lawyer."

"Of course," said Vance Allatore. The courtroom veteran wasn't about to risk the biggest case of his career on technical points and reversible errors. This was his Super Bowl. National attention was coming. Maybe even live TV coverage of the actual proceedings. It could happen, he bragged to colleagues. Meanwhile, the ambitious prosecutor prayed to God that he'd get a jury trial. No pleas. No bargains. Vance Allatore wanted Wesley Dean Theroux to stand up at the arraignment and throw down the gauntlet with a "not guilty" plea.

"Would you like a lawyer assigned to you?" asked Vance Allatore, more than happy to ring the L.A. County Public Defender's Office. "Or do you have someone else in mind?"

"I do, yes," said Theroux.

"A name would help."

"God," said Theroux. "I would like God to be my lawyer."

The request cracked the room into a dangerous state of laughter. The tough-guy faces were gone. This was a killer with a sense of humor.

"I'm not sure God has a license to practice law in this state," countered Allatore.

"That's a pity," said Theroux, his shackled palms turning toward the ceiling. "Then in God's stead, I shall represent myself."

Stitches. Vance Allatore saw stitches in the form of a small cross in each of Theroux's palms. Christ, he thought. This asshole's a first-class crazy. And entertained by all this. Five minutes into the interview and his Super Bowl case was already turning into bad performance art. The rare nutjob who could somehow convince a superior court judge to permit self-representation turned the courtroom into a nightmare, a mockery of justice, and was no goddamn fun at all.

"Fine by me," said Allatore. "But a judge will require a

psychiatric evaluation before he allows you to represent yourself. Are you sure you don't want the court to appoint you a capable attorney?"

"Oh, I'm plenty capable," said Theroux with a smug wink and his right hand over his heart. "Bring on the shrinks. I'm ready."

And bring on the shrinks they did. Psychiatrists, psychologists, neuropharmacologists, and forensic analysts conducted three months of jailhouse interviews, tests, and hearings before the case judge. Allatore dutifully fought every ridiculous and Hail Mary motion filed by the defendant.

Theroux made Allatore so bloody angry that, amongst his colleagues, the lawyer vowed to drop the gas pellets on the asshole himself when the time came.

Five months after the mass suicide, on a rare starry evening in the Los Angeles suburb of La Cañada, Vance Allatore shared Coronas and lime with his friend and Theroux's court-appointed psychiatrist, Jim Felton. They were on Allatore's southern-facing deck, overlooking the skyscraper lights of downtown Los Angeles. Allatore's wife and daughter were inside watching a prime-time sitcom.

"Okay," began Allatore. "Let's dispense with the surprises. When the judge asks you if Theroux's competent enough to know that if he represents himself in a court of law, that he would be at a tactical disadvantage . . ."

"I'll answer yes," said Felton. "He *is* competent. But at a disadvantage?"

"What?" laughed Allatore. "You saying he can beat me in a courtroom?"

Felton sipped his beer and chose his words carefully. "Follow me. I've spent better than three months with this subject. And I've found him symptomatically empathic, a classical sociopath—"

"Empathic?" asked Allatore.

"Remarkably intuitive. Almost psychic. Shall I continue?"

"Go on." Allatore was amused.

Felton counted off on his fingers. "He's an *empath*. He's

a *sociopath*. He's a *psychopath*. He's got a Technicolor photographic memory. And if that's not enough, he's got this doozy of a messiah complex that's good for at least four chapters in an institutional primer."

"So he's fuckin' crazy," confirmed Allatore.

"He's a mind-fucker without equal," said Felton. "He got off on how many times he could make me twist in my chair. That, and he's articulate as hell. Off the IQ scale. He can quote Freud, Shakespeare, New Testament, Old Testament, Nietzsche, and some guys you've never heard of. I'd say better than a legion of Ivy League professors. And I can guarantee the social worker's gonna testify that he's a product of twenty-five years in foster homes, juvenile lockups, and male prostitution."

"She's seen the juvenile file?" asked Allatore. "That shit's supposed to be sealed."

"She hasn't seen the file," said Felton. "But she'll go on the very convincing history as he tells it."

"Jesus," said Allatore. "What the hell am I dealing with?"

"I'd say W. D. Theroux is as whacked as the factory makes 'em."

"Is that your clinical opinion?"

"My clinical opinion is that if he wants to represent himself, there's nothing in his behavior to prove that he can't do so without understanding the risks."

"Yeah," said Allatore. "But what's your gut tell ya?"

"My gut tells me that if he gets his wish and goes to trial, you will expand for him a giant game board upon which he'll be able to move his little chess pieces."

"Chess pieces?" asked Allatore.

"You, me, the judge, jury. It's how he views the world. We're all little subjects in the Kingdom of Theroux. Except for a fixation that deifies his dead mother, the rest of us walking around the planet might as well be molded from plastic."

"Mother fixation? He a homosexual?"

Felton had to rub his scalp for an answer. "Neither. As in homo or hetero. He's got a distinctly asexual vibe. As if the subject doesn't interest him at all."

"Sounds like a sick little boy," said Allatore. "I'll tell you this much. When I get done with him, there won't be a lotta tears when the jury comes back with a decision to fry his sorry ass. You just watch."

Swilling back the rest of his beer and gazing up to the heavens, Allatore toasted himself. "Hey, God. Here's to fifty and zip."

Felton, who sat on a fence somewhere between atheism and agnosticism, merrily clinked his bottle with Allatore's. "Funny. Theroux says he talks to God, too."

Allatore let his endearing grin that had charmed forty-nine juries shine. "Guess it's gonna be up to the jury to tell which one of us he's listening to."

Nine months later, Vance Allatore went to trial.

Eight and a half weeks after that, in front of a cable TV audience of millions, Vance Allatore won a death penalty conviction for Wesley Dean Theroux for the murder of eighty-eight of his followers.

And that very night of the verdict, the blooding began.

The judge, butchered.

Six jurors and two alternates, butchered.

Theroux's assisting legal counsel, butchered.

The court stenographer, butchered.

Two court-appointed deputies, butchered.

Three *Los Angeles Times* writers, butchered.

One court observer, butchered.

And as Theroux had instructed, it was as if the eleven remaining disciples had awakened when the death sentence was read. They murdered and fled. Within a week, five were captured, but unlike Markus the Judas, each committed suicide before questioning. The six survivors—Izzy, Starr, Clem, Timothy, Jack, and Sheila—would remain at large for years.

The bloody courtroom coup made headlines all over the planet. And Wesley Dean Theroux was very, very pleased.

At dawn, Allatore woke from the dream unfazed but weary. Conscious or not, his memory always delivered the same, sad ending. It was a TV rerun with himself, the ego-driven prosecutor, star of his own horrifying melodrama. Sometimes the episode continued through to his ugly and public divorce and the spontaneous nervous breakdown which had followed. Other times, it ended when he'd woken to KTLA's early morning news and live images of one of his butchered female jurors.

The reinvented, reformed, and rejuvenated version of Vance Allatore pulled on his one and only jacket, crossed the street to a coffee shop, and ordered the early-riser sausage and eggs special for his main, daily meal. In the rest room he produced a toothbrush and soap from a Ziploc bag, washed up, and ran a comb through his salt-and-pepper beard, none too thrilled that it was the only hair he had left on his head. He'd filled out in his ten-year absence from the limelight. Twenty pounds, he reasoned. His face was puffy. His eyes were tired and lined. He gassed up the Mazda at the Texaco station next door, and was back on the road by eight.

California lay ahead. Los Angeles and its San Fernando Valley suburb of Reseda, where he would find everything just as he'd left it. The Rupert's U-Store-It lot. A horseshoe-shaped, two-story structure surrounded by cyclone fence and razor wire. The ten years of rent had been paid well in advance under the fictitious name of Alan Vanderbilt. No ID was required. Just the proper combination to the Master lock. That much he had kept in his head. His mother's birthday. Easy. Once there, he would lift the heavy door and look upon history. All of it, right in front of him. Files. Memos. Videotapes. Transcripts.

Bad, bad memories.

He had forgotten about the three cartons left over from his final, dark days as an L.A. County deputy district attorney. The boxes had been marked with a bold, black felt-tip marker: DESK, CORRESPONDENCE, and DIVORCE.

The man once called the finest prosecutor west of the Rockies kicked aside the last box, then with the tip of his worn-out Nikes tilted the box until the lid popped open and some of the contents spilled onto the concrete. Out poured sour memories, including silver-framed photos of his wife and child. An autographed picture of Ronald Reagan. And a mock trophy crafted in his daughter's third grade art class:

VANCE ALLATORE:
WORLD'S GREATEST PROSECUTOR!

Vance Allatore, prosecutor extraordinaire, was dead and gone, he told himself. Slaughtered along with the rest of Wesley Dean Theroux's victims. As he swept the contents back into the box with the full intention of closing the lid forever, he spied one last item. A severed wristband with his name neatly typed in capital letters. Instead of hospital blue, it was institutional pink. County USC's version of the city funny farm.

"Finish what you started," God had demanded on a bristling cold February night. *"The demon is still at work."*

With that, he unfurled a swatch of red velvet from his pocket. Inside was a silver whisky flask filled with holy water from Lourdes. In the sign of the cross, Vance Allatore sprinkled the room, uttered a blessing in Latin, and went on with his work. He sorted through the key evidence along with some of the videotapes, then crammed the boxes into the trunk and backseat of the rented Mazda. He would need a place to stay. He thought maybe Panorama City or somewhere in Van Nuys. Plenty of cheap housing up there in exchange for green cash. The anonymous refuge for the majority of L.A.'s increasing illegal alien population. No problem. He would hole up there for the month and begin sorting through everything. Reliving the mystery. He could feel the precious time bleeding away. Less than a year, he figured. A date for execution had been set. And if he'd been right about who and what he'd found in Dallas, Theroux had just outlined the final act of his grand play. At the end of which he'd be executed, but living on through the eyes of a child.

The cozy streets of Brookline, Massachusetts, were coated with leaves. October in New England was beginning with a shock of subfreezing cold, knocking down the last of the colorful leaves in one windswept weekend. Expensive four-wheel drives and European sedans forded the streets, stirring the dead leaves with each passing gust.

On the morning of October 6th, Gwen's red Ford Explorer was still parked in the driveway at a time when she would usually be well on her way to the office. Upstairs, she was in the master bath, robed in cream chenille and seated on the toilet as she cried her gray eyes out. The damn stick was blue. Baby blue. Pregnant blue. Positive. And next to the sink were three other pregnancy test sticks, each bearing the same result.

Blue, blue, and blue.

She'd gone through four boxes of pregnancy tests to get the same perfect result.

Jeez, girl. You are so *knocked up.*

She tried to calm herself. She knew the realities. Though it had been so very long since she'd gotten results, there was still the risk of miscarriage ahead. The perilous first trimester.

Oh my God. I'm pregnant. Sweet Jesus.

She gathered the sticks, pocketing them in the robe, then went to the phone. She thought to call Will, but first called her gynecologist, Dr. Hannah Rosen.

"Is this the service?"

"Yes, it is. Would you like to leave a message for Dr. Rosen?"

"What time does she get in?" asked Gwen.

"Nine o'clock."

"What time is it now?" Then Gwen answered her own question. The clock radio next to the bed read 7:44 A.M. "Please leave a message for Dr. Rosen. Tell her Gwen Sullivan will be in to see her at nine-thirty."

"I'm just the service, ma'am. I don't take appointments."

"Just tell her I'm positive."

"Excuse me?"

"I'm pregnant," said Gwen, a smile spreading across her lips. "I'm finally pregnant."

The woman's voice at the other end of the line warmed in a single heartbeat from monotone to a sudden, contact thrill. "Well, congratulations, ma'am. Hooray for you."

"Yes," said Gwen. "Thank you."

I'm pregnant. Praise Mother of God.

7

Wesley Dean Theroux spoke evenly, but softly. "How's this? Can you hear me now?"

Forty-seven years old, he appeared fit, seated as elegantly as humanly possible in a brushed aluminum desk chair, patiently allowing the technician to clip the lapel microphone to his neon-orange jumpsuit. The killer couldn't assist. His wrists were bound to a waist chain, his ankles cuffed to the chair.

"Can you speak a little louder?" asked the cameraman, his index finger offering a visual by tapping his headset.

"This is how I talk," said the convicted killer.

The cameraman didn't argue. He simply increased the volume level on his new digital Ikegami and kept his eye to the monitor. It flickered with a color image of the well-manicured prisoner. Aside from the numerated jumpsuit, the only indication that the subject was a criminal was his bone-white skin. Sunlight didn't penetrate much of Rancho Seco's concrete-bunkered death row.

"How about some makeup?" offered the cameraman.

"That would be nice, thank you. Natural Beige, please."

The camera assistant, a young woman with earthy looks, nervously popped open a tackle-box-turned-makeup-kit. She couldn't believe she was about to apply some Joe Blasco to the face of a mass murderer. One who already knew what tone worked best for him under the flat, TV camera lighting.

"I promise not to bite," said the killer, as if reading her mind. "As you might guess, I've done this before."

The prison guards laughed. Yes, indeed. He'd done this before. And they were always right alongside him. It was easy duty with the easiest, most compliant inmate. And oftentimes they'd get to meet major TV personalities. This week it was Harve Langer of MSNBC. A cable host. Not quite a celebrity highlight. Upon hearing it was NBC, the guards had hoped it would be Jane Pauley or Katie Couric.

MSNBC was only cable. Not exciting enough to tell the wife about, thought one guard. "Harve who?" he'd said, to the camera crew's amusement.

But W. D. Theroux—or *Deatheroux* as he was called by the tabloids—had never met a camera he didn't like. Since the trial, there had been plenty of lights, camera, and TV action for the convicted killer.

The MSNBC segment producer, Zach Schumwat, was finishing up the pre-interview with Theroux. "I'm sure you've heard a bunch of these questions before."

"I'm sure I have," said Theroux.

"But we're tailoring this piece to fit in with a series we're doing on the recent increase in U.S. executions."

"I understand."

"Yours is when?" asked Schumwat a bit too coldly.

"June twenty-third."

"Seven months to finish all your appeals?"

"Actually, I'm looking for a presidential pardon," deadpanned Theroux.

The guards laughed again. Theroux was damn funny. A murderer with a killer sense of humor.

"Harve should be right along," said Schumwat.

"Harve is here," proclaimed the reporter, appearing behind the camera, suit pressed, hair coiffed, and bearing a distinct nonstick attitude. Harve Langer was an on-air *personality*. That meant he bore the pedigree of Teflon. And not even America's most notorious serial killer could put a scare into him.

Especially one as camera-friendly as W. D. Theroux.

"Hi. Harve Langer. Nice to meet you." The dope had his hand stuck out as if Theroux could reach out and shake it. "Oops. I didn't see the chains."

"It's okay," smiled Theroux, who in his ten years of incarceration had suffered men more foolish than Harve Langer. But there was time. The interview hadn't yet begun.

Harve Langer sat to the camera's left, his own microphone clipped and ready.

"Gimme a level, Harve?" asked the cameraman.

"This is Harve Langer, MSNBC," said Harve in his anchor-ready voice.

Zach Schumwat handed the list of questions to Langer, who briefly perused them before giving his approval. "Okay, let's do this. You ready, Wes?"

Wes? It's Mr. Theroux to you, asshole.

"Go right ahead," said the killer.

A nod from the producer and camera rolled tape. Harve Langer started at the top of the page. "Mr. Theroux. What do you think of the recent forty-percent rise in state-sanctioned executions in the last three years?"

"You're asking me because I'm on the list? Or because my opinion counts?" asked Theroux, offering his best Tony Robbins smile.

Harve fired a look over to his producer. The response wasn't on his script. Schumwat gave back a shrug.

"Well, both," answered Harve Langer.

"As one who's on the list, I'm innocent. And recent polls show the twenty-five percent of those familiar with my case still think I'm innocent. That gives the state a three-in-one chance of being wrong. So to answer your question, I think every execution that makes haste puts at risk the murder of an innocent man."

"Such as yourself?"

"In answer to the second part of your question, does my

opinion count? Well, that's up to you and your viewers. After all, you wanted to put me on TV. But I will remind you that while I'm unjustly incarcerated, I'm unable to participate in the real debate. And that's the right to vote."

Harve Langer looked at the script. The follow-up question didn't fit Theroux's answer. Schumwat leaned in and whispered in Harve's ear, "Just wing it and come back to the page later."

"Is that something you miss?" asked Harve. "The right to vote?"

"Before I was arrested, I never missed an election," lied Theroux, straight-faced and without the slightest hint of deceit.

Ah. If they only knew. Before Theroux had set eyes on the radiant image of Gwen Corbett-Sullivan, the acclaimed killer had barely a gnat's interest in politics, let alone casting a bloody ballot for some plasti-formed liar in a blue suit and a red tie. Politicians?

Little tin gods.

"I love politics," said Theroux with gusto. "I've always been fascinated by those who are attracted to public service."

"That . . . uh . . . That might be considered strange," said Harve, still winging it.

"What's strange about it?"

"Famous cult leader misses his right to vote."

"Cult. Now there's a buzzword. What's a cult? Dean Theroux taking care of the love and feeding of a nonnuclear family? Is that really a cult?"

"Okay," said Harve. "So let's call it a family. By your count, three out of four people familiar with your case think you murdered eighty-eight members of your family."

"It was suicide," said Theroux. "And in court, the evidence proved as much."

"But didn't a jury think otherwise?"

"Six of those jurors are dead. Four have recanted. And two more of those who convicted me haven't been accounted for in over five years. I'd say that's evidence enough for a retrial. Don't you?"

"Let's get back to cults."

"Answer me this, first. By your definition, what would you call government?"

Harve Langer was suddenly lost for a follow-up of any kind. So Theroux continued.

"For example. And I'm using your definition. What could be more cultlike than, say, the Republican or Democratic parties?" asked Theroux, dancing around the hot coals in his theory like a practiced *spin-meister*. "You *vote* their party. *Believe* in their party. And once you're *in* the party you rarely leave. What better definition would one have for a cult?"

"Is that *Webster's* definition of a cult?"

At the mention of *Webster's,* Theroux could picture the exact definition in his mind's eye.

"I prefer the fifth," said Theroux.

"What? That means you don't want to answer my question?" asked Harve.

"No, I mean Webster's fifth definition of *cult.* 'Noun. A great devotion to a person, idea, or thing; especially such devotion regarded as literary or faddish . . .' Blah blah blah. In essence, *politics.*"

"That's how *you* define cult . . . er, I mean, politics?" asked Harve, unnerved to say the least.

"I'm saying that's how *Webster's* defines the word *cult.* Dean Theroux defines it as an ambiguous word used non-ambiguously by uninformed television journalists."

Harve shook off the insult and tried to move back to the text. "Can we please get back to the script—"

"Tape is cheap, Harve. And you're gonna cut all this out anyway. But let's talk. You and me. Who'd you vote for in the last election?"

Harve looked to his producer. Another nod from Schumwat. "I voted for Addison."

"The Democratic ticket. That makes you the classic liberal-slash-journalist. Very good. So would I if given the constitutional opportunity. Minus, of course, the journalistic credentials. I think Addison is good for America."

"But he also believes in the death penalty," added Schumwat from the wings.

"A true believer is one kind of man. *Living* your beliefs is another," Theroux stated.

"You really are up on the news," said Harve, trying to appear impressed. For some reason, he wanted the killer to like him. "Do you read the newspapers or watch television?"

"Actually, I get most of my news off the Internet," said Theroux. He was fast becoming a huge fan of a Web site called *A La Mode* and its chief proprietor, Gary F. Modetti. A secret he would decline to share.

"I'm sorry," said Harve. Surprised, to say the least. "But I didn't know they allowed computers on death row."

"As a rule, they don't," said Theroux. "It began back at San Quentin. As I'm still my own court-appointed attorney, I was having storage problems. The warden was required by the court to dedicate an entire cell next door simply to accommodate all my case files and transcripts. When the prison demanded the space back, I made a compromise offer that, in exchange for a computer, I would download all my files to CD-ROMs. The prison obliged. Next, I petitioned the court for a telephone modem and the right to communicate with my outside cocounsel in the adopted manner of today's legal world. Electronic mail. So now I have an IBM ThinkPad and ten minutes of court-approved download and upload time per day, excluding Sundays—"

"Tape's out," said the cameraman. "Gotta reload. Let's save the lights."

The camera assistant cut the lights while the cameraman fished into an equipment case for a fresh tape. In the meantime, Zach Schumwat pulled a chair up next to Theroux.

"It's going well?" asked the killer.

"Actually, no," said the producer. "The interview's all over the map. You think we could limit it to the questions in the script?"

"The script?"

"You know. What we went over in the pre-interview."

"What for? I'm sure you've got hours of those answers in your library. I thought we could talk about something different. If politics isn't to your liking, how about religion? My guess is there's also a cult angle there, too."

"We're not looking for the *cult* angle. We're looking for the *execution* angle."

"For May sweeps," confirmed Theroux.

"That's right," said Schumwat.

"But I'm not going to die," said Theroux, as resolute as he was calm.

"The state of California says otherwise," argued the producer. "Of course, you're still thinking appeal."

The killer's smile vanished and his eyebrows arched toward a well-defined dimple in his forehead that seemed to form a third eye of sorts. "Let me tell you something. They might take Dean Theroux's life. But Dean Theroux will not be dying. Of *that* I can assure you."

"Fine." Schumwat nodded. "Can you say that to Harve?"

"Okay, camera's up," said the cameraman. "Let's have those lights again."

"Okay," said Harve. "So where were we?"

"Let's talk about the pope," said Theroux. "Now, if there ever was a cult leader, he'd be the first to get my vote."

8

"The TV's workin' just fine. It's the cable that ain't connected," snapped Bill La Roy, annoyed that when the meeting was over he'd have to hightail it back to the Marriott Long Wharf. Either that or find a local sports bar and bribe the bartender to swivel his satellite dish so he could catch the remainder of the first-round NCAA matchup between Charlotte and UNLV. La Roy had laid off a five-hundred-dollar bet on Las Vegas through a part-time bookie working for the Teamster lobby. And hell if he was going to miss it, cable or no cable.

"Hooking up the cable's not on Gwen's list of priorities," confided Will during a break in the meeting. He was banging around the unfinished kitchen, looking for the coffee filters.

"House is too big for a common man," said La Roy.

"Me? Yeah," acknowledged Will. "But we both know there's nothing common about Gwen."

The new house was all her idea. The six-figure payment cashed out their combined savings. A low-interest loan was paying for the requisite remodel of the seaside Marblehead

Queen Anne. Once Gwen's pregnancy was confirmed, her priorities had changed in an instant. As if a "things to do" list had suddenly materialized in her head, a memo appeared the next day, mobilizing her troops to find the happy couple a proper place to raise their child. Real estate agents were interviewed, hired, fired, then rehired until a suitable home was found in Marblehead. Just north of Boston on a craggy coastline, the burg was provincial, old money, but most importantly boasted great schools and an easy commute by rail into the city.

The house itself was modest by Marblehead standards. A semi-rambling, seaside Victorian, it boasted two corbeled chimneys, steeply pitched gables, and triple windows with original stained glass adornments. The flat surrounding acreage offered many possibilities for improvement. Three-hundred-year-old fir trees naturally landscaped a plateau overlooking a lower shelf and, beyond that, the Atlantic. With a Boston-based architect, Gwen had quickly mapped out a new design, modernizing the interior, cutting in hidden skylights, and baby-proofing everything between the wainscoting and the hardwood floors.

Will's two cents had been limited to redesigning his study to accommodate his favorite pieces from his Civil War collection. He'd wisely left everything else to Gwen. Unfortunately for La Roy, that included calling the cable company to hook up the TV.

"Know what you oughta get?" asked La Roy.

"A maid would be a good start," said Will. Geneva, who'd been Will's housekeeper ever since he'd graduated from Harvard Law School, had not wanted to move far from her grandchildren. Luckily for her, the new owners of the Brookline house had four kids of their own who'd instantly taken to her as if she were Mary Poppins. Will and Gwen were both pleased to see her stay with the house.

"You oughta get one of them mini-satellite dishes," continued La Roy. "Eighteen inches and a hundred bucks? You can get every hoop game from sea to shining sea."

"I'll have Gwen put it on the list."

"I was thinkin' about today," said La Roy. "I'll bet you

there's an eight hundred number you can call that gets some inbred local white boy to install it by the time the meeting's done."

"I'll bet you're right," said Will, giving up on the coffee filters and shouting out into the stairwell. "GWEN?"

Gwen appeared from the opposite doorway, five months' pregnant and just starting to really show. Unlike some women who liked to hide it until they were seven months and oh-so-ready to have it over with, Gwen wore her pregnancy like a badge of honor. Tight jeans and one of Will's rarely worn Polo shirts.

"I'm right here."

"Sorry. I thought you were upstairs."

"Well, I'm not," she said. "I'm in a meeting, *remember?*"

"Then who's interviewing nannies?"

"Yvonne," she said. "I'll bet you're looking for the coffee filters."

"You read my mind," said Will.

"We're out. Why don't we send Wild Bill out for cappuccinos?" said Gwen, hands on her hips, staring at the Seminole cowboy.

"Because he won't come back," said Will. "*He's* got money on a basketball game and *we* don't have cable."

"Stop talkin' about me like I'm not standin' here," griped La Roy. "Gwen? You seem relatively in charge around here. What do you think about getting a little-bitty satellite dish?"

"Are you in this meeting, Bill?"

"You already know how I feel. I vote nay. *Nyet*. Negative. Bad deal. I say we wait four years and invade New Hampshire with no baggage."

"Well, do us all a favor and lend your opinion *in the meeting*," said Gwen. "Either that or be a good ol' boy and go get us some coffee."

"She's messin' with me." La Roy grinned at Will.

Gwen smiled, showing off more of *the glow*. "I'll send Sophie."

"Good idea," said La Roy, patting Gwen's protruding stomach as he passed by. "You're namin' him Bill, am I right?"

"In your dreams," jibed Gwen. She held the swinging door open for her husband, who stopped to give her stomach a kiss. "What about me?" asked Gwen.

"Sure. Why not?" said Will, kissing Gwen on the lips while giving her arrogant chin a little tug. "I love you, you know."

"And I love you back."

The meeting was in the eastern-facing solarium off the den, one of the few finished rooms in the new house. It was furnished in antique wicker with plush floral cushions. Attending were Will, Gwen, Bill La Roy, and two White House representatives. One was Manya Colby, President Addison's senior policy adviser. The other was Jim McDonald, the new head of the Democratic National Committee.

Also in the room, uninvited, was Will's father, Sully. Where he'd gotten the tip that such a meeting was going to take place was beyond anybody's scope. The old pol had simply shown up and set himself down in the meeting as if he'd belonged there all along.

The president of the United States, Del Addison, was on the speakerphone.

"Harper's finally out," said Addison of his politically wounded vice president. "We've made a deal with the attorney general. She'll keep those Republican wolves who're howling for a special prosecutor at arm's length. In exchange for that, Harper will resign in June. Save some face. And this whole Gavelgate thing will be deader than a box of hammers."

Ugh, thought Will. *Gavelgate*. And the Slammer Sisters had bagged another one. This time the vice president of the United States.

If there was a scandal, the press had to add some kind of *"gate"* to it. Will hated the shorthanded sound of it. It trivialized even the trivial. And it shot him back to the first time President Addison had dangled the vice presidency on a stick. It had been in a private conversation in the Oval Office. After the conclusion of a domestic security roundtable, Addison had asked Will to stay behind. Bending his arm around Will's shoulder, the president had confided that it would be over his dead, decaying body that his VP, James Harper, would finish the term. The tacit suggestion was that there would soon be a neon vacancy sign over the office of vice president.

"Harper's up to his ass in this bench-trading mess," the president had said to Will. *"And I refuse to let it get inside the White House."*

That was Gavelgate.

House Republicans had been pressing the attorney general to assign a special prosecutor to investigate charges that political favors were being traded for federal bench appointments. And Vice President Harper was fast gaining center stage.

"If the A.G. assigns a special prosecutor," the president had said, *"I have no intention of standing in her way. The last thing I want or need is that little viper setting her sights on the goings-on inside the White House. That means by springtime, I might be forced to look for a new number two. Someone to share the podium with in Atlanta. I'm lookin' to you, Will, to fill the vacancy."*

Atlanta. The site of the next Democratic Convention. From that moment on, Will had let himself dream of taking the podium and giving the speech of a lifetime. After which, the president would appear to a fifteen-minute standing ovation, and give his own acceptance speech. The fantasy ended with the president standing before the country, his hand enjoined with Will's and raised to the ceiling. Win or lose for Addison, it would leave Will as the odds-on nominee a mere four years later.

The thought crossed Will's mind that he could be president of the United States before he turned forty-eight. Some feat.

"It's Jim McDonald here, Mr. President."

"Go ahead, Jim," said the president over the speaker.

"I've been telling Will that it's all up to him. He can say yes or no."

"And I've got all of tomorrow to think about it?" asked Will. "You said it yourself, Harper's not out until June."

"Tomorrow *and* Monday," said the president. "I won't be making the announcement anytime soon. But we need you in the slot. Because if you're gonna say no, it means I gotta start looking for another running mate. And the pickin's ain't so good out there."

"On the record, Mr. President. I'm all for it," chimed a beaming Sully.

"Who's that?" asked President Addison.

"Danny Sullivan, sir."

There was a brief silence. Obviously, nobody was there to whisper in Addison's ear, to remind him just who Danny Sullivan was.

"That's my father," Will awkwardly explained.

"Oh, *Sully!*" said the president. A nervous laughter filled the room. The slight embarrassment passing as quickly as it had arrived. "How's it goin', you old son-of-a-shamrock?"

"Couldn't be better . . . or prouder," answered Sully.

"Well, get your boy to give me a yes vote," said Addison. "His commander in chief needs him."

"His country needs him," returned Sully, caught up in the moment and sounding too foolish and a little too damn patriotic for anybody in the room.

Will leaned in toward the speaker box. "For the record, sir. You know I'm going to have to talk it over with Gwen."

"Is she there?" asked the president.

"I am, Del," said Gwen. She was her casual self with the man. In person *and* over the phone. Had been ever since she'd been co-finance chairman with him when she was at the DNC.

"The First Lady's askin' how big are you?"

"Soon I'll be big as a house," Gwen said proudly.

"That's just swell," said the president. "But tell me, Gwen. What does Will need to hear so I can get him to come on board?"

Gwen turned to La Roy. "Do you want to ask him? Or do you want me to ask him?"

"Be my guest," said La Roy, knowing the question, but content to suck on his coffee.

"Ask me what?" asked the president, as if he didn't know what was coming.

"It's Gavelgate," said Gwen. "Just tell us it stops at Harper."

"It *stops* at Harper," said Jim McDonald before the president could answer.

"I'm asking your boss," Gwen cut in. "I'm asking *you*, Del. I don't want my husband signing on to a poisoned ticket."

"So ask."

"Did you know?" asked Gwen. "Did you know anything about Harper's bench trades?"

"You sound like you're warming up for that job as special prosecutor," teased Addison. The man was smooth as the silk shorts he was rumored to wear in bed. Some of Addison's extramarital conquests had even confirmed the silk shorts in publications like *Penthouse* and *Esquire*. Using the bully pulpit of the presidency, Addison had fended off the questions of character and infidelity along with numerous other "afflictions of the office." Being the president, Addison would privately say, was just like the Gary Larson cartoon where a deer had a bummer of birthmark in the shape of a target. When the press would refer to the current White House as being "awash with scandal," Addison would simply warn, "Better *awash* your hands after y'all throw so much mud in the air."

Will jumped into the conversation. "I'm asking you, Mr. President. Am I signing on to a sinking ship?"

"Will?" said the president. "You know how I feel about you. I would never do anything to ruin your career. You are the future of the Democratic Party. When you take the job as vice president, it'll be a new dawning and, in my humble opinion, the springboard that puts you into the Oval Office."

"Bet that's what Harper thought," grumbled La Roy.

"Who's that?" asked the president.

"Bill La Roy, your highness," said La Roy with far too much disrespect in his voice for anyone's comfort zone. Sully stood up, glaring at La Roy, ready to strangle him on the spot.

"I'll be blunt, Will," said the president. "You take the job, Bill La Roy goes back to consulting in Tampa."

"Actually," said La Roy, turning up the sarcasm, "I was thinking that if Will took the job, I'd go back home and run my black ass for Congress. That way, when Will needs a running mate after your impeachment, I'll be duly elected and available for greater public service."

For that comment, La Roy drew more stares. The contempt La Roy felt for Del Addison was no secret to anybody in the room. He'd hated him when he was in the House, when he was in the Senate, and when he was governor of Florida. Sure, Addison was a Democrat. But in La Roy's opinion, he was also a racist, Southern, elitist prick who'd crawled into the White House on the backs of the partisan poor, only to throw back bones when the time came to put up or shut up.

"Sir? Bill La Roy goes where I go." Will's stance shocked those present. He wouldn't give up La Roy at the drop of a hat. He owed the man too much. And in his opinion, politics was pliable. So would be this vice presidential deal. His loyalty brought out La Roy's trademark white-toothed grin.

"Oh, I'm sure we can all work this out," said Jim Mc-Donald, trying not to sound discouraged.

"Yes, I'm sure we can," underscored President Addison in a reticent pitch. "Just say yes, Will."

Will looked from La Roy, to Sully, then to Gwen. Her arms were crossed, signaling that they'd talk about it later.

But Will answered anyway. "Yes."

Sully beamed, stood, and slapped his son on the back. But Gwen turned on a heel and left the room.

"Good to hear it," answered the president. "Jim will fill you in as we go along. A kiss to Gwen."

The meeting was over. Sully was throwing a bear hug around his boy. "I'm so proud of you. My son's gonna be president."

"*Vice* president," corrected Jim McDonald, already pumping the senator's hand.

"Number two," growled La Roy. "And we all know what that smells like."

"I thought we were going to *discuss* it?" fumed Gwen.

Will didn't want to fight. It was closing on midnight.

He'd avoided the inevitable confrontation all afternoon and evening, and now he didn't want to engage when it was so late. It would stress him out and make it impossible to get to sleep.

"I said 'yes' to our president."

"Maybe you didn't hear me. *We* were going to discuss *it!*"

"We both agreed that the White House was a goal—"

"The White House!" Gwen stepped from the master bath and waved a toothbrush at her husband. "And it was in *four years*. If not then, in eight years. But I don't want to move *this* year."

"You disagree with the opportunity?" asked Will.

"It's not a matter of opportunity, Will. It's a matter of partnership. We discuss, we negotiate, we agree."

"Are you talking as a wife or a consultant?"

"Both!" she said, turning out the bathroom light and crawling into bed. She pulled up the covers to her neck and rolled to her side—away from Will.

"You want to end it like this?" asked Will.

"I want to sleep," she said. "Then I want to wake up in the morning to find out today's been nothing more than a shitty dream."

The room was cold. The fieldstone fireplace in the upstairs master bedroom was half-demolished and barely taped over with plastic sheeting. The architect's plans called for replacement brick to be salvaged from a two-hundred-year-old schoolhouse in Salem that had recently come under the wrecking ball. The contractor had just bid on a few pallets of the gloriously aged brick earlier that week.

Resolved to table the debate until daylight, Will closed in behind Gwen, cuddled her under the goose-down duvet and German flannel sheets. At first, she shrugged him off. She was formally pissed. Will reasoned that he'd be apologizing for a week and that he might as well start as soon as possible. He whispered at her ear, "I'm sorry," then slid his left palm over her belly. "I want him to kick me," he said.

"Dr. Rosen says *she'll* start kicking when she's good and ready," said Gwen.

"You really don't want to know?"

"Not until I'm supposed to."

"What if *I* can't wait that long? What if, as the father, I *demand* to know? I could file suit and take you to court. I'll bet Harper knows a judge or two—"

"Well, you're going to have to *wait*." With that, she turned over, cupped his face, and kissed him, as if to infuse him with patience as well as to signal her forgiveness. "But if it's a girl, I kind of like the name Erin."

"And if it's a boy?"

She didn't have a name. She didn't want a boy as much as she wanted a girl, unsure whether it was her maternal instinct talking or her contempt for Sully's occasional drunken demand that she bear him a grandson. What made the conflict even worse was that she really liked the name Daniel. Danny was a good boy's name. A little boy. Irish-American, like his father.

"So make it up to me and read," she said.

"No boy's name?"

"Just read," she said, passing Will a book from her nightstand. *Your Baby, Week by Week.* Maybe focusing on the baby would dilute the acid that had been boiling in her stomach ever since Will's knee-jerk decision to jump on the vice presidential honeywagon.

"Where are we?"

"The page is marked," she said, her eyes closing while both her hands rested palms-down on her stomach.

"Here we are," said Will. " 'The twenty-first week . . . Your baby now weighs nearly ten and a half ounces. Roughly the size of a cucumber.' Nice image. My son, the cucumber."

"Your *daughter,*" said Gwen, her voice sounding contented and dreamy. She elbowed him gently. "Keep reading."

And Will did. The entire chapter. Just as he'd done for the past four months. Each weekend he'd fly up from Washington. They'd curl up in bed on Saturday nights and he'd read aloud from a book that had taken on biblical proportions in their relationship, cultivating in the couple emotions that had long been stuffed. Both Will and Gwen were feeling a tug that was tightening the laces of their marriage. All from that mound, stretching Gwen's skin to smoothness unlike anything he had ever touched. No woman had ever felt so feminine. It was pure magic.

With the chapter finished, Will switched off his light and turned his body back to hers. She held his hands to her belly. "If it's a boy," she whispered, "you can name him Daniel if you like."

Will was stunned. It was totally unlike Gwen to slice off such a large piece of her pride. Especially to someone who annoyed her like Sully. From day one the two had locked horns over everything from politics to the taste of Southy's drinking water.

"He'd like that," was all Will could think to say in the moment, unsure how he himself felt about it.

"Then so be it," she said, before nodding off to sleep.

9

During her second interview, the nanny-candidate estimated that there were four hundred and eighty-six
cards in the double Rolodex. This was difficult to accom-
plish, but compulsively practiced. She'd counted roughly
twenty in the space of a quarter-inch, then multiplied it by
an approximation of the total circumference of the barrel,
then quadrupled the number.

"There's good news and bad news," Yvonne had begun,
seated behind her desktop where there was one bottle of
chewable vitamin C with seventeen tablets remaining. "Bad
news first. Ms. Sullivan has already chosen a nanny. I'll remind you, though. You were *my* first recommendation."

*Three-ring binders, one computer monitor, one Nissan
stainless steel coffee thermos, one* Roget's Thesaurus, *a six-
ring calendar.*

". . . But Gwen? Her favorite aunt was an English nanny
and, as it happened, there's another candidate that she really
likes."

*One five-line telephone unit, six scattered press clip-
pings, four framed photos featuring Yvonne's two boys at*

approximately eleven and nine years old, then at their high school graduations, and later with their girlfriends.

"The good news is that the senator and Ms. Sullivan have purchased a very large old home that will need a great deal of attending to. They're going to need a full-time, live-in housekeeper who can baby-sit once or twice a week. It pays nearly as well as the nanny position and, I might add, puts you in first position should there be a problem with their primary choice."

Six sharpened pencils in an old paint jar, four ballpoint pens, two felt-tipped pens, one water bottle, a twelve-inch ruler, one desk lamp with two forty-watt bulbs, and ten stems' worth of fresh roses in a beveled glass vase.

Yvonne gazed across at the polite candidate, unaware that every stitch of her being had been logged and accounted for, all while she was pitching a job that the other woman would've said yes to in a heartbeat.

The plot was simple and Dean's orders had been succinct. Get as close to Gwen Sullivan as humanly possible.

"What's more, the housekeeping job starts immediately," said Yvonne.

"I'll have to think about it," said the woman who'd chosen to call herself Isabelle Leconte. Izzy for short. It had been ten years since anyone had called her by that name.

Izzy had come to the audition with near-perfect credentials, appearing to have worked for the last ten years in Bermuda for an English family whose children had grown and were either in college or boarding school. Since then, *Isabelle* had moved to Massachusetts to care for her aging mother, twice divorced and living on her late husband's disability. Her child-care credential were enhanced by nursing experience, advanced training in emergency infant CPR, and some lactation consulting.

But where her research for the role had been dead-on, her calculation had been slightly off. Since Yvonne had been the one conducting the interviews, Izzy had concluded that Yvonne's own experiences as a child and mother would weigh heavily in the final decision.

Yvonne had been born on the French island of Martinique to a white U.S. diplomat. She was black in complexion, but only half in blood. And so, coincidentally, was she, Izzy had lied. Yes, her hair was jet-black and permed to resemble locks more genetically kinked, but her skin was syrupy-brown with mild splotching. A skin condition, she'd told Yvonne, that she'd suffered since her childhood on the island of St. Maarten. The truth was, for the last three months, she'd boiled her skin at a San Diego tanning salon. Seven days a week for up to three hours a day. She would sustain the coloring with dangerous doses of the not-yet-FDA-approved drug Salypson-D. A self-tanning medication developed in the Netherlands that increased the production of melanin in the epidermis, making it extra-sensitive to UV radiation. The side effects were increased irritability and the instant possibility for cancerous melanomas. Dean had done the research and passed it on to Izzy. She knew the risks and questioned nothing. All for the role of *Isabelle,* the half-black, Caribbean-flavored nanny.

At night, Izzy had brushed up on her French and Dutch, inflecting the rhythms into her daily speech until it was pat and habitual. She'd memorized a personal history, the names and birthdays of her eight younger brothers and sisters, the last three of whom she'd practically raised herself. A San Diego plastic surgeon had removed her breast implants, leaving her smaller, slightly sagging, and hardly looking like her original California-angel self. To complete the transformation she had to turn her former junk-thinned body into that of a matron who'd never found the right man to make her happy and give her children of her own. Estrogen therapy proved helpful with the weight trick. An overdose of hormones, Domino's Pizza, and milk shakes from Burger King had turned the formerly fat-free body into that of a born-again Botticelli, carrying thirty-five extra pounds and rounding out a makeup-free face.

Dean had been pleased. She'd scanned and downloaded a naked Polaroid of the new Izzy and sent it to him over the Net. He'd sent back an electronic cyber-kiss. *Just for luck,* he'd written.

"How long do I have before I need to give you a yes or no?" Izzy asked.

"As soon as possible," said Yvonne. "We're up to our ears in work here and the new house is under quite a bit of reconstruction. Gwen is going to need a lot of help."

"Would I still need to meet her?"

"Yes. But at this point, I can assure you it's just a formality," said Yvonne. "She's picked her nanny. But moving into the house, I promise, will give you time to grow on her."

"You think so?"

"I've got a good feeling about you," Yvonne admitted with a rare giggle. "It's as if we were cousins or something."

"Who knows? Maybe we are," joked Izzy. "You know. The *men* down there?"

Yvonne laughed. Oh yes, Izzy had done her homework well. And soon it would pay off. First thing tomorrow morning, she'd call Yvonne and accept the position. It was all pending on a meeting with Gwen, of course. But that would be fun, thought Izzy. She could hardly wait to meet the mother-to-be.

March. Washington D.C.

Still fresh from the Boston affiliate, Vanessa Curran's speedy rise at the network was being stymied by the shortage of good, meaty stories. The shine in her blonde hair was quickly wearing thin on the CBS executives who had placed their hopes on her in the ongoing prime-time news magazine ratings wars. Her New York agent had copped her a top-dollar contract. A three-year, mid-six-figure guarantee for her lanky good looks, easy diction, iridescent blue eyes, and—at least on her compilation tape—a fearlessness when confronting local politicos and elected officials about their daily misdeeds.

On camera, she was golden.

Off camera, though, she was getting a fast rap as a stone-cold bitch. In the first quarter of the year, she'd pissed off Dan Rather and just about every prime-time features producer. Even the morning program didn't want her. And when the promised appearance on Letterman's *Late Show* didn't materialize, she'd called in sick for a week, only to return when network lawyers threatened to terminate her contract.

All this despite a stellar reputation for giving the finest blow jobs east of the Hudson. The big buzz was that years earlier, she'd traded in her nicotine-stained teeth for a set of pearly-white dentures, easily removable at the drop of the most convenient zipper. Her technique had worked well in Boston where standards, along with viewership, were obviously lower. But at the network—in D.C.—her special gift only got her in the door. Talent reigned, product was king, and the story was still the most important thing.

For most of March, Vanessa had been pitching producers all over the Eye a story she didn't exactly have in the bag. She wanted to call it *"Camelot Rising: The Miracle Pregnancy of Senator Will Sullivan and Gwen Corbett-Sullivan."*

One problem. Along with his drinking, Will had stopped screwing around on his wife. Vanessa hadn't quite the access to him that she'd had when he was a philandering drunk. Cooperation would be difficult. Will wasn't returning her calls and her story had run into a roadblock down Dallas way. The very discreet fertility practitioner, Dr. Harvey Bertrand, was not only unavailable for an interview, but was proving impossible to track down.

"Will?" Vanessa whispered, having sneaked up behind him at a downtown Washington, D.C., restaurant called Habitat. He was seated at a table for four that included the secretary of the interior, Senators Allen of Arizona and Shutte of Idaho, and the House Speaker, Philip McCallister. "I've got something personal you might want to know about," she whispered within earshot of the others.

Will didn't even need to look around. And though he'd been drunk as a skunk the one time he'd been intimate with her, he still recognized the perfume. "Gentlemen? You know Vanessa Curran." Nods all around. Oh, they knew all right. Senator Allen was already attempting to get a glimpse of her teeth while Phil McCallister was standing with his palm out. "Ms. Curran. It's a pleasure."

"Pleasure's all mine, Congressman McCallister." Vanessa knew the faces *and* the names. Old homework from the network. Then she whispered again to Will. "Two minutes. That's *all* I need."

"You'll excuse us," said Will, leaving his napkin on the table.

She led him to a semi-private spot under the awning just outside the restaurant's back door, protected from the fifty-three-degree drizzle.

She torched up a Marlboro Light. "You don't return my calls."

"You oughta know why," said Will. "You're a big girl in the big town. Is this what you interrupted my lunch for?"

"It's about a story I'm working on."

"I won't confirm anything for you on or off the record," said Will, always critically careful with any member of the press. Especially those with a potential ax to grind.

"I pitched a story to the network brass about you and Gwen," said Vanessa. "You know. The *baby* thing?"

"And you didn't ask me if it was okay?"

"You wouldn't return my calls!"

"There are channels, Vanessa."

"I want the story. The network loves the idea. It would be good PR for you and you know it."

"Depends on the spin," said Will.

"Pro-science. Pro-Sullivan. It's a consultant's wet dream," said Vanessa. "Prime time and you're not even running for anything."

"Call La Roy," said Will. "Sell him and he'll hand you off to my communications director—"

"Sandra Corwin," said Vanessa, trying to impress Will with her prep work.

"*Then* we'll talk," finished Will. It was his way of saying that his staff would check out the story, the spin, the time slot, et cetera. Sniff the air and see if there was a sandbag ready to swing from the wings.

"That's all fine," she said. "But I want to do pre-interviews with the Dallas clinic."

"I can't keep you from doing that. But this doctor isn't

exactly into his own PR. He's about making lemons out of lemonade—"

"I can't find the doctor."

"Why don't you call Information?"

"Will, I'm saying, I can't *find* him. In Dallas. No forwarding number. No address."

"I'd say recheck your phone numbers."

Vanessa counted off on her fingers. "Called him. Faxed him. Certified-mailed him. Zip, Will."

Will didn't quite know what to say. He was briefly lost, reorganizing his thoughts. Thoughts that were instantly with Gwen, who was on some nest-furnishing, antique-gathering junket up in Maine.

"Could you talk to Gwen?" asked Vanessa. "I'm sure she knows all about it."

"Okay. I'll ask her."

"And Gwen? How does she look?"

"She thinks she's going to be big as a house. But I'd say when it comes to dress sizes, she's still a single digit."

"She's a cutie, your wife," purred Vanessa. There it was. She'd had the same look in her eye after she'd kissed Gwen.

"It'll never happen," defended Will.

"As long as you stay golden," she teased. "Don't fuck it up, or I'll be right there with a helping hand."

"Let's leave it there," he said. "I'll call you when I get a number. In the meantime—"

"I'll talk to La Roy," she finished, clicking her Dolce & Gabbana heels together as Will returned to his lunch.

As March blanketed Washington D.C. under a daily wash of bone-chilling rain, Dallas skipped spring altogether and vaulted straight into summer. The weather stirred the dormant winter nesting, causing a mosquito hatching unlike anything the Lone Star state had ever experienced. Windows were closed, air conditioners were switched on high, and bug repellent was on back order.

"It's like the Alamo," joked Jason Levin, a New York transplant working for the Texas wing of the DNC. "But the mosquitoes are the Mexicans and nobody's safe outside the walls of the city."

Allison Flannery wasn't amused. She didn't know this guy from Adam. He was simply a name on a carnival of colored Post-It notes stuck to the frame of her computer monitor. A name who was now returning her call. "Did you do as the senator requested?" said Allison, sounding more than businesslike and, possibly, a bit arrogant with her U.S. Senate staff position.

"What I'm saying is that I've got the mosquito bites to prove it."

"Fine. You left the DNC office under a March mosquito siege. Is that your report? I'll pass that along to the senator if you'd like," she bluffed. "Let's just make sure I've got your name spelled right."

"Look. They got bugs down here the size of B-52s, that's all I'm saying," he insisted. "What's it like in D.C.?"

Ugh, thought Allison. Was this guy trying to *work* her or what? Ever since she'd been promoted from the Boston office, it seemed like everyone she'd ever walked precinct with or had any contact with outside the Power Grid was angling for an inside track on a Beltway job. With the monumental success of the FDA hearings in the fall, she'd gone from Washington wannabe to a staffer with "leverage." One who *had the senator's ear.* She'd done a bang-up job as liaison between Will's office and committee staffs, penned a hell of an opening statement, and risen quickly past the ranks of the lowly "ferrets" to the position of legislative analyst.

"It's raining up here," answered Allison.

"I'd take some rain right now," said Jason Levin. "I miss the East Coast. Did you know I'm from New York?"

"Upstate," said Allison. "You told me when we first spoke."

The day before, Allison had called the Texas DNC headquarters to ask a favor. At Senator Sullivan's behest, she needed someone to take a quick walk or drive or bicycle ride—whatever mode they used in Dallas—over to the Harvey Bertrand Reproductive Clinic and answer some very simple questions. Were they still in business? If not, had they left a forwarding number or address? It required little more than some office peon taking a long lunch to get the information and report back.

"What did you find out for us?"

"Not much, I'm afraid," said Jason. "I went over there, just like you asked—"

"And you got the mosquito bites to prove it."

"I sure did."

"So what happened?"

"Nothing," said Jason. "Address you gave me is some teleconferencing group under the name of something like United We Call. I didn't find any clinic."

"Did you talk to the building manager?"

"He was out to lunch."

Allison wished she could reach through the phone and spank the faceless little prick. She was certain he was barely twenty-three, wore thick glasses, and had a face covered in volcanic acne. What made it worse was that guys just like *him* were always asking *her* out.

"Did you wait for him?" she asked.

"Of course I did. That's when I got all the bites."

And I hope you scratch them till you bleed.

"And what did the manager say when he got back from lunch?"

"Lemme get my notes."

Allison wanted to hang up, dial Jason's boss, get the little shit fired, then start all over again with someone who could give an answer without so much prompting. That's how it was done, she thought. You're given an assignment, you deliver the goods. No. You *own* the goods.

Accountability.

After a bit of paper shuffling, Jason answered the question. "The building manager said that Dr. Bertrand moved out of his office at the beginning of February. He left no forwarding number or address."

"Is that all?" asked Allison.

"Nope. He also said the clinic left behind most of their medical equipment. You know, those beds with the stirrups. Sterilizers, stuff like that."

As annoyed as Allison was, the news struck her as odd. She wasn't exactly certain why Will had requested the information. The task had been passed on by Myriam, not unlike any other research query. Still, something chilled the young staffer. She knew the senator and his wife had gone to Dallas to get pregnant. Her assumption was that Dr. Bertrand had done the procedure. And now the man and his clinic had packed it in with no forwarding address?

"Anything else?" she asked.

"Yeah," said Jason. "You know of any positions opening back there?"

"Sorry."

"I hate Texas."

"Everybody has to start somewhere."

"Where'd you start?"

"In my mother's womb," said Allison. "Thanks a lot, Jason. We'll call you if we need anything else."

Allison hung up, rolled her chair back, grabbed a legal pad, and swiveled her saddled young hips through the daily chaos that was the Bull Pit—a thrash-and-trash square of government cubicles, phone lines, and computers that made up the rear portion of the Senate office. A right turn down a tight corridor led her to the oak-paneled part of the suite which included the executive offices, a kitchen, a substantial reception area with a leather couch and antique oil renderings of Civil War battles, then Myriam's office, behind which were the double doors leading into Will's inner sanctum. Allison waited for Myriam to get off the line.

"Yes?" said Myriam.

"I've got that information from Dallas," said Allison.

"Is it in the form of a memo?"

"I thought you wanted a verbal," fibbed Allison. She was already learning the game. Memos got passed through. Verbals sometimes got you an audience with the senator.

"I wanted it on paper," said Myriam. "Plus the senator's on the phone with his father."

Allison looked down at Myriam's telephone unit. Will's personal line went from green to red.

"He's off the phone," said Allison, pumping up and down on her tiptoes.

With standing orders from her boss to reward persistence, Myriam sighed, stood, then reluctantly opened the door to Will's office, leading Allison inside. Will dropped his reading glasses and looked to Myriam first. "Mark Fulgham wants to fly Gwen and me down to Palm Beach this weekend on his corporate jet. I said thanks, but we both know he's under about three F.E.C. investigations."

"Want me to book you commercial?"

"First call Gwen and see if she wants to go. Two, check with somebody in Elections Oversight and see where they're going with it. If it's looking square, we'll take the free ride. If it's not—"

"American or United?"

"Whichever we can upgrade on," said Will, leaning back in his chair, arms behind his head. "Allison, my dear. What do you got?"

Allison delivered. "Dr. Harvey Bertrand closed down his clinic. No forwarding address or number. *Nada*. He even left some of his medical equipment. The space has been taken over by a teleconferencing center."

Will held his thoughts for a moment, all the while staring right through Allison. It was unnerving. But Will was just letting his brain catch up with the information, all the while masking the nerves which tingled behind his ears. "Swell job," he smiled. "Thanks."

"Is that all, Senator?" Allison asked, hoping for a follow-up assignment.

"You got your ten seconds," said Myriam. "Now don't let the door hit you in the caboose."

Allison feigned a smile, then closed the door as she left. Myriam waited for instructions.

"Call Steve Salinas," said Will. "I think you have enough to ask the right questions."

"Should I put a call into Mrs. Sullivan for you?"

"No," said Will, sifting through his feelings while still juggling political matters in his head. "Businesses go belly-up every week. Gwen is on track with her own OB. No reason to worry her over what's probably some kind of embarrassing foreclosure." Will shook his head. "Poor Dr. Bertrand. Nice guy trying to help nice people."

Myriam turned on a pump heel and exited just like she did about a million times a day, leaving Will to his own awkward silence.

But so much the more malign and wild does the ground become with bad seed and untilled, as it has the more of good earthly vigor.

Why the thought? Will hadn't the faintest. But he found himself thrown a bit off his usual keen track. Unable to focus on the legislative reading before him. His eyes stung for no reason. So he closed them and reasoned his way through the puzzle.

Dr. Harvey Bertrand, like many "nice men," would most likely prove to be a lousy businessman, screwed over by a healthy divorce judgment that had foreclosed him into early retirement. Sad, thought Will. *How many more childless couples might he have helped? The kind man had finally given them what Gwen had prayed so long for, rekindling something between a husband and wife who might otherwise have drifted even further apart.*

"Myriam?" called Will through the intercom.

"Yes, Senator?"

"Put in a call to Alan Hobbs over at the NIH. I want to talk to him about current federal funding for reproductive research."

"Yes, Senator."

Done, thought Will. If some vengeful wife or creditor had put Dr. Bertrand out of business, maybe he could save the old miracle worker with a government grant. A little reproductive pork.

"How much?" asked Gwen, her breath fogging the sub-freezing air. Spring had yet to appear in Maine.

"Two ninety-nine," said the dealer. She was over fifty, two-hundred-plus pounds, and wore three layers of plaid flannel. They stood toe-to-toe in the woman's wind-rattled barn, haggling over an English pine armoire. The air was so iced that the snow flurries which sneaked underneath the rusted roof didn't so much as melt when they hit the concrete floor.

"Too much," said Gwen. "That, and there's the cost of shipping."

"My husband's got a truck. If ya fill it, he'll do the trip for free."

Gwen was cold. She had Will's goose-down jacket wrapped over a fleece turtleneck. But she'd forgotten her gloves. And every time she'd point at something that caught her eye, she'd have to re-place her hand before it cracked. The heparin, she'd been told. It left her skin dry and split-ting. Three times a day she'd do the lotion dip. Hands, face, neck, then her growing tummy. Dry skin was no fun. And the threat of stretch marks forced her to be that more dili-gent about skin care.

"When ya due?" asked the dealer.

"End of June," said Gwen, working her way toward a rather provocative-looking dining room set. She was good with antiques, and read books nightly on furniture, pottery, and other collectibles before turning out the bedside lamp. Still, she couldn't put a date on the rough-hewn oak table and nine chairs stacked on top of it. "What do you know about this piece?"

"Not much, I'm afraid. My husband might know. He buys. I sell," said the dealer.

"How much?"

"With the chairs . . . I'd say two thousand."

"That's a lot without knowing what it is," said Gwen, moving on.

"Look at it this way. It could be worth more."

Hardly, thought the mother-to-be. "Is that a high chair back there?"

"Looks like it." The dealer crawled behind the dining room set and slapped a rag at it. A gagging dust billowed. "Oh, I remember this piece. A lotta sentimental value in this item."

Don't grind me, thought Gwen.

When the air cleared, Gwen slid herself around to get a closer look at the chair. Carved into the seat back was an *S.*

For "Sullivan," she thought. *Oh God, now I have to buy it.*

"You like it?" asked the dealer. "I'd part with it for five hundred."

"And I'd say you're at least three hundred dollars too high."

"Like I said, ma'am. It has sentimental value."

"What's your best?" asked Gwen.

"I'd go four-fifty."

"How's this? Three hundred and your husband doesn't have to drive all the way to Boston."

"That what you call incentive?" laughed the dealer. "Hell, I love it when he's gone for the day. Gets him outta my hair and I don't have to fight him for the TV."

"Three and a quarter," said Gwen. "And that's as high as I'm gonna go." Heels dug in, her arms crossing her chest, just above the five-month swell in her stomach. As much as Gwen loved the high chair, she'd rather not yield than get screwed.

"Well, bein' that you're expectin' and all," said the dealer. "I'll go three seventy-five."

"Have a nice day." Gwen turned and squeezed past the dining room set. She was heading for the door without looking back.

"Three-fifty," offered the dealer.

Gwen stopped and turned. The dealer wanted the sale. She'd given up her hand a hundred dollars ago. For Gwen, it was just about timing her exit.

"Okay. Three and a quarter," said the dealer, but insisting, "But that's cash."

"Of course," said Gwen.

The dealer smiled, returning to the high chair. "I'm gonna need a hand getting it out of here."

"Izzy?" Gwen called out.

"Yes, Mrs. Sullivan?" came the voice from outside the barn. Izzy had been sneaking a quick smoke. Nicotine was the only thing that seemed to take the edge off the constant doses of estrogen and Salypson-D. That, and she needed the

UVs to keep her skin dark. She flicked the butt into the snow and returned inside.

"Can you give us a hand with the high chair?" asked Gwen.

"Yes, ma'am."

While Gwen dug through her pockets for her wallet, Izzy and the dealer lowered the backseat of the Explorer and loaded the high chair into the rear.

"You a smoker?" asked Gwen, more interested in confirming the fact than asking an open-ended question. They were headed back to Marblehead. Izzy behind the wheel. Gwen in the passenger seat, cell phone at one ear, waiting for Yvonne to hook her up with another call.

Izzy took a moment before answering, knowing she'd been busted, but wanting to make sure her responses were lined up properly. "Yes, ma'am," she began. "But I would never smoke in your house or near the baby, Mrs. Sullivan."

"That's not a worry," said Gwen. "It's just the health risk. My father died of lung cancer."

"I'm sorry," said Izzy, as if she didn't already know. For when it came to Gwen Corbett-Sullivan, there wasn't much Izzy hadn't researched, read, or assessed in her brief employ. Gwen's parents were Andrew and Amelia Corbett. Her father, a wholesale dealer of commercial windows, died of lung cancer in 1981. Her mother, a part-time professor of art history, expired one year later from kidney disease. Because money was tight and her father had died while on the brink of Chapter 11, doctors found it difficult to find Gwen's mother a suitable kidney for transplant.

"To tell you the truth, Mrs. Sullivan," said Izzy, "I'm afraid if I quit, that I'll gain even more weight."

"Cigarettes as a diet pill," said Gwen. "Oh, I know all about that."

"You used to smoke?"

"In college for about ten weeks," said Gwen. "I think I vomited my way through an entire quarter. I guess that means I lost weight due to tobacco-induced bulimia."

Both women laughed. Gwen's laugh was especially easy

and comfortable. Izzy's, on the other hand, was well-disguised and practiced from years of deception.

Gwen rubbed her belly. "Thanks for driving."

"Not at all," said Izzy. "Whenever you want. I like driving."

The driving part had been Izzy's idea. Only her fourth day on the job and she'd braved a suggestion to the mother-to-be. When Gwen informed Izzy of her plans to spend the day antiquing in Maine, Izzy returned a pained expression. When Gwen asked why, Izzy asked if the airbags in the Explorer had been disconnected. When Gwen answered no, Izzy went on to explain the dangers of pregnant women and driver's-side airbags. Apologizing for her meddling, Izzy recommended that Gwen drive her car, an '85 white Cadillac Seville that belonged to her mother.

But there was no cell phone in the Seville. And as much as Gwen looked forward to any time devoted to furnishing the nest, she'd planned to work the phones from the road. Return calls. Shuck for campaign dough.

So Izzy volunteered to drive Gwen's Explorer.

And in that very instant, for the first time in God knows how many months or years, Gwen felt taken care of by someone other than Yvonne. Watched over that day by none other than her new housekeeper. Izzy from St. Maarten. Yvonne had chosen well, thought Gwen. Izzy drove. Gwen burned cell phone minutes all the way to Ogunquit, Maine, and back.

"Is English your first language?" asked Gwen, taking another break from business and warming her chapped hands in front of the Explorer's heater.

"Is that how I sound?" returned Izzy.

"If it's not, you speak it very well."

"My father owned a hotel on St. Maarten. The tourists were mostly English-speaking. So it was French for breakfast, Dutch at dinner, and English the rest of the day."

"And where's your family now?"

"Well, my mother, you know, is in Boston. My father, he's dead from an accident. But he died a long, long time ago."

"Brothers and sisters?"

"Everywhere," smiled Izzy. A big, broad grin. "Wait till you see the postcards I get. Beautiful places."

"We'll show the postcards to the baby."

"Do you know if it's a boy or a girl?"

"I don't want to know," said Gwen. "Not until . . . you know. It happens."

"But you have instincts, yes?"

"I have dreams."

"And what do your dreams say?"

Gwen bit her lower lip. She hated to say, only because she hated being wrong. That, and she didn't want to create any kind of internal expectation. But . . .

"I think it's a boy," said Gwen.

"Hallelujah," said Izzy.

"You like boys, do you?"

"I like *all* children. But there's something about a boy child that . . ." Izzy stopped. "Listen to me. I'm going on and on. I wish for you and your husband a healthy, perfect baby. No matter about the sex."

Yes, Gwen said to herself. No matter.

"You'll meet my husband this weekend," said Gwen.

"The senator?"

"The father," Gwen found herself correcting Izzy.

"Yes," said Izzy. *"The father."*

10

Gary F. Modetti stuck his foot inside the Lincoln and bellowed, "C'mon, Will. It's raining, for Christ's sake."

Will had to think about it. Like many in Washington, he despised Gary Modetti. No political reporter had recycled more bullshit into column inches than Gary "Give-a-Fuck" Modetti. He was formerly of the *Post,* formerly of the *Times,* and formerly of just about every other D.C.-based bureau. And although Gary F. Modetti might have lost his press credentials, he'd recently gained a massive following as a gossip columnist for his own Internet tabloid called *A La Mode.* From that platform, Modetti had turned his journalistic irresponsibility into a profitable new low. He'd print embarrassing photos, rumors, and despicable innuendos alongside legitimate links to AP, UPI, and Reuters news services. It was believed that though most of Washington woke up to the *Post,* when they hit their desks and logged onto their computers to collect e-mail, the movers and shakers secretly hooked up to Modetti's gossip column, appropriately titled *Below the Beltway,* for the latest in morning sludge.

Will was enjoying watching the rain soak Gary Modetti.

"Want me to drive off?" asked LBJ.

Will released the door and slid over. Whippet-thin and soaked through to his blue cotton shirt, Modetti climbed in, dropping the copy of the *Post* he was using as an umbrella.

"I wish the rain would stop already. It's supposed to be springtime, for Christ's sake!"

"Where are we dropping you?" Will asked.

"Anywhere you're going."

"Not likely," said Will. "So name your destination and it better not be more than ten blocks."

Modetti quickly did the math and leaned forward so LBJ could hear. "You know where Lila's is?"

"I know it," said LBJ. "It's more than ten blocks, Senator."

"Then get Mr. Modetti ten blocks closer to Lila's. What's on your mind, Gary?"

"So what's this talk I hear about you being the top pick for vice president?"

Will warned the writer, "Don't confuse my good nature for being stupid. No comment."

"Can I quote you?" joked Modetti.

"LBJ?" asked Will. "How many blocks left?"

"About eight and a half, sir."

"I might suggest, Gary, that if you want to make the entire ten blocks that you keep conversation to the public domain."

"Hey. What's more public domain than being a heartbeat away from the most powerful job on the planet?"

"Look. We both know you didn't hitch a ride because you wanted to ask me stuff that any moron knows I wouldn't answer with a gun to my head. So get to it."

"Hey, those FDA hearings were a home run," said Modetti, shifting gears. "I hear that Justice is gonna be handing out indictments like they were campaign buttons."

"And?" said Will.

"I hear one of those indictments has *your* name on it."

"For what?" asked Will. "Picking up hitchhikers? Beej? How many blocks?"

"Six, sir."

"The same FBI source," continued Modetti, "says that your chief of staff, Bill La Roy, is so paranoid he carries a gun in his right boot."

"Now, that's *not* true," said Will. "La Roy knows my stand on handguns. I'm on the board for Stop the Violence."

"My source says she saw the gun early one morning, right around the time he was crawling out of her bed."

"Stop the car," said Will. LBJ wheeled the car toward the curb. "Get out."

"Two more blocks," pleaded Modetti.

"Have a nice day, Gary."

"It's a shitty day. Look, Will. It's rainin' like a mother-fucker."

"I'd say it's raining *on* a motherfucker."

Modetti sat there for a moment, looking out at the rain, then back at Will. Reluctantly, he scooped up his copy of the *Post,* tented it over his head, and stepped out of the Lincoln.

"C'mon, Beej," said Will. "We're late already."

"Yes, sir . . . Sorry, sir." With the left blinker switched on, LBJ eased the Town Car out into traffic.

Bill La Roy was already seated in the bar adjacent to the Severino Grill, his seat squared in the direction of the mounted TV. North Carolina had beaten two top seeds to make it to the finals and get a shot at Villanova. La Roy had laid off his usual bet. Five hundred dollars and the points on the contest.

"So if you think it's fixed—" began Steve Salinas, off the FBI clock and well into his second bottle of Heineken.

"I don't *think* it's fixed," said La Roy. "I simply acknowledge the possibility."

"But you've got how much on the game?"

La Roy held up five thick fingers.

"Five hundred dollars? On a game you acknowledge the possibility that it *might* be fixed?" Salinas was looking for logic and finding little.

"Doesn't matter," said La Roy, eyes glued to the TV. "Just as long as you don't know which way it's fixed, it's still a roll of the dice."

"Your money, pal," said Salinas.

"Damn right." In the meantime, La Roy had charmed the cocktail waitress into going around the corner and bringing him back a large Americano with nonfat milk and one sugar. When she'd returned with the cup, Will was already seated and ready to order a tall Pellegrino and an order of nachos.

"Good boy," said La Roy. It was halftime, so the chief of staff could give his boss the full attention he deserved.

"Don't move," said Will, sliding his chair next to La Roy's. He reached down and squeezed the top of La Roy's right cowboy boot.

"Wanna explain your sudden interest in my footwear?"

"I heard a rumor," said Will.

"That horseshit again?" La Roy was clearly annoyed. "In Jacksonville? Back when I was a mean ol' drunk? From time to time, yeah. I packed heat. Big whoop. But now that I'm sober and a respectable employee of Uncle Sam?"

"Sorry," said Will. "Didn't mean to doubt you. I just can't take the risk of you getting nailed for some conceal-and-carry violation." Will moved his chair back and shifted gears all in one smooth move. "Jeez. Last time I was here, I think I was plastered. Remember? It's when I got that DNC alert that it looked like the Republicans were going to take over the House."

"It wasn't *that* bad of news," volunteered Steve. "I kinda liked it when those ol' boys upped the FBI budget."

Will laughed. He'd forgotten it was the Republican budget increase that got Steve his transfer to the Office of Public and Congressional Affairs, an FBI division servicing federal crimes relating to the House and the Senate. Will had made the call on Steve's behalf, acquiring his old college chum a transfer from Oklahoma City to Washington D.C. Who knew he'd end up working full time for the Slammer Sisters?

From his jacket pocket, Steve pulled a piece of copier paper on which he'd scribbled his notes with a red Sharpie.

"Well, one thing's for sure. Your doctor is definitely MIA. As of now, I don't exactly have the authority to send agents running around Dallas looking for the guy. But electronically speaking, Dr. Bertrand hasn't registered a blip in over thirty-seven days. No activity on his bank account, credit cards, telephones, passport. Wasn't hard, but I found out he was a heavy user on the MedNet bulletin boards. And it's the same thing. He hasn't posted anything under his own name in over a month. Hasn't paid a bill, rented a car, or used an ATM machine."

La Roy grumbled before the words came out. "Sounds like a description of a dead man."

"Hate to agree with him," said Salinas. "But yeah. Missing persons like this usually turn up as floaters or John Does in some morgue until the fingerprints get their turn in line."

"And there's nothing with the Texas medical board that would lead to this kind of disappearance?" asked Will.

"Not in Texas," said Salinas, his voice turning reticent. "But go right next door to Arkansas? About fifteen years ago, the same Dr. Harvey Bertrand pleaded a *nolo contendere* to possession of illegal narcotics.

"As it sometimes happens with doctors," continued Salinas, "and I think you see where I'm going . . . The record gets sealed if the well-intended physician pleads no contest and goes into rehab."

"So you're saying Dr. Bertrand was in rehab?" asked Will.

"No. I'm saying the record is sealed. That usually *means* rehab."

La Roy joined in again. "So, for all we know, this old coot coulda been using again and wound up dead over a drug deal?"

Salinas turned to Will. "How paranoid can one man be?"

"Not paranoid," said La Roy. "My mind just works in worse-case scenarios. What I'm paid for."

"It could be a simple case where the doc's using again," said Salinas.

"But he'd be paying for drugs," said Will, thinking he'd found a hitch in the FBI agent's theory. "Then he'd have accessed his bank account by now."

"Not necessarily." Salinas grinned. "My information is that physicians who do drugs keep cash available so they can hide their transactions. Not unlike habitual gamblers."

The cheap shot wasn't lost on La Roy. "You think 'cuz you went to Harvard that makes you less a Mexican?"

"No," said Salinas. "I think I'm just enough of a Mexican that I was able to take advantage of our country's late, great affirmative action programs. That, and I was able to kick a lot of black affirmative action asses in my training at Quantico."

"You couldn't kick the First Lady's ass," jabbed La Roy.

"Will you both leave it alone?" asked Will, his sense of humor wearing as thin as the reasons La Roy and Salinas needed to cross swords. "I'm gonna have to tell Gwen *something*."

"Well, don't tell her he's dead," said Salinas.

"Even though that's what you think," said La Roy. "That *is* what you think?"

Salinas tried to choose his words carefully. But he was tired and came up with what his gut told him. "Yeah. That's what it looks like."

"Can I request an investigation?" asked Will.

"You could," said Salinas. "But I wouldn't. You're not family, so that means you can't file a missing persons."

"What about the FBI investigating?" asked Will.

"Does it matter?" asked Salinas. "Gwen is pregnant. Everything's fine. Am I right?"

"Everything's *perfect*," corrected Will.

"Then it's my unofficial recommendation that you wait and see what turns up. I promise to keep my finger on it."

"Good enough," said Will, his appetizer arriving just in time for the second half of the ball game. The trio hung around to watch Villanova thump North Carolina with a twelve-point overtime surge, beating the spread by five points. Will autographed a napkin for the manager, then offered La Roy a ride home but only if he promised not to grouse anymore about "the fix." La Roy declined. By the time LBJ dropped Will off at the Georgetown condo, it was well past one in the morning.

Will undressed in the bathroom, sat on the edge of the bed, and thought foolishly of calling Gwen to kiss her and the baby good night, only noticing the time just before dialing the final digit. After he hung up, he remembered to check his e-mail. He willed himself off the bed and steered his tired tail into the next bedroom, booting up the computer and logging on to the secured congressional WebNET.

The computer was still glowing from the last time he'd used it. A rarity, he thought. He must have forgotten to turn it off twenty-four hours earlier. As he cursed the late hour, he auto-dialed the Web and keyed in his personal user ID. The computer screen blinked, then scrolled down a message. There were two new pieces of correspondence in Will's mailbox. The next morning's call sheet was first, neatly scanned in by Myriam's new assistant. Will moused the pointer to the print icon. The laser printer hummed to life and spat out the list. He'd read it in the morning, returning the crucial calls from the car.

Then Will pulled up e-mail number two.

At first glance, the words on the screen looked filtered. As if his brain had somehow turned dyslexic or he was reading through a prism. He rubbed his eyes, shook off the fatigue, then stood back to try and shoulder the strangely familiar chill in the room.

But the message didn't change:

THE CHILD IS NOT YOURS . . . IT IS <u>HIS</u>!

Will felt the air evacuate from his lungs. In a heartbeat, he found himself seated and hacking uncontrollably. His eyes watered from the fit. What had come over him? It was a prank. Just a crimson, goddamn political prank.

When he looked at the page again, he scanned for the return address box, only to find computer hieroglyphics:

ηξΦλσ>∴τιεο//___∴θδσσκφζδσ]

He slapped the laptop's lid shut. Then after a moment of contemplation, he opened the unit again and shakily maneuvered the mouse to the "save mail" icon and double-clicked the message into a file folder.

That's right, asshole. Fuck you.

He stuffed the urge to send some kind of pissy return. But where would he send it to anyway? Would his computer know the sender's address? In any case, sending prank mail or threats over the secured congressional system was a felony. The retort in his head would be considered criminal if he actually sent it.

The adrenaline shot straight to his skull. He was up, pacing. Churning his guts and wishing for some way to come down. Something liquid to calm the snakelike nerve that started at his cortex and spiraled all the way down to his tailbone. His body screaming for an alcoholic epidural, Will reached for the telephone and dialed Lane Allejandro. When she answered, he was out of breath and near panic.

"It's me."

"You okay?" asked the congresswoman. "You don't sound okay."

"I wake you?"

"Wouldn't you like to think so?"

"I don't want to be a bother."

"You're not bothering. What's up?"

"I want a drink," admitted Will. "I can see three vodka martinis. All lined up and ready to go. One, two, three."

"Don't we all?" she said. "Except I want mine with two olives. You know why I like two olives?"

"If it's sexual, I don't want to hear it."

"Then don't ask."

"I didn't ask. You volunteered."

"You know, if you weren't such a smoothy, I'd . . ."

"You'd what?"

"I thought you didn't want to know," she teased.

Will exhaled. She'd done it. Broken the spell. He was calming, suddenly distracted, and laughing with both lungs. God bless her. They talked for another hour before practically falling asleep on their respective receivers. When Will closed his eyes, though, the words burned on the back of his eyelids.

THE CHILD IS NOT YOURS . . . IT IS <u>HIS</u>!

11

Where running down missing doctors wasn't in Special Agent Steve Salinas's FBI job description, investigating breaches in Beltway security was. His visit to Will's office the following afternoon was on official ground on official terms. He'd brought along a very young computer analyst named Wayne, who was dressed for the office in a bowling shirt, Wrangler jeans, and a pair of black suede Nikes.

Will had invited Benjamin Yao.

"What's he doing here?" asked Salinas.

"I'm here at the senator's request," answered Benny, arms crossed and seated on the arm of the leather couch.

"He's here," corrected Will, "because we were just cleaning up some FDA matters. I asked him to stick around and lend an opinion. The FBI can still *handle* opinions?"

A former senior agent in the Bureau, Benny Yao had quit to start his own private security and investigative service. He'd had all the blessings of his colleagues until he'd taken on the FDA gig. It was considered a turncoat's slap in the agency's face.

"FBI dress code *ain't* what it used to be," said Yao of young Wayne, who was already rubber-gloved and booting up Will's laptop, the senator leaning over his shoulder.

"He's a subcontractor," said Salinas.

"You don't have your own staff of computer geeks?" shot back Benny Yao.

"Not enough to meet the demand in computer crimes," said Salinas. "Anyway, the Bureau's low on geeks since you quit."

And just when Salinas was about to impress Will with his knowledge of Internet crimes—how the crisscrossing of phone signals on the information highway had come under the FBI's understaffed jurisdiction, Wayne stepped up to the plate.

"Okay, so what's the problem?" he asked.

"What's the problem, *Senator?*" corrected Salinas. The boy's lack of formality was bordering on antisocial.

"Don't worry about it," said Will. He pointed out the encrypted message in the return address box.

"That's your problem?" asked Wayne.

"We need to know who sent it," said Will. "Can you crack the code?"

"That ain't a code," said Wayne. "It's just some router droppings."

"What kind of droppings?"

"Router droppings," repeated Wayne. "It's your computer's way of saying it doesn't recognize the sender."

"We thought it was some kind of encryption," said Benny.

"Sorry to pop your bubble, Mr. Former FBI dude," said Wayne. "But it's a lotta nothin'."

"Did you check the source code?" asked Salinas, betraying the unfortunate extent of his computer literacy.

"I don't need to check the source data," said Wayne. "I know where the message came from."

Everyone was listening.

Wayne shrugged. "It came from the *senator's* computer."

"Are you saying *I* sent the message?" asked Will.

"Not hardly," said Wayne. "I'm saying it was sent from your laptop. *This* computer right here. It's kind of a memo function. Here. I'll show you. I'm typing an e-mail to the senator's address from his own computer. Let's call it 'Test mail one.' "

Wayne typed: TEST MAIL ONE.

"Now I send it. Click. Wait about three seconds." Wayne sat back, arms briefly crossed, until the computer screen showed that Will had new e-mail. "Now I click on the mail. And hello-whaddayou-know, there she is."

TEST MAIL ONE

Will saw it before Salinas or even Benny. In the return message box was the exact same sequence of computer hieroglyphics:

$$\eta\xi\Phi\lambda\sigma{>}\therefore\tau\iota\epsilon o//\_\_\_\therefore\theta\delta\sigma\sigma\kappa\phi\zeta\delta\sigma]$$

Salinas tried to get it straight for himself. "You're saying that message was sent from *this* computer."

"Yup," said Wayne.

"And it couldn't have been done to make it *look* like the senator sent it to himself?" asked Salinas.

"Look," said Wayne. "When it comes to cyber-messaging, there's no such thing as impossible. It's just a matter of likelihood—"

"The computer was on when I got home," interrupted Will. "And I was pretty certain I'd shut it off the night before. I usually do after I pick up my mail . . ."

A unifying thought struck them all. The senator had suffered a break-in. Someone had been in his condo. It was on all their faces.

"Bag it!" said Salinas to Wayne. He reached for the phone and dialed a five-digit extension. "This is Special Agent Steve Salinas from the OPCA. How soon can I have an E.R.T. on deck?" Then Salinas put his hand over the receiver and snapped his fingers at Will. "One. I need the address of your condo. Two. If I were to send in an Evidence

Response Team to dust, is there anything in there you *don't* want them to see?"

"Like what?" asked Will.

"Like what? His collection of Swedish pornography? Or them salad bowls he's got full of crack cocaine," said Bill La Roy from the doorway, his smile turned up to its full caffeine-whacked wattage. He'd just returned from lunch, afternoon dose of joe in hand.

"It's not funny, Bill," said Salinas. "The senator had someone *inside* his home."

"No," Will answered earnestly. "Nothing in there that can hurt me."

"Okay," said Salinas. "You want to come along or you want me to handle this?"

La Roy tapped his watch. "Senate budget conference. Ten minutes."

"Want me to supervise?" offered Benny.

Will saw the proprietary look Steve Salinas was sending. He tossed his old friend his keys. "Try not to leave a mess."

Wayne slipped the Toshiba into a plastic bag as Salinas strode up to La Roy. "I expect you to explain to him how serious this is."

"Oh, you know me," said La Roy. "Everybody's a suspect."

"Be real for once," urged Salinas. "Try not to tie this into one of your assassination theories."

"Gotcha." La Roy winked, smiling far too broadly for a man who'd dropped five hundred dollars the night before on a game he thought might be fixed. Will recognized all too well the twinkle in La Roy's eyes. The ol' Seminole had lost money, but had clearly gotten laid in the process. In La Roy's book, that meant he'd broken even on the night.

Before Benny said so long, he had to stick it to Will and La Roy about the fabulous scuba-diving vacation in Bali he was putting together. Paid for with all the dough Will's FDA committee had ponied up for his exclusive service. Benny promised to send a postcard and left.

Slumped in that massive political-prop-of-a-desk-chair, Will sat flanked by flags of Massachusetts and the U.S.

Stars and Stripes—de rigueur in congressional decorating. In his somewhat less-than-statesmanlike posture, he floated the obvious question. "So who would do this kind of thing?"

"Name your enemy," said La Roy.

"That's *your* job."

"Like I told our favorite G-man, everybody's a suspect," said La Roy before firing imaginary bullets from his index finger. "And don't forget. You're number one on the short-list for the number-two job."

"I want an enemies list," said Will. "A *real* one."

"Ooh. That sounds Nixonian," said La Roy, eyebrows arching. "I like it."

"And while you're on your way out, can you ask Myriam to come in?" asked Will. "Scratch that. Just tell her I want the first shuttle home."

"How much are you gonna tell her?"

"Gwen?"

"You married to someone else?"

Will was in no mood for sarcasm. He glared until La Roy tempered himself.

"A little advice?" asked La Roy.

"Sure. Why not?"

"Wait to see whose fingerprints show up in your bedroom."

"I'm way past that kinda behavior," said Will. "You should know that by now."

"Just checkin'," said La Roy, grin intact. "Enemies on the way."

"Shut the door behind you."

As a regular on the U.S. Airways shuttle to Logan, Will was polite and familiar with most of the ticket agents and flight crews. As a rule, the mostly female contingent was charmed off their Aerosoles by the senator and, on the rare occasion when he requested to be seated alone, they so willingly complied. Sometimes they even bumped a reserved passenger to meet the senator's personal needs.

Such were the perks.

A platoon of eight-ounce Diet Cokes sat upright on the tray next to him as he drank himself into a quiet repose. His mind whirred and tracked backward. The drive home from the Severino Grill with LBJ. Walking through the door. Lights on, up the steps into the living room, a right turn after that, then a straight shot up to the lofted bedrooms. Had the intruder been in the condo when he'd entered? Had Will been watched as he'd tossed aside his jacket and tie, kicked off his shoes at the bottom of the stairs, and loudly belched his way into the bedroom?

Jesus, the violation of it.

His mind sped ahead. Who would pull such a prank? Why? And to what end?

Who were Will's true enemies? By tomorrow, La Roy would fax him a memo. A guaranteed hit list of the far left and right and everybody with a political ax to grind in the middle. A list that might even include the president. Sure, Bill La Roy was certifiable. But that was his gift. A wild imagination that left no rock unturned. Will needed to hear the options, lop off the extremes at either end, and focus on the center.

So who was in the center?

Despite the caffeine injection, fatigue eventually forced his eyes to close. His head tilted toward the window. For nearly the rest of the flight, he dozed and dreamed of petty policy ideals, engaging in a weeklong filibuster on the Senate floor, then a horrific parade of women leaving bloody fingerprints in his Georgetown condo bedroom. The Navajo-white walls were slathered in crimson palm prints, names written in red, a top ten list corresponding with notches in the senator's mental bedpost and, marked on the ceiling, dripping in neon-orange:

THE CHILD IS NOT YOURS . . . IT IS <u>HIS</u>!

It was seven forty-five when the limo dropped Will at the top of his Marblehead drive. He was quick to notice the posted order. It was encased in plastic and tacked to the wooden gate:

CONSTRUCTION SUSPENDED UNTIL SAFETY INSPECTION

Will briefly skimmed the finer print. Something about the site being unsafe due to "geological anomalies." It was signed in red ink by a county inspector whose name Will could not make out. It looked as if the crew had, in choreographed unison, suddenly dropped what they were doing and marched off the site. Concrete had even been left to harden in a wheelbarrow that Will found parked near the front door, a shovel frozen in time like a spoon in a thick bowl of chili.

As for Will's early homecoming, Myriam had kindly called ahead so, for Gwen, there was no surprise when he walked in on a Wednesday evening instead of the scheduled late Friday night. The same couldn't be said for Will, who was met at his own front door by his father, Sully. A surprise attack. The old man's pump was already primed with a half-pint of Bushmills. It made Will wish someone had had foresight enough to warn him.

"Be nice," were Gwen's first words. "Your mother's here, too." A kiss hello and she was swinging the door wide open. Will's parents had stopped by unannounced. It was always conveniently around dinnertime. Sully's excuse was some crap about "that's the way it was *still* done in the old country." On the other hand, Will's mother gave no excuses. She didn't speak a word, nor had she since 1988.

A stroke had left Corrine Sullivan seventy percent dysfunctional and without the use of her vocal cords. She was mostly paralyzed but for the use of her left arm which she used to wave off her irritating husband and maneuver her motorized wheelchair about the bottom floor of their five-room Southy condo.

"Mom," acknowledged Will, kissing her cheek and taking his place at the dining room table. Her one good eye flashed a hello and, closely inspected, the left corner of her mouth lifted a millimeter in what passed for a smile. He was her only child. She loved him. She was proud of him for who he was.

As usual, Sully did the talking for her. "Your mother can't express how excited she is about the baby."

The baby, groaned Will's stomach. It had been churning for some twenty hours. He'd looked forward to walking through the front door, kissing his wife, and settling in for a calm night. They would talk as partners. Gwen would finally understand the fear that was scorching the walls of his belly.

Dinner proved to be without much incident, prepared by Invisible Izzy, the housekeeper who Will had yet to meet. As usual, Sully did most of the talking over the meal. And much to Gwen's surprise, Will stuffed the caustic tone he'd come to reserve for his father. For once, patience prevailed. That was it, thought Gwen. She'd wondered if her husband had finally matured into the perfect politician for the coming millennium. Raised and trained in the practical art of pliability, Will had learned how to patronize all the annoying characters he might need in a crunch one day. Even his father.

"Can you bring the cocoa butter?" Gwen called out as she turned back the bedcovers. Sully and Corrine had long left the expectant couple alone. It was finally the way Will had planned. Just the two of them. Alone. And Gwen hadn't an inkling as to what was coming 'round the corner.

"Where is it?" asked Will.

"I think it's on top of the toilet," she said.

Swell, thought Will. She wanted him to massage her belly with lotion. Not that it was tough duty. It was about stretch marks. The baby. The whole package. It was just that he wanted to spit out the bad news. He'd been holding it in long enough.

"Look, before we get started down the baby trail—"

"Something wrong?" she jumped in, her voice sharpened. Gwen didn't miss an inflection.

"I wanted to tell you earlier, but—"

"Surprise attack by your parents. Right. So get to the point."

"Ease up, will ya?"

"I can hear the bad news coming." Actually, she could feel it. As her belly grew, she thought, so did her instincts.

"You didn't even wonder why I came home on a Tuesday? While we were in session?"

Tuesday. She'd totally missed it. After the construction crew had walked off the site, the day had gone downhill. Then in her haste to accommodate her ambushing in-laws, she'd forgotten what day it was. Tuesdays, Will was in Washington. Yvonne had left her a brief message that he was coming home early, but with no information other than his ETA. Gwen had briefly wondered why, but had forgotten to ask.

"What happened?" Her tone was grave and short.

"It's about Dr. Bertrand."

From there he began, telling her all about Vanessa Curran's puff story, his cursory investigation, followed by Steve Salinas's unofficial FBI report on the missing doctor and his theory that Dr. Bertrand might be a user.

"So you're afraid for our baby?" asked Gwen, somewhat incredulously, seated dead center on the bed, pillows propped around her. Will stayed at the threshold, shoulder propped against the jamb, wearing nothing more than knit cotton boxers. His arms were protectively crossed.

"At the risk of sounding paranoid," said Will, "I'm wondering if the baby's really mine."

"Just because Harvey moved his office?"

"Last night, somebody broke into the condo and left a message on my personal e-mail. The note was pretty cryptic, but it said the baby wasn't mine."

"Broke in?"

"The FBI's investigating."

"They have any idea who?"

Will shook his head. "It could just be a prank."

"The hell you think," said Gwen. "Why else would you be taking this posture?"

"Look. It's hard for me not to wonder."

"You're just feeling guilty because you weren't there."

"That's right," said Will, his voice rising above the usual level. "I *wasn't* there! And now Dr. Bertrand's up and gone to God knows where. All his records have disappeared—"

Gwen was five steps ahead of Will. "I won't do another

amnio. I already had the one. The baby's fine. End of discussion."

At twelve weeks, Gwen had had an amniocentesis. And the idea of having another scared the shit out of her. A local anesthetic had been pricked into her stomach near the navel to numb her skin. Then, as Gwen turned her head away from the monitor, choosing not to watch, the eight-inch ultrasound-guided needle pierced her belly and made its way into her womb. It might as well have been a harpoon. A sample of the amniotic fluid was extracted. Two weeks later Gwen had the results. A healthy baby with the sex known only to her OB and some lab technician somewhere upstate.

The optional DNA paternity portion of the test was never offered, or ordered.

"I'm talking what if," said Will. "Just what if there'd been a mistake? What if it wasn't my sperm?"

"It was your sperm," said Gwen.

"But how do you know?"

"Because it *tasted* like yours," Gwen snapped. "For Christ's sake, how am I supposed to answer that? There was this frozen vial. Your name was on it."

"Mistakes happen."

"Yes, they do," Gwen conceded. "And so what if one happened here and the baby wasn't yours? Would you love it any less?"

"That's not the question," Will said. "WHAT IF IT ISN'T MINE?"

"You're a vain prick!"

"None of this bothers you?"

Gwen tried to sound collected. "We've had the amnio. The baby's fine. I was there. It was *your* sperm. I'm sorry for all the prospective parents out there who lost money or won't have a baby because Dr. Bertrand's dead or gone or whatever . . ."

You don't give a fuck because you're pregnant, Gwen.

It was as if both of them had the same exact thought at the same exact moment, but neither would say it to the other. Silence thickened the room. The only sound was the ticking of the space heater and that of the plastic sheeting covering the fireplace—billowing, then retreating like cellophane over a sucking mouth.

"Sit down," she pleaded. "Please . . . Just sit."

After a measured pause, Will broke free from the doorjamb and did as instructed, sliding onto the bed next to her. She swiveled on her hip and laid her head in his lap.

"Now, gimme your hand," she said.

With one hand, she pulled up her XL T-shirt. With the other she placed her husband's hand on her belly. "Feel that?" she asked, but without waiting for an answer. "That's *our* baby. Yours and mine. Nobody can take that away."

Will's jaw tightened as he tried so desperately to believe it. His long fingers palmed her stomach like a basketball.

"Ours," she repeated.

"And the message on my computer?"

"You said it. A prank," said Gwen. "Think about it. Vanessa Curran tells you about poor Harvey. You tell the FBI who, we all know, loathe the *popular* senator from Massachusetts. The FBI confirms Dr. B.'s missing. And suddenly, there's a message on your computer.

"The part that worries me," Gwen added, "is that *somebody* broke into the condo."

"It's overtime for Bill La Roy. This is the kind of stuff that gets him hard. He's working on an enemies list right now."

"And the leak's in the FBI?" she asked before answering the question herself. "More than likely somebody heard of a Dallas fertility doctor's misfortune and—bingo—that same somebody finally finds a way to rattle the slippery senator's happy little cage. I'll give you two prime suspects. Margie Van Hough and Lois Freehold."

The Slammer Sisters.

She could see the wheels turning behind her husband's eyes.

"It's just politics, sweetie."

"I wish it were that simple," said Will.

"If it were simple," joked Gwen, "they wouldn't pay us consultants those big, big bucks."

Will palmed a fistful of cocoa butter and spread it over her stomach. It melted over the stretched skin.

"You're using too much," she said.

"Not too much," said Will. "Not enough."

With that, Will moved northward, under her shirt, spreading the goo over her growing breasts, between them, and around her neck and shoulders. He was straddling her and she was giggling. "You're supposed to be doing my tummy."

"Your tummy?" repeated Will. "You mean Mount Everest here?"

"I'll be that big soon enough," she said. "Don't make me bigger than I am."

"Fine." With that, Will lay on his side and, with both hands, worked over the arched surface. From left to right, sternum to pubis, until she was waxed and glistening.

"Did you feel that?" she asked.

He did. But found himself strangely mute.

"Was that—?"

"The baby?" she finished. "I think so."

"Was that the first kick?"

"I think so. I never felt anything like it before."

"Wow." Will grinned. "Do it again!"

"*I* didn't do anything. The baby did."

Will kissed the ever-growing mound. As sweet as a caress. For over an hour they lay there, in the dark, Will's hands exploring her stomach, hoping for just one more tiny thump. But nothing followed. Only the stillness of Gwen's breathing, then sleep. In the darkness that soon followed, Will kissed the baby again, promising himself to repeat the gesture every night. With Gwen. Over the phone. It wouldn't matter. He would have her hold the receiver up to her belly and he would kiss the child good night. Every damn night. Until the child was born.

His child.

the mister worries the child is not his.

IS HE SUSPICIOUS? OR JUST PARANOID?

i can't tell.

YES. BUT WHAT DOES YOUR INSTINCT TELL YOU?

how could the mister know <u>anything</u>?

AS MUCH AS THEY DISLIKE HIM, THE MISTER HAS A FRIEND IN THE FBI.

> how could the fbi know anything?

I CANNOT TELL. BUT SOMEBODY IS TALKING. I CAN SENSE IT.

> it's all in control. i'm here as you instructed.
> to watch the flower and stay close to her.
> she likes me. will soon trust me. she
> is in such a bloom. you should see her.

SOON ENOUGH . . . WHEN DO YOU MEET WITH CLEM?

> tonight.

HE HAS HIS INSTRUCTIONS.

> as do I, lover.

KEEP AN EYE ON HIM. HE'S A JEALOUS BEAST.

> only of you.

I SAW YOUR NEW PICTURE. THANK YOU.

> i look like a fat old hag.

YOU DO. AND FOR THAT I LOVE YOU EVEN MORE.

Izzy closed her laptop, her eyes squeezing shut as she tried to recall what he'd looked like the last time she'd seen him. They were in a visiting room. He, the convicted murderer. She, masquerading as one of the constantly shifting members of his appeals counsel. She'd carefully chosen dark brown contact lenses to match her newly Clairol-colored mane, a conservative, A-line dress, heels to add three inches to her height, and thick, designer optical frames to obscure her face from possible FBI recognition.

The scripted encounter appeared to witnesses as nothing more remarkable than the standard grind of lawyer-client legal-speak. Nobody but Izzy was watching for Dean's signals. A wink. A flared nostril. And on cue, Izzy launched from her chair and kissed Theroux full on his open mouth. That's when the seed was passed. From Dean to Izzy. The guards rushed in and pried the two apart. Izzy was pinned to the wall while Dean was knocked to the floor, his laughing maw pried open and swept for contraband. They'd found nothing. Certain he'd swallowed a narcotics balloon, Dean was rushed to the infirmary for X rays while Izzy was held for little more than a perfunctory questioning. She'd artfully claimed that she'd been overcome with an urge unlike anything she'd ever experienced. That the madman had drawn her near.

For it was Izzy who'd swallowed a tiny prophylactic balloon. Dean's precious seed had been passed from *him* to *her*.

In the blackness of her room, Izzy tried to remember the touch of his lips to hers. Then as she was about to leave the house, she realized she'd forgotten her keys. They were on the buffet near the big dining room table. Having already memorized the layout of her new home, she navigated the darkness from her housekeeper's quarters, passing through the kitchen into the dining area. Once there, she bumped into a dining room chair. It was turned toward the double fireplace which served both the dining area and the living room where, less than an hour earlier, she'd sat and listened. The old chimney was a straight cavity that emptied into the master suite. From Izzy's silent post she could listen to Will and Gwen trade intimacies. Sure, she could've been far more sophisticated, obtaining and planting a listening device in the couple's room. She'd done it before. The bugs could be picked up in many electronics stores or, for that matter, in the baby department of any K Mart. A simple Fisher-Price baby monitor plugged into the new nursery down the hall could easily be modified to pick up the Sullivans' romantic whispers.

But the open fire-pit worked nicely. In the semidarkness of the downstairs, Izzy could be seated at the dining room table and tune a keen ear to the words upstairs. The unfiltered voices traveled cleanly down the bricked shaft. An unabridged conversation between married intimates who were awaiting the birth of their first child.

If they only knew.

Izzy gathered her keys from the buffet and headed back to the kitchen, intending to exit through the back door.

"Going out?" Will was standing, bare-chested, in the refrigerator's stark light.

Gathering her wits, Izzy feigned shock at first. "I'm sorry. You must be Senator Sullivan."

Will extended his hand. "And you must be Julia Child."

Somehow the reference was momentarily lost on Izzy. Will went for the saver. "The dinner . . . it was terrific."

"I'm sorry, Senator. But you scared me half to death."

"Please. It's Will." Will glanced down at his boxers. Not exactly a dignified way to meet the new housekeeper. "You must forgive me. I get hungry after midnight," he said. "I see you've got your keys."

"I have a date."

"A date?" asked Will, sounding surprised, but the words came off slightly suspect.

"This fellah? He manages a Burger King," she lied coolly. "They close at midnight so, you know, I get to see him when I can."

"Must leave you short of sleep," said Will.

"Your missus? She gave me the morning off tomorrow. So I can sleep in."

Will closed the refrigerator door. "I'm sorry. I'm keeping you. Drive carefully."

"I will, sir," she said. "Good night."

"And watch out for drunks. Between midnight and four, one out of three drivers on the road are legally lit, if you know what I mean," warned Will, warm smile intact. "Good night. I'll lock the door after you."

"Thank you, Senator."

"Will," he reminded her. "When you're in my house, my name is Will."

And then, ever-so-politely, without meeting his eyes, Izzy answered, "Thank you, *Mister* Sullivan."

"Okay," he relented. "A compromise."

Will locked the door after her, then leaned back into the refrigerator for a little late-night inventory. Leftover chicken, tuna salad, and day-old lunch meat.

"Screw that," said Will. He dove into the freezer and found a half-gallon of mint chocolate chip. Gwen's private stash.

"Well, look who got all fat and ugly," said Clem. Those were the first words out of his filthy mouth. His teeth were as crooked as ever and his beard flecked with more gray than its original dirty blond.

"It's for the part," said Izzy, sounding vain and fatigued from the long day. "Anyway, Dean likes me this way. Told me himself."

She'd been late, making Clem wait for her at a North End bar called the Sweeper. She'd found him against the back wall, seated on a cut-down stool and feeding quarters into a video game. As always, Clem was rail-thin with hair that looked as if it hadn't been washed since the day they'd all split up. The foam from his third beer was stuck to his thick whiskers.

"You gonna play this game or are we gonna talk?"

"Just passing the you-know-what," said Clem, picking up his mug and leading her to a corner table. "You want something to drink?"

"I'm clean. I gotta stay straight until Dean says otherwise," she said. "What do they got to eat here? Do I smell onion rings?"

"Dean don't say shit to me."

"Maybe that's 'cuz you don't mean shit to him."

"He brought me back from the dead. Just like he did you," said Clem. "So let's not get competitive. We all got our seat at the table."

"Mine just happens to be closest to Dean."

"Fuck that," moaned Clem. He'd heard it from her before. She was a prima-donna bitch who thought she was Dean's one and only love. As if when he'd returned them to the living, she'd been the only one he'd meant to resurrect. The rest had been some kind of mistake. Izzy was more like a cold fuck, he thought. "Dean knows I get it done. Otherwise, he wouldn't have resurrected me."

Izzy straightened, propping herself on her elbows. "What do you know?"

"Dean's knocked up some fancy broad," said Clem. "He wants us around her. Protecting the you-know-what."

"The baby," she said. "I need to know what you can do."

"You name it."

"No bullshit. These are hot-shit people with hot-shit tastes. You might have to cut your hair and shave." Then after she thought about it: "Yeah. You *have* to get a cut and shave."

"Yeah? And what else?" asked Clem.

"What can you do?" It was late. Izzy was rubbing her eyes.

"You know, the last time I saw you—"

"Let's stick to the script as Dean wrote it," she interrupted.

"All I was gonna say is that you were a sight for a sore dick."

"You can't be crass around these people." Then she figured it out. "Pool man. Yeah. I think I can get you a job doing the pool."

"I'll need a truck."

"I'll get you cash and fresh ID."

"I got plenty of fresh ID. But money, sweet-chunks," said Clem. He let it hang. It had been an issue since the big split. The money. Dean controlled it. Money was wired from Dean-knows-where to Western Union and cashed whenever one of them was tapped out.

"You'll get what you need."

"But will I ever get what I'm due?"

"When it's done," she said. "Dean promised."

"It'll never be done!" spat Clem. "I swear to God, he'll die and leave us alone with absolutely nothing!"

"Not nothing," said Izzy. "A baby. *His* baby!"

"What for? So we can feed it and change its diapers? It makes no sense."

"He'll tell us why when he's ready," said Izzy. "And now's the time we must keep our eye on the prize. We *must* protect the mother *and* the child."

"And why *her?*" he asked. "If you're so precious to Dean, why not you? Why aren't you the one he knocked up? Or Sheila?"

The question hurt. What's more, Izzy didn't have an answer for him. She only had the pat response. "Ours is not to ask why. Only to accept our place at his table."

Though Clem understood, he showed some resentment. Izzy sensed it. Was it still love that kept him in line, or was it fear?

"Pool men work once, twice a week," said Clem. "Maybe I should sign onto the construction crew. I did some landscaping for a while in Colorado."

"In a minute. I gotta pee."

As Clem watched Izzy embark for the rest room, he tried to remember how many times she'd walked away from him. Usually after he'd made some kind of awkward advance. Oh, how he'd coveted her tight ass ever since she was nineteen. All the way back to when they were squatting in empty houses in the Hollywood Hills. But he'd never fucked her. Nobody in the family had. She was always saving *it* for Dean. And he hadn't so much as touched the snotty bitch. Dean, man. He was all tease. He had everybody on a string, always wanting more, but never ever letting a man or woman get close enough to see inside him.

Now, it was stuffy Boston and Izzy was looking dumpy, ugly, and wide in the pants. For the role? Sure, he thought. Why the hell not? What Dean wanted, Dean got. Messiahs had that unearthly privilege. But in Clem's eyes, the bitch had let herself go. Eventually, all bitches did. Dean had said as much that same night they'd first met up in a Tiny Naylor's on the east end of Sunset Boulevard. That was some fifteen years back. A time when Clem still had dreams of playing guitar in front of thousands of screaming girls. Each and every one with nothin' but sex on their minds and a willingness in their jeans.

It was the end of the millennium. Rock and roll dreams were dead and buried. As was Clem. He'd been resurrected, but only to serve as slave-boy to his imprisoned master. He could run, turn his back on the family. Turn his back on Dean. If only Dean wouldn't come to him in his dreams, he might've been brave enough to call it quits. Most every damn night, Dean appeared in quasi-color. Talking to Clem. Teaching Clem. Promising a world beyond imagination in exchange for just one more day of servitude.

In those dreams, Clem would suffer his enslavement and scream in Dean's face, "YOU ARE NOT GOD!"

Dean would appear either unfazed or as if he'd never heard Clem's words. He always answered with an angelic smile. "Yes," he'd say. "I am not God. But I know *him,* he knows *me,* and we both know *you,* Clem. We both know Clem is a *killer.* And you will do just as we say!"

12

Planning on staying in Marblehead through the weekend, Will had Myriam cancel the rest of his week. For the first time since getting pregnant, Gwen put her business on hold and gladly filled her husband's calendar with day trips to antique stores, lunches on Newbury Street, and shopping expeditions for the expanding nursery. Will was game enough, dutifully lending his opinion when asked about his taste in cribs and changing tables. But he drew the line when it came to the registry. He'd leave those decisions to Gwen and Yvonne, who'd picked a weekday afternoon in mid-May for a baby shower. Will was doubly pleased to find out it was a girls-only affair and he was *not* invited.

And though he was occasionally recognized by a constituent, he remained mostly anonymous in the shadow outside his wife's unearthly halo. Between choosing a layette and sucking back paper cups of designer coffee, Will accepted his ornamental role and the repetitive chitchat of saleswomen.

"How far along are you?"

"When are you due?"

"Do you know if it's a boy or a girl?"

"Are you going natural or epidural?"

The weekend itself proved peaceful, providing some long-lost quiet time, hand-holding, and even some surprisingly tender lovemaking. Will cooked a pasta meal and the couple talked Pampers more than politics. As the sun set on Sunday, Izzy volunteered to drive Will to Logan Airport. He kissed Gwen good-bye, then the baby in her stomach, and waved from the passenger seat of Gwen's Ford Explorer.

"You love your baby," said Izzy, comfortable behind the wheel. "I can tell such things."

"As much as I can," said Will. "I mean, it's not exactly a baby yet. It's this kicking little beast in her stomach."

"I think it's a boy."

"Why do you think that?" he asked.

"Just a feeling," she smiled. "A very good feeling."

"From your mouth to my father's ears," said Will.

"Your father?" she asked. "Was he also a famous senator?"

"My father's a famous pain in the ass," said Will. "But I love him just the same."

Izzy gave a practiced laugh. The kind she used to give when she was still a stunner, seated on a bar stool and working a potential victim. But tonight, Will wasn't buying. He seemed to have drifted off into his own thoughts. Izzy thought it best not to continue the conversation. She would keep her mouth shut, drive the Mister to Logan, drop him at the terminal. She offered to pick him up on the following Friday. He thanked her, said he would call, then had one more request.

"Do me a favor," said Will.

"Yes, Mr. Sullivan?"

"While I'm gone, take care of my wife," he said. "She trusts you."

"Oh, yes, sir. I most certainly will."

That Sunday evening looked as if it would come to a customary close when a D.C. cab dropped Will off at his Georgetown condo. But on his doorstep, Will found a thick, messengered packet bearing the usual markings. A gray envelope, his name scripted in Myriam's precise handwriting, and the red stamps of the congressional messenger service. Just a light bit of night-table reading, thought Will—an evening preparatory for the next day's business, compiled as a loose-leaf potpourri of pending or proposed legislation, legally notated by his youthful squad of legislative analysts, with handwritten memos in each margin from various members of his staff. Green ink from his own administrative assistants. Red from Sandy Corwin. Blue ink if it was Bill La Roy's scratchings on policy.

Will tucked the heavy package under his arm, turned the key in the lock, and swung the door open to a nightmare courtesy of the FBI. His first clue was the gagging, baby-blue feather dust hanging in the air. A reminder that the FBI Evidence Response Team had given the space a once-over, lifting prints and fiber in hopes of identifying the computer perpetrator. But Will hadn't expected the seemingly ceaseless tagging. Switching the lights on, he found his stuffed quarters practically emptied. As if a moving company had stopped by over the weekend and removed most of his furniture, kitchenware, sheets, and toiletries, not to mention his rare and costly Civil War collectibles. Where there had been property, Will found pink FBI evidence receipts.

What the hell?

The couch was there, but the cushions were gone. The stereo and VCR were there, boxed at the center of the living room floor, but his tapes and compact discs had been confiscated.

In the kitchen, notepads had been removed, replaced by tags. The fridge was tagged. The cupboards, tagged.

Even the walls were tagged. Right where his valuable sabers had hung in Civil War glory. The muskets, flags, boxes of belt buckles, all missing, but accounted for with those pink tags.

Will hurried up the stairs to his lofted bedroom. Pink tags and blue dust covered nearly every surface. The carpet was swatched and tagged. The contents of his bathroom, either boxed or tagged as received. Swinging around into his home office, he saw that the room had simply been emptied.

Everything was gone. Files. Disks. Even the chair and desk. The room was utterly vacant but for one pink FBI tag taped to the door.

His gut wrenched. His subconscious straightened the hair on the back of his neck. The condo smelled far more of opportunity than it did an actual investigation.

Hustling back to the bedroom, Will reached for the phone, but it, too, was gone. No tag, though. Will kicked over boxes until the unit tumbled out. He found the plug, got a dial tone, and punched up a familiar number. The line at the other end rang endlessly.

"Loose-dick prick!" said Will of La Roy. Plus the guy didn't even have an answering machine. *Loose-dick controlling prick.* From memory, Will dialed La Roy's pager, programming in the number of the condo followed by the number 9-1-1. Code for emergency. Call me now!

Next Will dialed Steve Salinas. He was alone, awake, and tuned into an ESPN women's beach volleyball rerun. The sound coming over the TV was so loud, Will had to ask Steve to turn the volume down.

"What's with my condo, Steve?" Will's voice left no room for interpretation. He was boiling over.

"We dusted. We're investigating," he said.

"Don't bullshit me," said Will. "I've got more of your pink little tags than I have property."

"They dusted for prints. That's it."

"It's like Allied Van Lines did a friggin' number on my home. Now, what's the deal?"

"I, uh . . . I wasn't there," admitted Steve. "I don't know."

"You weren't here?"

"I got called to testify in an Ethics Subcommittee hearing. I had your keys. I opened the door and left explicit instructions. They were supposed to dust for prints on the door, the landing, and your office and that's all."

"I got a tag here that says they booked my toothbrush as evidence."

"I don't get it," said Steve. "Gotta be a mistake."

"No, Steve," said Will. *"Better* be a mistake. You hear me?"

"You don't need to take that tone, Will. We got history, you and me."

"That's right," said Will. "I trusted you."

"And you said you had nothing to hide," Steve's voice rose over the phone line.

"My office. Tomorrow! Nine o'clock!" Will slapped the phone into the cradle. He hung around another half hour waiting for Bill La Roy to return the page. When he didn't, Will grabbed his overnight reading and a bundle of dry cleaning, including a fresh suit that was luckily still wrapped in plastic, protected from the choking dust. A cab picked him up and delivered him to the Marriott on 12th Street. He checked into his room, dumped the mini-bar into a wastebasket, left it outside the door, and then paged La Roy one last time. He didn't expect to hear back. He just wanted Bill to wake up with his pager buzzing before he hit the nearest Starbucks.

An hour passed.

As he switched off the light, hoping to get some sleep, Will heard a quiet shuffling outside the door, then the sound of something being slid underneath it. Bolting from bed, he ignored the note and threw the door open. Before him stood a frightened bellman, barely thirty years old, his belly straining at the hotel-issued vest, utterly terrified at the sight of the panicky senator.

"Fax for you, sir." The bellman pointed at Will's stocking feet. Will was standing on the envelope. "I'm sorry, sir. I really didn't mean to disturb you. I hope you don't think—"

All Will could think to say was "I'm sorry, too," and then, "Thanks. Good night." He shut the door and tore open the envelope, unfolding the message while fumbling for the overhead light. Unable to find the switch, Will resorted to the bathroom. Once there, under the harsh, fluttering fluorescent strips, he saw more cryptic words expressly designed to rattle his soul cage:

YOU MUST ASK YOURSELF,
HOW DEEP IS YOUR FAITH?

Will's eyes shot to the top of the fax for a return number. It bore a Washington, D.C., area code and a downtown prefix. Bingo. From the phone next to the bed, Will dialed the number, waiting to hear a voice, an answering machine, or the distinct electronic handshake that signaled the ready modem or fax machine.

Instead, Will got the switchboard.

"Good evening, Marriott D.C. Can I help you?"

"I'm sorry," said Will. "I must've dialed incorrectly." He hung up and carefully dialed again.

"Good evening, Marriott D.C. Can I help you?" asked the hotel operator.

Stuck for words, Will was trying to figure out how he'd misdialed again.

"May I help you?"

"Yes," said Will. "This is Senator Will Sullivan in room 1209. I just received a fax."

"Is there a problem, Senator?"

"I think the return number on top of the fax is the same as the hotel's."

"That means, sir, that the fax was sent inter-room."

"From within the hotel?"

"Yes, Senator."

"Is there any way to find out who sent it?" asked Will. "Or from which room?"

"Let me ask," she said. "Please hold."

Will waited, rereading the fax and the number printed faintly across the top, looking for some kind of clue or hint. The hotel operator clicked back in. "Senator Sullivan?"

"Yes," answered Will.

"The night manager says she's sorry. But there's no way of telling which room it was sent from."

Will didn't speak nor did he hang up. He just sat there as if the operator's answer was insufficient.

"Will there be anything else, sir? Perhaps a wake-up call?"

After another lengthy pause, Will responded. "Yeah. Please. Seven-thirty." That was before he checked his watch and saw just how late it was. 1:44 A.M. "Do me a favor and make that eight."

"Eight A.M., sir."

"Good night."

With his right hand Will wadded the note into a ball and flung it at the mirror. It bounced and rolled underneath the bureau.

You are seriously fucking rattled, Will.

"Screw you!" Will shouted back at himself.

The shout pierced the wall to the adjacent room, loud enough for the hotel guest to clearly make out the "Screw you!" Seated for nearly an hour at the end of his king-sized bed, occasionally praying, but mostly staring at the common wall he shared with the senator from Massachusetts, the road-rumpled Vance Allatore waited, counting all along on that well-worn rosary.

For an entire hour.

That's how long it had taken the fax to go from room 1207, through the switchboard, and from the main fax machine to the front desk, into a sealed envelope, and delivered back up to room 1209. Will Sullivan's room.

One hour.

The former prosecutor had been relieved to hear the bell-man walk past his room, the slight thump of the bed as Will had rushed to door, the short and muted conversation which followed, the bellman leaving, and silence broken by Will's muffled call to the hotel operator. The "Screw you," he figured, was merely some elective enunciation. Oh, Will had the right to be frustrated, angered. The whole deal. The senator's psyche was being royally messed with. Mind-gamed into utter mental asphyxiation. But it was still the beginning. There was so much more to be done. So much for the senator to unlearn before starting over. This was only the beginning of a very difficult learning curve. The same learning curve Vance Allatore had followed once he'd exiled himself from government service.

Frustration, Denunciation, Education, and then Belief.

The prescription for the true believer. Time was waning. From now on, he would need to stay close. Very close.

13

As cherry blossoms burst against gray skies and the ominous pull of tax deadlines, the media was holding an executioner's ax over the head of the IRS director, Kenneth G. Durrant. His three-year, five-billion-dollar revamping of the collection office had turned into a political nightmare. The computers didn't work. His plot for tax filing via the Touch-Tone telephone and the Internet had twisted phone lines into Ma Bell hell. People were terrified of missing their deadlines and trial lawyers were mobilizing nationwide for class action suits against the agency.

Durrant, the first African-American appointed to such a post, was also fighting a federal grand jury subpoena. The FBI was investigating investments made by his wife—in particular, stock in a Boston-based software company named AmeriTech Systems, which had designed the failed IRS operating systems.

Durrant was standing before Will's desk, hat in hand. "*Your* office recommended we give AmeriTech the contract—"

"C'mon, Kenny. My office *recommended* a Massachusetts designer be allowed an *opportunity to bid*. Nothing more." Behind his desk, Will feigned a relaxed posture, hands behind his head.

"They put money in your campaign?"

"I had no discussions with AmeriTech about money. Soft *or* hard."

"What about Bill La Roy?"

"You trying to squeeze me?" asked Will. "We've known each other a while, Kenny. If you want something just spell it out."

The forty-eight-year-old, six-foot-six, former All-American from Georgia Tech bent at the waist and gripped the edge of Will's desk. Bony white knuckles rising through his mocha skin. "You're tight with President Addison. You got his ear while he's not returning my calls. I understand that. He wants to keep himself clean before the convention." Durrant straightened. He was a proud man and asking for help was hard. "I thought you could make my case for me."

"And that case would be . . ."

"I'm going through a divorce I can't afford. And now the grand jury? I can't pay for defense attorneys." Durrant pointed a finger at Will. "Get Addison to call off the dogs and I'll resign without turning this into a race thing."

"The dogs?" asked Will. "Are we speaking of the A.G. and the FBI director?"

"That grand jury they got impaneled?" complained Durrant. "It's like a Roach Motel for government officials. Politicians go in, but they don't come out."

Will hadn't thought of it that way. He smiled and made a promise. "Okay. I'll talk to Addison and see what I can do for you. Now, if you'll excuse me, I've got 'em lined up all the way to Constitution Avenue."

Will offered the IRS director the privilege of leaving through his private door.

"He'll have a fight if I go down," insisted Durrant.

"Let's hope it doesn't come to that," said Will, shaking the director's hand before returning to his desk. He punched up Myriam on the Amtel:

WHO'S NEXT?

Myriam pushed through his office doors, reading from a steno pad. "Tour group from Fitchburg. They've been waiting an hour. Phil Sumner from the Right to Die Coalition. Plus we got four Arizona state legislators here to talk to you about your vote on amendments to the Wildlife Act. They're doing rounds so I can ask them to come back."

"What else?"

"Joe Kingsley's in Bill's office," she said. "He wants to see you."

Will's mind sped through his mental Rolodex. Joe Kingsley. Timber lobbyist. Big-ticket hawker for the party.

"I'll see him when Bill's finished taking his dough."

"Oh, and a camera crew from NBC just arrived. I think they're chasing Durrant and this IRS bug."

Bug.

God bless Myriam, thought Will. That was the perfect name for it. Scandals would come through the Capitol, infecting the place like a cold virus, running their course before the system's own defenses could flush them out.

"I'll see the crew and the tour group. Tell them they've got five minutes and then I'm out to lunch," said Will, checking his hair in the mirror before repeating a criticism he once received from a *Post* columnist:

"Will Sullivan. Never met a TV camera he didn't like."

And that was just the morning. The afternoon would bring more lobbyists, corporate elephants bearing bags of money for party coffers, textile industry leaders, abbreviated subcommittee hearings on Cuba and education, a domestic security briefing, countless phone calls about the president's push for Medicare revisions in next year's budget proposal, and a rehearsal with Bill La Roy and Karen Younger, the White House media stylist. Will was prepping for his second weekend in a row on the TV pundit circuit. The word was finally out. Senator Will Sullivan was the odds-on pick to replace the unofficially outgoing vice president. Every news director wanted his ten-second opinion, be it on the trouble brewing in Korea or the threatening baseball strike.

For the crucial four months leading up to the August convention, *the Big Team* wanted the telegenic Will Sullivan front and center, serving up carefully crafted answers that would assure both the pundits and the public that the president and his designate were in perfect *policy sync*.

And no matter how often Will was asked to go on the record about his chances at the vice presidency, his answers always sounded relaxed and off the cuff.

"Let's be fair. The president and the vice president are good friends of mine. We have many conversations on personal and policy issues. And most of them, as you might guess, are off the record. But sure. If come August the president asks me to dance, I'll be the first to see if he knows a good jig."

All the while, Will did his best to keep his mind off the baby and his nose in the business of government. He tried to forget that radioactive nugget he'd unwillingly swallowed, praying it wouldn't burn a hole in his stomach. Should he dwell on it too much, his gut might up and turn septic. The Big Team didn't need an ulcerated, unfocused player. For that matter, neither did he. So he stuffed the creeping fear to the point that whenever Steve Salinas called with investigative updates, he would pass him off to Bill La Roy. La Roy would inform Will only if there was any progress. But so far, it was a zero-sum game.

As for Will's personal property, it was returned to the condo in neat cardboard boxes covered in shrink-wrap from the FBI lab. From linens to Civil War artifacts. And the apology? A curt note from the director along with a personal call from the attorney general herself, Margaret Van Hough. It was all chitchat with very little mention of the agency's snafu or the bitterness of the FDA hearings. Dinner was discussed, but had yet to be confirmed. Both Will and she were just too busy.

Business as usual.

The weekend neared. With it, most of the city's political populace climbed onto their favorite outbound arteries, ditching the nation's murder capital for the quieter calm of Virginia, Maryland, Delaware, or a home state. For those who stayed, the work wouldn't end. As La Roy had once waxed about his weekends in Washington, D.C., there was nothing else to do but sell drugs, buy drugs, smoke, shoot, or inhale drugs, or stick around and write legislation designed to stop drugs.

On late Friday, Will found time for Steve Salinas. La Roy was present along with Benny Yao.

"Let's forego the lack of fingerprints and get to who's sending the love letters," Will began.

La Roy played ringmaster. "We can start with either Steve's political laundry list or we can look at Benny's psyche-profile."

Thanks, pal, thought Will. Already he was forced to make a choice between Benny Yao and Steve Salinas.

"I'll hear the profile," said Will. "But only for amusement's sake."

Benny Yao went from zero to full reportage within three syllables. "There's the basic stalker stuff. Fixation, developing a kind of transference. A sort of proprietary interest in your affairs. In your case, a belief in your political agenda. Transferred to your personal life. Then when feeling betrayed, he sees it as permission to act out. That leads to the Melrose note, the e-mail, and then the fax from the Marriott. Shall I continue?"

Nods from Will and La Roy. Salinas kept his arms crossed but chose not to object. Benny Yao might have been an FBI turncoat, but he was also a fine investigator.

"Well, Bill was right about the note from the Melrose Hotel. It wasn't biblical. It was from *Dante's Inferno*. And as you suspected, it has to do with tilling the soil with bad seed. On its own, it makes little sense. But on to the phantom e-mail. Self-explanatory, I think. The author wants you to think the child your wife carries is not your own. But his, maybe? Or somebody else's? He's clearly trying to hit you where you live."

"What about the last note?" asked Will. "The fax."

" 'How deep is your faith?' " reread Benny Yao. "The third message itself wasn't what stumped the shrinks. Just the order in which it was delivered. They thought the third message should've come second. Like some kind of warning. Then the second message should've come third, 'The child is not yours.' Is this making sense?"

In fact, it cooled Will's veins. "How about we get back to some reality," he said. "I find it difficult to believe that I could inspire *that* kind of passion."

"Movie stars do," said La Roy. "Why not a handsome, nationally known, camera-friendly hack like Earnest P. Senator?"

"Reality?" reminded Will. "Political reality. Let's stick to the obvious. Steve?"

"One," began Salinas, "it could be someone close to you. On your staff. Or a former staffer with an ax to grind. Wants to play with your head."

"Don't believe it," said Will. "Next."

"The other extreme is political. The furthest of which is a Republican or a coalition of Republicans. Dirty tricks team from the central party. They might see you as an obstacle in the years ahead. They might be looking for mental weaknesses to exploit."

"Bill?" asked Will.

"You know me," said La Roy. "I'll believe everything and nothing. But I agree with Steve. Whatever it is, it's most likely a weak prank. It ain't goin' anywhere. And it's too damn personal for a buncha Republicans. My bet is that it's from our side of the aisle."

"Branch?" asked Will.

"Congress," said La Roy, none too thrilled to be the one who states the obvious. "Somebody else wants the number-two spot. Or he doesn't want to see you in it."

"I thought you said it was a *prank*," moaned Salinas.

"I was speculating *if* it was a prank," corrected La Roy. "If you ask my *opinion?* It's somebody sending a message."

Will wanted to stay in his tidy political comfort zone. From there, he could command. From there, he could keep control. "I just want to know which shoulder I should be looking over. My right or my left?"

"Friends or foes?" asked Benny Yao.

"You got an opinion? Let's hear it," said Will.

"Friends," said Salinas.

"Friends," agreed Benny.

La Roy looked miffed that nobody would even consider his "message" theory. "Friends," he finally conceded. But he had one more name to add. "Hell. If you call the White House a friend."

"The administration?" asked Salinas. His tone was incredulous.

"Dey's got da means," spiked La Roy, playing his own silly race card.

"But what's the motive?"

"Fuck if I know," said La Roy. "Earnest's condo gets broke into by some pro. Then he tosses Special Agent Steve-o-rino here some house keys. *He* opens the door so the FBI can lift a coupla fingerprints. Instead, the FBI turns over the whole joint. What's up with that?"

"Wait a minute—" said Salinas.

"When it's *been a minute,* I'll let you know," continued La Roy. "Could be the White House is using this crap as an excuse to test the reliability of the product. They got themselves in a heap a shit with Harper and Gavelgate. When it comes to the next four years, I figure they might wanna kick the tires of their first-round draft pick. Make sure there's no snakes rattlin' around in ol' Earnest's closet. Know what I'm sayin'?"

"Sorry," said Salinas. "That's a lot to swallow. And, on the record, I have no knowledge—"

"Yada yada yada," said La Roy. "You're a fed. And we get where you're comin' from."

"I'd say after the FDA stuff, the FBI's got far greater motive to mess with Will than the White House," offered Benny Yao.

"You bet," said La Roy. "and it's outta respect for Steve-o here that I didn't even go that way. He gets a little pissy when it comes to matters like conflict of interest."

"That's it, Bill . . ." Salinas was on his feet. "What the fuck did I ever do to you?"

Will fired a look at La Roy like a master would a guard dog. "Steve's just trying to help."

"Then why doesn't Mr. Helper tell us what he's gonna do?"

"That's up to Will," said Salinas, standing between his seat and the doorway. A lungful of air and he calmed himself. "I want to put a team on your wife up in Boston. And I can put a team on you down here. Mildly protective in case this *prankster's* on the extreme. But anything further—"

"Would be official and draw undue attention to the Bureau or the A.G.'s office," finished Will. "The A.G. would talk to the White House and, if they're not involved in any of this, which I'm certain is true, then they'll start to wonder about the product and *really* start kickin' the tires.

"We can't tell Gwen," said Will. It was an executive order to all present.

"You can tell her the FBI car's a precursor to Secret Service protection," said Benny Yao.

Will groaned. "That oughta go over big."

"What are you worried about? If they're a coupla straightlaced boys like Steve-o here," said La Roy, "she surely won't give a shit."

Gwen had long ago accepted that marriage to a politician would be relegated to weekends, vacations, and the odd junket. And as much as she had excuses *aplenty* to head south to Washington for business or pleasure, the fact was that she couldn't stomach the city, finding it dirty in both mind and business. Rotten to the core, she'd say the second she even thought of the place. The only chance for the future of the country, she reasoned, was for the service-minded citizens *outside* the walls of Washington to send in their finest warriors to do battle. Gwen knew she was not a warrior. Only an architect of war, with a preference for managing local candidates. National campaigns were too large, unwieldy, and the antithesis to the health of the republic . . .

. . . and, of course, motherhood.

If nesting was an instinct, Gwen found herself on full tilt. The pull of home was as powerful as anything she'd ever experienced. Sure, she'd work her usual week. But to make things that much easier for the mother-to-be, Yvonne had

set up office in the downstairs den of the Marblehead house.
From there they'd roll calls, boil the overnight polling digits, return faxes, and whip campaign troops from Portland,
Maine, to Portland, Oregon. During breaks they'd peruse
baby catalogues, ordering up everything from Huggies in
bulk to *Consumer Reports'* "best bet" in jogging strollers.

Ahead was the second weekend in a row without Will.
Gwen would catch glimpses of herself in every reflective
surface, each time as if noticing the growing bump for the
first time. She'd rub it, talk aloud to it. Play it her favorite
music. Sing it lullabies. Every so often, Izzy would appear
and join in. As it turned out, Izzy knew practically *all* the
words to *all* the lullabies Gwen could think of. Izzy proved
good company.

On Saturday, she asked a favor.

"Mrs. Sullivan?"

"It's Gwen, Izzy." She was kneeling on the floor of the
nursery, applying a second coat of semigloss to the baseboard.

"I hesitate to ask . . ."

"Don't hesitate," said Gwen. "Just ask."

"I have a friend coming for the weekend. A girlfriend
from St. Maarten."

"And . . ."

"Like you, ma'am, she's pregnant. But she's going
through a bad patch with her husband. He's not very nice.
Doesn't even want the baby. I tried to talk her out of the
marriage. Everybody did."

Perceptive, Gwen prodded. "Ah. So she's run *away* from
the asshole? Was it your idea?"

"It was. Yes."

"And you want to know if she can stay here?"

"Oh, no, ma'am," lied Izzy, laying down her cards just as
Dean had instructed. "She can stay at a motel. Only she
doesn't have money. This is why I hesitate for a favor. I was
going to ask for an advance on my pay—"

"So she can stay at a motel? I won't have it," said Gwen,
not once looking up from her baseboards. Each stroke perfectly horizontal. "It's a big house. Nobody here this week-

end but us girls. As long as she doesn't mind roughing it. How far along is she?"

"Almost the same as you," said Izzy. "She'll stay in my bed. I'll take the floor."

"We have guest rooms and guest beds," said Gwen. "Do we have clean sheets?"

"We do, ma'am."

Finally, Gwen turned so Izzy could see her face. Her smile was genuine. "I'd like very much to meet Izzy's girl-friend from St. Maarten."

The compliment wasn't lost on Izzy. In just a few weeks, the mother-to-be had bonded with her new housekeeper. Months before the English nanny was scheduled for her first day's work, Gwen was already having second thoughts about her choice. Izzy's simple, caring nature had molded comfortably with Gwen's premium-blend personality.

Even if Gwen's "Izzy" was just a facade.

"How about I invite Yvonne over for dinner?" Gwen asked, returning to her work. "If she can pry herself away from her boys, we'll make it a foursome."

"Does Miss Yvonne eat brisket?"

"If you haven't noticed, Miss Yvonne eats everything," said Gwen.

"If you haven't noticed," vamped Izzy, a hand on her overly shapely hips, "I eat everything, too."

"By the way. What's your friend's name?"

"Starr," said Izzy. "Her name is Starr."

If Yvonne had been there to hear Gwen, she would've countered with a blistering "And I've *earned* the right to eat everything. I don't want no man. So no man in his right mind's ever gonna want me!"

At fifty, she'd survived two husbands. One dead, one for-gotten. Put two kids through college and herself through law school. And was woman enough to admit she still pined for the one fellah who got away. A married professor from Boston College. A man whose name she'd never disclose to anyone. Not even to her boss and best friend, Gwen Corbett-Sullivan.

When Yvonne wasn't working or nosing about the sex lives of her two sons, she was holed up in the same rent-controlled apartment she'd lived in for fifteen years, either watching a recent video rental from the corner Blockbuster or one of her own golden oldies. Musicals were her favorite. M.G.M. classics from the thirties. On Saturday nights, she'd stay up until four in the morning, legs propped on a foot-worn ottoman, her head settled into the crook of her mother's old wing-backed chair.

It was Yvonne's little piece of heaven on earth.

But at the drop of a dime, Yvonne was there for Gwen, whether she was in the mood or not. Dinner up in Marble-head with amiable Izzy and her oldest pal sounded fine enough. Gwen would surely call it a night by eleven and Yvonne could be home by twelve and rolling a video by twelve-fifteen.

As she pulled through the gate and down the Sullivans' gravel drive in her newly minted Saturn, a joint Christmas gift from her sons, Yvonne had entirely missed the government-issue Chrysler parked nose-forward and perpendicular to the driveway. She set her brake in the usual spot and let herself in through the front door with her own set of keys.

But where Yvonne missed the government car, Starr had not. Starr made the FBI sedan as far back as the first turn up the asphalt grade. Instinct caused the redhead to slow just enough to draw a bead on the car, but she made it look as if she was merely checking addresses. When she finally found the Sullivans' drive, she made an overt point to drive past it, pulling right up alongside the government car. Starr rolled down her window, gesturing for one of the two FBI men to do the same. Her voice was a throaty, cigarette-infected wisp. " 'Scuse me. Is this the Sullivans' house?"

The FBI agents had no authority to stop people from driving onto the property. Their strict orders were to record activity while providing protection from any obvious threat. The redhead in the Toyota looked too much the waif and too little of anything else.

"Are you a friend of the family?" asked the agent in the passenger seat.

"Friend of the housekeeper," said Starr. "You know Izzy?"

They knew her. Izzy was listed as the "housekeeper." The agents passed Starr along, making notes as she parked her car, removed a Nike duffel bag from the backseat, and rang the bell. Izzy answered in a heartbeat, throwing her arms around Starr as if she hadn't seen her in a lifetime. The agents could hear the squeals of girl-talk lift and vanish as Izzy escorted Starr into the house. The time was logged at 6:22 P.M.:

Unidentified Caucasian female. Age 30-35. Red hair. Blue eyes. Approx. six months pregnant.

14

"So how long have you and Izzy known each other?" asked Yvonne, slicing into a second helping of brisket.

"Forever," said Starr. "Since . . . I dunno. I was five, you were—"

"Eight," answered Izzy.

"It was just vacations," said Starr. "But we'd write the whole year. In January, I was always thinking about June."

"Starr's parents had a summer home in St. Maarten," added Gwen. She'd already gleaned most of the history from Izzy.

"Summer home?" said Starr, looking Izzy over like she'd never met her. A hitch in the story? Hardly.

"I thought that's what you told people," cued Izzy. It was all part of Dean's script.

Starr turned back to Yvonne and Gwen. "My daddy cooked, my mother cleaned, and my two brothers worked in the resort's laundry." Then Starr made an obvious elbowing gesture at Izzy's ribs. "You are *such* a liar."

"I didn't lie," Izzy defended herself. "I told Gwen you had a summer house. I didn't say you *owned* it."

Yvonne segued. Another question, her interest sounding a note more ulterior than simply curious. Something about Starr rubbed her the wrong way. "How old are your brothers?" she asked.

"Younger," said Starr. "Miles is thirty-one and Mitch is twenty-seven."

"Just north of my boys," said Yvonne with a feigned smile. "You close to your brothers?"

"We talk some," said Starr. "But all of us, we're so spread out. The whole family." Starr dug at her beef, but ate little. "Both think I should stay married to the asshole. For the baby, you know?"

"Asshole?" asked Yvonne. "Strong word."

"That's what I called him," said Gwen.

"Nicer than 'fuckhead,' " added Starr, inadvertently breaking the table up. The women laughed until it hurt.

"What's the problem with him?" asked Yvonne when the laughing settled, her curiosity unsettled.

Gwen interrupted, "Don't go trying to fix something that's none of your business."

None of my business? thought Yvonne.

Yvonne liked Izzy from moment one. Felt an instant kinship with the imposter and had practically hired her on the spot. But the redheaded Starr, pregnant and wearing skin the color of a newborn piglet—something about her startled Yvonne. She was over-animated and a little too open.

"Oh, I don't care who knows," said Starr, sticking with Dean's scripted answers. "He said he wants his firstborn to be a boy. But cuzza my age I had . . . you know, the thing with the big needle?"

"The amnio," helped Gwen.

"That's it." Starr continued with her charade. "My doctor said I was having a little girl. And my husband? He went, like, totally ballistic. He even drove me to Planned Parenthood for an abortion."

The tailored lies stuck like glue. At that point, neither Gwen nor Yvonne could possibly imagine the real truth. Not even in their worst nightmares. Starr was pregnant at Dean's command. The father was the all-too-willing

Clem, who'd taken to the duty with the relish of a lusty mongrel. Lucky for little Starr, she hit the mark in the second month. And she dusted Clem off like a case of dandruff.

Dean was pleased. The plot was moving as predicted.

"And why didn't you?" asked Gwen, cautiously polite about the issue of abortion. "I mean, if you don't mind me asking."

"Have the abortion? Well, it's not 'cuz I hadn't done it before. I mean, lots and lots before," said Starr with far less shame than Izzy would have liked. They were still on the script, but Starr was treading very close to truth. "It's just that I was told after so many, I might never have a chance to go full-term, you know? So this time, when I got pregnant . . ."

Gwen was nodding with understanding.

Then Izzy improvised, "Starr got knocked up every summer when she was on the island. From thirteen years old to nineteen."

Starr picked up on her cue. "I'd have the abortions when I got back to Michigan. Dad was *always* pissed. He wouldn't pay for the last two."

"I sent her the money," said Izzy.

The awkward silence made Starr blush. Her pink skin turned magenta. What a performance. "Oh, my God. I haven't offended anybody, have I?"

No, she hadn't. Not even Yvonne who was staunchly pro-life in her personal beliefs. Still, Yvonne sat back from her plate, arms crossed in judgment. Was it the cavalier manner in which Starr spoke of her abortions? Or was it that she reeked of white trash and Yvonne's racist reserve was breaking the surface?

Whatever it was, Izzy didn't miss Yvonne's body language.

Starr looked at Gwen, rubbing the top of her own belly rather obviously. "So you understand why I'm keeping my little girl."

"Of course," said Gwen. "Will and I went through a lot to get to this point. Pushed the scientific envelope, so to speak."

Starr couldn't help but ask. But this time, she turned on the requisite emotion. "And is it *everything* you hoped for?"

"Honestly?" asked Gwen. "Yes . . . and more."

"From your mouth to God's ears," said Izzy. "Starr would make the *best* mom." Then with perfectly pitched embarrassment: "Present company excluded, of course."

"So you're best friends?" segued Yvonne again. "You and Starr?"

"You could say that," affirmed Izzy.

"How about you, Gwen?" asked Starr. "You have a best friend?"

"Besides my husband? I'd say Yvonne's my best pal. Knows everything about me. She's the keeper of all the secrets."

"And I *likes* it that way," said Yvonne. "I'm the mystery. She's the boss. I think it keeps us in *good* balance."

"I'll drink to that," said Gwen, lifting an iced tonic and lime. Starr joined in with her ginger ale. Izzy and Yvonne toasted with a fine Merlot Gwen had chosen from their soon-to-be-cellared wine stock. Glasses clinked.

Starr wanted to see the nursery that Izzy had described over the telephone. And Gwen was all too proud to show it off. The large room was wood from floor to ceiling, skylit, brush-painted, with recessed halogen lights cut in like tiny stars in the sky.

Then Starr boldly picked up a paintbrush. "Okay. So what's left to do?" she asked.

Gamely, all four women pitched in and painted until Gwen called it a night on account of her own exhaustion. As Yvonne had predicted, Gwen was in bed by eleven, leaving Izzy to lock the door after her.

ARE YOU BOTH IN THE NEST?
    we are. yes.
AND ARE YOU BOTH THERE TO STAY?
    yes.
THE MISTER?
    in washington.
TELL ME OF THE COURTIER.

yvonne. she is even closer and of a more suspicious nature than we expected.
IS SHE AN OBSTACLE?
yes.
I UNDERSTAND. DO YOU UNDERSTAND?
i do, my love. clem has his instructions.
I SENSE SOMETHING YOU ARE NOT TELLING ME.
there are 2 feds watching the house.
WATCHING YOU?
we don't know. they arrived today.
I'LL SLEEP ON IT AND ADVISE.
when we sleep, we will dream of you.
I KNOW.
and when we wake, we will serve your needs.
I KNOW.

Izzy and Starr were leaning over the computer, waiting
for more from their Dean. But none came. He had signed
off and was obviously working out a new script based on
the two FBI agents parked at the end of the driveway. With
the lights out, Izzy and Starr both cuddled on the floor.
  "Like the old days," whispered Starr.
  "Before we were dead," whispered Izzy.

Clem didn't wait for long. As Izzy had meticulously calculated, Yvonne arrived back at her Rutland Street apartment just shy of midnight. It had been a long week and a
long Saturday—from faxing campaign missives to prepping
for the upcoming power shower, Yvonne had been on the go
all day. Keys in the door, she threw back the deadbolt and
entered into darkness. She could maneuver the space blind-
folded, her course already plotted. Bedroom, bathroom,
robe, kitchen, a two-liter bottle of Coca-Cola, tape in the
VCR, then Tom Cruise, here I come. The first show of the
evening was *Cocktail.* She'd already seen it three times. A
lousy movie, but a guilty Tom pleasure. So due to the lack
of decent titles on the shelf at Blockbuster, Yvonne had
opted for the old Tom Cruise standby. After which, she'd
cap off the night with something from her own collection.

Perhaps *Broadway Melody of 1936*. Eleanor Powell and Robert Taylor, and Buddy Ebsen tap-dancing long before he'd taken on the career-typing role of Jed Clampett. After the second movie would come bed. She'd sleep until noon, scratch up some blueberry pancakes for breakfast, and call her two boys.

So much for planning.

Yvonne barely made it past the first threshold of her apartment. Clem kicked the door shut behind her and drew his right arm high around her head, burying her face in the crook of his arm so that when she screamed, her voice was muffled by his heavy coat. As he expected, she brought both arms up in a reactive attempt to pull herself free. It was a natural impulse and the opening Clem had waited for so many times before. With her breastbone exposed and a kitchen carving knife in his left hand, Clem slid the blade between her fourth and fifth ribs. He twisted the knife upwards to the hilt, slashing her aorta and pulmonary vessels in one clean sweep. Yvonne struggled briefly, then slumped from his arms to the floor.

Just another blooding in Dean's ten-year crusade to quicken the end of the world.

All Clem had to do next was fake the forced entry, easily accomplished by wedging a chisel between the jamb and the bolt receiver. With the entry door cracked open, the soft wood splintered away, looking as if the door had been shoved or kicked in. Only Clem's method was far more quiet. The neighbors didn't hear a thing. Clem left the knife next to his victim, pocketed his gloves, and walked down the single flight of stairs to the stolen car.

The rest had been cake. He'd already loaded up the stolen Acura's trunk with Yvonne's TV, VCR, compact discs, and shelf-stereo unit. A picture-perfect burglary—only the quick and the obvious were taken. Nothing was pitched over. Nothing was broken and there were zero signs of struggle. Boston PD would merely conclude that Yvonne had happened upon some crack addict scoring barely enough electronics to cover his next day's rock collection.

Clem's coup de grace had been the method of his killing.

Swift, the coroner would surely write. A total surprise. Experienced with knives. The assailant would be scored as left-handed where Clem was right-handed. Possibly with military experience. And the investigation would slam into a dead end. No fingerprints because the killer had worn surgical gloves. Any trace evidence, fibers, matching clothes, et cetera, would be found on some downtown homeless man who'd been quick to accept the anonymous gift of warm clothing. The stolen car would be found abandoned, but the stolen property would never be recovered.

The case would remain open—but unsolved.

Ten A.M. on Sunday, Yvonne's youngest son, Evan, bravely called. Knowing his mother didn't care to be disturbed before noon on Sundays, he just couldn't wait with the good news. He was engaged to be married. The thrill of it would jar his mother awake and he planned to invite her out to celebrate over a champagne Sunday brunch. Evan didn't expect the machine to answer. He tried again at eleven, eleven-thirty, then noon. Partially concerned and partially anticipating his mother's thrilled expression at the news, he got in his Honda and drove up from Hartford.

Evan was first to arrive on the scene.

15

That same Sunday morning, a network-ordered limousine waited outside Will's Georgetown condo. By 7 A.M. the senator had showered, shaved, and been prepped over the phone by a junior White House policy adviser on the morning's headlines and the spin he was expected to serve up on his three scheduled shows. First up was *The McLaughlin Group.* Taped at nine but aired in different slots all over the nation. After that, Will was due to appear on the first segment of ABC's *This Week,* a live slot at ten o'clock Eastern. And finally, *Inside Politics Weekend* on CNN, where he was scheduled for the segment at the bottom of the hour.

The bitch of it all was that LBJ had weekends off. And each program sent their own driver. So Myriam had to schedule the pickups and dropoffs for each show. There was a driver for *The McLaughlin Group.* Another for *This Week.* And a third scheduled to pick Will up at the ABC Washington Bureau at eleven-fifteen sharp to deliver him to CNN.

So far the morning had gone smoothly enough. Under all the glare and bluster of McLaughlin's lineup of Sunday assassins, Will had remained collected and bone-cuttingly articulate. The pundits lined up to take their pokes at the young senator, lobbing softballs from the left and magnum-powered gun blasts from the right. If they wanted to disagree, Will politely let them. But if somebody tried to cut him off, he insisted that he be heard. He would never argue or trade barbs. It was always, no matter what the subject or how hard the gust, the senator on political point.

With the first program in the can, Will moved on to what he liked to call *The Glamour Show,* referred to by the local elite as *This Week Without David Brinkley.* Since the old master's Clinton-hashing exit, the show had been handed over to the likes of Cokie Roberts, George Will, and former policy adviser turned media darling George Stephanopolous. Today, the senior anchor on the show was Sam Donaldson, wearing his swirl of plaster-formed hair atop caterpillar-shaped eyebrows and enough foundation to make a cadaver appear ripe.

All the questions on the show felt rehearsed. Even the hard-bitten Donaldson's lines played as if they were entirely TelePrompTered. There wasn't the ease or flavor of Koppel's tough-rooting conversations. Or even Buddy Prince's charmed-to-still-be-here rhetoric. The show was a flat setup for Will Sullivan's spin-doctored answers. The young senator was in and out with barely a handshake or hello. A reminder, thought Will. He was on *their* show. And *they* were the stars.

After *This Week,* Will was bristling for a serious challenge. A chance to spin for the Big Team *and* talk. With two shows under his belt, he was feeling that kinetic charge that came from having TV cameras aimed at him. The adrenaline pulsed. A better high than a good dose of vodka, TV was a certain celebrity rush.

Wolf Blitzer would be next to put Will under the lights. No dummy, Will reminded himself. Blitzer was a White House veteran who played a fair game on TV, but still liked it loose and, most importantly, informative for the viewing audience. All questions would be as carefully sculpted as Will's answers.

Driver number three held the limousine door open. Will slipped out the back door of the studio, ducking from the drizzle, and slid onto the leather seat.

"You know where we're going?" asked Will, seeking nothing more than confirmation.

"Yes, sir," said the driver.

They eased through the gate, then left onto 17th Street. Then another left on New Hampshire. After a moment Will reminded the driver. "We're going to CNN."

"Yes, sir," said the driver.

"You know a better way?" asked Will.

"Yes, sir," repeated the driver, wheeling the limousine into a hard U-turn, crossing the meridian and launching the big Lincoln up the Whitehurst Freeway on-ramp.

"Where in God's name are you going?" barked Will. "CNN's back the other . . . I've got twenty minutes to—"

The driver answered by locking the doors with a solid, hydraulic thunk. The Town Car swerved into the center lane and accelerated. Will's electric-adrenaline-TV-charge vanished in a heartbeat. He was flushed, pressed back into the rear seat, his limbs and cheeks prickly and tingling. He fixed his eyes on the rearview mirror, trying to carve a mental picture of the driver. Dark eyebrows arched over aviator Ray-Bans. A thick salt-and-pepper beard. Cracked lips.

It would have been difficult for anybody, let alone Will, to recognize the driver as former Los Angeles Deputy District Attorney Vance Allatore.

"Do you have a clue who I am?" asked Will.

"United States Senator Will Sullivan. On his way to CNN for a live interview with Mr. Blitzer."

"But we're not going there?" Will found himself confirming.

"Let's say you'll be late."

"This is kidnapping!"

"Not exactly," said the driver. "Kidnapping is a felony defined by an abduction, followed by a demand. This is more like a temporary hijacking."

"I think you should stop the car right now."

"I respect your request, Senator. But I can't do that. It's already gone too far."

"Whatever it is," said Will, "you can stop it before it gets worse."

"You don't understand. I had to speak with you."

"There are other ways to talk!" Will's voice was sudden, acerbic, and arrogant. Stupid, he thought, instantly regretting his tone.

"What was I supposed to do?" asked the unrecognizable Allatore. "Make an appointment? And how would that work? A letter? A formal introduction? Or would I get passed off to an assistant? Wait. I've got it. Maybe if I showed up at your office with a paper bag filled with cash—"

"Who are you and what do you want?"

"You don't have a clue," said the driver. "But I expected that. It makes sense that you wouldn't know. Right now, you're afraid. That's good. I want you afraid. I want you to be very afraid. Are we understood?"

"You got my attention," said Will, trying to sound brave. "So what more do you want?"

"I want you to know what you believe in."

Believe in?

It struck Will in a single mental hammer-blow. The image of a short man scurrying down the hallway at the Melrose in Dallas.

"Believe in?"

"Do you believe in God, Buddha, Allah, Deepak Chopra? Simple question. I ask. You answer. What do you believe in?"

Wacko, thought Will. La Roy, Salinas, and Benny Yao were all wrong. The notes weren't anything near a political prank. They were the work of a lone nutcase. A nutcase behind the wheel of a car traveling at sixty-five miles an hour down an asphalt parkway. "Believe in?" asked Will again, a prisoner inside his own tightening skin.

"How about yourself?" asked Allatore. "Let's start there. Do you believe in yourself?"

"What's your point?"

"Without belief there is no faith. Without faith there is no hope. Without hope, there is only evil. And when evil rules, the world is lost. Do not pass Go. Do not collect two hundred dollars."

Will wondered how he could've missed it. Hanging from the rearview mirror was a rosary. It swayed with the gentle roll of the speeding Lincoln. Not a wacko, thought Will. A religious nutjob.

Will chose his next question carefully. "What is it that you would *like* me to believe?"

"Good question," said Allatore. "But like our time, your capacity for understanding is short and shallow."

"Try me."

"I want you to believe what I'm about to tell you is true. Believe that you are in danger. You, your wife, and the child she carries."

"You sent the messages."

"Yes," said Allatore. "Now I ask you of your wife. Does she have any new friends?"

Will blocked the question. His brain was still in hyperdrive. One hemisphere, figuring the angle. The other, looking for a way out of the car. He tried to roll down the window, but it was locked in position. The tinting would make it impossible for anyone to see in—to see Will pounding on the window, screaming for help.

"Your wife!" continued Allatore. "Does she have *any new friends*? Women friends? Employees? Nannies? With a reason to be close? Just hanging around her? Women you don't know?"

"I'm a United States senator. You're committing a serious felony!"

"Believe me when I tell you I know the difference between a crime and an act of faith. Question is, do you?"

Stuck for an answer, Will kicked at the floorboards and tried to breathe, trying to calm himself. His skin tightened even more.

"Let me help you. You are a United States senator. You have certain powers. Leverage. You can start things and you can stop things."

A shakedown, Will thought. Suddenly, the kook was

starting to sound like he wanted to make some kind of deal.

"What is it that you want?"

"For you to *HEAR* my message. *BELIEVE* what I'm about to tell you. And most of all, be *FRIGHTENED.*"

The ego of the prick, thought Will. "And why should *your* message frighten *me*?"

With a sudden twist, the former prosecutor wheeled the car to the right, steering it sharply across two lanes and slamming on the brakes. The Lincoln skidded along the shoulder, scraping the guardrail with an angry screech of metal. Dust billowed around the car, fogging it from traffic. Then the driver spun around to face Will, his Ray-Bans twisting off his face. Heavy brown eyes locked onto Will's. Tired eyes. Seen-too-much eyes.

Eyes that belonged to Vance Allatore. Will recognized him. Not from the book jacket. He just . . . recognized him.

"Why should you be frightened?" asked Allatore. "Because unless you are frightened, you will not believe. And unless you believe, you will not be saved! Nor will your wife. Nor will your child. Of this, I swear."

The ending to the former prosecutor's opening statement was, upon his later reflection, a bit over-the-top. Operatic, even. Defense attorneys would have objected and judges would have privately complained. It was a matter of style, the old Vance Allatore would have argued. A good drama opened the pores of a jury so the truth might seep in that much deeper.

Will Sullivan was such a jury. As expected, Vance Allatore had found him distant, scared, and suspicious. Righteously so. But since time was so terrifyingly short, a sudden shock of fire and brimstone had been in order. First the messages—cryptic subpoenas addressed to Will's soul, ordering him to appear. Then the hijacking, the opening statement, and finally, the hard-to-swallow presentation of fact.

Allatore recounted for Will the quote with which he'd end each opening address to a jury:

"The truth is a snare. You cannot have it without being

caught. You cannot have the truth in such a way that you catch it, but only in such a way that it catches you."

The former prosecutor left the shaken senator at the service gate of the Washington CNN bureau. As the scarred Lincoln sped off, the gate guard cautiously stepped from the booth. "Can I help you, sir?" It was then that he recognized the strangely catatonic senator. The guard had been expecting Will for the last half hour. The program producer had been calling down to the gate every five minutes, anticipating the arrival of their on-air guest. In case of delay, she'd moved her third-segment guest up to first position, bumping the senator from Massachusetts to second.

"Senator?" asked the guard. "Are you all right?"

In the softest voice, Will answered. "Call 911."

"Excuse me, Senator?"

"Call the police. I was just hijacked."

"The limo?" asked the guard, instinctively lunging out into the street, looking in the direction of the speeding Lincoln, hoping to glimpse the tags. But the car was already gone. Out of the guard's sight. "Come with me, Senator. They're waiting for you upstairs."

Once inside the studio, Will felt the chill subside. The monitors hanging over the makeup mirrors put him at greater ease. Wolf Blitzer was interviewing Kevin Albrecht, the secretary of agriculture. And the familiar sound of political punditry briefly brought Will back into himself. His heart-rate slowed. The fresh coat of makeup encased the frozen beads of sweat that continued to creep to the surface.

"Are you sure you can go on?" asked the attractive young producer. She was the classic CNN single girl. Late twenties. Short. Brown eyes. With a body hardened from non-stop motion, she was professional to a fault. La Roy's favorite type, Will thought. "The D.C. police are on their way. I can make sure they wait until you're off air."

"I'm fine," stammered Will. He was obviously lying to himself and to her. But Blitzer's voice brought his mind back to the task at hand. Spinning for the Big Team. The subject matter, normalized relations with North Korea. Will knew the ins and outs of the foreign policy debate. He could fake his way through a twelve-minute segment before facing detectives from the police department.

"Okay," said the producer. "You're on in three."

Will was led around the rear of the set where, during the break, he did a quick, thirty-second schmooze with the secretary of agriculture while being miked by the stage manager. On set, he said his hellos to Wolf Blitzer as he was seated on a stool to the anchor's right.

"Sixty seconds," called out the stage manager.

The robotic cameras swiveled into position while Wolf Blitzer quietly rehearsed his introduction on the TelePrompTer.

"Hold for new copy," barked a voice from the booth.

Then that pretty young producer barreled through the stage door, hustling over to Wolf Blitzer with an eight-inch TelePrompTer sheet. "The senator has an emergency telephone call."

"I said I was fine for the segment," argued Will.

The producer ignored Will, quickly going over the copy with Wolf Blitzer. "It's just an intro and we'll go to tape."

The stage manager was leading Will from the set, out a side door, and into a glass-encased office to a blinking telephone line. "It's for you, sir."

Before picking up, Will could see two D.C. detectives and one uniformed cop standing across the newsroom. All eyes were on Will. He reached down and picked up the line, pressing the blinking button. "This is Will Sullivan."

"It's me," said Gwen, her voice already cracked and worn. "You gotta come home."

"Is it the baby?" Will's reaction was instinctive.

"It's Yvonne," said Gwen. "She's been murdered." With that said, she let loose a horrific sob. Will heard mumbling in the background. Moments later, a strange voice was on the line. "Senator? Gwen needs you. Can you come soon?"

"Who is this?" asked Will.

"I'm Starr. Izzy's friend."

"What happened to my wife?"

"Izzy's having her lie down. For the baby, you understand. Can I tell her you're coming home?"

"As soon as I can," Will said. As he heard the line click at
the other end, his mind was already beginning to race.

Hustled in a police cruiser to Andrews Air Force Base,
Will and one of the DCPD detectives were joined by Bill La
Roy and Steve Salinas. Upon hearing the grave news, the
White House had graciously loaned the services of *Air
Force Two.*

"Can you describe the man?" asked the D.C. detective, an
elder department statesman by the name of Rolley Means.
Totally professional, he was the man the FBI called when a
crime involved a member of government, victim or suspect.
So cool and collected was Detective Means, he could have
been in his own living room, let alone a leather upholstered
captain's chair on *Air Force Two.*

The senator was having difficulty keeping focused. The
morning had been a nightmare. He didn't answer the detective.

"Senator," said Detective Means. "Do you need a drink,
maybe?"

La Roy interrupted, "The senator doesn't drink." Then he
flagged down the flight attendant. "You got any coffee?"

"Will. Listen to me. Do you remember what he looked
like?" asked Steve Salinas.

"Fifty . . . fifty-five," said Will. "I remember a beard. His
eyes were . . . black."

"Weight, height?" asked Detective Means. "We realize he
was seated in the front, so it might not be easy."

"I can't say," said Will. "But he looked like . . ." His voice
trailed off. He knew the answer, just couldn't believe he was
about to say it.

"Looked like what?" asked Detective Means.

"He looked like this L.A. prosecutor. The famous one.
Vance Allatore."

"You're kidding me," said Steve Salinas.

"You wanna spell that?" asked Detective Means.

"I don't know," said Will.

"V-A-N-C-E A-L-L-A-T-O-R-E," answered La Roy, well
aware of who Vance Allatore was.

"Are you saying he *was* this Vance Allatore fellah?" asked Detective Means. "Or are you saying he *looked* like this Vance Allatore fellah?"

"It was Vance Allatore," said Will.

Detective Means was lost. It was clear everybody but himself knew who the man was.

La Roy elaborated. "Former Los Angeles assistant D.A. Star prosecutor back in the eighties. Had something like a fifty-and-zip conviction record before he wrote a best-seller, had a nervous breakdown, then disappeared." La Roy knew more, but shut up. This was Will's interview.

Salinas jumped in. "If it was Vance Allatore, that means he's not dead."

"You heard he was dead?" asked La Roy.

"You know, that cult thing," said Salinas. "They killed him like they did the others."

"Cult thing?" asked Detective Means. "Am I missing something?"

"All you're missing is a picture of the hijacker," said Salinas. "And one shouldn't be hard to find of Vance Allatore."

Detective Means picked up the questioning. "And during the hijacking, what exactly did he say or demand?"

"He . . . He wanted to know what I believed in," said Will.

"Believed in?" asked Salinas.

Will didn't *believe* it himself. It was all so far-fucking-fetched. Crazy. Mad, out-of-one's-gourd insane. But the picture permanently drawn in his mind was as clear as crystal. Vance Allatore, the former superman of the L.A. D.A.'s office, had hijacked him for forty minutes, and asked him what he believed in. All before encouraging Will to believe *him*. Believe in God and . . .

Here comes the hard part, Will.

. . . and believe the child in his wife's belly was not his own, but belonged to the same mass murderer Vance Allatore had put in jail and used to buy himself fifteen minutes of Warholian fame. Wesley Dean Theroux.

"It doesn't matter," said Will. "I don't believe it. The man was out of his mind. Probably ripped on something narcotic."

"So it's the lone-wacko theory after all," La Roy attempted to confirm, nudging Steve Salinas.

"I'm concerned about this so-called message," said Salinas. "Vance Allatore *admitted* and proved knowledge to sending the three messages. The hotel in Dallas, the condo, and the fax from the Marriott. Am I correct?"

Will stiffened a bit, forming the answer first in his mind, and then speaking with such practiced spin that he might as well have been standing at the podium in front of the White House press corps. "The message was about my wife. And considering her current state of mind, I'd rather not say, for fear that the information about this lunatic might get back to her before she and I could talk."

Detective Means sighed loudly. As if just when he was getting to like the senator—bang—Will proved to be more of a politician than a willing witness to a crime. A mother of a self-proving, self-promoting self-preservationist. In Detective Means's view, Will had shown that all politicians were cut from the same Machiavellian cloth.

"Without the full text of this so-called message," Detective Means was forced to say, "my report will be incomplete."

"Only temporarily!" spun La Roy, properly deflecting for his boss.

"Do me a favor," said Will. "Let me take care of my wife. In the meantime, you've got my description of the guy. I'll bet by the time I return to Washington, the good detective will have him in custody. Yes?"

"Are you saying you're too distracted to continue?" asked Salinas. "Or just unwilling to fully disclose everything?"

"I think I've made myself clear enough." Will stood from his seat. "Excuse me. I gotta go to the bathroom."

The attendant showed Will the way. Meanwhile, Salinas huddled with La Roy and Detective Means. "Okay, Bill. What's going on?"

"Your guess is as good as mine," said La Roy. "But I'd give him a break. He's had a tough morning."

"I don't get this Vance Alliota thing," said Detective

Means. "Sounded to me like he thought it really *was* this fellah driving the car."

"Vance Allatore," corrected Salinas. "And whether or not it really was the former L.A. deputy district attorney? I don't think so. I think it was just a good description. But I'll get a recent picture for you to go from."

"Good luck," said La Roy.

"What's that supposed to mean?" asked Salinas.

"Like you said," La Roy continued, "after he wrote this book, see, Allatore up and vanished. You heard he was dead. Others say he turned into a drunk and committed himself. My bet is that he was cut into pieces by the same nutjob he put behind bars. You know? The one he wrote the book about."

"Oh, wait," said Detective Means. "This is coming back to me now. They made a TV movie out of the book. Scared the shit outta my ex-wife. Gave her nightmares for a week."

"Wesley Dean Theroux," said La Roy. "I think it started with something like *True Believers,*" he went on, knowing full well he was one hundred percent correct. It was part of the ever-growing nonfiction collection that he kept shelved in his bedroom library. Vance Allatore's *True Believers: The Killer Cult of W. D. Theroux* was considered a classic piece of true-crime literature that fit snugly alongside books on the Kennedy assassination, the Black Dahlia murders, and *Helter Skelter.*

"*True Believers.*" Detective Means wrote it down. "Can I still get it?"

Will wanted no more of the D.C. detective's Q and A. Once he'd finished in the restroom, he'd continued forward in the cabin until he found the attendant. He had her hook him up to the secured Airfone. His first call was to Gwen. She seemed more at ease than before.

Gwen relayed the very little she actually knew about Yvonne's murder. Will then dialed his father. Old Sully had connections nose-deep in the Boston PD. He'd dig up all there was to know for his statesman son, reporting all the grislies the minute *Air Force Two* touched down at Logan.

Will spent the rest of the flight on the phone with Myriam, who rolled calls for him from her Chevy Chase living room.

It all proved a strange distraction. A morbid respite that kept him from thinking about the murder. His brief abduction that morning. The speeding Lincoln. Vance Allatore. And that bizarre second message that was turning over like some endless loop inside his skull.

THE CHILD IS NOT YOURS . . . IT IS HIS!

Once on the tarmac at Logan, Will politely shook hands with Detective Means, Steve Salinas, and Bill La Roy. He promised to be in touch the next day, then deplaned through the rear stairwell to the waiting unmarked police car flanked by two motorcycle escorts. Sully was in the backseat.

"The escort wasn't necessary, Pop," said Will, climbing in.

"Maybe not," said the old man. "But it sure *looks* good."

"Let's go," said Will.

As they began the thirty-minute drive to Marblehead, Sully filled Will in on the details of Yvonne's murder. For the most part, the crime looked utterly happenstance. A burglary gone bad. Nothing more. The story, tragically familiar. He showed Will a copy of a faxed police report. Will folded it, stuck it into his coat pocket, then asked the driver if he wouldn't mind stopping at a nearby bookstore. Sully waited in the car while Will went inside. Will was quickly directed to the true-crime section. There he found three paperback copies of Vance Allatore's one and only book. At the counter, Will paid seven ninety-five in cash, stuck the receipt in the pages for future use as a bookmark, and was gone without having been recognized by the Sunday clerk.

"What was that about?" asked Sully.

"Just some light reading," said Will. "Haven't been sleeping well."

"Still off the sauce?" asked Sully.

"What do you think?" Will bristled.

"Thatta boy," said Sully, scratching for more things to yak about. There was at least twenty more minutes left on the drive to Marblehead. "*Air Force Two,* huh?"

"It's just a plane, Dad."

"The vice president's plane," Sully boasted. "Reminds me, Fred Dolgen from the Department of Commerce was through town the other day—you know, some of those old bureaucrats still stop by to pay your old man their respects. Anyhow, he was talking me up about this North Korea fiasco—"

"Pop," interrupted Will. "Your heart's in the right place. But right now, your timing sucks. If you don't mind, I'd like to close my eyes for a minute."

"Not a problem," said Sully. Without missing a heartbeat, he was leaning forward and accosting the cop behind the wheel. "Radio work? See if you can find the Red Sox game, will ya?"

With his eyes shut, Will could see Vance Allatore plain as day. In the Lincoln, eyes afire, dressing him down with more information than he'd ever care to know. More images came. A younger, clean-shaven Vance Allatore on TV. Nice suit. In court, he was giving a final summation to an unseen jury. Taking calls on *Larry King*. By satellite on *Nightline*. Stumping his book on *Oprah*. Sure enough, Vance Allatore had been the man behind the wheel.

"Vance Allatore," he'd finally told Will before dropping him at the CNN gate. "You can call me Vance."

"Sure," said Will. "Why not?"

But the other? The man called W. D. Theroux? Will tried to picture him but couldn't. A haircut was all he could imagine. Simple, brown, somewhat conservative. The book would have pictures. But Will wouldn't dare pull it out. Not in front of Sully. All that would follow would be another barrage of unnecessary questions.

No. First Will needed some answers. Then he might talk about it. Until then, he'd keep his mind available and his mouth shut. Offer the proper, consoling shoulder to Gwen—grieve with her over the loss of her friend . . .

"The truth is a snare. You cannot have it without being caught. You cannot have the truth in such a way that you catch it, but only in such a way that it catches you.

"And most importantly," the former prosecutor had continued, "keep your eyes and ears alive, but listen only to your heart. God's in your heart. And he will never lie to you."

With the words of a newly minted religious zealot ringing in his ears, Will's eyes popped open to a blast of Marblehead sunshine.

"Been sleeping, son?" asked Sully. "We're just about there."

"What time is it?" asked Will.

"Time to hold your wife and tell her that when you make it to the White House, you're gonna make it a better world for her and your baby."

Then Sully couldn't help adding, *"And my grandson."*

"I don't think it's a good idea if you come in," said Will.

"I understand," said Sully. "Just give her a hug from me and your mom. Tell her she's in our prayers."

"I'll do that," said Will. He gave his father the rarest of embraces, stepped from the police cruiser, and, as if on some sort of obligatory remote, took a moment to shake hands with the driver and the two motorcycle cops.

"Don't forget your *light reading.*" Sully was holding Will's copy of *True Believers.*

"All in the eye of the beholder," said Will. He retrieved the book from his father, shoved it into his coat pocket, then started down the short gravel drive toward his house. Will gave a politician's wink and wave to the stationed FBI vehicle, then disappeared inside.

"Gwen," called Will. "I'm home!"

PART | TWO

1

Izzy counted.

Thirty-seven mourners, five of which were family, including two distant cousins and Yvonne's two grieving sons. One minister, twelve coworkers, four neighbors, eleven close friends, a senator, his wife, and two shallow acquaintances named Izzy and Starr.

Twenty-five of the mourners were women. Twelve, men.

Twelve men, she remembered. *Like the Apostles. Dean had changed that, breaking down the two-thousand-year-old gender barrier and giving women a seat at his own sacramental table.*

Nineteen of the twenty-five women wore black. The rest, something dark. Navy or brown. Two of the men wore gray sport jackets. One man wore a deep blue pinstripe. Inside the church there were forty rows, twenty-nine of which were empty. Near the altar lay a single casket. Inside, Izzy counted one dearly departed. Two eulogies were given that Wednesday and one communal reciting of the Twenty-seventh Psalm, followed by the Lord's Prayer.

The temperature in the church, Izzy calculated, was

roughly sixty-nine degrees Fahrenheit. Outside it was fifty-four.

As a final notch in her mental score, Izzy noted one copy of Vance Allatore's nearly forgotten best-seller, *True Believers: The Killer Cult of W. D. Theroux,* bulging in the senator's coat pocket. It hadn't left the senator's side since he'd returned home on Sunday afternoon. She computed his progress by the yellow MasterCard receipt he'd used as a bookmark. Izzy determined that Will had just about made it up to the part where Dean had taken the witness stand in his own defense. A grand moment when the TV viewers could gaze upon the face of her immortal father. A man greater than men. Wesley Dean Theroux.

She also calculated that the book in Will's pocket was no coincidence. Somehow, he *knew*. But did he know about her? Who was talking to the senator? Izzy couldn't calculate that as of yet. The FBI? Another reporter? Or a Judus *inside* the family? A survivor. Dean would need as much information as she could collect and submit. Then *he* would decide what to do next.

Following the memorial, Gwen was faithfully flanked by Izzy and Starr, each never further than a whisper away. Right there if she needed them, playing the roles of her closest comforters. That, too, was part of Dean's script.

Divide the courtiers, then close the circle.

The wake was a tastefully catered event held on the ground floor of Gwen's Beacon Hill office. Tears were openly shed by most of the staff. Yvonne's surviving sons were ever-so-gracious. All were impressed that Yvonne, a single mother, had done such a fine job of raising her boys up into manhood. She would be missed by all.

After merely an hour, Gwen experienced hot flashes and sudden weakness. She excused herself. Will drove the Explorer home. His left hand on the wheel, his right hand holding Gwen's. In the rear, Izzy and Starr rode along like obedient ladies-in-waiting. Hands in their laps. The perfect demure attendants—seen but not heard.

"Will you interview?" asked Will. "Or promote from within the firm?"

"I can't answer that right now," said Gwen. "She meant too much to me."

"I know. Just let me know where I can be of help."

"You're helping," she said, gripping his hand that much tighter. "You're here. I *am* wondering, though, for how long?"

"We can talk about that later," he said cautiously, holding back a fusillade of frightening thoughts while checking out the strangers in the rearview mirror. Izzy and Starr seemed distracted by the scenery. But something instinctive inside Will thought it wise not to discuss anything personal in front of them.

"Does she have any new friends?" Vance Allatore had asked. "Employees? Nannies?"

Between all the shoulder-crying and hand-holding of the last three days, Will's mind was stuck in an endless cycle of text from Vance Allatore's book and reminders of the cryptic limo ride. It took most of his willpower to hide his anxiety from Gwen, who'd surely dismiss his thoughts as utter paranoia. She needed him calm, present, and right next to her. Sure, he was fifty percent facade. But so far, she hadn't noticed the difference in him.

At Marblehead, Izzy vanished to attend to her chores while Starr engaged Gwen in a distracting game of gin rummy. It left Will time to check in with his Washington staff. He retired to his unfinished study, a former attic space with angled, open-beam ceilings and a window seat overlooking the rear yard. From the high perch, he rolled calls via a D.C. conference line while watching Clem ever-so-slowly rake the recently contoured yard in preparation for new sod. For a moment, Will and Clem locked eyes, but the landscaper broke contact quickly and returned to his work.

"Anyone unknown to you with immediate proximity to your life, your wife, the child?"

Will fanned the paperback, daring himself to read on, but locked it in his desk drawer instead. Enough already, he bemoaned. It was time to leave the lousy dream and return to reality. Which was, as Will's overriding intellect ticked off the argument, as follows:

I was not hijacked by Vance Allatore. Only some poor lookalike who thought he was the former L.A. prosecutor.

Therefore, the child Gwen carries is mine, and not, as the hijacker had phrased it, the child of a demon. The child of Wesley Dean Theroux.

Harvey Bertrand's disappearance was no conspiracy, but merely a sad coincidence, seized upon by a lone madman who penned the three puzzling messages, then hijacked me on the way to my interview at CNN.

The cult, as described in the book, mostly died in a mass suicide with the exception of Wesley Dean Theroux. Those who didn't fled for fear of further prosecution.

Wesley Dean Theroux would soon die by lethal injection in California's Rancho Seco prison on June 28th. And that would be the end of him.

More arguments raged in Will's mind.

Senator Will Sullivan will join the Democratic presidential ticket at August's convention. After which, the Addison/Sullivan team will march on to victory in early November. Come January, Gwen, our child, and I will move to Washington to occupy the residence of the vice president of the United States of America.

End of argument.

Then Will added one more mental entry.

If all that is true, then why not tell the FBI the whole truth? Why not call Steve Salinas and the able Detective Rolley Means and empty his troubled mind?

Because for one single, God-fearing, marrow-thinning, bone-freezing moment . . . something inside Will Sullivan had believed.

"I'm here, Senator, because God has demanded that I finish what I started ten years ago."

"Well, I'm afraid God and I aren't on a first-name basis anymore. I don't even know if I'd be considered Catholic anymore," Will had said defensively. "I'm Irish. I was raised in the church, but . . ."

"Trust me when I say you weren't chosen because you're Catholic," said Vance Allatore. "I don't have all the answers yet. And we may not when all is done. But what I've

*said is true. I once made the mistake of thinking Theroux
was less a man and more of a psychopath. I've since
learned otherwise. Theroux is between a god and man. He
is a demon. And thinks the way he will survive the execution
is through his seed."*

"And I'm expected to believe all this?"

*"Not at first," said Vance Allatore. "But if you pray. If
you close your eyes and open your heart to the Holy Spirit,
the truth will be known to you. Of that, I can promise."*

"You're pretty darn confident," mocked Will.

"It's called faith, Senator."

"I'm afraid you found the wrong pragmatist."

"Answer me this. Do you love your wife?"

*Will was looking for the hook in the question when Vance
Allatore grew impatient, swerving the speeding Town Car
as if to spill an answer from his passenger. "Is it that hard
of a question?"*

"Of course," said Will. "Of course I love her."

"You love her above yourself?"

"I would like to think so."

*"Then believe in that," said Allatore. "The rest shall fol-
low."*

"Gotcha." Will cursed himself for his mocking tone.

"You will post a watchful eye over her?"

*"Okay. Fine. A watchful eye. Anything else?" asked Will,
the cynic returning despite his reservations.*

*"Do I have to spell it out?" asked Allatore. "The FBI
won't admit to it, but they have a file on Theroux and the
survivors of the cult. They've kept an open ear but little
more. You need to convince them to find the missing doctor.
Find the doctor and you'll find the link to Theroux. After
that, the network. How Theroux communicates with the rest
of the cult."*

"And my wife is saved. Simple as that?" asked Will.

"They will kill her and keep the baby," said Allatore.

*"And the baby?" Will couldn't help asking. "I mean, if
it's really not mine . . ."*

"That, my friend, is between you and God."

Between Will and God? The idea itself that the child his

wife carried might not be his was awful enough. The prospect that the child might be a killer's . . .

"You son of a bitch!" said Will, as if Vance Allatore were seated across from him. Instead, he kicked at his desk, unlocked the drawer, and retrieved the paperback. For a moment, he stared at the inside of the back cover. There was that same picture of a younger Vance Allatore. Sparkling eyes. A prosecutor at the top of his game, vexed only by the fact that, despite the conviction of Theroux, he'd never been able to prove a motive for such a horrible crime. Even if it was just to himself.

Or God.

Will curled himself into the window seat and read on, deeper into the tale, oblivious to the stares he'd been getting from the yard below. Clem was on watch. Keeping an eye on the man Dean liked to call *the Mister.*

"You can't fire her!"

"I'm not firing her," Will said defensively. "It's a *temporary leave* until she passes the preliminary FBI security check." Gwen had cooked up a huge mess of fettucini *alla checca,* feeling grounded for the first time in days. She'd even squeezed out her own spinach noodles. Will was rinsing dishes and placing them one at a time in the dishwasher. The activity kept him on an even keel while Gwen flew into her inevitable fit.

"I hired her. *You* can't fire her," said Gwen.

"I'll say it again," said Will. "I didn't fire her. I told her it was only temporary."

"You're not even on the goddamn ticket yet!"

"It's what the White House wants," lied Will.

Fact was, he'd been crossing swords with La Roy all afternoon. The chief of staff had sounded the reality alarm. The cursory investigation on Vance Allatore had shed some light on the mysterious character. Psychologically speaking, his brain had suffered a compound fracture—at least that's what the admitting psychiatrists had written. Significant depression. Episodes of verbal schizophrenia. Then two weeks after being self-admitted to a psychiatric hospital, Vance Allatore had up and vanished, leaving behind everything but his toothbrush. Officially, he hadn't been heard from until he'd hijacked Will.

"Don't blame yourself," said Will. "I didn't see it coming. And neither did you."

"That's right," said Gwen. "You're so fucking blameless!"

"You think I don't like her?" Will spun it back his way. Liking Izzy had nothing to do with his decision. After plowing through the rest of Vance Allatore's book that afternoon, then banging skulls with La Roy for over an hour, Will found himself in what La Roy liked to call a "pragmatically paranoid" state of mind. Will was alarmed and covering his ass. Overall, he didn't believe the tale Vance Allatore had told him. It was too far-fetched. Even La Roy thought the story, despite its high entertainment factor, was most likely the dubious hallucination of an addict's mind. He was well informed about what the hard stuff could do to a failing cranium.

"I have an idea," said Will, unfolding his own plan as if it were a spontaneous thought. "This nanny you hired. Bring her on early. If you really need the help, maybe she can pick up the slack until we get Izzy her clearance."

Gwen stood silently, arms crossed, leaning against the recently installed butcher block at the center of the kitchen. Her lips were tightly creased.

"And the *nanny's* clearance . . . ? This is about Izzy, isn't it?"

"Is there something you're not telling me?" asked Will, dodging Gwen's astute question with one of his own.

"I'd decided . . ." she began. "I'd decided to bump Izzy up to nanny and give the housekeeping job to Starr."

"To Starr?" Will said incredulously. "You barely know her."

"She's been a big help the last few days," defended Gwen. "I think Yvonne liked her and, between you and me, she's been a real comfort. It just made sense—"

"Sense?" asked Will. "She's a bloody houseguest! That and she's knocked up. What, she's going to hold the baby with one arm, vacuum the floors with the other?"

"It's just temporary! And she's Izzy's best friend, so—"

Mockingly, Will wiped his hands on a towel and put a cool palm to her forehead as if to take her temperature. Gwen shoved it away. "Not funny, Will."

"Since when do we take in strays? For Christ's sake, you haven't hired anybody in five years. You left it all up to Yvonne."

"I trusted her," said Gwen, starting to sob.

"I know, I know . . ." Will found himself suddenly backpedaling. He tried to hold Gwen but she slipped away, keeping that butcher block island between them.

"She was *my* best friend!" bellowed Gwen. "And some faceless prick took her away from me!"

"I'm sure they'll catch the guy," said Will.

"Shut up!"

"Fine. I'm sorry," said Will. "I was just trying to—"

"Stop trying to make me feel better!" said Gwen, gulping back the sobs and grabbing hold of her nerve. "You know what makes me feel better?"

"What?"

"Izzy and Starr," she said, winding up for her big shot. "They've been my *only* comfort."

In that moment, something about Gwen crystallized for Will. A part of her he had never understood. Gwen knew about half the Democratic Party. Her head was a virtual Rolodex of politicians, pundits, money managers, media players, and party soldiers. At a crowded convention, she could recognize an old college classmate at a glance from across the room, share a glass of Chardonnay, and never lose a conversational step. Yet at the end of the day, Gwen had so few friends. None of them were close. Now that Yvonne was gone, Will was all she had left.

And now her husband was lying through his teeth to her. To protect her feelings, he told himself. He didn't want to scare her with his momentary fits of "pragmatic paranoia." All he wanted was an FBI check on the new housemates.

Will cursed Vance Allatore. How could he predict such a thing as *new friends*? In his argument with La Roy, they'd compromised and simply gone tactical. An FBI proctology exam would take care of Will's fear in a heartbeat. Izzy and Starr would come back clean and all would be well in the Sullivan household.

Right?

"I'll make you a deal," said Will, circling around toward Gwen. "One week. Izzy and Starr move out. The FBI does their check. And I'll stay here. With you."

"Don't make me laugh," said Gwen with a dose of pure derision. "The free world can't survive without you for that long."

"If you can make it work," said Will, "then I can make it work." His hands found her tummy, one palm to either side, caressing her. Then he let his arms stretch around behind her, pulling her close. "I can do this."

"You'd stay here?" she asked. "A whole week, just for me?"

"For you *and* the baby," he said. All at once, Will sounded twenty-four karat. Conciliatory, proprietary, and genuine as a Mercedes-Benz.

"A week," she confirmed.

"I'll get Myriam on it first thing tomorrow."

Will kissed the leftover tears, held her firmly for another minute, then promised to bring her a cup of tea after he finished cleaning up the meal.

Meanwhile, his mind replayed the scene over and over for details of the pitch. It had gone well, even if not perfectly according to plan. He had barely a week to make the nightmare disappear. Based on his description, the FBI or DCPD would hopefully track down Vance Allatore. At the same time, he'd have Salinas run checks on Izzy and Starr and, for that matter, everybody else involved in the renovation. While he was at it, thought Will, he'd include Gwen's office staff. Of course, the FBI gears might grind a bit. In the eyes of the Justice Department, Will wasn't exactly senator A list. But he was the odds-on heir apparent and future vice president of the United States of America.

As Will turned off the kitchen lights and climbed the stairs with the tea, he heard keys in the back door and familiar voices. Izzy and Starr were returning from their evening out. Earlier, after having politely informed Izzy of the FBI check and her pending leave of absence, Will had fished into his pocket and peeled off a crisp hundred-dollar bill. He suggested Izzy take her best friend, Starr, out for a nice dinner and a movie. Izzy had demurely said she understood the situation, being that Will was *such an important man of government and things.*" Will and Izzy briefly discussed restaurants in the area and what movie they might want to see. In the end, Will had left the decisions up to the women. He'd simply wanted them out of the house. He'd wanted to be alone with his wife. And he'd wanted space enough to maneuver should Gwen not have taken the bad news so well.

By the time he made it upstairs, Gwen was already reading in bed. He handed her the tea before changing his clothes in the master bath, washing up, and brushing his teeth. As he crawled into bed, Gwen shoved a paperback in his face.

"What the hell is this?" she asked, holding up the Vance Allatore book.

Will took a moment, as if his eyes needed to focus. "Something I was reading," was all he could muster. "Where did you find it?"

"Izzy fished it out of the trash."

"Why the hell would she—"

"She wanted to know if you'd mind if she read it."

The line struck Will cold. After finishing it, he'd dumped the book in the trash compactor in the kitchen, burying it deep into the garbage. He cursed himself for not burning it.

"This is entertainment?" Gwen asked of the book.

"What's wrong with it?"

What's wrong with it? Since Gwen had known Will, he hadn't picked up a book like Vance Allatore's crime tome. On the rare occasion he took the time to read something other than a newspaper or magazine, it was either historical in nature or a biography of some sort. "It's odd," said Gwen. "It's not you. Not to mention that it's kinda creepy."

"Well, it *was* in the trash, wasn't it?"

"You're evading."

"I was bored, okay? It's just something I borrowed from La Roy," lied Will. "I needed some distraction and that's what he happened to have with him."

"I didn't know he got off the plane with you."

"He didn't," said Will.

"Then explain exhibit B," said Gwen, pulling out the yellow MasterCard receipt Will was using as a bookmark. She waved it inches in front of his nose. "Boston Booksellers. April 16th. That was Sunday, mister. And you are *busted.*"

"Okay," he relented. "*I* bought it."

"Then why lie to me about it?" Her hackles were up. The issue was minor for anyone other than the wife of a reformed philanderer and alcoholic. She was, and would always be, wired for suspicion. "You want to explain this to me?"

"For some reasons that are best left unsaid for now." Will snatched the book from her, crawled over her to shut off the light, then flipped the book across the room where it careened off a chair and landed face-up on the floor.

"Don't tell me it's because I'm pregnant, that suddenly makes me a delicate little flower?"

Will tried to joke. "I wouldn't say *little.*"

"You know what I mean. And if that's your answer, you are either too sweet or a lying sack of shit."

"You would be wise to pick the former and forget the latter," said Will.

"I won't let you sleep until you tell me why you lied."

Suddenly she was out of bed, retrieving the book from the floor, then propping herself up next to Will. She opened the book. *"True Believers: The Killer Cult of W. D. Theroux.* By Vance Allatore. Prologue. 'Wesley Dean Theroux scares me as much today as he did the day I first cast my eyes upon him—' "

"I can't believe you're doing this," groaned Will.

"I just want to know what the big deal is," said Gwen, prepared to torture Will until he told her the truth. He was momentarily saved by a soft knocking on their bedroom door. "Yes?"

"It's me," said Izzy from the other side of the door.

"It's okay," said Gwen. "Come on in."

Cautiously, Izzy entered, eyes dipping to the floor as she crossed the threshold. "Senator Sullivan. I'm very sorry. But I was wondering if I might get a word of advice from you?"

Briefly dumbstruck, Will couldn't imagine what kind of advice Izzy might need. "Can it wait until morning?"

"I'm packed up to leave tonight. Starr is driving us to my mother's. We decided *she* could use the company," said Izzy. "Please. It will take just a moment."

Gwen nudged Will. It was the least her husband could do for kicking them out of the house for a week. Will pulled on a T-shirt, stood, glanced back at Gwen. She was still holding the Vance Allatore book. "Well?" he asked Gwen, arm outstretched. "Izzy asked if I'd let her read it. And I can't see why not."

Gwen cut him a sore-loser's frown and handed the book over to Will, who then gave it to Izzy. "Thank you, Senator," said Izzy. "I've always wanted to read it."

"I'll be right back," Will said to Gwen. "And you better be sleeping."

In the darkness that was the nursery next door, Starr waited under the hand-painted Caribbean sky until Will had followed Izzy down the stairs. Taking another beat to catch her breath, Starr entered the master suite through the rarely used side door. Gwen had just switched out the light. At first, she thought Will had returned.

"That was quick," said Gwen.

"It's Starr, Mrs. Sullivan."

Gwen was startled. "Starr? What are you doing here?"

Will was strapped down with silver duct tape. His feet bound to the legs of the chair. His left arm strapped behind him. His right arm on the kitchen's butcher block, taped at the wrist and hyperextended. His elbow felt as if it was going to snap. If it weren't for the dishrag balled into his mouth, Gwen might've heard him screaming.

"You want *me* to find the vein?" bitched Clem.

"Fuck you," said Izzy as she took over. Her St. Maarten

patois extinguished. "If I wanted, I could find a vein in your asshole." She slapped Will's forearm until it throbbed, demanding a vein to rise. Her expert fingertips probed his skin until she found the requisite bump. "There's a nice big one for Aunt Izzy."

"Then stick him!"

She was way ahead of Clem. The syringe was right there where she'd left it. Top right kitchen drawer. Izzy flicked off the plastic cover with her thumb, then drove the needle into Will's vein. Blood backed up into the barrel of the syringe. "Bull's-eye."

"C'mon," said Clem. "Slam it and let's get him in the car."

"Shut up, you dumb fuck. This is hundred-proof ethanol. Dean says it's gotta go slow or he'll either clot or go into alcohol shock."

Clot? Shock? Will knew a bit about ethanol—just enough for speech-making. It was the pure alcohol compound found in the blood gasses of a drunk driver. In his public battles alongside Mothers Against Drunk Driving, he'd fought to lower the levels of ethanol found in blood to a national legal standard of .08. He'd lost that fight. Now, he was fighting against the rush of heat boiling up in his arm. He bucked against the chair, throwing his weight left, then right. Izzy lost control of the needle, leaving it wiggling in Will's shaking arm.

"Hold still!" She smacked Will hard across the face, then moved in, eyeball-to-eyeball. "I'm not up for killing you, Willy! At least not tonight!"

Clem maneuvered in behind Will, throwing a hammerlock around his neck. The extra weight seemed to anchor Will long enough for Izzy to finish the job. With her thumb back on the syringe, she slowly depressed the plunger, a quarter cc of the solution at a time. A cold sweat broke out on Will's forehead. A chemical reaction. The warmth spread from his right arm to his torso. The chill vanished and his head went temporarily numb. His ears tingled. His eyelids dropped as he lost consciousness. That's when his stomach began to convulse.

"Aw, fucker!" said Clem. "He's gonna puke!"

Izzy tore at the tape which held the dishrag in Will's mouth. The gag came loose just in time for Will to douse her in a sudden wave of regurgitated fettucini.

Clem laughed. "Guess that was him sayin' you're fired, bitch."

"Shut up," said Izzy. "And keep his head between his knees. We don't want him choking on his own dinner."

Izzy stripped right there in front of Clem, stuffed her clothes in a heavy-duty garbage bag, and left to grab a pair of jeans and a fresh T-shirt from her bag. As she was leaving, Clem couldn't help but comment. "Damn, girl. You went and got yourself a big ass."

"All for love, asshole!" she said. "All for love."

2

In the emergency room of Shrewsbury's St. Patrick's Hospital, a young resident wearing flexible wire-rimmed glasses was playing a game of finger roulette with the patient.

"C'mon, Senator. How many fingers am I holding up?"

Three fuzzy fingers was the correct answer. About that, Will was certain. Instead of answering, though, his eyes swiveled away from the triple digits to pick out the other individuals surrounding him. He spotted what looked like two nurses in kelly-green surgical scrubs. Leaning up against the back wall he could make out the hefty figures of uniformed cops. White short-sleeved shirts, noticed Will. Not Boston cops. Where the hell was he?

"Just gimme a finger count," urged the resident. "How many fingers?"

"Three," whispered Will, thinking the test would be over.

Instead, the young resident wanted to double-check himself. He held up both hands, two fingers on his left, four on his right. "How many this time, Senator?"

"Six," said Will a bit louder. His voice radiated up

through his skull, sending a ripple of shock waves through his nervous system. His mouth tasted like cold vomit, his tongue was dry and thick. "Where the hell am I?"

"In a hospital," said the resident. "You were in a car accident. But you're okay."

"What car—"

"Now that you're conscious we're going to take you downstairs for a quick series of X rays and, if we can find a technician, an MRI. Okay?"

Before Will could answer, something familiar caught his ear. A voice. His father's voice. To his left, Sully was talking loudly. Beyond some curtain. His boyhood radar picked out the familiar pitch of Sully twisting somebody's arm. Will's terrified gut wanted to know whose. Whatever his father was doing, whoever he was speaking to, Will instinctively wanted it to stop right there and then. Sully's search-and-destroy flavor of politics didn't fit his son's life.

"Gwen?" The words spilled right out of Will. "Where's my wife?"

That's when one of the uniformed officers stepped up. He was a roundly decorated captain in the Shrewsbury PD, who had been snoring in his wife's ear only twenty minutes earlier. "Captain Sam Cundiff, Senator. Glad you're okay."

"My wife," Will repeated.

"Your father gave us the number and we called," said the Captain. "No answer, I'm afraid. But it's still early, so I expect she's sleeping. So I took the liberty of sending a unit up Marblehead way to make sure she gets the news that you're okey-dokey."

"I'm in Shrewsbury?" croaked Will, making out the embroidery on the captain's shoulder patch.

"You are, sir. Why? Well, that doesn't matter." The captain winked. "We all fall off the wagon sometime. I'm just awful glad my senator's gonna be back in the fight ASAP!" The captain showed Will a fisted gesture of encouragement.

Will's antenna wagged, setting off the "ass kisser" alarm. But what was all this wagon shit? The captain was a cop. Didn't he know what happened? Will was drugged. A needle slammed into his vein by some bitch and the landscape guy named Clem. There'd be evidence at the house. And what about Gwen? How could she be okay? Or even sleeping? How did the SOB know so little about so much?

"Drugged," said Will. "I was—"

"I know all about it," said the captain. "I'm a proud Twelve-Stepper myself. And I wouldn't have been able to face my own demons if you hadn't gone public with your own problems."

"I said drug—"

"You bet it is!" said the captain. "The one that comes in a bottle is the worst drug of all."

"Let's get a move on," said the resident, unlocking the wheels of the bed. The nurses pitched in and the room swiveled. Will felt like he was going to puke again.

"Go ahead and try," said a nurse. "But I promise, ain't nothin' more in there to come up."

Will coughed after his own dry heaves. The lights above trailed by like speeding headlamps on the autobahn. The last thing he heard was Sully barking, "Bullshit!"

"That's absolute, unmitigated bullshit and you know it!" spouted Sully. He'd cornered himself a private audience with the hospital's chief resident, the head ER nurse, the hospital's head of security, and the Shrewsbury chief of police. Sully's boy was in trouble and Daddy was giving the marching orders. "It's been done for every son-of-a-Kennedy, and by God, it's gonna be done for my boy."

"His blood alcohol tested at point two-one," said the chief resident, a rosy-cheeked fellow with bulletproof-thick glasses and a nose worthy of Mount Rushmore. "And I'm not going to be a party to sweeping that kind of abuse under a rug."

"The heck you won't," said Sully. "The only person he hurt was himself. Now, answer me this. Who owns the hospital?"

"I don't see what that's got to do—"

"The Morgan-Williams Group," interrupted the head nurse. "It's a managed care company."

Sully nodded his thanks, but kept his focus on the chief

resident. "This HMO that owns your butt. It got any federal, state, or county contracts?"

The chief resident's lips pressed together as his arms crossed his chest.

"I'll take that as a 'most likely,' " continued Sully. "So here's how it goes. You want to keep your contracts, you'll keep this quiet. My boy Will is a United States senator. He's an important man and, as you well know, he's the national poster boy for sobriety."

"Some poster boy," fired back the chief resident.

"By going public about his battles with booze," argued Sully, "Senator William Sullivan has brought more drunks *out* of the closet and *into* rehab than anybody—and I mean *anybody*—in the history of this country. Now, compare how many lives he's saved by his public act of courage to some dented utility pole out on your local two-lane."

Sully pushed himself in a bit closer, invading the chief resident's personal space. "Convincing, ain't it? But if I'm not getting through, maybe I should be talking to the hospital administrator. Better yet, I'll betcha inside fifteen minutes I can get four of your medical review board members on the horn. How'd you like to see me line up them apples?"

A slam dunk, thought Sully. But he thought it best to let the doc cool for a minute. So he disengaged, turning to the chief of police. The cop's face was still creased from his pillow. "Your turn."

"Look. If the hospital loses the blood test," said the chief of police, "what can I do or say? It's *their* problem."

"What about the boys from EMS who scooped your boy up?" asked the head of hospital security. "They could smell the liquor."

"They do a sobriety test?" asked Sully.

"Blood test was performed here," said the ER nurse, a fifty-ish woman who'd seen it all in her career. She was unflappable from her Nikes to the kelly-green hair-sock on her head.

"So we could say that Will was driving fatigued and had a reaction to, say, a flu medication," ventured Sully. He nodded, as did the others. "Good."

"I won't tear up reports," said the chief resident.

"Don't be an asshole," said the police chief. "Nobody was hurt."

"You can keep me from talking," said the chief resident. "But I won't be a party to destroying medical documents."

"You won't have to," said the nurse. "Just go back to your office and play with your Game Boy."

"Oh, I get it," said the chief resident to the head nurse. "You *voted* for the SOB."

"Watch yourself," warned Sully, his Irish balling into a human fist. "That's my boy!"

"I *did* vote for him," answered the nurse, proud as hell. "And you know what? One day he's gonna make a hell of a commander in chief."

The chief resident wiped his glasses, then replaced them on his fabulous nose. "I'll be up in the office if anybody *doesn't* need me."

"You're doing the right thing," said Sully.

"Go fuck yourself," said the chief resident. It was his parting shot in a losing battle.

That left Sully to finish concocting his Kennedy-styled cover-up with those who mattered. He'd personally supervise the destruction of the blood evidence, hospital forms, and doctor's statements. By the time Will emerged from the MRI cylinder, he'd be clean and sober once again with nobody the wiser.

As for the two uniformed cops assigned to inform Gwen of Will's accident, they weren't in quite the hurry that their chief had expected. They were shift-weary and hungry, so they 10-24'd themselves to a Denny's in the North Boston suburb of Saugus, just west of Lynn. After a couple of caffeine pick-me-ups and two free Breakfast Slams, the cops followed a map they'd picked up from a local Mobil station to find their way out onto the peninsula. By the time they'd arrived at Marblehead, the construction crew had blocked the gravel drive with two pickups and a cement mixer. The only place to park was behind the FBI surveillance sedan. In their written request for overtime pay, the two Shrewsbury uniforms reported encountering a pair of FBI agents with whom they shared information about Senator Will Sullivan's drunken encounter with a Shrewsbury telephone pole.

And with that, the cat was out of the bag.

"Doc says you've got your airbag to thank," said Sully.

"Did you talk to Gwen?" pressed Will. He was propped up in bed in a private room.

"The headache part," continued Sully. "Doc says that's gonna take a few days to get rid of. Not to worry though. MRI says it's just a mild concussion. Got your bell rung good by that phone pole."

"I don't remember a phone pole."

"Point two-somethin'," said Sully. "Hell, I wouldn't remember my own name if I was that potted."

Will's blood pressure rose. He felt his face flush with blood. And with it, the pain in his head. "I wasn't drinking, Pop. Now, where's my wife?"

Sully's mouth turned up on one side, half frown, half bad news. Will knew his father's tics too damn well. He'd been reading them since he could remember. "I had one of my staff go over to your house," said Sully, looking for a little credit. "Part of my little cleanup campaign."

"What the hell are you talking about?"

"First, it was getting the hospital to lose the blood tests and paperwork. Had a problem with the chief resident, but he fell in line once I—"

"Gwen!" shouted Will. The noise of his own voice hurt his head so bad he thought his brains might leak onto the pillow.

"She wasn't there," said Sully, pulling up a chair and placing a gym bag on Will's lap. "Like I was telling you, one of my staff went over. The house was open. I guess your contractor has a key. Anyway, my assistant was getting rid of the evidence—"

"What evidence?"

"The vodka bottles," said Sully. "Two empty fifths of Absolut, she told me."

"That's bullshit," said Will. "You know I don't keep liquor in the house."

"What I'm trying to say is that she found a note." With that, Sully unzipped the gym bag. "I had her bring you some clothes. Pajamas. Stuff like that. The note's on top."

Reaching into the bag, Will's free hand withdrew an unsigned, word-processed paragraph. He couldn't read it. His eyes were scrambling the letters and his brain couldn't translate. "Read it, will ya?"

"Already did," said Sully. "You wanna talk to your old man about it?"

"Read it again," said Will. "To me! Please."

Will handed his father the page. Sully extracted his reading glasses from his breast pocket, cleared his voice as if he was about to give an oration, then read:

WILL,

IT'S WITH GREAT SADNESS THAT I WRITE THIS NOTE. BUT WITH THE RESUMPTION OF YOUR DRINKING, I DON'T THINK IT'S BEST FOR EITHER MYSELF OR THE BABY TO BE AROUND YOU OR YOUR ADDICTION. PLEASE. FOR THE SAKE OF OUR MARRIAGE AND OUR CHILD, GET YOURSELF TOGETHER. I LOVE YOU.

GWEN

Will's eyes were on hyper-scan, as if searching for an explanation out of thin air. Sully lowered the note along with his glasses. "I'm afraid it's a familiar pothole in the old road called marriage. Don't worry yourself, son. Everybody hits one or two—"

"They've got her," Will found himself interrupting. He didn't care to hear a word of Sully's self-serving little speech. In his muddied memory, he'd been replaying the night's events. Izzy's invitation downstairs. The landscape man who'd strapped him to the chair. Izzy'd called him Clem. And where was Starr? Will asked himself. Where the hell was Starr?

"I'm sure Gwen is fine," said Sully. "Like I was trying to

tell you, she's just gone *hormonal* on you. Happens with some pregnant women."

"Christ!" cried Will. His hands to his head. He couldn't think straight.

"Not to worry, son. Like I said. It's all been fixed. As far as anybody knows, you had a bad reaction to some cold and flu medication—"

"I wasn't drinking!" shouted Will. "I was drugged!"

"You've had a concussion—"

"You don't understand. They've got her. They took her and the baby!"

Sully stood and put a solid hand on Will's shoulder. "I talked to one of the docs," he whispered. "Paranoia, denial. Standard side effects for a fellah who returns to the bottle after a long dry spell. Just let it go, son."

As a sudden reflex, Will's hands reached up to push his father away. In doing so, he nearly yanked over the IV stand. The IV needle tore from his arm and blood geysered.

"Oh, shit," Sully said, rushing for the door and shouting, "Nurse!"

"What the fuck's happening to me?" screamed Will, begging to wake up from the nightmare.

"It's okay, son. It's going to be okay. Just stay calm and wait for the nurse." Sully jumped into the hallway and yelled even louder, "GODDAMMIT! WE NEED A NURSE HERE!"

3

Bill La Roy's desk was an awful embarrassment to his personal assistant, Kevin Charles. The more Kevin fussed to keep charge over the piles of interoffice exchanges, correspondence, policy memoranda, and legislative analyses, the more of a mess La Roy would plot. It was all an organized effort on La Roy's part to amuse himself at the expense of his anal assistant. On odd days, before he'd leave for lunch, La Roy would purposefully shuffle files, mixing the likes of grease-stained takeout menus with important policy papers. All just to see the shape of things upon his return. Kevin would surely be annoyed, but would never give La Roy the satisfaction of knowing. Upon his return, La Roy's desk would be totally reorganized. Files stacked and memos feathered and facing his chair in four neat rows. White House memos on the left. The two middle rows were both houses of Congress, Senate on the left and the House on the right. And the far right row was always a miscellaneous gumbo of letters, faxes, hand-jotted notes on yellow legal pages, and an updated call sheet.

But La Roy still couldn't find that goddamned fax!
"K.C.!"

"Yo, sir," said Kevin, sounding about as Negro as vanilla
ice cream. And hardly military. Everything about him had a
haughty air of homosexual surliness. Not that La Roy
minded that Kevin was the office's token gay activist. Be
proud, thought La Roy. It was just that Kevin's presence
was a daily reminder of his most irksome concession to Will
Sullivan. The deal wasn't that La Roy had to "hire a homosexual," just that he "couldn't have any woman under his direct employ." La Roy was a good old-fashioned sexual
harasser. All bark, no bite, with an uncontrollable tongue in
the presence of a personal secretary. Foreseeing a scandal
somewhere down the road, Will had made the deal with La
Roy, and Myriam had hired Kevin from the available pool
of legislative staffers.

"The fax," pressed La Roy. "The one that was here before
lunch."

"Haven't seen it," said Kevin. "Did you take it with you?"

"Why would I take it with me?" asked La Roy, answering the question in his own head. He wouldn't take it with
him for fear that he might inadvertently leave it someplace.
The fax had the explosive potential of melting nitroglycerin
and now it was nowhere to be found.

"I can look for it again," said Kevin.

"I'll find it," said La Roy. "Now what's the word on our
senator?"

"Just got word from Shirley up in the home office. She
got some people over to the hospital before any of the media
got wind," said Kevin. "So I guess there's plenty of spin to
go around."

"And Sully?"

"Neu-tra-lized," vamped Kevin. "We got him a ride back
to his office. They're baby-sitting him."

Good, thought La Roy. The idea of Sully commanding
the media rotation on such a powder keg was terrifying. La
Roy had already gotten the report from Sully on the morning's events. He had to admit that so far, the old man had
done well. But give the old pol a little too much poop,

thought La Roy, and he'd be on TV saying God knows what to some *ditzoid* from CNN's Boston bureau.

"And how about Mrs. Sullivan?" asked La Roy, half-afraid to hear the answer.

Kevin could only shake his head. "Nobody knows where she is."

That fucking fax. How could Gwen do something so untimely and pissy?

"What shuttle am I on?" asked La Roy. "Oh, yeah. Got it here."

"The senator called while you were out to lunch."

Lunch. Why the hell did I go to lunch when Will was laid up in the hospital?

The détente lunch had been with the White House assistant press secretary, Kelly Anne Reyes, and deputy attorney general, David Butler. At Will's request, La Roy was trying to schmooze his way back into the good graces of the Justice Department *and* the West Wing. La Roy's acid tongue had gotten him into trouble with some White House staffers during a Gavelgate panel on *Rivera Live.* He'd been way too impolitic on the subject, practically openly accusing President Addison of making the vice president the fall guy. If Will was to be chosen as Addison's running mate, it was paramount that La Roy make amends. Even if it did mean from that day forward he'd have to wear a suit. Shit, thought La Roy. There was always a catch in politics.

"And . . . ?" prompted La Roy.

"He said he doesn't want you to come up," said Kevin. "He wants Steve Salinas from the FBI ASAP. But he needs you here to run the office."

"He needs me *there,*" corrected La Roy. "The numb-nuts needs his sponsor by his side and talkin' him down from any more white-boy foolishness."

The foolishness. The fax. They were clearly interconnected. La Roy had to get on a plane and start patching up the marriage before it came unraveled in front of the entire *Jerry Springer*-watching nation.

"The fax was on my desk before I left. I hope you didn't read it."

"Guilty as charged," said the assistant. "It kinda sizzled, don't you think?"

"Then if you know what's good for your rectum, keep your mouth shut about it," said La Roy, finger pointed. "You *never* saw it!"

"I didn't see what?"

"Just find the damn thing!" The coy little shit had read the fax. God knows what he'd told the women in the office. Gwen had sent their boss an ultimatum. Stop drinking or it was over. But why be so indiscreet? thought La Roy. It wasn't Gwen's style to fire something so personal from her PC. Could she be that mad at Will? La Roy wondered if Will had reneged on his promise to stay in Marblehead for the week.

What mattered right now was that the fax was missing. Nowhere to be found. And that made things worse. If it ever made it out of the office? God knew what La Roy'd be reading the next morning in the *Post*.

"Get me on the next shuttle," shouted La Roy. "I'm going up there tonight!"

By Thursday afternoon, St. Patrick's was humming. Television trucks were parked outside, their masts raised skyward in preparation for live spot coverage of what amounted to a nonevent. The on-camera talent was prepping their stand-ups, reporting little more than that the young and beloved United States senator Will Sullivan had been involved in an early morning car accident, suffering a minor concussion, and doctors would be holding him overnight for observation.

Inside the hospital, reporters tried their best to dig deeper. Sully's fabricated story would play on the five, six, ten, and eleven o'clock editions, leading into alarming pieces on how fighting the common cold could turn deadly. Nevertheless, speculation was running high that Senator Will Sullivan had fallen off the wagon. That he'd gotten drunk and smashed his wife's car. The questions being fired at the hospital staff ranged from the mundane to the highly speculative. Had Senator Sullivan been drinking? Had he been with another woman? And what the hell had he been doing in Shrewsbury anyway?

"*It's been reported that . . .*"

"*An unnamed hospital source said . . .*"

"*We have an unconfirmed report that . . .*"

In an effort to "make the story," Boston news directors sent more field reporters over to the Shrewsbury PD to get interviews from the cops. But those who'd been on duty that night had been sent home. The same went for the fire department paramedics called to the scene. The only actual interview anybody scored was from the milk truck driver who'd reported the accident. The driver, of course, was unable to corroborate a single rumor. He'd had his deliveries to get to. He'd only stuck around long enough to give his name and address to the arriving officers. Standing outside his small clapboard house in Framingham, the driver grinned and played hero for any camera crew hungry enough for a playable sound bite:

"*Anyhow,* I was on my Thursday route. Shrewsbury first, North Grafton, then I gotta backtrack and swing my way up to Boylston. *Anyhow,* my headlights caught a look at a busted-up Explorer. So I stopped, you know? *Anyhow,* the right front end was pretty mangled up. Lotsa steam. Didn't know there was no senator inside. Don't vote. So to me, it was just some fellah bleedin' from the head. *Anyhow,* I got on the horn to my dispatcher. Her name's Callie. She's the one who called the nine-eleven. After that, musta been ten minutes until I saw the police cruisers."

Anyhow. From the semidarkness of his private room, Will watched the reports on the lousy wall-mounted television. The swelling had nearly closed his dominant left eye, so the images were mostly a blur of dull colors. He listened some, but spent most of the time tracing his thoughts between the painful thumps in his head. Cops blocked the outside of the door. And Will's requests to be left alone were mostly obeyed by his Boston staff, headed up by Shirley Cartright, who'd handled most of the afternoon spin for the TV cameras.

Blackouts. That's what Will was thinking about. He'd had only one in his entire alcoholic life. It was on a college ski trip to Stowe. He'd mixed tequila with rum with vodka with beer, topping it all off with a colorful pageant of exotic liqueurs served in shot glasses. He'd cooked himself good that night. Thus, his one blackout. According to friends, he had risen the next morning with a gleam in his eye and skied his brains out. It wasn't until noon and he was cuddled up next to a Vermont spruce that he regained actual consciousness.

Tales of blacking out were popular AA testimonials. They were not only frightening, but all too common. Will remembered one where a high school principal had fought with his ex-wife, returned to the bottle, blacked out, and hallucinated himself an entirely new reality to replace the drunken episode. To a fault, the principal remembered the fight, but not the aftermath. He'd insisted that he'd gone on a trip to Disneyworld with their three children. The AA shrinks labeled the behavior as alcoholic denial. It often occurred when an ex-addict fell off the wagon, and out of guilt subconsciously concocted a completely fabricated scenario to explain the lost time.

Could that have been what happened?

If it was all some kind of guilt-induced hallucination— Clem, Izzy, the duct tape, the chair, the needle—then where was Gwen? *Could* he have fought with her, found some long-lost fifth of vodka and drunk himself into a near-fatal car accident? And in Shrewsbury? What in God's name was in Shrewsbury? And now it was all some horrible episode that, in the best of political traditions, was being covered up.

Will's head hammered. His thoughts warped. And he found himself lucid only between the waves of pain. Guilt pulsed throughout him. Memories of his drinking days and all those blistering fights with Gwen rushed in. He would get angry, drink, drive. It had been a matter of luck that he'd never been pulled over and issued a DUI. A political career killer if there ever was one. Never mind the danger of injuring or *killing* another human being. But then Bill La Roy had entered his life and offered a helping hand. A sponsor. A former addict who knew the troubles he was experiencing. Alcohol had broken up both La Roy's marriages. He'd been damned if he'd let it break up Will's.

"Some headache, huh?" said a voice.

Will heard the words, distorted through the rushes of pain. Disinclined to move his head, he waited for whoever was talking to eventually appear in his impaired field of vision.

"I talked to the attending. Says you're gonna be okay. I just need you to sit up."

Swell, thought Will. Another specialist. He felt a gentle hand slip behind his neck, supporting him as he pulled himself upright. He tried not to scream with agony. It was as if all the blood in his body had mainlined to his skull. "Now what?" he groaned.

"We're going to get in the wheelchair."

"You get in it first," joked Will, as if something funny would kill the pain.

"Let's compromise. You get in and I'll push."

Will slid his feet off the bed, turning toward the voice. He saw shades of green, an ID badge, and a stethoscope slung over the shoulder. Hands gripped under his arms as the doc, or nurse, or whoever he was, helped him into the wheelchair.

"Careful of the IV," said the voice.

Automatically, Will grabbed the IV stand and rolled it next to him. "Got it. What's your name?"

"Here we go," continued the voice. "I'd close my eyes, though. The hallway's kinda bright."

As suggested, Will closed his good eye. He felt himself being wheeled backwards through the door. He heard the sounds of a hospital corridor, the rubber wheels of the chair chirping against the checkerboard of linoleum tiles. He heard a cop say, "Hey there, Senator. How ya doin'?"

"Fine," came his croak.

No more questions, please.

"Figured we'd take the back road," said the voice. "That way you won't be doing a personal appearance around every corner. How's that?"

Will nodded, suffering another hellish crush of pain. He heard the ding of an elevator, felt the car shudder as the doors shut behind him, then the de-gravitation of the elevator working its way downward. He tried to calculate floors with each bell. There were nine in all at St. Patrick's. Not including the basement. That's where he figured he was going. Back down for more X rays. Instead, the elevator stopped two floors short by Will's count. Second floor. The doors opened and he was pushed out.

"Where we going?" asked Will.

"Almost there," said the man.

"Almost where?"

Will felt the wheelchair spin a careful one-eighty, then head backwards through double doors. There was a rush of air and a sudden warmth. He could tell that this room was darker than the corridor. Comfortable for his eyes. Typical, he thought, of radiology.

But radiology was in the basement.

"We're here," said the voice. "It's pretty dim, so you can open your eyes."

"Got only one that works," said Will, opening his right to a remarkable surprise. This wasn't radiology. Before him was a fixed source of light coming from behind stained glass. A large crucifix was suspended above an altar stacked with electric candles. This was the hospital chapel. Hardly larger than a jail cell. Wood-paneled walls, four pews, and a kneeler in front of the shrine. Will found his chair parked directly across from Vance Allatore. This time the former prosecutor was disguised in surgeon's scrubs and a disposable bonnet.

"I hope you don't mind," said Allatore. "But it's private in here. I'm afraid God doesn't do as much business as he used to."

"You!" said Will, wondering if he was suffering another blackout. A hallucination.

"I owe you a grave apology," said Allatore.

Will huffed. "I should call a cop."

"That wouldn't help your wife."

Speaking killed Will. Sentences ached. Each uttered word torqued up the pain meter five notches.

"Poisoned you good, didn't they?"

"I had a blackout," said Will, still trying to convince himself.

"Is that what you think? You drank yourself into this?" Allatore was nodding in agreement. "Makes sense. When alcoholics blow their sobriety, they look for some kind of rationale—"

"Oh, now there's the rub," said Will. "At this moment I'm *not* very rational."

"That's good. Belief isn't rational. It's a matter of knowing your heart."

"For a moment, I was *believing* what you said."

"And now?"

"I don't know."

"The apology," continued Allatore, "is for not warning you sooner. I had no idea they were so close. I thought they'd leave her be until she was ripe."

"They?"

"I think you know who *they* are," said Allatore. "I think we need to start with names."

"I think we need to start with you, *Vance*!" angered Will. His blood pressure peaked and his head swelled from the excruciating cranial pressure.

"I'm not important," said Allatore.

"Tell that to the FBI."

"You've talked to the FBI?" asked Allatore. "About me?"

"You committed federal crimes!"

"I've *committed* myself to God!" said the former prosecutor.

"I'm so happy for you!" snapped Will.

Allatore's eyes shut briefly. He wanted to choose his words carefully. Talking about himself didn't move the ball forward. He'd cast away his former self so long ago . . .

"After Theroux's conviction," began Allatore. "The bloody aftermath, then the book . . . While I was touring, my wife met another man and took my little girl—"

"You had a nervous breakdown."

"I was in the hospital. And there I found God—strike that," he said, still sounding like a courtroom litigator. "God found me. He's been directing my life ever since."

"And I'm supposed to *believe* he directed you to me?"

"That's a politician talking. Who says he directed me to *you*?" Allatore stared Will down. "God has directed me to finish what I started when I first accepted the Theroux case."

"Which was?"

"The destruction of this singular evil."

"And this is all because you never proved motive?"

Allatore showed a brief moment of recognition. His voice lifted. "You read my book? Paperback or hardcover?"

"Let's say, for argument's sake, I believe you," pressed Will. "What does any of this have to do with me or my wife?"

"I'm not certain it has anything to do with you *personally*," said Allatore. "But once I found Sheila, I knew it was about a baby."

"And who's Sheila?" asked Will.

"Sheila Fernandez. One of Theroux's surviving disciples. I found her working as a nurse in Dallas at Harvey Bertrand's clinic under the name of Elena Valenzuela. Do you remember her? She was supplying the old doctor's heroin habit. And then I knew. I knew Theroux's plan to play God through a child. I knew he thought this way, he would never die. A true resurrection."

"But why us?" Allatore's theory stretched credulity to an extreme. "Why *our* child? Why not somebody else?"

"I'm sorry, but I'm sometimes compromised by the fact that there are some few things that God does not tell me." Then he rephrased. "At least not yet."

"Swell." Will was trying hard to get a grasp on Vance Allatore's concoction of religion and paranoia.

"It's a hard pill to swallow," said Allatore. "But I firmly believe that the facts in evidence will be proof enough."

"Facts in evidence?" stopped Will. "*You* send me these . . . messages. *You* break into my home. *You* hijack me. Now, my wife is kidnapped? I'd say the *evidence* points right at *you*."

"Sure. Why not me as a suspect? Former prosecutor turned public pariah. There's not much in the crime game I haven't seen. I could've arranged your accident, kidnapped your wife. Question. What's my motive?"

"You tell me. Money? Opposition loyalty?"

"Opposition loyalty?"

"The Republican Party," said Will. "They see me as a White House threat."

"Oh. A dirty tricks campaign. I see," mocked Allatore.

"Damn you, look at this from my perspective," angered Will. "I'm a public figure. I'm in politics. My wife's in politics. My father's in politics. My life is about political problems and political solutions." His mouth was moving despite the pain. He focused to keep his words on point. "All this is about some psycho's ambition to have a child? My child? It makes no sense."

"You still think this is about you?"

Will caught the subtext. Allatore was calling him a vain SOB. Well, so be it, thought Will. He was who he was. A politician, a power broker, a man who mattered in the world.

"I mean, how could this be true?" continued Allatore rhetorically. "After all, if this killer simply wanted to have a child, it would've been far easier to knock up the wife of some nobody."

"You saying this is a *coincidence*?"

"Why not?" asked Allatore. "Lightning strikes twice. People win lotteries every day. And bad things happen to good people, regardless of gender, race, economic status, party affiliation, or the fact the somebody thinks he's going to be the next president of the United-damn-States."

Allatore continued the attack. "My question is, what is it in *you,* other than some kind of bullshit politician's pride, that makes *you* insist that all this is about *you*?"

"Because otherwise it doesn't make sense!" said Will.

"Maybe not in an earthly sense," agreed Allatore. "But in a spiritual sense? Listen to me when I ask, if God works in mysterious ways, why then shouldn't the man who *pretends* to be God?"

"You wanna try and sell that to a jury of twelve?" shot back Will.

"I don't need to sell it to anybody other than an egomaniacal, thickheaded senator who thinks—"

Enough. Will reached for the wheels of his chair and tried to move. He wanted to get the hell out of there. But the brakes were set. He couldn't move the chair an inch.

"We're not finished," said Allatore. "We have work to do."

"I'm an alcoholic!" spat Will. "I had a fight with my wife,

I drank myself stupid, and I blacked out. The work I have to do is about going back to step one. Get back on the wagon and get on with my life."

"For God's sake, son! Stop thinking about yourself and start thinking about *her!*" Vance Allatore knelt before Will's chair. On both knees. "Look at me. I'm a broken old prosecutor, resurrected as a servant of God. To anybody else, I'm a ghost. All I have is my faith and my wits. You, on the other hand, are—"

"A United States senator."

"Yes! You have power. You have resources. Only *you* can save your wife."

"You're just trying to scare me again."

"Precisely!" admitted Allatore. "But soon you'll realize that your wife is *not* in some comfy hotel, waiting for her precious husband to dry out and come pleading for her forgiveness. She and the child she carries are prisoners—"

"I blacked out—"

"Bullshit!" Vance Allatore revealed an envelope. From it he withdrew photographs. "These are old pictures. But the faces you may still recognize. Can you see them?"

It was dim. Will had trouble enough with his good eye.

"Look," said Vance Allatore. "Elena Valenzuela, also known as Sheila Fernandez. You might recognize her from the Dallas clinic?"

Will was looking at an old black-and-white booking photo. Sheila was made up like a Sunset Strip hooker. Heavy mascara. Lip gloss. Will couldn't place her from anywhere. He shook his head.

Next were pictures of the twins. Timothy and Jack—before they'd shaved their heads. This was a family snapshot from when the boys were just teens, arms around each other. Wide smiles as if they shared a guilty secret.

"No," said Will.

"This one's name was Starr," said Vance Allatore.

The name turned Will's skin to gooseflesh. But when he looked at the ten-year-old mug shot of a smacked-out, hollow-eyed hooker, he couldn't see the plain-faced, freckled, pregnant Starr.

"No," said Will.

"Isadora," pressed Allatore, holding up an actress's head shot, a black-and-white, eight-by-ten glossy of a gorgeous California blonde. There was no resemblance to the house-keeper Will knew as Izzy. But the name . . .

"Izzy," said Will.

"So you recognize her?"

"Only in name," said Will. "Starr and Izzy. They were at the house."

"How about this guy?" asked Vance Allatore. "His name's Clem." He was holding up one last photo. A mug shot of Clem. Unkempt, unshaven, and changed oh-so-little in ten years.

Will felt deathly cold. It crawled up from his feet, crossed his pelvis, then choked him when it got to his larynx. "My God. That's the landscape guy."

"You know him?"

Will stared at the mug shot. He knew him all right. His memory found a new clarity. Will hadn't blacked out at all. The trick in his brain vanished. "Clem," confirmed Will. "She called him Clem. He held me down while Izzy stuck me with the needle."

"Now do you believe?"

It was hard. The chapel was so damned dim with Vance Allatore crouched and shadowed from the light of the stained glass behind him. Will's one good eye tried hard to focus. To look into the man's face and see some kind of truth. All he got was a notion, though. A feeling. Something warm and trusting. Something . . .

. . . *Holy?*

"Your book said the survivors weren't ever identified."

"You're a good study," said Allatore. "And yes. That's what the book said. But we—the FBI and the Los Angeles D.A.'s office—we didn't want any of the survivors to know that we'd identified them."

"The FBI has a file?"

"Yes! Get them to show it to you. They might have more recent pictures by now. You might be able to identify Izzy or Starr."

Will slumped. Winded. The pain was growling between

his ears. He'd gone full circle from being convinced of his blackout to now *believing* Vance Allatore's tale. "If I buy this story. If I go to the FBI, I expect you'll be there to corroborate what you know?"

"I would be an obvious liability to your credibility."

"What are *you* scared of?"

"Listen. You have suspicions your wife was kidnapped. These are the suspects," pressed Allatore. "Get the file. If there are photos, composites, descriptions, any identifying marks you can attribute to the abductors—who cares who figured it out? Your wife will be the subject of a nationwide FBI manhunt. What more could you want?"

"To know for certain that this is not a hallucination."

"Maybe not a hallucination," said the former prosecutor. "Maybe a vision. God's talking to you, son. I think it's time you listened."

While Clem drove the RV, Izzy counted fence posts. Postured in the front seat of a '90 Winnebago Chieftain, they played the happily married pair. A couple of lottery winners named Marve and Mary Weisberg from Long Island, spending their million-dollar ticket traveling America's highway until old age caught up with them and they'd have to retire to Orlando and learn to play golf. That was the script Dean had written for them. And those were the parts they were playing.

They'd left Marblehead at seven-thirty in the morning amidst the tangle of arriving construction vehicles. When Clem was asked to move his dented gray Econoline van to clear the way for the cement truck, the FBI didn't take note that he'd never returned. It was all so very neat. Because inside Clem's van were Dean's actors: Izzy, Starr, and one very terrified Gwen.

By eight, they'd dumped the van in the parking lot of a Shaw's supermarket just outside Salem, where the Winnebago was parked and waiting. Izzy pulled the motor home alongside the van, waited for traffic to diminish, then signaled a transfer that took less than three seconds. Gwen was bagged head to toe in breathable canvas, whisked on board the Chieftain, carried to the rear, and secured to the bed with Velcro straps. She'd been gagged with a mouthful of cheesecloth and duct tape. Then, straddling the mother-to-be, Izzy slapped Gwen hard across the face. Open palm. Five times. Then with a balled fist, she popped Gwen one in the eye.

"I've been wanting to do that for a month," Izzy giddily admitted.

Aside from the premeditated beating to her face, the orders from Dean were not to sedate Gwen for fear that drugs would bypass the placenta and damage the growing fetus. Just smack her enough to raise a readable welt, bind her, then sweet-talk her from then on. Keep the mother-to-be as calm as possible. But tell her nothing. Neither their direction nor destination. During the journey Gwen wouldn't need to eat. Instead, she would be fed through an IV stuck expertly into her arm by Izzy. The tinted windows were further blackened by layers of tinfoil. The ride was relatively smooth.

By Gwen's own calculation, she'd run out of tears sometime before sundown. Afterwards, a dull shock had set in along with a slow-surfacing sick fear for the baby's life. *What the hell was going on?* The more still she was, the easier it was to feel the child bump inside her. The quieter she was the easier to distinguish the difference between the baby's kick and a ripple in the road. It was alive. She was alive. Concerned the fetus wasn't getting enough oxygen, Gwen leveled her breathing. She even tolerated Starr's soft hand to comfort her. If only for the baby.

"It's all going to be *wonderful.*" Starr beamed. She hadn't left Gwen's side since she'd crept up on her in her bedroom. "We're going to be beautiful mothers with beautiful babies."

For the long trip, Starr had stocked up on children's books which she read aloud to Gwen. She insisted the babies were listening through their own special subconscious, remembering the words and her voice. But by the second nightfall, Starr was fading. She'd curled herself into a fetal ball at the foot of the Winnebago's bed. If she'd had the mind to, Gwen could have kicked her in the head. Maybe killing her with an accurate strike to the base of the skull.

But to what end? Izzy and Clem were only footsteps away, wired on enough crystalmeth to kill any sign of road wear. That, and Gwen had been informed that the tiny, lipstick-sized camera mounted over her head was connected to a small black-and-white monitor concealed in the RV's center console. Periodically, Izzy would lift the lid and catch a quick peek at Dean's chosen flower.

Gwen's thoughts slipped from the safety of the baby to Will. Was all this part of some political plot? A new wave in Beltway blackmail? Could this explain his odd behavior of late? And most importantly, where in God's name was he? She feared they must have killed him. While Starr had been apologetically holding her at knifepoint in her own bedroom, she'd heard shouting from downstairs. Izzy and Clem, bitching at one another. Something about what to do with Will. Soon after, she'd heard the distinctive sound of the Explorer's engine turning over and Clem's heavy footsteps on the stairs. What had Izzy done with her husband? She had vanished for what seemed an eternity, returning a nudge before dawn only to confirm to her cohorts that the *"work had been done"* and *"nobody had seen me."*

Gwen cried aloud for Will. All day until she thought she was done. And suddenly, she was crying again. What madness had spurred such a conspiracy? Will had suspected *something*. That much was clear. Yet he'd chosen to keep it from her. The tears spilled over her face and wet the pillow at her temples. Then the baby kicked her hard just above her cervix. Her baby. Will's baby . . .

. . . Or was it? Will had his doubts, after all.

"Wake up!" said Izzy, shining a flashlight into Starr's face. "We're stopping for gas and I need you *awake*."

Starr languished, unnerved by Izzy's shout. "Forgive me, Miss Perfect, but I don't have the luxury of eating speed."

"So take some," said Izzy, offering up a half-eaten blister pack of Purple Hearts, a low-budget amphetamine.

"It's bad for my baby," said Starr.

"Your baby don't count," said Izzy. "So screw the little fucker and stay awake. *Please?*"

"I won't take it," said Starr.

"Fine," said Izzy. "Drink coffee. Have a Snickers. I don't really give a shit. Just keep it lively while we're stopped."

That's when Gwen heard it. As if her ears had been uncorked and all sound was unfiltered. Izzy's voice. That St. Maarten patois had vanished in the course of twelve hours, replaced by a harsh, distinctive American blend. From where, Gwen couldn't tell. Hardly Caribbean, though. Izzy was a fraud and had been since day one. Gwen's thoughts reeled back to Yvonne and her strong recommendation to hire Izzy as the housekeeper.

She found herself gasping, nearly sucking the cheesecloth into her larynx. Yvonne. Had *they* killed her? Jesus Almighty. Could they have killed Will too? The thought caused an ache in the back of her skull. When it subsided it left her numb.

"How much farther?" asked Starr.

"Clem figures about twenty-one hours."

"Nonstop?" asked Starr. "Twenty-one hours?"

"We're staying under the speed limit and stopping for gas every three hundred miles. This ride's a fuckin' pig."

Izzy's eyes caught Gwen's. Steering the flashlight back onto Gwen's face, she inspected the budding black eye. Gwen squinted.

"You're gonna have one helluva shiner," said Izzy proudly. "Starr tell you it's all gonna be okay?"

Gwen nodded silently.

"It's my voice, isn't it?" asked Izzy. "You can tell."

Once again, Gwen nodded.

"Well, I'm not usually this fat, either," said Izzy. "You'll see. When I get down to weight I'll have Dean's true eye again."

Whose eye? Gwen wanted to ask. Did she say Dean? Who the hell was Dean?

And as if Izzy had bugged Gwen's brain, she answered. "It's not for me to say who *he* is, honey. But I promise— you'll know soon enough."

Switching off the flashlight, Izzy returned to her post in the front passenger seat. Starr took her place alongside Gwen, holding her captive's hand. "Don't mind her. She's just jealous."

Of me? thought Gwen.

"Jealous of anybody else who catches Dean's eye."

Lightning strikes twice.
People win lotteries every day.

Fatigued and nearly unconscious, Will was discovered by a maternity ward nurse, his wheelchair parked near the curtained windows of the nursery. She'd recognized the senator and quickly alerted the hospital authorities. As a precaution, a CRASH team was called as if responding to the scene of an accident. In minutes, Will was surrounded, helped onto a gurney, and rushed back to his room for reobservation. He'd lost sense of time. He had no idea how long he'd been left alone by Vance Allatore to feast on another helping of humble pie.

And bad things happen to good people.

Yet Will's subconscious continued to howl, why me? Why Gwen? Why not somebody else?

It was still Thursday. 8:49 P.M.

Shortly after nine-thirty, Will awoke from a short nap. His focus seemed better, the pain in his head subsided to a six out of ten, and he found himself flanked by Bill La Roy and Steve Salinas.

After sucking back a lungful of fresh oxygen, Will sternly addressed La Roy. "You're supposed to be in D.C."

"Sponsor first, chief of staff second," said La Roy with a big, confident smirk. "Welcome back to step one, asshole."

"I didn't fall off," said Will.

"Don't make me take away your chips," said La Roy.

"I didn't fall!" said Will, emphatically now. "I need you to believe this."

"Look," said La Roy. "We can spin this all day for the rattlesnakes and say it was an OD on . . . what was it? Tylenol PM? But facts is facts, Earnest. We gotta go back to zero and work the steps. Make some amends. Gwen'll come back. I promise."

Will rolled his eyes and turned to Steven Salinas. "I was slipped a mickey. Ethanol injection. Here. Look at the bruise on my arm."

"In the program we call that 'stinkin' thinkin',' " added La Roy. "And the harder the fall, the fouler the smell."

"Shut up," said Will, growing more aggravated with La Roy by the microsecond. "Steve. I want you to listen. Gwen was kidnapped. This much I know for sure."

"By whom?" asked Salinas.

"This is the hard part," said Will with a weak finger pointed at La Roy. "It's going to sound irrational. I'm not sure I believe it myself."

"This have something to do with Vance Allatore?"

"You know something?" asked Will.

"I did some checking," said Salinas. "La Roy was right. After the Theroux trial he went kinda bat-shit, then poof. Gone with the wind."

"He said there's an FBI file," said Will.

"Allatore said what? A file?" asked Salinas. "On who? You know, on the plane, you didn't say anything about a file."

"He was here, wasn't he?" said La Roy, catching on quickly. "Is this guy still stalkin' you?"

"He says there's an FBI file," repeated Will. "On the Theroux cult. If it exists, I want to see it."

"Whoa!" said Salinas, holding up his arm. "That's way out of my realm of magic. I'm assigned to *legislature oversight*. I know some folks. I can make some calls. But pulling files? Active or inactive? You gotta go upstairs. And friend? Last time I checked, they don't like you much over at Justice."

"If I have to do it myself, so be it," said Will, disappointed and unafraid to let Salinas see it. "This is about Gwen. I'll crawl across glass . . ."

La Roy pulled up a chair and held Will's hand. "You, my dear friend, are encountering some classic Humpty-Dumpty shit. I say you rest, let those of us who are clean and sober spin this thing back into the light. You and I can do the rest from here. Like I said, we'll work the steps. Get Gwen back—"

"Why the hell are you my sponsor?" asked Will.

"Because you need me," said La Roy.

"And what did you say to me when I was rock-bottom drunk?" asked Will. "I remember what you said. Do you?"

"Sure enough," said La Roy. "I said I believed in you."

"Then believe in me now!"

"A sponsor's job is to see the sunshine through the shit."

"You either believe me or you're fired," said Will. "What's it gonna be?"

La Roy exchanged pained glances with Salinas. He was up against the wall and not beyond patronizing his boss if, as sponsor, he was acting in Will's best interest. "Sure," he relented. "Why not. I believe in you."

Back to Steve Salinas, Will asked, "How do I get the file?"

"Anybody in the chain of command *above* Special Agent Steve Salinas," said the agent. "You're the U.S. senator. I'd call over to Justice. Hell, call the A.G. If there was a file, dead or otherwise, she could have it on your desk inside the hour. Question is, will she?"

Will nodded to La Roy. "Get Margie Van Hough on the phone."

"It's almost ten, Earnest," said La Roy. "You think we can wait to call her until the morning?"

"Call her now! For Christ's sake, my wife is gone! I want this moving by midnight."

La Roy complied, making the requisite calls. Not for the sake of his job. But out of sheer loyalty. As he expected, the A.G. was unavailable. So were those under her immediate command. La Roy gave up at eleven after Will had been overtaken by sleep.

Keep your mouth shut and let the boss's demands play out. That left La Roy's secondary issue on hold until morning. The missing fax. Upon his arrival at the hospital, Sully had shown La Roy the note allegedly left by Gwen. La Roy's hackles spiked as he instantly saw the note was identical to the one he had received that very morning. It was obvious to the chief of staff that amongst the day's labyrinth of events, from Sully's cover-up to the suspect reappearance of the mysterious Vance Allatore, a bizarre undercurrent was moving beneath the earth's surface. Something was leaking. The dark feeling left La Roy craving something more than caffeine. Some cocaine, maybe. A lousy sign.

4

WHERE ARE YOU?
        grid 49 by 21.
YES. I KNOW THAT PLACE. YOU ARE
HALFWAY TO YOUR FINAL DESTINATION.
        we are, my love.
COMPLICATIONS?
        none, my love. it feels like family.
SOON, THE OTHERS WILL JOIN AND
WE WILL ALL BE ONE AGAIN.
        i am breathless with waiting.
AND MY FLOWER? HOW IS SHE?
        she is scared. but nothing that you didn't have us prepare for.
GOOD. YOU <u>ALL</u> HAVE DONE SO WELL.
        soon we will all be blessed.
PRAISE BE.
        to you, my love.
AMEN.

G*ive-a-Fuck.*
    Gary Modetti loathed the moniker. It was crude, crass, and didn't take into account that he had children in

public fucking school that one day might have to hear such trash. To his three kids, the eldest a teenager, Modetti was a crusader for truth and justice. One who tore at the walls of hypocrisy that enslaved the American government.

Modetti's three kids clearly didn't know the truth—that their father defined *cavalier* and was willing to print any and all hearsay in the name of news.

Lucky Modetti, thought the reporter.

While D.C. fax machines worked overtime, U.S. Senator Sullivan's office was besieged with requests for confirmation on the authenticity of a phantom document. Journalists all along the Potomac scrambled to make a story out of what looked like a marital ultimatum given to America's favorite Saint of Sobriety.

But legitimate newspapers still required multiple sources and substantial lead time to break a story. And for TV and radio to run the story, they required taped statements from talking heads, either denying or confirming the rumor. However, an Internet-zine like *A La Mode* needed little more than a high-quality scanner and a formerly credentialed reporter named Gary F. Modetti. Within minutes of filing the story from the comfy converted den of his Bethesda bungalow, there it was—the fax—right there on the Internet for absolutely anybody to access. And once something was "reported," no matter how dubious the nature of the source, it theoretically became legitimate enough for other news services to "report the report." By midnight, Modetti's story was a blurb on the major wire services and a page-three question mark in an uncredited gossip column inside the conservative daily, the *Washington Times*.

Saintly, Sober Senator <u>Falling Down</u> on His Home Life?

The short column went on to report the coincidental nature of Senator Will Sullivan's "accident" and the alleged fax from his politically savvy and pregnant wife, Gwen Corbett-Sullivan.

The piece sent Washington tongues into full throttle before

inbound traffic reached its usual Friday morning crawl. Myriam called Allison Flannery, waking her up, lighting a fire and demanding she get her sleeping tail down to the office to dial every number in La Roy's Rolodex until she came up with the senator's chief of staff. Fortunately for Allison, a nurse in the private ward where Will spent Thursday night found Bill La Roy's motel room telephone number written on a pink Post-It at her station. Allison's conversation with La Roy set the rest of the morning into overdrive. By 6:00 A.M., La Roy had Will checked out of the hospital, wheeled from the rear elevator and into a waiting police car. As the cruiser roared out of the parking lot, La Roy was certain he saw the first news truck at a nearby stoplight, waiting for it to turn green. Under the wire, he thought. Another bullet dodged.

Surely, La Roy reminded Will, there'd be scores of rattlesnakes waiting outside the Marblehead house. "Right now, I couldn't give a damn," said Will. "I just want to find my wife."

"Who knows? She *might* be there," said La Roy, trying his best to sound encouraging. A difficult deed for the notoriously cranky SOB.

"You talk to Salinas yet?" asked Will, who was looking more human—the swelling greatly reduced, but still black and blue from his left cheekbone past his hairline.

"It's six in the morning, Earnest," said La Roy. "Give him a chance to throw some water on his face."

"I'm gonna want to be talking to the A.G.'s office by eight. After that, I'm gonna want to talk to Addison. If this fax thing blows out of proportion, I want to do the damage control myself. Plus he's got a relationship with Gwen. I give him the straight talk, the quicker I get the file."

"Ten four, Earnest," said La Roy.

"I'm also going to ask the FBI to put on a search for Vance Allatore," said Will. "I can't have this son of a bitch popping in and out of my life at his own convenience. If he's telling the truth, he can be a stand-up guy and help. Otherwise he's—"

"A suspect?" confirmed La Roy. For La Roy's money, Vance Allatore had proven a far more mysterious and dangerous character than this Izzy or Starr or Wesley Dean

Theroux. After all, Theroux was locked up somewhere west of the Rockies.

They arrived at Marblehead before the construction crew. Surprisingly enough, no news teams were visible from the upper drive. At the bottom of the drive was Will's Thunderbird, parked right where he'd last seen it. The house was dark. The porch lights, switched off. Most likely because they'd never been turned on in the first place.

Entering the unfinished house, Will felt cold and sick to his stomach. It wasn't home. It was empty. A lifeless, hollow shell that he'd visited from time to time. Instantly he knew Gwen was nowhere inside. And though La Roy promised to do a cursory once-around, Will suspected the chief of staff's foremost agenda was to do a sponsor's inventory. A search-and-destroy mission, scouring the place from floor to ceiling. Find any and all booze and dump it down the kitchen drain. From the den, Will dialed Myriam, listening to the cabinet doors banging in the kitchen, drawers opening and closing, footsteps pounding up the staircase. La Roy was dutifully turning the place inside out. Cleaning the environment of abusable substances. Then they would start with step one of twelve.

"I ADMIT THAT I AM POWERLESS OVER MY ADDICTION."

And then on to step two:

"I BELIEVE THAT ONLY A POWER GREATER THAN MYSELF CAN RESTORE ME TO SANITY."

When had he lost God? For a micro-moment, Will thought he'd felt Him in the hospital chapel. A womblike warmth that momentarily filled the empty place in his heart . . . But now he was drifting, losing focus. He shook himself back on course, dictating his agenda to his Washington staff. One by one, he gave them orders, but offered no explanations. Their job was to do and never question why. That suited the situation just fine. The boss was doing plenty of questioning himself.

La Roy had begun in the basement and worked his way up. He dumped laundry baskets, sniffed bottles of Clorox, and sifted through powdered detergents. It was Inventory 101:

An addict will go to any length to hide his addiction.

In his sponsor's class, La Roy had heard stories of alcoholics hiding half-pints of liquor under loose floorboards, in jumbo jars of mayonnaise, even inside their own children's stuffed Barneys.

Once he'd finished in the basement, La Roy moved on. He turned over Izzy's room, then Starr's. Both downstairs bathrooms. Gwen's filing cabinets in the unfurnished living room. The cushions in the chairs and couches, then moved into the kitchen, where he opened and shook every box of cereal, rice, Bisquick, sugar. Every jar and bottle in the fridge was sniffed or stirred. The cupboards were emptied, the drawers swept clean, the pipes under the sink tapped for odd sounds. La Roy was desperate to trust Will again.

Dead center in the kitchen floor was a two-foot-square brass register. A duct into which the central air and heating had long ago been connected. When the thermostat kicked in, a blast of warm air rose from the floor. La Roy stood upon the register.

If I were hiding my booze . . .

On his knees, La Roy was about to unscrew the grate with a butter knife when he heard the slightest buzzing. He put his ear to the register. The sound grew louder. A bottle or can, maybe, vibrating against the duct?

The one screw twisted out easily. A sign, wondered La Roy, that the grate had recently been loosened. The register was heavy. It hinged open, resting against the butcher block island. Without a flashlight, La Roy had to reach in and feel around. He lay on his belly and bent his arm into the shaft and under the floor. He found the bottom of the shaft with his fingertips, then slid them back and forth in search of the contraband.

"I've got you, Earnest," he said quietly, semi-thrilled at the prospect of discovery, while ruing the possible disappointment he'd feel about his charge.

La Roy inched deeper into the hole, inserting his shoulder to the collarbone, sweeping with his hand, certain he'd find a bottle, a can, or a flask. Instead, he found a sharp prick and a pain that drove from his index finger all the way up to his armpit.

"Son of a BITCH!" La Roy jerked himself upright to find an eighteen-inch gauge hypodermic needle stuck into the first crease of his forefinger. There was no barrel, no plunger. Just a single disposable needle. La Roy first thought tetanus. How long since he'd been immunized? Then AIDS. It *was,* after all, a needle. As he quickly plucked the spine from his flesh, he suddenly understood the significance of his find. He was in the kitchen, on the exact spot where Will claimed he'd been shot up by Izzy and Clem.

Jesus.

La Roy bounced into the den. "Lookee what I found."

Will put Myriam on hold. He turned and saw La Roy gripping a bloodied dish towel. "What happened to you?"

"Recognize this?" With his left hand, La Roy gingerly held up the needle between his fingers.

"Where'd you find that?"

"I found it where my right hand shouldn't have been lookin' without a flashlight."

"So what? You suddenly believe me?" asked Will.

"I think if my hair weren't so damn curly, what's left of 'em might be standing straight on end."

"We got work to do," said Will.

"And then some," said La Roy. "Question. Why don't you look terrified?"

"I am," said Will. "I just think my head hurts too much to show it."

"I'm serious, Earnest," said La Roy. "On a shit scale of one to ten, we're lookin' at a thirteen."

Will stopped, inhaled slowly, deeply, and amidst the carnage that was his insides, tried to give a thoughtful response. "What scares me is being so damn frightened that I can't function. And if I can't function, I'm afraid I won't ever see Gwen again."

The spanking-new Rancho Seco Correctional Institution showed few scars from the twelve-year battle it had taken to be built. A state bond referendum initially raised the cash, which then sat in escrow for nine long years while the California State Legislature crossed swords over where to break ground for the high-tech prison designed for the state's worst felons. No city or county wanted the facility, and each sent lobbyists, councilmen, mayors, supervisors, teachers' groups, and even schoolchildren to Sacramento to testify in front of corrections committees. It seemed nobody particularly wanted killers living in their backyard.

Making matters worse, another citizens' lobby filed a class action lawsuit on behalf of the voters for malfeasance of bond funds. The suit demanded that the California secretary of state either release the funds or build the damn prison. Push came to shove and shove came to an election-tilting issue in a contentious gubernatorial race. The newly elected governor, Dana Florsham, the first woman ever to occupy the state's highest office, decreed the prison would be built during her first term. Twenty miles southeast of Sacramento, a site was forced upon the small town of Ione, in the shadow of the Rancho Seco nuclear power plant's fading twin towers. A place where the grasses turned brown at the first warm winds of spring and the summer heat topped out in triple digits.

The only concession to the local community was the exterior design. The four painted domes, three stories high, surrounding a three-acre yard, would comprise the entirety of the facility. Circling the compound, eucalyptus trees would mask the wire and concrete structure, not to mention the one thousand horror stories that were captured inside.

The inmates were divided by domes along mostly racial barriers. Blacks, Hispanics, whites, and then those on death row where skin color didn't matter. The same went for yard time. Three hours per day per population. That included the death-row populace, which was divided into three tiers: the conforming inmates, otherwise known as "grade A"; the nonconformers or *"problem customers,"* defined as "grade B"; and the third-tier group, "grade C," those who were considered so dangerous they were only let out of their cells to shower and exercise. The rest of the time, they were confined to their cells.

Wesley Dean Theroux was a "grade C" inmate.

With barely ten weeks left before his date with a lethal dose of sodium thiopental, his exercise time had been increased to five hours per week. He was also permitted a modest half hour every Sunday in the prison chapel. Outside his cell, he was never without waist chains, leg irons, and four guards monitoring his every move.

All this, claimed Theroux, for a man who'd done nothing more than assist his family in "leaving this earth before the oceans turned red with blood."

"Your lawyer's online, Wes," said Fred, one of Theroux's favorite daytime guards. "Got anything to upload?"

"I do, yes," said Theroux. His cell was standard—concrete, six by twelve, fold-down bunk, toilet, washbasin, and over a small desk was a single shelf that was quadruple-stacked with books. More books were under the bunk. Even more volumes piled into the corners. Theroux unplugged his laptop and carried it over to the metal carrier tray on which his meals were delivered. He opened the lid, booted up the IBM ThinkPad, then waited for Fred to hand him a telephone line to jack into his internal modem. The new-tech prison was equipped with personal phone jacks assigned to each cell. That's how C-grade prisoners received their legal telephone calls. Simple enough. Instead of moving the prisoner to the phone, the phone was delivered to the prisoner, plugged in by the guard, then monitored from the CSD, the Central Security Depot.

In addition, Theroux's able attorneys had lobbied an appellate judge that their client was so vitally involved in his case, he should be provided with a portable computer from which to communicate with his legal team. And because the data to be exchanged was privileged information between client and counsel, the prison was ordered not to monitor the transfer.

A sweet deal for the prisoner, thought most legal experts. But Theroux wasn't fooled. Without court supervision, nothing could keep some tech-head in the CSD from capturing his data transfers on a zip-drive and secretly forwarding them to the Los Angeles County D.A.'s office or the FBI. Therefore, Theroux was careful. He was certain to make sure the notes to his attorneys were benign. Nothing that he wouldn't want public. Just standard-issue pleas of innocence, suggested language for new writs, and friendly notes of encouragement to "keep up the good fight."

"Hooked up?" asked Fred.

"I'm ready," said Theroux.

Theroux double-clicked the SEND icon and away went the data. With the high-speed modem, it all took less than five seconds.

"Thanks, Fred," said Theroux.

"That's it?" asked Fred.

"A dying man learns to be concise," said Theroux with a whimsical smile. Oh, yes. Theroux was certain he was going to die. With only weeks remaining, he had little faith left in the appeals process. The odds of winning the state lottery were far better. Especially in a state such as California which, along with the production of the high-tech prison, had publicly committed to increasing its execution rate by the millennium. That and W. D. Theroux was a popular choice for execution. He was notorious, photogenic, and guaranteed to garner the sitting governor a strong rating on crime and punishment.

"So what do you do on that computer when you're not playing lawyer?" asked Fred.

"I write in my journal, mostly. Play some games," said Theroux. "Solitaire came with the Windows program."

Of course, he was lying. When the guards were gone and the prisoner was alone, he'd command the computer to engage a second, internal modem with a satellite cellular chip. This allowed Theroux to dial outside the walls of the institution, hook into the Internet without the slightest detection, and leave his daily, detailed instructions to the remainder of his disciples.

The steep cellular phone bills were charged to a trust account managed by a Seattle-based attorney who'd never actually met his client. His instructions were to never ask questions, communicate only when communicated to, and execute the trust to the letter.

"Ever win?" asked Fred.

"Solitaire? Only when I cheat," smiled Theroux.

"How do you figure you can cheat a computer?" Fred was casual enough with the prisoner to lean his long, slender self against the heavy-gauge, galvanized mesh.

"Computer's just like any man," said Theroux. "Programmed by a mommy or a daddy. Once you learn what buttons to push, it's just a matter of time before it comes around to your way of thinking."

"That so?"

"God's truth," said Theroux. "Let's take you, for example."

"What about me?"

"Your father died last week, yes?" asked Theroux, completely offhanded. "Lymphoma."

Fred did a double take and stepped back from the mesh, his eyebrows arching toward two creases between his eyes. "Who said anything about my old man?"

"You did."

"I did not!"

"Not verbally. But your insides are screaming. Be a man. Hold it in. But it's coming out of your pores. I've been waiting for you to come talk to me about it. Do you wanna talk to me about it?"

"I *wouldn't* talk to *you* about it," said Fred, turning red and angry. "I wouldn't talk to no death-row con about my old man."

"But you should," said Theroux, sitting upright, his hands on his lap, one on top of the other. "After all, I'm dying, too. I know how *he* felt. You can say to me what you wanted to say to him. The things you couldn't."

"Fuck you. You're no shrink," said Fred. "And I might like ya. But you're still a damn killer."

"Maybe yes. Maybe no. But I'm the one who listens. I'm the one who watches you. Sees your pain. There's not much else for me to do, Frederick, but *watch* and *listen*."

"I just want to know who told you," raged Fred. "Was it that shithead Roger C.?"

"Look at me," said Theroux.

"I'm looking," said Fred. "Know what I see?"

Theroux chose not to answer. He simply sat on the edge of the bunk, eyes open, benign yet fixed on Fred's. Before

Fred could break the gaze, he saw tears spilling from Theroux's blue eyes.

"Jesus," said Theroux. "You weren't even there."

"I wasn't where?"

"With him," said Theroux. "When he died. He was calling for you."

"My sister was there."

"And he called for you. The eldest child. His firstborn son was not there when he died."

"This is too fuckin' weird, Wes." Fred slapped at the mesh. "You're freakin' me out."

But Theroux's tears turned to sobs. Real tears. Then from deep within the con came a tangy, guttural voice rich with Tennessee. "Don't carse yerself, son. Ah understand. And ah lo-ove you."

"You son of a bitch!"

"That's good, Fred. Don't curse your father. Curse me."

"You're not my father!"

With that outburst, Theroux buckled at the middle, rolling sideways on the bunk. Clutching his belly, fetal and weeping. Fred crashed another first into the mesh. "Fuck you!" His voice echoed all through the concrete tier, followed by fading foot-stomps as he charged down the clanging gangway.

Theroux waited a good thirty seconds, closed his mouth, and inhaled through his nostrils until his muscles eased. He shifted over onto his back and fully reclined, let the warm satisfaction saturate his entire being. The feeling was absolutely splendid. Not only did he still have *it*. But *it* was better, speedier, and more facile than when he was on the outside.

Those shrinks at the L.A. County Jail had diagnosed him as an empath. What a bunch of psycho-shit. It was nothing more than a gift from the Almighty. Just like his ability for photographic recall. Another gift. And so useful. If he'd only known how powerful it would all become once he'd been incarcerated. His death sentence had crystallized him into a living god. Free of mental or sexual restraints. His divine thoughts flowed as swiftly as the Intel Super Chip that revved his computer.

Theroux sat up again, retrieved the ThinkPad, and opened a subdirectory titled "GUARDS" and a file appropriately named "FRED." Flawlessly, Theroux recalled his performance with Fred to the most subtle gesture, recording the encounter with copious notations. He dated it, closed the file, then decided to visit some of his other favorite places. He had logged observations about his attorneys, doctors, nurses, and even some of the neighboring cons. Vast, expansive notes on behavior, opinions, idiosyncrasies, and, oh yes, their petty politics.

Ah, what a tonic.

"THE POLITICS OF MAN"—Theroux's favorite new directory on his ThinkPad. From there he track-pointed his way to a subdirectory titled "GWEN." A simple double-click brought up a two-megabyte volume of words, photos, and QuickTime video. The powerful ThinkPad loaded up a six-month-old file, located the correct plug-and-play function, and began the video application. Theroux's colorful screen blinked, then switched over to monochrome as a black-and-white video played images captured from a camera hidden in the ceiling of the Harvey Bertrand Reproductive Clinic in Dallas. Theroux gazed at the replay of Gwen's insemination. His seed. Harvey Bertrand performed the procedure, his gentle Southern voice soothing the radiant patient as he delicately replaced the fertilized egg inside the mother-to-be. Through the grainy video, Theroux studied Gwen's face. Beautiful. Perfect. The mother of his child.

The mother . . .

He imagined what it would be like to kiss Gwen's lips. Touch her eyelashes with his. Taste her. If only, thought Theroux, she could feel his touch. Then he would be complete . . .

. . . and so would she.

Interrupted by the squeaky wheels on the oncoming meal cart, Theroux threw his eyes open, closed the lid to the computer, and placed it on the shelf above the small desk. He'd watch her again later. The beautiful Gwen. His blooming flower. Then at midnight, an update. A talk with his family. So much to look forward to. So little time left.

5

"Kidnapped," said Will. With that, he hoped the strong word would cut through all the tension built up during the FDA hearings.

He said the word *on* the record and *to* the enemy—the Justice Department and the FBI. From that point on, there would be no turning back from the pronouncement.

By noon on Friday, the Bureau had asked local authorities to send the construction crew home and seal off the Marblehead estate, pending an investigative team. In the meantime, Will and La Roy had shuttled from Logan to Dulles, and been driven directly to the DOJ. As a favor to Will, the White House had called ahead and cleared a spot on Attorney General Margaret Van Hough's calendar. Attending were FBI Director Lois Freehold, the deputy attorney general, Hal Willoughby, and Ralph Bedletter, the FBI's top kidnapping profiler. Bill La Roy was there, and Will Sullivan, who was dressed in a dark gray Senate uniform, punctuated by a stately red tie. But sweat beaded off that purple lump seemingly glued to his forehead. Listening over the speaker was the former

DNC chair, recently named White House chief of staff, Sean McGeorge.

"We're all attorneys here," said Margie Van Hough. "So I hope you can appreciate me getting this straight and on the record."

"I'm no lawyer," volunteered La Roy, wearing the smirk on his face like a badge of bloody honor.

The attorney general was well aware of La Roy's loose mouth. And that she could either patronize him or ignore him altogether. She chose the latter, looking to Will for confirmation. "It is your opinion that your wife was abducted by this cult?"

"I have strong suspicions," said Will. "And if there is an active file that I can look over, I might be able to identify the abductors."

"But so far there have been no demands?" asked Hal Willoughby.

"Not yet," said Will. "But I have an idea what they'll ask for."

Looking thoroughly uncomfortable in a straight-backed federal chair, the FBI director rose, standing five foot ten inches, with shoulders as broad as a linebacker's. She favored custom suits made from bright fabrics. Orange was a favorite. And high collars in order to wear her trademark opal-in-gold cameo. She was a sharp contrast to the delicate and feminine attorney general.

"What will they ask for?" asked Lois.

There, the road between truth and conjecture split. Will chose to depart from Vance Allatore's theory in exchange for something he could sell. He had to see the FBI's file. "Wesley Dean Theroux is due to be executed in California in ten weeks," said Will. "I believe, because of my close association with the president, that these cult members hope that their leader's death sentence might be commuted in exchange for my wife's life."

"Holy Mother," said Sean McGeorge over the phone. He'd heard some wild stuff during his political tenure, but this somber account from Will was downright chilling.

"Once again," said Margie Van Hough. "On the record. You are saying this note from your wife—"

"It's a fake," said Will. "To buy time. She didn't sign it. And she would *never* leave something so private on paper, let alone fax it to my Washington office."

"So the two of you," she continued. "You and Gwen are getting on fine?"

"We're expecting a child," said Will.

"Yes, congratulations," said Margie, somewhat on political autopilot. "And this talk that's going around—"

"About the drinking?" confirmed Will.

"Questions of the senator's sobriety have nothing at all to do with the commission of a federal crime," said La Roy.

"I have to ask these questions, Senator," said Margie Van Hough.

"I understand," said Will.

"The accident," said Hal Willoughby. "Your office said it was cold medication."

"Off the record," said Will. "And I mean, this is *off the record.* Before I regained consciousness, my father—and we all know Sully, okay? My father succeeded in having the actual blood evidence destroyed." Will appeared embarrassed. He was talking about a father whose heart-in-the-right-place actions equaled a felonious destruction of evidence. "He did it to protect me. He thought I'd fallen off the wagon."

"Wait," said Lois Freehold. "You're saying that the blood work showed that you *were* drinking?"

"The kidnappers injected me with pure ethanol. That's how they were able to—"

"Actually injected you?" interrupted Hal Willoughby. "With, you know, a needle and syringe?"

"I can vouch," said La Roy. "Found the needle myself. We left it with the Boston Bureau for testing. Should come up positive for ethanol."

"Again," said Margie. "*On the record.* You were *not* drinking. *Have* not been drinking. At all. This is an important credibility question, Senator."

Nodding that he understood, Will affirmed, "I have not had a drink in five years."

"I can vouch again," said La Roy. "I'm his sponsor. And if I didn't believe him, I woulda kneecapped him just for lyin' to me."

"That's a comfort," said the attorney general. "Back to this cult stuff. Your source information is?"

"Vance Allatore. The guy who prosecuted Theroux. A bit of a dubious character, I admit," said Will. "I've had trouble believing him myself. On the other hand, he showed me some old photographs. Mug shots. And from them I was able to identify one of the conspirators. Clem, our gardener."

"Can I butt in here a second?" asked Ralph Bedletter, the FBI profiler. "Now, Senator. If there's been a kidnapping, it's best to investigate any and *all* suspects as quickly as one can get the operation up and rolling. If I can liken it to tossing a pebble in a pond. You always want to start near the very first ripple."

"And that ripple would be Vance Allatore," confirmed Will.

"Yes," said Bedletter. "In my book, he's the most suspicious character you've described so far. You are aware of his history?"

"I am. But what if he turns out to be a resource?" asked Will. "If he's correct and he has key knowledge, I don't want to send him running back into the shadows because he took some illegal steps in bringing me this information."

"Vance Allatore running for the shadows?" said Bedletter. "Ten years ago, yeah. He might've been a smart guy. But now he's a certified head case. Then, from outta nowhere, he breaks into your condo. Leaves funny messages. Hijacks you in broad daylight so he can tell you God knows what nonsense. Forgive me, Senator. But if I were you, I'd wanna throw a net around the SOB and grill 'im till his ears bleed."

"So far, he's been accurate," said Will. "He described the cult. Their behavior. And what might happen to—"

"And guess what? It all went down just as he described!" said Bedletter, his pitch turned up three notches. "How'd he know? Hmmm. Lemme guess. Think maybe he was in on it? Think maybe ol' Vance Allatore thought it up himself? I'll lay odds right now that, *if* your wife was abducted, and *if* there's going to be a ransom demand, it's going to be for money or some political payout. And should you decide to pay, that the guy who gets the payoff is guess-the-heck-who? Vance Allatore."

"Your opinion is clear and appreciated, Mr. Bedletter," accepted Will, forgiving the insolent tone and letting his eyes drift back to Lois Freehold, before holding firm on Margie Van Hough. "Let's be frank, Margie. My office and yours haven't exactly been on solid ground lately. We can change all that by your showing me the file."

Lois Freehold piped in, sounding more patronizing than concerned. "Of course you'll see the file. And I think I speak for all of us when I pray that it provides something probative to the investigation. We just wish you'd listen to Mr. Bedletter. He knows what he's talking about."

"We're talking about *my* wife and *my* child!" barked Will.

"No disrespect, Senator," said Bedletter. "But this is *my* domain. I've got an idea how trying this must be for you."

"The hell you do!" Will's voice betrayed the cracks in his usual statesmanlike pose. He could feel the prickly heat swelling around his collar. The fear was starting to bleed out.

"Will," said Sean McGeorge over the speaker. "It's going to be hard to keep this quiet. You're already taking hits on this fax deal. Lotta media speculation. Drinking, divorce. It's the White House's recommendation that you take a strong public position."

"That can't be the safest thing for Gwen," said a concerned La Roy.

"It's a Big Team play," said McGeorge. "There's a groundswell of crappy press to beat back before we make the official announcement that you've been chosen as running mate. Of course, if Justice or the Bureau thinks we're putting Mrs. Sullivan in further danger . . ."

Margie Van Hough looked to Ralph Bedletter. It was his call.

"It's been what? Almost forty-eight hours?" surmised

Bedletter. "And so far, no ransom demand. Yeah. I'd agree with a public statement to the effect that Mrs. Sullivan has been kidnapped. Nothing more is known. The FBI is in charge and the senator is cooperating in any way he can."

Will let his crowded brain run it down. If Vance Allatore was telling the truth, there'd be no ransom demand. Theroux wanted the unborn child. That was the scam. But Bedletter was making decisions based on how Will had spun the story, having left out the most frightening and unbelievable element. That the real father of the child Gwen carried was a mass murderer. It strained at credulity.

"Okay," answered Will. "We'll prepare a statement."

"The president," said McGeorge over the speaker, "has authorized me to offer you temporary quarters in the White House. The Lincoln Bedroom is there for you if you need it."

Quarters, thought La Roy. McGeorge's military stripes were showing. Since when was the Lincoln Bedroom *quarters*? La Roy could already smell the press announcement:

White House Offers Sullivan Shoulder to Cry On.

Biting his tongue, La Roy found himself burning to ask McGeorge if they'd refurnished 1600 with military bunks.

"Thank you," answered Will. "I'll keep that in mind."

"Will!" commanded a voice over the speaker. A voice that snapped the entire office to sudden attention. It distinctly belonged to President Addison. "Don't mind me horning in here. But I was just walking by the chief of staff's office and, well, let me put it this way. Me and Mrs. Addison are sick over this whole episode. Don't think, Willy. Just do yourself a favor and come on over to my house. We'll have ourselves a late dinner and I promise you the privacy you'd surely expect at this crucial moment. That's, of course, if you don't have plans to return to Beantown and wait this out up there with your old man."

"I'm here for tonight, sir," said Will. "Tomorrow? I guess the only thing I can do is see what Justice comes up with."

"So I'll take that as a yes," said the president. "I'll see you after your press conference."

"Yes, sir," said Will.

"You're in good hands, Will," said the president.

"I appreciate the confidence, sir," said Margie Van Hough.

Good hands? thought Will. Addison was scared to death of the Slammer Sisters. Since when did they garner a lick of his confidence?

"I'll see you all later," said the president.

The speaker line went dead. Control of the meeting was returned to the attorney general. "Unsolicited advice, Senator. Make your statement and then bunker your office. Brief your staff that any queries are to be referred to either Justice or the Bureau."

"When do I see the file?" asked Will.

"If there *is* a file," reminded Lois Freehold.

"Madame Justice is about to twist your arm, Earnest," said La Roy.

"I'll forget you said that, Mr. La Roy," said the attorney general, turning back to Will and ever-so-slightly leaning over her desk. "We're stuck on one last point."

"Vance Allatore," guessed Will.

The attorney general was firm. "You want to see the file? I suggest you swear out a complaint against him."

Will tried to be unguarded with his answer. But something instinctive told him not to give up Vance Allatore. Then again, Gwen's life was at stake. She was gone. As he asked himself for an answer, the emptiness inside him echoed. After a quiet, contemplative minute, Will capitulated. "What do you want to know?"

The Capitol's east-front plaza. In the shadow of Crawford's *Statue of Freedom*.

Vanessa Curran and her three-man crew nearly steamrolled over Gary Modetti in order to get a position at the noon press conference. Her newest assignment as talent-on-loan to the local CBS affiliate had gotten her off the back of network management and back into the TV trenches.

By Modetti's count, there were sixteen camera trucks crowding the northeast front at Constitution Avenue, their masts raised, and microwave feeds hot and locked. The tape crews and print media pressed their way into position for Will Sullivan's statement.

Standing before a cluster of microphones, the young senator waited for the assembly to settle. To the rear on his right was Bill La Roy. Ralph Bedletter was on his left. "Good afternoon," Will said in a clear voice. "Contrary to popular rumor, my wife, Gwen Corbett-Sullivan, has not left me. Nor is she planning a divorce. She has been kidnapped."

The been-there, done-that press corps erupted at the announcement. Motor drives whirred. Flashguns exploded. Hands with tape recorders stretched forward, reaching for more information. And questions were shouted out in a screeching cacophony. Will held up his arms. "I will not be answering *any* questions. I am working with the FBI. And I am also looking for your help. We will make available to you a photograph and description of a man named Vance Allatore, a former Los Angeles deputy district attorney. We have reason to believe that Mr. Allatore might be in possession of some information that might prove helpful to the investigation."

As Will removed himself from the microphones and La Roy stepped in to run block, Vanessa Curran ditched her crew and ran around to the outside, her long legs bounding two steps a stride. "Will!" she shouted, trying to catch up with the fleeing senator. As if he could hear her over all the other bellowed questions blasted his way. This time, when she bumped into Gary Modetti, he gave no ground.

"Slow down, sweetie. He's not answering *any* questions and you know it."

"We're friends," she said snidely, trying to edge by.

"Like it matters."

"Excuse me," she said, pushing on.

"Hold on," said Modetti. "I *believe* you're his friend. I just don't get this kidnapping deal. Some pretty harsh return spin, don't you think?"

"I don't think it's spin at all."

"No?"

"I don't have time for you, Mr. . . ." Vanessa leaned in to read his press tags. But he had none.

"Gary Modetti," said the underground columnist. "Heard of me?"

"Hardly," dismissed Vanessa. Will was already gone, back inside the Capitol's east doors. Now she had to get back to her crew to do her live stand-up before she missed her on-air window.

"But I know *you*," said Modetti. "And I've got sources that say you could use something special. Something that gets you back in the pink with senior management."

Modetti's sources were the anonymous gossipmongers who'd e-mail him bags of loose-juice in hopes of reading it in the *Below the Beltway* section of his Webzine.

"Get out of my way. I got a live shot I don't want to miss."

"Will Sullivan was *drunk* and he was *driving*."

"How do you know?"

"I got a pen pal who knows more about Sullivan than Sullivan knows himself."

"My network won't go for deep throat sources."

"My pen pal? He gave me the name of the doctor who saw the blood test."

Vanessa's instinct flexed. "What's in it for you?"

"We'll talk," said Modetti.

She didn't have a card to hand him. "You know me? Then you know where to find me."

"Oh, I will," grinned Modetti. Standing on the highest Capitol step, he watched her hips pivot all the way back to her impatient crew. They'd already cued up the feed and quickly handed her the mike as they counted down to air. Vanessa took four seconds to primp her hair and check her makeup. By the time her camera operator gave the number one finger, she was ready and ripping through her twenty-second wraparound. Some piece of work, thought Modetti, who packed it in for the day and returned to his Bethesda bungalow to file his afternoon column. Before he switched off his computer, his e-mail in-box was blinking hello.

To: GFModetti@alamode.com
From: penpal@cyrus.net

> SUBJECT: FYI

> Dear Gary,
> I saw Sullivan's press conference live.
> Don't be fooled. It was a total sham.
> Nothing but a whitewash of Sullivan's
> Humpty-Dumpty act. Divorce in the works.
> Suspect charges of spousal abuse.

> Pen Pal

Theroux had easily downloaded the short text of Will's live press conference over an Internet newsgroup. Just reading Vance Allatore's name was enough to scorch the killer's gullet. Suddenly, he wasn't divine. He was *confined*. Like so many others, Theroux had thought Allatore had fallen into some bottomless abyss from which he'd never, ever return. Instead, he'd resurfaced, somehow uncovered part of the plot, and found a willing ear in the Mister. How much did he know? Theroux turned to his ThinkPad, signed on, and sent the note to Gary Modetti. After which, he accessed a far more secured site which required double password confirmation and a custom encryption stroke. From there he sent a missive to his dormant boys, Timothy and Jack. His precious twins.

To: TwinTowers@mobius.com
From: FatherFigure@Allentown.net

> SUBJECT: VANCE ALLATORE

> My sons,

> He is back in the game. Find him.
> Cut him in pieces. Don't forget
> to send me pictures.

> Dad

*   *   *

"Forgive him, Jesus," asked Vance Allatore, reacting to Will's televised news conference in a muttered prayer. Then he added a little addendum when, flashed on the screen, he saw a ten-year-old picture of himself—the superstar prosecutor of the eighties. "And a little courage wouldn't hurt, either." If Theroux hadn't known who'd been working Will, he would surely know now. The cult survivors would know. As would the FBI, the DOJ, and all of the news-chewing population across the nation. "Shit. He had to up and go political on me."

As at peace with himself as he'd ever been in his fifty-odd years, politicians still made Allatore's teeth grind. He'd dealt with them daily during his twenty-five years in the D.A.'s office and the politics had been thick after Theroux's calculated bloodbath.

Surviving members of the cult were still on the loose, he had explained at a news conference. Unfortunately his statement only led to a further public backlash. Who were these phantom killers and why hadn't they been arrested along with Theroux in the first place? They'd never been identified, he'd later explained. There was only scant evidence and theories. Theories, critics argued, didn't save lives. The city of Los Angeles was running scared from the invisible clan. Those involved with the case who'd survived the murder spree were thinking of moving out of town, changing their names, purchasing better home security systems, buying handguns. Mostly, they were unified in finding somebody to blame for *the blooding*. Vance Allatore fit the description. He was arrogant, tough, not exactly camera-friendly, and unrepentant in his prosecutor's zeal. It wasn't long before Vance Allatore was taking a temporary leave of absence and writing his side of the story. He could break down the rest of his life into a trilogy of pieces.

The book.

The breakdown.

The call from God.

"I'm checking out early," the former prosecutor whispered over the motel telephone. "Could you slip my bill under the door, please?"

Once again, he would have to move on. He'd leave the cash-friendly Sturbridge motel he'd been camped in, pack up the Mazda, and find some other hole in which to burrow and pray his way through the muck. His closest mortal ally had foolishly dropped a very large dime on him.

"The idiot!"

Maybe, he prayed, Will had given him up in quid pro quo exchange for the file. Hope filled him as he swept the dungeonlike motel room, packing boxes and preparing to hit the road. If the FBI snagged him, it would help to have something tangible to bargain with.

"God," he prayed, wrapping a rosary around his fist and gripping the ebony cross until his knuckles turned white. "Please, show me the way to go." Vance Allatore listened, nodded gently, and said his thank you. "Amen to that."

6

The family dining room in the residence wing of the White House was rather unremarkable, thought Will. A typical Colonial-styled room. Cabernet-colored wallpaper. Oak floors and wainscoting. Two large nineteenth-century oils faced each other from behind the twelve-seat maple table. Pork chops were served with a side of vegetable pasta. Mrs. Addison was seated across from Will. The president was to his left at the head of the table. The conversation was polite and, for the most part, political in nature. Gwen was barely mentioned.

The First Lady retired after the meal, while President Addison treated Will to a private screening in the White House theater. It was a recent Hollywood release. Will quietly suffered in his own thoughts for the duration of the benign romantic comedy. Here he was in the house he coveted most. The Mount Everest of all his political ambition. But naturally Gwen was all he could think about. What kind of conditions was she forced to endure while he sat in the lap of presidential splendor? The picture was all wrong. Somewhere along the line, he'd made an awful mistake. He didn't belong here. In the White House. He belonged in Boston, next to the phone, losing sleep alongside his father and some hardworking FBI agents.

The movie ended and Will, afraid the lights would come up and catch him with red, cried-out eyes, stood quickly and thanked his fatherly host. "I think I should get some rest."

"Of course you should," said the president. In the flicker of the movie's credits, Will could see Addison's confident smile, the same visage the older man had ridden all the way to the White House. For a brief moment, Will was reminded of the comparisons between the two of them. Everybody saw it. It's what scared most Republican organizers. Will was the obvious heir apparent.

Will thanked his host. "Good night, Mr. President."

"See ya later, Willy."

But it wasn't exactly good night. Will showered in the Lincoln Bedroom's opulent bath and dressed in a pair of shrink-wrapped navy blue pajamas reserved for overnight guests. Before he could turn out the light, there was a soft knock at the door. The president entered before he could answer. Addison was draped in a regal red robe. In one hand, he held two long-necked beers. In the other, a bottle opener.

"Thought you could use a nightcap." The president popped a cap and offered the beer to Will.

Will stiffened. "Sir. I'm an alcoholic. I don't drink anymore."

"Just checking." Addison winked, withdrawing a third bottle from his right robe pocket—a nonalcoholic Sharps beer. He handed it to Will. "It's a twist-off."

"Thanks," said Will. He found himself on guard. The ruse with the beer struck him as odd and out of the president's usual genteel character.

"I was talking to the missus. She thought you might have some trouble sleeping tonight. So I thought we'd have a chat." The president pulled up a desk chair, sat, and put his stocking feet up on the bed.

Will placed himself at the edge of the bed near the headboard, legs crossed. "What do you want to talk about?"

"I don't know. How about the next four years?"

"I'm looking forward to them," said Will.

"With Gwen?" asked the president. "Or without her?"

Shocked at the bald frankness of the question, Will found a brave face, staring down his commander in chief. "At this point, I'd rather not consider the latter."

"An indelicate question, I know," said the president. "But this job, as you might expect, requires harsh questions and even harsher actions."

"Is this a test?" asked Will.

"Back home in Jacksonville? They'd call it a gut check. I talked to my FBI director today. You know, the Slammer Sister who looks like a side of beef in hot pink."

The line was meant to make Will loosen up. Laugh. He didn't.

Addison continued. "I asked her for the straight skinny. She told me that eight out of ten abductions don't have happy endings."

"Thanks for the good news, sir."

"Good news, Will? I'd love some good news. But that's not the job. The job's about *bad* news. Every day. All day. So bugger up and get used to it."

"We're talking about my wife, sir."

"And *my* friend," said the president. "Hell, I knew Gwen before you did. She's not just special. She's a goddamn star in my book." The president guzzled at his beer.

"I don't know," said Will. "Am I missing the point?"

"No, you're not, Will. The point's very clear."

Crystal, thought Will. "You want to know, if Gwen turns up dead, whether or not I'm still on board."

"The country needs you, son."

"If Gwen were here, she'd tell you to shove the rhetoric up your ass."

The president smiled. "Yes. I believe she would."

"But you still want to know what *little Willy* thinks?"

"Willy thinks first, talks second," said the president. "It's one of the things I most admire about you."

It was just as the president described. A gut check. Will was living through a personal hell—Gwen even worse— and the leader of the free world wanted to know if his heir apparent had what it took to make the hard choices. It was a prick's move. One Will wondered if he'd respect when this was behind him.

"You know my answer," said Will. "Or you wouldn't have asked me in the first place."

"We don't need a liability on the Big Team."

"I'm not a liability," said Will.

"And you weren't drunk Wednesday night when you crashed your car?" said the president. "The truth, Will."

"Leave the other bottle," said Will. "See if it's here in the morning."

"Touché," grinned the president. "I think I'm gonna like sharing the podium with you."

"Likewise." Will forced a smile and clinked his Sharps with the president's empty bottle.

"Ah, hell," said the president, standing up. "I'll drink the other one myself. Good night. Sleep tight. Don't let the FBI bite."

"Good night, sir," said Will.

The president stood, returned the chair to the desk, then closed the door behind himself.

"Fuck you very much," said Will to himself, raising his bottle toward the door. He took a sip, placed it on the nightstand, and switched out the light. As he lay awake, eyes open and staring, he wondered if sleep would come. And if it did, what ugly nightmare would ride in behind it?

Intermittent beeping cut into Gwen's REM sleep. That's when she asked herself if the nightmare was ending.

No, was her answer.

The beeping became familiar as she surfaced into consciousness. The sound was a fetal heart monitor. She recalled the unit had been strapped across the basketball that was her abdomen. Was she still there? In that musty vault? Her eyes stared at the gray-painted water pipes which striped the arched ceiling above her. Shifting her focus to the right, she saw the dextrose-saline drip line snaking into her taped forearm. Beyond that, concrete walls stained from some kind of flooding. How old? she wondered. When had this vault taken on water? And where in God's name was it, anyway?

The restraints were looser, slack enough that she could scratch an itch or roll to her side, but not enough that she could cross her arms or legs. Her arms ached from lack of use. Her legs felt weighted and bloated. The air was thick, but cool. She sucked it in, glad to find she didn't cough. She wasn't sick. That was good. She heard Dr. Bertrand's voice in her head:

"You take care of your body and your body will take care of the baby."

"I promise," he had added. But the voice was not in her head. It was directly to her left. She jerked, her focus trailing a second or two behind. Gwen could barely make out Dr. Bertrand's gentle features, illuminated softly under the dim bare bulb. He put his hand on her forehead. "There's my girl. Now that I've got the baby's pulse, how about I get yours?"

He took Gwen's left wrist into his practiced fingers, checking her heart rate against his antique Hamilton. She stared at him, eyes unblinking with disbelief. When she tried to speak, her mouth was as dry as a vacuum.

"That's the drip makin' your mouth dry," he said. "How about some water?" He bent a cup straw toward her mouth. Gwen sucked up some water and swallowed. The first gulp stuck and ached in her throat. "Easy," he said. "Little sips."

She sipped some more, drinking easily now. He withdrew the straw. Then briefly examined the welt underneath her eye where Izzy had socked her.

I'm safe. Saved. My doctor is here to help.

"Where are we?" whispered Gwen.

"Never mind where," he said gently. "You and the baby are safe. And that's what matters."

Safe, yes. We're safe.

"Is my husband—"

"Can you hear the heartbeat?" interrupted the doctor. Gwen nodded. "Good, good."

She went to rub her eyes, but the restraints scratched. Why was she still in restraints? For her own protection?

Was Dr. Bertrand afraid she'd do something to hurt her baby?

"Can you take these off?" asked Gwen.

"I'm afraid not," said the doctor.

Reality arrived with a hammering pain behind her eyes. "No. Not you," she said. "Not you. You didn't do this to me."

The old man's eyes tilted with a consciousness of guilt. "I did what I did," he said. "I'm not proud of it. But in about ten weeks, it'll all be over. Your life will return to what it was and we'll be done with all this."

"With what?" asked Gwen, exasperated after only a few short sentences.

"Don't overwork yourself," said Dr. Bertrand. "If you hurt yourself, you'll hurt the baby."

"My baby?"

"Your baby, yes."

"Are you the father?" she asked. Gwen had read news accounts about egomaniacal fertility specialists who'd planted their own seed inside their patients. They'd been arrested, tried, and tossed in jail. Forever, she'd hoped.

"No. I'm not the father. I'm only a small pixel in a very large picture. A fragment of a man whose sole purpose is to take care of you. You must trust me to do this one task."

Trust? With her left hand, Gwen reached over and started tearing at his sleeve. He pulled away and stood up. "I want to see them!" she demanded.

"See what?"

"The track marks!"

The old doctor's eyes closed. She knew! It was as if all the air inside him bled out in a single sigh.

"It's true, isn't it?"

Dr. Bertrand relented, rolling up a sleeve. "I don't shoot it into my arms, see?"

"Where then?" she asked.

"Does it matter?"

"That you shoot drugs?" she asked. "When you say you're supposed to take care of me?"

"As addicts go, I'm a very old soul," said Dr. Bertrand.

"But at this point in my life, it's only to keep me alive. As long as I'm supplied, it won't affect my practice."

"And *they* supply you?" Gwen shook her head. She was too wiped out to play games. This was too hard. "You know," she said. "Them. Izzy. Starr. The landscape man."

"Yes. They're helping."

Gwen started to sob uncontrollably. The nightmare was worsening. The small, arched vault, the fetal heartbeat. Only now did she notice that she was in an electric hospital bed. In the far corner was what looked like an ultrasound monitor. The far shelves were stacked with white boxes stenciled with red crosses and blue words she couldn't distinguish without her contacts. Dr. Bertrand was practicing, all right. In the vault. The one with the steel door.

"It's okay," he said. "We're both here for the duration. And then, as I promised, it will be over."

"I want to die," she found herself saying.

"No," he said. "You don't want to die. Here. Feel." He guided both her hands to her stomach. "There's life in you. It's against your instinct to end it. It's against *my* instinct to let you. That's why I'm here. To make sure life survives."

"Whose life?" she pleaded. "My life or the baby's?"

"Both," he said softly and with assurance. "They've promised me that you aren't to be harmed. They only want the child."

Clunk-screep! The harsh sound of the bolts twisting from their grommets startled them both. The door opened. Izzy entered, a Polaroid camera in hand. She didn't mince her words. "Did you ask her?"

"We're having a talk," Dr. Bertrand answered defensively.

"You were supposed to *ask* her," said Izzy.

Dr. Bertrand's chest heaved. Then he obediently swiveled back to Gwen and asked, "If I remove the IV, will you eat?"

Gwen's eyes never wavered from Izzy's. She felt such contempt at the mere sight of the evil bitch. Already, though, Gwen could see the transition. Izzy had quit the pigment-altering medication. Her skin was lighter. And she had quickly begun to rid herself of the thirty extra pounds required of her St. Maarten character.

"He asked you a question," said Izzy, unwavering and remorseless in her returned stare. When Gwen didn't answer, Izzy answered for her. "Fine. Stick with the needle. I found it's always been handy for keeping the extra pounds off."

"Gwen. You really should eat if you can," the doctor coaxed.

So angry she could bite her tongue, Gwen turned away from both of them. The baby was healthy. That much she could tell. The heartbeat sounded strong and, when it kicked, it felt stronger with each and every new blow. Screw them, she said to herself. She couldn't imagine eating a damn thing Izzy had concocted.

"Okay, Dr. B.?" said Izzy. "We have our answer."

"I think I should stay a little longer." Given more time, Dr. Bertrand thought he could talk Gwen into eating.

"You may have treated her," said Izzy. "But I *lived* with her. If she wants to eat, I promise—she'll eat."

"I'd like to watch—"

"That's what the video's for," said Izzy, giving a nod up to the high corner.

That's what it was, thought Gwen. The tiny red light she'd seen above the ventilation filter. A videocamera. They were still watching her. She was never out of their sight.

"I gotta pee," said Gwen.

Izzy just rolled her eyes. "That's bullshit."

"I said I gotta pee!"

"And I say it's BULLSHIT!" groused Izzy. "You wanna tell her, Doc?"

Dr. Bertrand took his usual time. He liked things to go along easy. Zero conflict. Life on a white, puffy heroin cloud. And Izzy had rubbed him wrong since day one.

"You've been on the dextrose solution for three days," said Dr. Bertrand. "Your bladder's empty. You might feel some pressure from the baby—"

"She doesn't have to pee," said Izzy, stepping around the bed and, before Gwen could even think to turn away, flashing the Polaroid. Zip, zip, zip. Three quick close-ups of Gwen's black-and-blue face.

"Now let's eat before Clem finishes the whole meal," said Izzy.

Another deep, defeated sigh came from Dr. Bertrand. He seemed ten years older than the last time Gwen had seen him. Was it the heroin? Or stress or disease? He slumped toward the door.

"Wait," said Gwen.

Dr. Bertrand stopped. His eyes casting hopefully upon the patient.

"I'll eat."

"That's wonderful," said Dr. Bertrand, hands clapping together in a genuine gesture.

"You are too stupid for words," said Izzy. "She just figured that if she eats, she gets to pee. If she gets to pee, she gets to leave the room. If she gets to leave the room, she *thinks* she might figure out how to get out of here."

Gwen's eyes were locked again on Izzy. Dr. Bertrand broke in. "Eating is good. Eating is good for the baby. Better than the IV. We agreed, yes?"

"Oh, sure," said Izzy. "Eating's fine. And then she can drink and she can pee and get a good look around the place. That way she'll see there's nowhere to go. No way out. No day, no night. Just the family. Us. That's all she needs and that's all she's got. Right, Gwenny?"

"Gwen," corrected the mother-to-be. It was a programmed response to an old grade-school tease. She reissued her request to Dr. Bertrand. "I'm hungry. I want to eat."

"Five minutes," said Izzy. "I'll send Starr back with something *yummy.*"

Dr. Bertrand gave Gwen a nod and a hopeful smile before leaving with Izzy. The door swung back closed with the bolts uniformly locking into place. Screech-clunk! Once again, it was just Gwen, the baby, and a mystery slowly unraveling in her mind.

HOW IS MY FLOWER?
    safe and sound.

EATING?
>yes.
AND THE BABY IS STRONG?
>yes.
I WOULD LIKE VERY MUCH TO SEE HER.
>we have video. would you like to download
>it from the site?
YES. AND SOON, SHE AND I WILL TALK.
>i think she would like that.
DO YOU REALLY THINK?
>what woman wouldn't want to chat with
>the father of her child?
SHE HAS A STRONG WILL, YES?
>yes. but not near as strong as yours.

And then, uncharacteristically, Izzy keyed:

>or mine, for that matter.
YOUR WILL IS STRONGER THAN HERS?
>i think so.
SINCE WHEN IS IT YOUR PLACE TO THINK?
>i was making an observation.

The response box on Izzy's computer screen remained blank for a full sixty seconds. Long enough for her to break out in a genuine flop sweat, wondering if she'd gone too far with her beloved Dean.

YOU ARE JEALOUS.
>i am.
YOU WISH I WOULD'VE PLANTED MY SEED
IN YOU INSTEAD OF HER?
>i love you more than life itself.
I KNOW. BUT YOU KNOW THE REASON.
>i do.
IN MY EYES, YOU ARE A DAUGHTER.
>it wouldn't be incest. it would be . . . perfect.
IT HAS ALREADY BEEN DONE!
>then why must i suffer this indignity?

YOURS IS NOT TO ASK WHY, BUT TO DO.
    i too am strong!
THE TIME WILL COME FOR YOU TO SHOW ME
YOUR STRENGTH.
    when?
SOON.
    but when?

Theroux didn't care to give Izzy an answer. He simply waited at the other end of the distant link for her to download the video and Polaroids of Gwen. When the connection was eventually terminated by the master, Izzy slammed the laptop lid and cut a rare tear. He'd picked Gwen over her. Why? Even after she'd personally swallowed the balloon carrying his seed, keeping it warm inside her until she could deliver it to Sheila. But even that wasn't enough for him. *She* wasn't enough for him, had never been enough and would never be. It had been eating at her for years. Yet the conflict within her wasn't raging—it was more like a creeping cancer. She loved him, needed him, and owed her second life to him. Yet another seed was growing within her. The one of human discontent. A fix would help her. A brief respite lifted from Dr. Bertrand's personal stash. A shot in the arm and the discontent would be temporarily extinguished. She would once again belong to Dean, body and soul.

7

"*The file*," said Steve Salinas, sliding the folder across the breakfast bar. LBJ had rescued Will from the White House at eight in the morning, and delivered him to Steve Salinas's bachelor-simple Garfield Park apartment—one bedroom, leather sofa, glass tables, and some seventies swap-meet kitsch.

"You looked at it?"

"I'm afraid so," deadpanned Salinas. "I don't think it's what you expected."

"What do you mean?"

"Hell," said Salinas. "It's not what *I* expected."

Will sat on a stool, put on his glasses, and swiveled the folder right side up. He took a deep breath, a sip of coffee, and turned to the first page. Before him were faxed file documents from the FBI. But they had absolutely nothing to do with the Theroux cult. Will quickly leafed through the papers, and with each turn of the page, a greater shock registered.

"This is *my* file!" said Will.

"No shit," said Salinas. "I make the call, right? Last

night. After your press conference. And over the fax comes this."

Will fanned through the file. Each page a more startling shock than the last. "Christ, they've got phone taps."

"I think it's a fuckup."

"Fuckup?" asked Will incredulously. "The FBI doesn't fuck up and make a file on somebody."

"I didn't mean it that way," said Salinas. "I think when I asked for the file for Will Sullivan, some mole over in Documents faxed over the Will Sullivan file. Either that or you've got a lone fan inside 935 Pennsylvania."

Will was scanning the first couple of pages. "I'm being investigated for campaign finance fraud? Illegal gift donations in the form of Civil War memorabilia?" He shot a scowl at his former roommate.

"When the E.R.T. boys turned over your condo, that must've been what they were looking for."

Will pressed on through the file until he landed on exact transcripts of his off-the-record meeting with Kenneth G. Durrant. The IRS director had been wearing a wire. The FBI had recorded the conversation.

"Yeah, I read that part, too," said Salinas. "Looks like they're trying to lure you into an obstruction of justice charge."

"For Christ's sake," said Will. "He was asking for my help!"

"C'mon, Will. You had to see this coming."

"Entrapment?"

"You stuck it hard and high to Justice during the FDA hearings," said Salinas. "They were bound to try and stick you back."

"It's bullshit!" said Will, shoving the file back over to Salinas. "They've got me linked to women in there I haven't slept with since Reagan was in office."

"Here's the kicker." Salinas cleared his throat, turned the file back around, then opened it to the last couple of pages. "In the Bureau's eyes, you haven't *stopped* drinking."

Jesus. Will snatched the file back. There it all was. Black-and-white pictures, entries from the Shrewsbury cops' comments to the FBI stakeout team, even Will's day-old, *off-the-record* admission that Sully had had the hospital blood-alcohol tests destroyed.

"The Ladies Justice are after your skinny ass."

"I can't believe it," said Will. "I asked for their help and they gave me their oath."

"Wasn't it La Roy who once said, 'There's no penalty for perjury if you're in government service'?"

"I can't deal with this right now."

"As your oldest friend in this stinkin' town," said Salinas, "I recommend you lawyer yourself up quick and good."

"The hell I will!" spat Will. "That's tantamount to saying I'm guilty as charged."

"You got a choice in the matter?"

"Yeah," said Will. "Like get out of Dodge and find my wife!"

"And you expect the FBI to help you?"

Will found himself stuck. Nowhere to go. He'd trusted the FBI to deliver him a file. The Theroux file. And now this?

"If there was a mistake . . . Just do me a favor, will ya? Find out where the file came from. If I have more fans inside the Bureau—"

"Whoa there, roomie. You're lookin' at a man who wants to keep his job," said Salinas. "If my own Bureau chief finds out I got faxed the wrong file, I'll be delivering subpoenas in Alaska by sundown." Salinas shut the file and held it out to Will. "If you don't take this with you, it goes through Stevie's shredder."

Picking up the file, Will couldn't help but say it. "With friends like you—"

"Sorry, man. But I got child support payments, you know?"

Will left without another damn word. He wanted out of Washington. He directed LBJ to drive him to Dulles. They'd barely made it onto the expressway when La Roy caught Will on the cell phone.

"Just get your ass back here," said La Roy. "And make sure to keep your head down."

* * *

On Saturday morning, the Gwen Sullivan kidnapping story was on the front page of nearly every major newspaper in North America.

By eleven A.M., a Boston attorney by the name of Sherman Stratford called an impromptu press conference at his stately downtown office. Crowded with as many microphones and hand-held tape recorders as he could cajole, the sixty-two-year-old, silver-haired divorce lawyer read aloud from a prepared statement.

"Under the proviso afforded me by the Massachusetts State Bar, I have been engaged by Mrs. Gwen Corbett-Sullivan in her pending divorce from Senator William Sullivan. On her behalf, I am filing divorce papers based on the grounds of estrangement, alcoholism, and spousal abuse. I'll take your questions."

"Are you saying Mrs. Sullivan has not *been kidnapped?"*

"I'm saying that this is her response to her husband's public allegation that she was kidnapped."

"Where is Mrs. Sullivan?"

"Mrs. Sullivan is obviously in hiding," said Stratford.

"From her husband?"

"Senator Sullivan is a powerful man with powerful friends. And as you might guess, since she's charged spousal abuse in her divorce complaint . . ."

"Does Mrs. Sullivan say specifically if the senator beat her?"

"She was not specific about aspects of her abuse," said Stratford. "Next question."

"Do you have evidence of abuse?"

"Forthcoming," said Stratford. "Next?"

"Have you spoken directly with her?"

"I have, yes," said Stratford.

"How was it that Gwen Sullivan came to choose you as her attorney?"

For that answer, Sherman Stratford preened. "I've known Gwen Sullivan for quite some time. That, and I am the most experienced divorce attorney in Boston. Who else would she choose?"

There were more questions followed by more pat answers that said so little, but implied so much. Sherman Stratford managed to delicately sidestep the fact that even though he'd spoken to a woman *claiming* to be Gwen Sullivan—a calm, but indignant lady who was both articulate and convincing in her complaint—he'd never actually met Gwen Sullivan other than exchanging a perfunctory handshake at a Democratic charity fund-raiser some six years earlier. A fifty-thousand-dollar retainer wired directly to his business account from an untraceable source was all he'd required to close the transaction. If Gwen Sullivan was happily ensconced in some private retreat, who was Sherman Stratford to demand anything more than a faxed signature on a faxed contract? Fake or not. With that and fifty grand, he was glad to be Gwen Sullivan's gun for hire and de facto media mouthpiece.

News of the impending divorce attracted lightning rod attention throughout Washington, D.C. Every lunch table in the city was abuzz with the sudden turn of Senator Sullivan's fate. That morning and the prior evening, he'd had the nation's sympathy in his back pocket. And the deepest concern of those working in the seat of government. Both parties, both houses, friend and foe had sent their good wishes to Will's Senate office. Politically speaking, the White House couldn't have purchased better PR for its vice-president-in-waiting.

The Gwen Sullivan kidnapping was, for that brief window in time, a unifying event. But less than twenty-four hours later, it looked as if the story was shaping up to be the wedge which could split Will Sullivan from his Washington career. The Sherman Stratford news conference made instant air as a *CNN breaking news event*. The electronic virus instantly spiderwebbed from Boston to the West Coast, hitting every satellite dish in between.

Then came the ambush. LBJ skillfully maneuvered Will's Town Car through the camera teams gathered at the Russell Building's underground entry. Flashguns blasted in attempts to penetrate the limo's tinted windows. Field producers and cameramen foolishly pelted questions at the moving car in hopes of some usable sound to match their pictures.

Safely parked in the underground garage, Will grabbed his briefcase and headed for the private Senate elevator. The operator, a black, thirty-year Beltway veteran named Miles, gave Will the same old smile he reserved for all senators on the right side of civil rights. "Afternoon, Senator."

"Afternoon, Miles," said Will, just as he had every day since he'd been in office. The doors closed. The elevator car started its upward climb, ringing in on the second floor. And without hesitation, in strutted Vanessa Curran, flaunting her sharp new Thierry Mugler suit, a large Coach satchel slung over her shoulder.

"Ma'am," said Miles. "This elevator is for Senate members only."

"Will?" said Vanessa, as if she expected him to reprimand the operator and give him the okay.

"Members only, Vanessa," said Will.

"I've just got one question," she said.

"Ma'am," said Miles. "Don't make me get security."

"Step off, Vanessa," said Will.

"I'll step off when you tell me you didn't do it," she said.

"I didn't do what?" said Will.

"You didn't get drunk and beat your wife."

"I won't dignify you with so much as an answer."

"So you did it," pressed Vanessa. "You beat her."

"I did no such thing!" said Will.

Miles was on the phone to security in an instant.

"Is that on the record?" asked Vanessa.

"On the record? Off the record? What the hell does it matter?" hissed Will. "I categorically deny that I have ever so much as laid a hand on Gwen. We are husband and wife. We are in love. And we are expecting a child!"

"So you're standing by the kidnapping story?"

"It's not a goddamn story!"

"Ma'am?" said the operator. "I've got security on the phone. They want you to stay put until—"

"No need," she said, stepping out of the elevator. "I've got what I came for."

"There's a protocol, Vanessa!" said Will.

"All bets are off. And if I find out you're lying, I swear to God . . ."

Will never heard the rest of it. The operator had thrown the lever and closed the door. "How about we make the rest of the trip a single, sir?"

"Thank you, Miles," said Will.

"They're all the same, sir."

"Women?" asked Will. "Or reporters?"

"A woman? A reporter? Apart, they're usually just fine an' dandy. Human beings. Likes you and me. But put the two of 'em together and, I tell ya, they're nothin' but capital *P* for Problem."

Will forced a smile. Miles had been entertaining the membership for years with his homespun wisdom. And when he had an opinion, he wasn't at all afraid to share it.

Capital P *for Problem.*

But Will hadn't the faintest idea *how much* of a Problem. He'd just been royally *had* by Vanessa Curran. From her Coach bag she'd carefully aimed prime-time TV's newest ratings grabber. An electronic best friend to ambush journalism. The camera was formally named an Ink-Mini. But in the trade, it was better known as a lipstick camera, aptly named for its size and shape. It was easily attached to the input port of any small, Hi-8 video deck, recording dynamite sound and a wide-angle color image that was fast becoming broadcast bullion. Hidden cameras were everywhere on the news, sparking a new style of "gotcha" journalism.

I gotcha, Willy, thought Vanessa.

And with that ten-second piece of video, she was about to get herself back in the good ol' graces of CBS senior management. Praise be to technology.

Bunkered in his Senate office with the phones turned over to the voice-mail system, Will addressed his entire staff. All of them. They'd bunched into his office. The room was stuffed, thirty strong with a mixture of experience and youthful eagerness. Legislative analysts, correspondents, speechwriters, and young spin doctors. Myriam was wedged near the door. La Roy was in his usual position. On the sofa, cowboy boots aloft, cup of coffee in hand. And Allison was front and center, seated on the rug, legs crossed, elbows on her knees, with her chin cradled between her hands.

"I'm sure you've heard it all by now," said Will, coat off, sleeves rolled up, and leaning on the edge of his desk. "The news reports, the hearsay . . . the gossip. But I thought before I asked you to pitch in and help, that you should hear the truth from me. So here it is."

Will tried to make eye contact with each and every one of his staff. He wanted them to know what he was about to say was the real deal. "One. My wife has been kidnapped. Anyone or any report that says otherwise is simply false.

"Two. I did not fall off the wagon. I am sober and have been for five years.

"Three. I am not getting a divorce from my wife, nor has she filed for one. This is probably nothing more than some kind of political opportunism which I expect this office to be at the forefront of rooting out.

"Finally. I did not—nor have I ever—beaten my wife, struck her, hit her, or touched her in any way that was unkind." And then Will gave his speech a punctuation point. "Not even when I was a fall-down drunk. Am I clear on this point?"

In return, Will received a lot of nodding heads and a smattering of supportive applause. He knew, amongst the team, there would be nonbelievers. Shameless Capitol staffers who would already be covering their collective asses and sniffing around for new jobs.

"Now," finished Will, his voice breaking and his eyes welling with tears, "I know we have pressing legislation. I know we have duties to the country and the state of Massachusetts. But right now, I want to know, who amongst you is going to help me find my wife?"

For the briefest moment, all the sound was sucked from the room. Then Allison's hand stretched for the ceiling. Her body followed.

"I will," she said. "I'll help you."

"You bet she will," said La Roy, on his feet. "We all will, am I right?"

The room suddenly filled with raised hearts and helping hands. The staff closed around Will, offering hugs and pledges of love and unconditional support. Will was so moved, he could barely speak out a word of thanks. He left the marching orders to La Roy. Eventually, the chief of staff hustled the whole crew through the door and barked out his commands, leaving Will alone with Myriam.

When it looked as if Will had composed himself, Myriam stepped forward. "Is there anything you need, Senator?"

"Has President Addison returned my call?"

"No, sir."

"Anybody from the White House?"

"No, sir."

That was the hardest stab. The swiftness of President Addison's silence spoke volumes.

Will forged through the list. "The attorney general?"

"No, sir."

"The FBI?"

"Not yet, sir."

The wind momentarily emptied from Will's sails. He slumped in his chair and tried to regroup. "Call them all again. And if they don't call back in ten minutes, call them all again."

"Yes, sir," said Myriam.

"And call my father. Tell him I'll be coming home tonight."

From his Bethesda bungalow, Gary Modetti watched the evening news. CBS was so thrilled with Vanessa's sneaky report, they couldn't help but share it with the rest of the electronic world. ABC had it for *World News Tonight,* giving credit to CBS. NBC had it. The same deal. CNN. CNBC. MSNBC. *Rivera Live. Larry King. Buddy Prince.* They were all doing the same twisted dance of the damned. Will was damned if he did. Damned if he didn't.

Did he hit his wife? Or didn't he hit his wife? Were they divorcing or not divorcing? Was she kidnapped? Was she not kidnapped?

Modetti was privately grinding that *he'd* started the snowball from hell rolling downhill, only to be left out of the fun once it had reached a critical momentum.

That, and Vanessa Curran had never returned his call.

Now she'd captured the only actual video of Will Sullivan denying the spousal abuse charge. It was airing everywhere and she was getting far more credit than she could ever deserve.

The alarm on Modetti's office computer bleeped, alerting him to incoming e-mail. But he held off on reading it until he'd seen how Larry King weighed in on the subject. At five past midnight, he dragged himself over to his computer and retrieved his e-mail.

To: GFModetti@alamode.com
From: penpal@cyrus.net

SUBJECT: SAVE THE ICING FOR LAST

Dear Gary,

Thought this might make your career.
Distribute it, sell it, copyright it,
take credit for it. But beware.
Others would <u>kill</u> to be in your position.

Pen Pal

P.S. Do you believe in God? You will,
once you open the jpg.file.

Sure enough, at the bottom of the e-mail was a hypertext link to an attached jpg.file. A graphic image for Modetti to download to his hard drive. Modetti clicked on the icon, waited while the screen momentarily blanked, then watched in awe as a pixilated image slowly formed. What he saw shook the reporter to his fluttering heart. Unfolding on his computer screen was a high-resolution picture taken of

Gwen Corbett-Sullivan. The wife of Senator Will Sullivan. In the photograph, sure as shit, she was black and blue from an awful beating. A huge welt bloomed under her left eye.

The son of a bitch was lying!

Modetti's heart skipped a very happy beat.

The son of a bitch Sullivan was lying and I'm the one who's got him!

Pulling up his home page, Gary Modetti started a new *Below the Beltway* column right on the spot, erasing the next day's scourge and replacing it with words to match the brutal photograph he'd already pasted.

Will Sullivan's career was about to crash and burn in a deadly pyre. And Gary Modetti was going to grab as much credit for it as humanly possible.

8

The original Polaroid had been anonymously FedEx'd to Sherman Stratford, who'd corroborated to the pouncing media that Gary Modetti's photo-scan and accompanying story were authentic *and* authorized. Within days, the photo would complement stories on practically every news program: morning shows, noon news, evening reports, and 11 P.M half-hours. In nearly every newspaper: national, tabloid, local, and even some global. And despite further denials from the Sullivan camp, more lousy headlines began piling up:

Page one. The *Washington Post*:

SULLIVAN DENIES WIFE'S ABUSE CHARGE
Is the Former Alcoholic Senator
Caught Between a Photo and a Hard Drink?

Page three. The *New York Times*:

SULLIVAN INSISTS ABUSE PICTURE IS FAKE
Wife's Attorney Offers Polaroid for Authentication

Page one. The *New York Daily News:*

DEMOCRAT'S WIFE:
MISSING OR DISSING?
Party It Girl Maintains
No-Comment Status Through Attorney

Op-Ed page. The *Chicago Tribune:*

MASSACHUSETTS SENATOR IN ABUSE SCANDAL
Sullivan May Not Be a Kennedy,
But Does He Live and Drink Like One?

Page one. The *Los Angeles Times:*

ALCOHOL AND ABUSE
Experts Ponder If Sullivan Wife-Beating Scandal
Just the Tip of a Washington Iceberg?

Page one. The *New York Post:*

"I WANT
MY WIFE
BACK!"
Sullivan Maintains
Kidnapping Yarn

The harshest of weeks ended with both *Time* and *News-week* using that compelling-as-hell Polaroid as competing cover art for generic coverage on spousal abuse. Each carried sidebar articles on the Sullivan abuse scandal, but with so little actual fact to go on, both publications thought it savvy peddling to use the cover photo, but prudent to go soft on the topic. In front of willing TV cameras, La Roy leaped to the fore and railed at *Time* and *Newsweek* for putting the unauthenticated photo on their covers, and littering news-stands across the nation with the indicting picture.

"This kind of crap is the apex of irresponsibility!" La Roy repeated on *Larry King, Washington Week in Review, Nightline, Rivera Live, Cochran and Company,* and *Buddy*

Prince. "Especially when such a photo is equally consistent with a kidnapping scenario!

"I remind you," La Roy would go on to say, "that we're still working with the FBI. Now, I ask America. If these abuse charges weren't specious and utterly suspect, don't you think the FBI would turn its high beams off the kidnapping and onto Will Sullivan?"

Then, just when it seemed things couldn't get any worse, the *Washington Post* delivered a slam-dunk headline. Page one, just below the fold:

<u>FBI INVESTIGATING SULLIVAN</u>
Justice Department Source Confirms Suspicions
that Senator Filed False Kidnapping Charges
as Part of Drunk Driving Cover-Up

And on page three, a small but devastating nail in Will Sullivan's coffin:

<u>NO TICKET TO RIDE FOR SULLIVAN</u>
White House Officially Says Senator is Off
Vice Presidential Candidate List

The newspaper that accompanied breakfast was neatly creased into quarters and used as a small tray under a plate of steaming buttermilk pancakes and two strips of bacon. The meal itself, which usually included a fruit, eight ounces of mineral water, and a handful of Dr. Bertrand's prescribed prenatal vitamins plus one capsule of folic acid, was always delivered by Starr. She'd inwardly giggle about how she'd wave the calorie-stacked meal right under Izzy's starving nose.

At a prompt eight in the morning, the vault door would clank and squeak, and in would come Gwen's pregnant counterpart. All smiles and rosy cheeks. After breakfast, Gwen would get her first bathroom break, and then be returned to her bed. The restraints were loosened to the degree where she could operate the electric gears. She could make the bed sit up and she could lie down and stretch. But she could never leave the confines of the mattress unless accompanied by Starr or Izzy.

The newspaper was Dean's inspiration. It was against Izzy's better judgment to include the *USA Today* in the morning routine. But Dean had insisted. All the comforts within reason, he'd ordered. His design was that he didn't care for the mother of his child going batty with some sort of confinement sickness. There'd been plenty of studies done, some of which Theroux had read and catalogued. Captives required light, dark, and a sense of time and place. As much as place wasn't an option, the *USA Today* was Theroux's idea of a mild tonic. For one, it came in Monday-through-Friday installments. And since it was a national publication, it would fail to give Gwen any hint as to her whereabouts.

That, and she could read about the travails of her priceless husband, "Swill" Sullivan.

It was a risk. Yes, reading about Will's tribulations could cause the mother-to-be undue stress. But Theroux was insistent. Gwen was emotionally stalwart. She would at least be relieved that her husband was alive. She might even take a rooting interest in Will's fight against the avalanche of bad press. Strong emotions befitting a stronger woman.

Every morning Gwen would eat her breakfast while reading the paper. She would pass over any news that didn't pertain to her husband, her abduction, or the alleged divorce without a second glance. But after a week, the paper proved a respite after repeating nights of crummy sleep and horrific nightmares.

Gwen would begin each meal at page one in her *USA Today,* slowly devouring every column inch until the paper had been totally consumed. When articles concerning Will popped up, she'd read them twice, sometimes three times. Happy that he was alive, desperately hoping that they soon might be united, and relieved at Will's intractable stance that she was not filing for divorce. That she'd been forcibly kidnapped.

Since the *USA Today* occupied barely an hour of her morning, Gwen had bravely asked for a TV. After discussions with Theroux, her captors complied, with Clem drilling a hole in the twelve-inch concrete and running a coaxial cable into the room. A twelve-inch TV was stacked on top of orange plastic milk crates. Gwen was secretly hoping to tune in some local news or commercials that would give away her location. Instead, the set was permanently tuned at channel 3 with but one signal piped in through an eighteen-inch satellite dish.

T.V. Land.

No news. No local commercials. Just a morning full of endless reruns of *Happy Days, I Love Lucy, Gilligan's Island,* and *Father Knows Best.* At noon, Starr delivered lunch and further reading materials. Usually a protein-rich sandwich, milk, fresh-baked cookies, and maybe a fashion magazine. At three in the afternoon, Dr. Bertrand would visit, give a listen to both Gwen's and the baby's heartbeats, then switch off the TV and urge the patient to nap. The lights would dim and Gwen would shut her eyes and listen to the faint sound of a gasoline-powered generator. It was her first real clue to the remoteness of the locale. The generator must be for electricity and that forced, dry air she'd been breathing for a week now. Eyes closed, she played her little game. She tried to remember what other facts and details she'd gleaned.

The flooding. The curved, corrugated walls of her steel, half-cylinder room bore three feet of rust near the concrete slab floor. It informed her that the room had been flooded at least once. Maybe more.

The stamp in the concrete. From her vantage, she couldn't quite make out what had been carved in the far corner. A date, maybe. It was partially covered by the do-it-yourself shelves bearing the emergency medical supplies: 8/18/19??

Then there were the serial numbers scratched into both the bed frame and ultrasound unit. Hand-engraved, bearing the respective numbers SMS433 and SMS1558.

Finally, the milk crates. Each was neon-orange and neatly stenciled—SUNNYSIDE DAIRY—but with no city or other identifying marks.

Gwen would repeat her recollections over and over until they were burned in her memory. Eventually her body surrendered to sleep. Starr would wake her for a snack—usually a cereal bar—and some mother-to-be talk.

But now it was Izzy waking her.

"Wake up. He wants to talk with you."

Her eyes fluttering open, Gwen couldn't help asking, "What time is it?"

"Time to meet the father of your child." Izzy was standing at the foot of Gwen's hospital bed, her laptop under her arm. Clem was behind her, snaking a telephone connector through the hole he'd drilled for the TV cable. Next, he attached an RCA connector to a small Sony HandyCam and handed the other connector to Izzy.

Gwen instinctively recoiled as Izzy flipped open the laptop at the foot of the bed and plugged in the telephone line and RCA plug. "It goes like this. I act as interpreter," said Izzy. "You talk, I type. He types, I talk. Get it?"

"What's with that?" said Gwen, gesturing to the camera Clem was holding.

"He not only wants to talk. But he wants to *see* you, as well."

A creeping chill began at Gwen's toes. She tingled all over as she drew her knees up under her belly and took a deep, cleansing breath. Agreement, she'd discovered, was the path of least resistance. No matter how foul the request, Gwen would simply give the okay as if everything was fine and dandy.

```
IS SHE THERE?
     yes, she is. can you see her?
YES. THERE SHE IS. I WILL ADDRESS HER NOW.
     okay.
```

Izzy looked at Gwen, but spoke for Theroux. "GOOD AFTERNOON, GWEN. YOU LOOK SO BEAUTIFUL TODAY."

"Good afternoon," said Gwen, her voice a bit shaky and not daring to look directly into the camera.

"I'D LIKE VERY MUCH FOR YOU TO LOOK AT ME."

"I'm sorry. I don't like cameras."

"I AGREE. THEY TAKE SOME GETTING USED TO. PLEASE. I'D LIKE TO SEE YOUR EYES."

Clem zoomed to a close-up of Gwen as she braved the lens, finally looking dead on.

"THERE. YOU ARE AS BEAUTIFUL AS . . . WELL, LET'S JUST SAY YOU'RE AS BEAUTIFUL AS THE FIRST DAY I SAW YOU."

Gwen swallowed. Her mouth wouldn't stop watering. She wanted to vomit. "Thank you," she said.

"I'M SURE THERE ARE SO MANY THINGS INSIDE YOUR HEAD THAT YOU'D LIKE TO ASK ME. SO PLEASE. FEEL FREE. THIS IS <u>OUR</u> TIME TOGETHER."

Gathering her wits, Gwen began with the most simple of questions. "Who are you?"

"I'M THE FATHER OF YOUR CHILD."

"And how do I know this?"

"YOU KNOW IT AS WELL AS YOU KNOW YOURSELF. SEARCH YOUR TRUE SELF. IT WILL TELL YOU THAT IT IS MY SEED WHICH GROWS INSIDE YOU."

"But whose seed?" said Gwen, the anger turning her voice to acid. "Who are *you*?"

"IZZY CALLS ME DEAN. OTHERS CALL ME WES. WHAT WOULD YOU LIKE TO CALL ME?"

"Asshole!"

"You want me to write that?" asked Izzy. But before Gwen could even give an answer, Theroux had already read her lips and written:

"DID YOU CALL ME AN ASSHOLE?"

Izzy laughed. Dean was as sharp as ever.

"I called him 'asshole,' " confirmed Gwen.

"YOU HAVE CAUSE TO THINK AS YOU DO. AFTER ALL, I'VE IMPREGNATED YOU WITHOUT YOUR PERMISSION, KIDNAPPED YOU WITHOUT SO MUCH AS A WARNING, AND SO ON, AND SO ON."

"Like I said . . ." Gwen continued.

"REALLY, NOW. I DON'T EXPECT YOU TO LOVE ME. I GET PLENTY OF LOVE FROM MY FAMILY. IZZY, STARR, THE REST. LIKE YOUR HUSBAND, I HAVE FANS. I AM TREATED AS IF I'M SPECIAL. IT'S WITH THAT KIND OF LOVE THAT I EXPECT YOU TO TREAT OUR CHILD."

"Right now, I want it to die."

"NO YOU DON'T, GWEN."

"If I could kill it, I would."

"THAT'S NOT TRUE, GWEN. WE BOTH KNOW THAT GOES AGAINST ALL THAT YOU ARE. ALL THAT YOU BELIEVE. YOU WANTED TO BE PREGNANT. YOUR HUSBAND PROVED UNSUCCESSFUL. SO I STEPPED IN AND HELPED A LITTLE—"

"A little? And I suppose I should thank you?"

"I'M NOT ASKING YOU TO THANK ME. I'M ASKING YOU TO APPRECIATE THE CIRCUMSTANCE."

"I don't understand the circumstance." Gwen was beginning to fold up, sobbing between breaths.

"IT'S SIMPLE. YOU WANTED A CHILD. I WANTED TO FATHER A CHILD. I PICKED YOU AS THE MOTHER. SOON, WE WILL BOTH HAVE WHAT WE WANT."

"But why *me*?" shrieked Gwen.

"WHY NOT YOU? WHY NOT IZZY? OR STARR?"

Izzy's jaw clenched. She hated reading it aloud. It was as if Dean didn't care if she was in the room.

"PERHAPS IF YOU'D MET MY MOTHER . . ."

"His mother?" Gwen was asking Izzy.

"SCRATCH THAT. THE ANSWER YOU SEEK IS SIMPLE. I PICKED YOU BECAUSE YOU WALKED THROUGH THE DOORS OF MY CLINIC."

Through her heaves, Gwen only heard half the sentence. "Repeat what he said?" she asked Izzy.

Izzy complied. "He said it was because you walked through the doors of his clinic."

"His clinic?"

"Dr. Bertrand's clinic," said Izzy.

"You mean I could have been anybody?"

"NOT JUST ANYBODY. A TRUE SOMEBODY. I HAVE EXCEPTIONAL TASTE IN WOMEN. I PICKED YOU."

"You picked me because I went to see Dr. Bertrand? At random?"

"I COULD GO SO FAR AS SAYING THAT I SEARCHED THE HEAVENS FOR YOU. AND IT WOULD NOT BE A LIE. BUT TO SAY I PICKED YOU AT RANDOM? I THINK IN A WAY WE PICKED EACH OTHER. SUCH IS THE NATURE OF CHAOS AND THE COSMOS. HAVE YOU READ THE WORKS OF THE GREAT PSYCHIATRIST CARL JUNG?"

"No," said Gwen. "But maybe if you'd picked a living shrink, a sick fuck like yourself might've gotten some help."

"JUNG SAID, 'IN ALL CHAOS THERE IS A COSMOS. IN ALL DISORDER, A SECRET ORDER.' ONE CAN SAY THAT CHAOS WAS WHAT BROUGHT US TOGETHER."

"You faceless prick! If I hadn't walked into that clinic I might—"

"AH, YOU MAKE ME THINK OF LORD BYRON. HE ONCE SAID, 'OUT OF CHAOS, GOD MADE THE WORLD, AND OUT OF HIGH PASSIONS COMES A PEOPLE.'"

"I've got a quote for you. Two words. Fuck you!"

"AH, BUT GWEN, YOU CAN DO BETTER THAN THAT. YOU ARE AN EDUCATED WOMAN WITH A BACHELOR'S IN LITERATURE."

Hell yes, she could do better. Out of her sudden rage, a favorite quote rolled to the end of her tongue. But she ordered herself not to say it.

The empath in Theroux watched her. Her body language spoke volumes.

"PLEASE, GWEN. FAVOR ME WITH YOUR KNOWLEDGE."

Prodded, she lowered her head like a bull about to charge. Her eyes fired and stared dead into the camera lens. Slowly, word by word, she began. " 'In order to master the unruly torrent of life, the learned man meditates, the poet quivers, and the political hero erects the fortress of his will.' "

"MEDITATIONS ON QUIXOTE! A VERY NICE SELECTION. I'M ASSUMING THAT, IN YOUR MIND, THE POLITICAL HERO IS YOUR HUSBAND?"

Gwen didn't answer. She kept her glare at the camera, full of fury and fiery contempt. She wanted to reach through it and strangle him.

"IN ANY CASE, AS YOU'VE PROBABLY BEEN READING, IT'S OVER FOR YOUR HUSBAND. POLITICIANS LIVE IN HOUSES BUILT OF CARDS. AS WE SPEAK, WILL SULLIVAN'S HOUSE IS CRUMBLING. PROOF, I BELIEVE, THAT WITHOUT YOU HE'S NOTHING BUT A CHEAP, BOTTOM-FEEDING POLITICIAN. A COMIC BOOK CHARACTER OF MACHIAVELLIAN PROPORTIONS—"

Surging from her coiled repose, Gwen unfurled her leg and struck the laptop with her bare foot. She sent it clear off the bed and crashing to the floor. Broken the instant it hit concrete.

"You bitch!" shouted Izzy.

Gwen hissed her retort. "Conversation's over."

Izzy crawled over the foot of the bed and was raising a fist to strike when Clem caught her arm. "Dean sees one mark on her that he didn't okay and . . ." Clem let it go at that. The implications were clear. To Izzy *and* Gwen.

"Get it fixed," said Izzy.

"I'm on it," said Clem. "Now back the fuck off."

Izzy turned back to Gwen. "I'm revoking your TV privileges."

"I'll be sure to mention that next time *the father* and I speak."

"Who says there'll be a next time?"

"He did," bluffed Gwen, shuddering underneath her skin while she put on a courageous show. "I can tell he likes me. Yes. I'm certain he'll want to talk again."

Izzy wanted Gwen dead. Instead, she wheeled and charged out of the vault, leaving Clem to pick up the broken pieces of the computer. Before leaving, he addressed the hostage. "Word of advice, lady. You might be able to come between Izzy and Dean, but you won't come between Dean and the baby. So behave. Understood?"

Gwen gave a most understanding, least resistant nod of her head.

"Not to worry about the computer," said Clem. "The twins'll take care of it. And in a day or so, we'll be right back on track."

"What *is* the track?"

Clem gave her a terse, one-question-too-many glare, then locked the door behind himself. Screep-clank!

The twins? Who were the twins?

And for that matter, who was this *father? They call him "Dean." Others call him "Wes."*

In the aggravating frustration of it, she squeezed her eyes shut and the image of a book flickered. A paperback. Will's paperback. She'd been grilling him about "the lie." That silly-assed, useless lie of his . . .

True Believers: The Killer Cult of W. D. Theroux.

Wesley Dean Theroux. Cult criminal and mass murderer. Gwen's eyes snapped wide open. Jesus God. It couldn't be.

"It *can't* be!" she screamed.

The Western Union telegram read:

Philip and Stuart Ramsey
15 W. Division St. #26
Las Vegas, NV 89101

Notebook busted. Need new hardware. Install and
send FedEx asap:
PO Box 655. Portland, OR 97204

The twins, Timothy and Jack, had long ago abandoned their shaven heads and let their hair grow out. Now that it was shoulder length, Jack kept his in a ponytail while Timothy wore dyed, dirty-blond dreadlocks. For five years they'd successfully posed as independent installers for the ever-growing Las Vegas teleconferencing business, rigging computers for boiler-room operations in exchange for easily laundered cash. Timothy was all about hardware. And brother Jack, given the opportunity, could program a toaster to calculate odds for the local bookmakers. The job was a great cover and gave them access to all the latest software and technology.

And now Izzy had broken another damned laptop. Her fourth in two and a half years. Jack would have to drop what he was doing to install and program the new unit. If only Timothy was there with him in the white stucco terra-cotta-roofed house. In a finger's snap, Timothy'd be able to set up the new laptop and ship it inside the hour. Instead, Timothy was in Massachusetts, waiting for brother Jack to hack the FBI database and get a fix on Vance Allatore's whereabouts. But Jack had yet to break the government's encryption codes. He'd put the word out on *the undernet*—the cyber-subworld by which so many techno-criminals corresponded—that he was looking for the codes and was willing to pay for them. There'd been many offers, but none were the real deal. They mostly stank of FBI stings. Before Jack would pay up, he'd need to sample the numbers. To date, nothing had shown up in any of his twenty-nine Worldnet e-mailboxes.

Timothy preferred to work with the guts of the machines. Microchips were his passion. Hyper-speed modems. And his newest arena—cellular transplants. He'd built his first prototype for Theroux, hardwiring a cellular chip and the corresponding electronic serial number into the ThinkPad's motherboard. A few drops of conductive solder and Dean was in receipt of a portable computer with a built-in cell phone. Totally undetectable and able to accept any new ESN entered on the laptop's keyboard. That meant that at any time of day, Dean could dial up an outside line from his computer, connect to the nearest cell, log onto the Web, and communicate without prison officials any the wiser. Those five-minute downloads to his appeals teams were just for show. While prison officials thought he was playing solitaire on his computer, the killer was actually plotting, communicating, and sending scripts to his players in the field.

It was Timothy's superb handiwork that allowed Theroux not only to direct Izzy, Starr, and Clem at the drop of a satellite-linked telephone line, but to send e-mail to the likes of Gary Modetti, and view the MPEG pictures of Gwen Sullivan's insemination. From his computer, Theroux could also manage funds long-hidden in a Dutch national bank in the financial haven of the Cayman Islands. Over ten years, that two-hundred-and-fifty-thousand-dollar kitty had grown to more than two million. Through a series of un-traceable accounts, Theroux could ably order wire transfers from the Caymans to his family, his attorneys, and even the one and only Sherman Stratford of Boston, Massachusetts.

All from a six-and-a-half pound laptop computer in his death-row prison cell. Hallelujah.

From his twenty-two-dollar motel room, Timothy logged onto the Web and waited for the words of his master to ap-pear on the screen. The TV rumbled in the background about a series of deadly twisters that, hours earlier, had torn a three-hundred-yard canyon through a town in southern Oklahoma. To Timothy's cataclysmic way of thinking, April was having its way with the planet. Flooding in the Dakotas. Eight-point earthquakes had cut loose in both Japan and Guatemala. The spring tadpole hatching in Saskatchewan had mysteriously produced six-legged frogs throughout the province. And a once-in-a-hundred-years ice storm was blowing through Eastern Europe, catching half the continent by surprise and killing nearly a thousand.

Something was happening. The end was coming. Just as Dean had long predicted, God was about to foreclose on Mother Earth. It was up to Timothy and the rest to help quicken the coming apocalypse. The child must be part of it. And that's all Timothy needed to know.

I WANT YOU TO STAY CLOSE TO THE MISTER.
I'VE HAD FEELINGS THAT V.A. WILL ATTEMPT
CONTACT THROUGH HIM.

then i shall butcher them both?
ONLY THE PROSECUTOR! THE MISTER MUST
REMAIN ALIVE! IF HE WERE KILLED
ACCIDENTALLY OR OTHERWISE, TOO MUCH ATTENTION
MIGHT BE DRAWN TO THE MYSTERY OF THE MOTHER
AND THE CHILD.

i promise to do what is required.
MY SON, WE HAVE WAITED SO LONG, AND NOW
WE ARE NEAR THE END, SO YOU MUST
PROMISE FIRST TO GET IT DONE. AND IF IT
SERVES ME, TAKE THE LIFE THAT NEEDS TO BE
TAKEN . . . AND THEN YOUR OWN.

but my brother will miss me . . . he needs
me. without me—
I NEED YOU!

yes, my love.
DOES HE LOVE YOU MORE THAN I?

he loves me as a brother.
AND HOW IS IT THAT I LOVE YOU?

you are god's love, sir.
I LIFTED YOU FROM THE DEAD! AND IF I
SO CHOOSE, I WILL SEND YOU BACK TO THE
GRAVE!

i will obey.
I LOVE YOU, SON.

i love you, father.

9

It was easier than even he could have expected. Where Gwen was Theroux's prize, Will was merely an amusing bonus round. A challenge. Oh, sure. Killing a man was simple enough. Or impregnating a woman from his jail cell. He could've picked anybody. But inseminating the wife of a U.S. senator? And then destroying him before the pagan altar of a rabid, media-hungry public? Now that was like running your tongue across a dripping vanilla ice cream cone. Theroux could taste it. It was, for him, the ultimate manipulation of mind and man. More succulent, even, than leading a hundred broken souls to their poisoned deaths, resurrecting twelve, and programming them all for later service.

Politicians. Little tin gods.

Paper tigers all. Easily ripped into tiny pieces. The proof was in Will Sullivan and the recipe Theroux had effortlessly concocted:

A syringe full of ethanol stuck into a famed alcoholic.

The public politician's wife . . . suddenly missing.

An unsigned note.

A cashier's check to a publicity-seeking divorce attorney. And finally, a well-timed Polaroid.

Of course, Theroux's plot wouldn't have played as well without Will's denials. Or Sully's cover-up. Or, for that matter, the FBI's vengeful interest in the U.S. senator. But to Theroux, these were the human elements that gave his concoction the flavor of believability. If he only had more time. What other dishes he could devise from behind bars . . . As the killer's life was getting shorter, the world was growing smaller. Nothing seemed out of his grasp.

The rumors piled up in Washington as quickly as the resignations on Will's desk. With the snap of Theroux's fingers and the well-timed Polaroid, Will had gone from the next generation's flavor of the week to political poison. Half his personal staff had quietly bugged out or called in sick for one lousy excuse after another—all afraid that Will's sudden stink would never wash out of their white shirts and khakis. It left Will numb and locked behind his office door. All while La Roy tried to keep his boss in political play. Lowballing lobbyists were dialing in, attempting to buy the senator while his stock was low. In the meantime, the short-sellers—the Teamsters, teachers' unions, national police organizations, and even Mothers Against Drunk Driving—all dumped their equity shares of Will Sullivan like hot rocks in the Sahara.

La Roy was knee-deep, trying to spin the most recent rumor circulating amongst the *politerati*. The current twist passed around was that a drunken Will Sullivan had first argued with his wife, and then, in lashing out, had accidentally killed her. The kidnapping story was little more than the panic-stricken senator's first botched explanation. And the more plausible divorce filing was a red herring manufactured by Bill La Roy to throw off the FBI. And to the rumormongers, that explained the FBI's sudden interest in the affairs of one very troubled U.S. senator.

In that depressing week, phone calls to the senator went unreturned. Will Sullivan was absent from the FDA Oversight Committee on which he was still the sitting chairman, and on the Senate floor he was a prominent no-show. In his determination to avoid the ever-probing eyes of the camera lenses, he'd taken to sleeping on his office sofa. Myriam delivered all his meals and fresh clothes every day.

Early Thursday morning.

Will remembered the strange hour as if he'd been levitated from the darkness of his office and delivered unmolested down the corridor, into the public elevator, through the Russell Building's main entrance, and into a waiting taxi. After that came blackness and strangely hollow emotions. He didn't recall checking into the Watergate Hotel under his own name, signing an autograph for the concierge, let alone crossing the threshold of room 1165.

Fortunately for Will Sullivan, La Roy was a habitual gambler.

The gentleman who was currently running book for La Roy was the Watergate's night manager, and a quiet courtesy call to his client set off alarms. LBJ was promptly paged. As he dropped La Roy at the Watergate's rear entrance, he was told to wait with the engine running.

With a key slipped into his palm by the night manager, La Roy took the stairs and eased into room 1165, finding it pitch black save for the open door of the refrigerated mini-bar. In the time it had taken La Roy to hightail it from his apartment on the other side of town, Will was already laid out flat and barely conscious. Scattered shot-sized bottles of vodka and bourbon surrounded him—all emptied in an alcoholic's revenge against his better self.

"Ya dumb fuck," said La Roy, tilting a bottle of chilled mineral water into Will's face.

"Fuck you very much," mumbled Will. "If ya didn't bring a bottle, yer not invited."

La Roy slipped a large hand around Will's collar and pulled him upright, then, with his arms underneath Will's armpits, was about to lift him to his feet when Will said, "I think I'm gonna puke."

"Be my guest," said La Roy, not caring a lick if Will puked or not. He dragged the drunk bastard backwards into the bathroom, flipped on the light with an elbow, and dumped the poster boy for sobriety into the bathtub before

turning on the cold water. Will screamed for a while, recoiled under the spray, and cursed La Roy a blue streak before submitting to the sobering treatment. He was off the
wagon. Plummeting toward another hard, rock-bottom
touchdown. And sobbing like a lost baby.

" 'S okay," said La Roy. "It's all gonna be okay."

"She's dead," cried Will. "I just know she's dead."

"She's not dead. Not until she gives what's-his-face his
baby."

"Aw, hell," said Will. "You don't believe that shit, do you?"

"I don't believe much, Earnest. But I still believe in you."

"Who's the dumb fuck now?"

"We're goin' home," said La Roy. "Back to Boston. So
let's squeegee off them clothes and get you out of here before the rattlesnakes get wind of your dirty breath."

Will lost La Roy at "Boston." As he stood, he buckled
over and finally vomited.

"What're we doing?" asked Will once he'd caught his
breath.

"We're going to find Gwen."

"Just you an' me?"

"If that's all we got, that's all we'll need," said La Roy,
throwing an arm around Will and helping him from the tub.

"You and me, huh?"

From the Watergate Hotel, LBJ and La Roy switched off
turns at the wheel, dutifully driving the eleven straight
hours up to Boston, and then Marblehead. The FBI car was
parked in the usual spot, the two faceless agents snapping to
camera-ready attention at Will's arrival. La Roy guessed
they weren't there to serve and protect but to keep a watchful eye on the suspect senator.

The driveway was roped off with yellow police tape. LBJ
tore it down and La Roy flipped him five hundred dollars
for his time and a local motel room. Since Will had no idea
where a spare key might be, La Roy busted through a side
window and helped Will upstairs to the master bedroom.
They both collapsed onto the king-sized bed, fully dressed,
with the chief of staff's arm securely around the senator for
safekeeping. The last thing La Roy needed was Will slip-

ping off in the wee hours to start another bender. They slept until noon, with La Roy waking to the sound of a coffee grinder and someone rummaging in the kitchen.

Thank God, thought La Roy. Gwen.

Creeping out the bedroom, La Roy sneaked down the back stairwell to the kitchen, only to find a small, unshaven fireplug of a man, barefoot and scrambling eggs in a skillet filled with tomatoes and extra-virgin olive oil.

"You must be the one and only Wild Bill La Roy," said Vance Allatore without so much as a partial glance.

"Deputy D.A. Vance Allatore, I presume?" returned La Roy, though he hardly needed an introduction.

"I prefer Vance," said the former prosecutor, wiping his hands on a dishtowel and extending an open palm. "I heard you two bust in this morning through the side window. Thought it was either the FBI, vandals, or one of the demon's whosits come to kill me. Lucky for me I saw the senator and yourself in the foyer."

"And you didn't think to say hello?"

"Hell, no. You both looked awful tired. Figured you needed some shut-eye before runnin' into the phantom former prosecutor from La La Land." Vance Allatore arched his eyebrows in mock menace.

"And lemme guess. You've been here the whole time?"

"Not quite. Just about a week now. Figured it'd be the last place anybody'd look," said Allatore. "After that press conference where your Senator Willy flashed my picture to the whole danged country, I had to figure the demon knew I was back in the fight. Send one of his own to put me down for the count, if you know what I mean."

"What's this demon?"

"W. D. Theroux."

"Oh," said La Roy, for a moment questioning who was more paranoid—Vance Allatore or himself.

"Hungry?"

"I start my day with coffee."

"Got some in the pot," said Vance Allatore, returning to the cooktop. "Why don't you run up and get the senator? We've all got us some talking to do."

"I say we let him sleep it off a little longer."

Sleep it off?

The thought struck Vance Allatore hard. He stood motionless as if in a deep and melancholy prayer. "Fell off the wagon, did he?"

"A mini-bar bender," said La Roy. "Last night."

"Then he's hit his bottom, you think?"

"Just one bender," said La Roy. "But by AA standards, that's a deep decline."

"It's time, then," said Vance Allatore. "The real work can begin."

"And what work might that be?" asked La Roy, the cynic in him punctuating every syllable.

"God's work," said Allatore, serving up a plate full of sausage and scrambled eggs. "Sit. Eat. If you're his true sponsor, you're going to need strength enough for the both of you."

La Roy bristled. "I know my responsibilities, *Vance.*"

"And Will knows *his* as a husband. And I know *mine* as God's humble slave. Now, you would think between the three of us we'd be able to get the good work done."

"And find Gwen," confirmed La Roy, who was as religious as a Sunday cockroach.

"Couldn't have said it better myself." Vance Allatore gave a big smile. Moving on like a man on a mission. "And Lord knows, I've been known to make a convincing argument or two in my lifetime."

Briefly charmed but wary nonetheless, La Roy sat and politely dug into the breakfast. Vance Allatore joined him, pouring a cup of strong brew.

"Lemme ask you something," asked La Roy, jabbing a forkful of sausage at the former prosecutor. "Story goes, you cracked up."

"The story goes."

"I'm not knockin' you," said La Roy. "Came close to wrecking a time or two myself. I just wonder, why all the God stuff? I mean, why not turn yourself over to Buddha or move to India or pay up the big bucks to Deepak Chopra or something like that?"

"Well, let's say I thought of moving to Tibet and becoming the Dalai Lama," said Allatore. "But wouldn't you know? I didn't quite have the pedigree."

La Roy laughed. He was getting to like Vance Allatore quicker than he was comfortable with. He could see why fifty juries convicted.

Saturday morning. Three TV trucks had already found their way to the top of the Marblehead driveway along with twelve photographers with their longest privacy-intruding telephoto lenses. Some of the shooters were legit news. Some were from the tabloids. All were waiting to get a shot at the fallen senator. Fighting off his hangover, Will appeared with a crackling smile, cordially waved to the cameras, opened the garage door, and stepped into his Thunderbird. La Roy was in the passenger seat. Vance Allatore was covered by a blanket in the rear. As expected, the FBI surveillance sedan followed them all the way to Southy and Sully's office above the Pintail Pub.

"To hell with damage control!" croaked Will. "I don't want to hear one more word about it."

With that said, Will broke into another pack of Camels, expertly stripping the cellophane and flipping up the lid for a fresh cigarette. He lit the tobacco and sucked back the nicotine, exhaling through his nostrils as if he'd never quit. All he had to do now was throttle back those conflicting instincts to save his career and drink until he was numb. Instead he had to focus on keeping hope alive. He had to keep those occasional shakes he'd get every hour or so under control. They weren't the real DTs—he hadn't slipped long enough for a thorough attack on his nervous system. They were ghost DTs found in some former boozers who'd fallen down for just one night. The one-bender shakes had been haunting Will since his self-sotting on Thursday.

"Self-fucking-preservationists," pissed La Roy. "Fish stinks from the head down, don't it? Everybody's credo is cover-thine-own-hump. From the Oval Office all the way down to the goddamn typing pool—"

"Please," begged Will. "Bill? So help me, I need you to

stay on point. If somebody doesn't want to help, then they can get the hell out of our way."

La Roy had been groaning about the doors that continued to close in Washington. His outgoing calls remained unreturned. And as more phantom stories continued to circulate, allies were drying up left and right.

Myriam had stayed on. She was a true "through-thick-and-thin" personality. As was Allison Flannery, who was stronger than Will had imagined. Either that or she was too young and too stupid to know better, hanging tight onto the coattails of one sinking U.S. senator.

There they were, crammed into Sully's office—Myriam, Allison, Sully, and a very reluctant Steve Salinas. Myriam had seen fit to uproot the FBI man from a deep sleep and badger him until he'd agreed to come. To escape the notice of Will's tail from the agency, Salinas had arrived hours early, entering through the rear of the pub and waiting upstairs before Will and the rest showed.

For the first half hour, Will had talked and paced and smoked and confessed until his guts bled. He hadn't time for an AA meeting, so his closest allies would have to do. He'd fallen off the wagon. About that he was contrite to all who'd trusted him. And, he admitted, he had little power over his addiction. They all stared as Will burned down one filtered Camel after another—an obvious pacifier and La Roy's idea.

"To think you voted for the FDA regulation of tobacco," joked Myriam during a moment of quiet tension.

"What about the private investigators?" asked Will.

"The good ones are slow," said Myriam. "And the fast ones are booked."

"Benny Yao?"

"Still on his sailboat."

"Well, get him off his sailboat," said Will. "He bought that boat with my money!"

"The Oversight Committee's money," reminded Salinas.

"Don't bust his hump," barked Sully. "Just get on with the report."

"Pop? Please?"

"It's okay," said Salinas, unfolding his notes and addressing Will. "You've seen the file the FBI has on you? From what I'm told—and if asked, I'll deny that you ever heard this from me—the file's just one of hundreds the Bureau's generated on members of Congress."

"Generated on whose orders?" asked Will.

"Your guess is closer than you'd like to hear."

"Addison?" asked Will.

A nod came from Steve Salinas. "But like I said—"

La Roy lashed out, "I was right all along—"

"We're talking about the president!" said Sully.

"Pop. Will you please shut up?" asked Will. "If this process is going to work, I want Steve to say what he knows without argument. So what about the kidnapping investigation? Is there one or not?"

"Yes and no," said Salinas. "My guess is it's just a PR smoke screen so that Justice can appear as if they're covering their bases. They did run forensics from the house. Best piece of evidence was the needle La Roy found in the kitchen."

"And it tested positive for ethanol," said La Roy, looking for confirmation.

"For *heroin*," corrected Salinas. "So you can see where this is going? Alcoholic senator. Falls off the wagon and turns junkie. It's all crappy news. Won't be long before *that* one gets leaked."

All this time, Will was spinning an antique ashtray on his index finger. It was black, bearing the U.S. attorney general's insignia in gold inlay. When Will angrily flinched and sent the ashtray flying, shattering into a corner, Sully was on his feet.

"Hey!" angered Sully. "That was a gift from Bobby!"

"You wanna help, Pop? Or you wanna cry over broken shit?"

"Know what I'm cryin' over? Your broken goddamn career. If you were more man than a whining boy, you'd march back down to D.C. and stump your story until you turn it around."

"It's not a story, Pop. It's real. It's my life. And if you don't think I'm man enough—"

"It's not that. If you don't like the spin," argued Sully, "spin it back until it goes your way!"

"This isn't about politics!" said Will. "It's about Gwen!"

"The hell it's not!"

"I wouldn't be so quick to disagree with your father," warned Vance Allatore, speaking for the first time since he'd politely greeted them all with a handshake and a husky hello, before retreating to the background. Seated on a corner stool underneath that massive rogues' gallery, Vance Allatore had remained nearly invisible until he'd carefully found his place to speak. "Will. Remember when I told you that you are a man of power and influence?"

"Past tense," said Will. "I *was* a man of power and influence."

"Power is one thing and influence is another," said Allatore. "And influence, I might add, is a gift. You are a public figure. People want to hear what you have to say. Whether they believe you or not, there's still a very strong curiosity factor. A pull, you see?

"Yes," continued Allatore. "The more I think about it, the more I believe your father is correct. You must take your gift—*your influence*—to the people. Go on TV. Any program that will book you. Take the hard questions, but fight the fight. Fight for Gwen. Offer a reward. Show those old pictures of Izzy and Clem."

"We can put up an eight hundred number," offered La Roy.

"And who's going to run down the million and one crank calls you *know* you'll get?" warned Salinas, foreseeing utter chaos as a by-product of what he worried was a dumb idea.

"I will." Allison was raising her hand like a teacher's pet. "At least I'll try. We can recruit help from—"

"You won't have to," said Allatore, shifting his posture slightly and leaving the others in the room to wonder which wheels were turning in his formerly busted brain. Those of the undefeated prosecutor? Or the religious nut?

Allatore continued. "As a D.A. I used to fool myself into thinking that I worked for the people. When all along I was working for myself. Driven by ego and my own political ambitions. I'm thinking, what makes the FBI any different? At the top there's always a director. Above her, the attorney general."

La Roy locked in on Allatore. "I got it. We remind the people just who the FBI works for. Mister and Missus John Q. Public."

"Does the *FBI* still have an eight hundred number for missing persons?" asked Allatore, his unwavering gaze aimed at Steve Salinas.

"Yes," said Salinas, not pleased at where this was headed.

Allatore simply let the idea sit on the table and take hold in the imagination of all present.

"No, no, no, no, no!" said Salinas. "Goddammit, I shouldn't have come."

"Don't be a pussy!" countered La Roy. "You love it as much as I do. Will takes his message to the people. Demands an investigation. Phone calls overwhelm Justice's fuckin' switchboards."

Salinas couldn't help but disagree. "It'll just piss Justice off that much more."

"Goddamn right it will!" seconded Sully.

Salinas turned to Will, pleading. "It could make things worse for you."

"Worse for me?" asked Will. "Worse for me? What could be worse for me, Steve?"

"How about an indictment?" asked Salinas.

"On false fucking charges?" Will was on his feet. "Bring 'em on!"

"That's it!" said La Roy, pointing at Will as if he was a boxer prepping for a title bout. "That's exactly the posture you take. On TV. In the papers. Will Sullivan's *da man*. Bring 'em the hell on!"

Will blazed up another Camel and spun around in Joe Kennedy's old chair. From some angles he appeared strong, in control. His old self. From others, he looked as if he might burst at the slightest pinprick.

"Tylenol," pleaded Will. La Roy tossed him a bottle. Will's hands visibly shook as he washed back a couple with the remains of a Snapple Mango Madness. "Of course I'll do it. I'll do it all. I'll do anything I can. I only wonder if it's enough."

Instinctively, Will searched for one face in the room. Not La Roy's. Not his father's. But that of Vance Allatore. The former prosecutor returned a transcendent nod, as if God himself were approving of the plot.

On returning to Marblehead, Will and La Roy discovered the media presence had swollen to five TV trucks and twenty-two print photographers. That very morning, they'd gotten barely a courteous wave from Will. Maybe that night, if pressed, he'd give them a comment. Crews blocked the driveway while lenses were bumped against the window of Will's Thunderbird with flashguns set to stun. Will flipped his passenger's visor down to block the repeating glare.

La Roy screamed out the driver's side window while revving the engine. "Each one of you I run down is a separate public service unto itself!"

A particular shooter, baseball-capped and wearing a tattered, hunter-green safari vest, stepped up and fired off multiple pictures of La Roy screaming out the window. But the photographer's motor drive whirred as if there was no film in the camera. La Roy knew cameras well enough. He'd had his face in enough of them. Nikons especially. He couldn't imagine a photographer worth a lick who'd forget to load his magazine. La Roy gave the shooter a shit-assed grin, then as he eased the Thunderbird past the TV crews, he tossed a final glance upon the lone shooter, stealing a look at his press credentials. FBI, figured La Roy, not knowing how far off he was.

The photographer was Timothy.

And Theroux had given Timothy meticulous instructions. Following them to the letter, Timothy had outfitted himself by renting an auto-focus Nikon with an 80-200mm zoom and a blaster flash attachment, and purchasing an old vest and battered hat under which he could stuff his hair. The coup de grace was the faked press credential. Jack had forged it on a Mac and expressed it overnight to Timothy's Boston hotel room.

As night descended on Marblehead, La Roy found Vance Allatore in the den, lying upon a new slip-covered sofa that had been delivered on the very day Gwen had gone missing. It was still sealed in plastic so Allatore paid no mind to resting his old sneakers on the cushions. *Wheel of Fortune* was on TV. Laced in Allatore's fingers was that well-worn rosary. It appeared to La Roy that the former prosecutor was playing cat's cradle.

"Teach you that in Sunday School?"

"It's not how you pray," said Vance Allatore. "It's how often."

"And in your case, it's during the commercials."

The remark slid off Allatore. "Is Will going to do the TV?"

La Roy plopped into the matching plastic-covered chair across from Allatore. "Networks are lining up like sharks at a bikini buffet. Half think Will's a Dalmatian short of a three-alarm fire. The other half think he's gonna up and resurrect himself in a public confessional, just like he did five years back with his drinking."

"Your idea?" asked Allatore. "The public confession?"

"Wish it was," said La Roy. "That way I could've taken all the credit with a clean conscience."

Vance Allatore twirled the cross of his rosary between his thumbs. "Where is young William, anyway?"

"I got him doing a Chumash Indian sweat," said La Roy proudly. "Steam shower ain't finished, so I got the hot water running while Earnest sits on the toilet and meditates over some burnin' sage."

Allatore was unimpressed, eyes on the TV as Vanna White turned another letter. "Think that'll help?"

"The sweat?"

"The sweat? The caffeine? The cigarettes?"

"You got any better ideas?" asked La Roy.

"Me? I close my eyes and ask the Almighty for strength. Answers come. He points the way. It's hard for some to grasp, but it's really very simple."

"Oh, I've read me a book or two on the old Roman Catholic Boys' Club," said La Roy. "I got an advance copy of a book that claims actual evidence that Mother Teresa's death came as a result of her deep belief that the pope was either A, possessed by the devil or B, under the thumb of the Russian Mafia. And that he was funneling millions of Vatican dough intended for the sick and poor into a golf and gambling resort on the Ukraine's Black Sea. And that the pope and/or the Russian mob had her killed before she could mobilize her secret Angels of the Lord to do the old demonic colonic."

Vance Allatore laughed again. "You mean an exorcism?"

"Believe everything, rule out nothing. That way, nothin' ever surprises Wild Bill."

"And William was going to take Wild Bill with him to the White House?"

"Hell no!" said La Roy. "Don't get me wrong. His intentions are straight up. But I know Earnest well enough. While dividing up the sacred middle ground, he'd cut me loose before I said somethin' too stupid to fuck up his chances at a second term."

"And you wouldn't have minded?" asked Allatore.

"Hey. That's politics and Earnest's a politician. You play the game, you live by the rules."

"Believe me when I tell you W. D. Theroux's a better politician than your Will Sullivan," said Allatore. "What you call spin, he calls mind control."

"Somethin's been buggin' me. How does W. D. talk to his followers?"

"Good question," said Allatore. "After the trial, I reviewed the videotapes. We later deduced that when the camera was on him, he was always tapping a finger. Even when he was on the stand and speaking, his right index finger would tap, tap tap, tap—"

"Morse code!" said La Roy, his eyes flaring at the conspiratorial thrill of it.

"He spelled out precisely who he wanted killed, who was to kill him, and in what manner it was to be carried out. Sadly, by the time we figured it out, it was too little too late."

"So now you're thinking what? Phone calls?"

"Monitored," said Vance Allatore. "I still have contacts in the L.A. office. Best I could get was that Theroux is still acting as his own attorney. In so doing, the court allowed him a personal computer with a modem. He downloads every day, sending and receiving information from his outside counsel."

"There's your answer," said La Roy.

"Not quite," said Vance Allatore. "It's illegal as hell, but the L.A. office still monitors all transmissions. There's nothing incriminating."

"It could be encrypted."

"It could be. But that would make his cocounsel complicit. But that's where the FBI comes in. If we could somehow get them to run the documents through some of their decoding software—"

La Roy glanced at his watch. "I better check on the patient."

"Remember," said Allatore. "We can help him. But he's got to carry the ball."

"He'll be ready," said La Roy, on his feet and charging upstairs.

Allatore thought to turn up the volume on the TV, but with only two letters turned, he'd already figured out the secret phrase. He spoke it aloud as if Pat Sajak could hear.

"Between the devil and the deep blue sea."

On the strength of the ultrasound, Dr. Bertrand first gave an encouraging smile to Gwen, then turned to nod to the videocamera. Clem circled around behind the doctor, zooming in on the monitor's high-definition screen. The neutral contrast images of fetal shapes in green and black changed with each expert twist Dr. Bertrand gave the wand. It slid across the transmission gel smeared over Gwen's exposed belly.

Starr hung over Dr. Bertrand's shoulder, a great grin spread from one ear to the other. All while Izzy was seated across the room, her new IBM ThinkPad on her lap. She read Theroux's words as they appeared on screen.

"ARE YOU CERTAIN YOU DON'T WANT TO KNOW?"

"And spoil the surprise?" feigned Gwen. Weeks ago she didn't want to know for the simple tradition of it. Now she didn't want to picture anything in her mind—boy or girl— that might resemble the man at the other end of the computer. W. D. Theroux. Deatheroux, she'd eventually recalled after hours of digging through her mental recesses. All she could get her brain to confirm was that Theroux was waiting for his end to come by some government-sanctioned means. How, she didn't know. The wheels of justice were clogged and rusty. She couldn't even recall where he was incarcerated. In what state. That could mean he had a date with a needle, an electric chair, gas chamber, or firing squad.

For you, Wes, it can't come soon enough!

She'd gone through fits of shock, anxiety, denial, then blame. Once she even imagined a blackness inside her belly—a fetus without form, possessed of pure evil. At another low moment she pictured it aborted and burned. Then it'd kick her so very softly. A gentle touch from deep inside. A reminder that it was alive and belonged to Gwen. Innocent, loved, and while unborn, protected in a bubble of amniotic perfection. In the end, she vowed to defend it with her life.

"SHALL WE CONTINUE?"

"Of course," said Gwen.

" 'OUR BABY WEIGHS ABOUT ONE AND A HALF POUNDS AND IS APPROXIMATELY NINE INCHES IN LENGTH.' "

The son of a bitch was reading to her from the *Your Baby, Week by Week* book. Just as Will had done every week. What didn't he know about her? What else had his spies told him?

" 'FETAL ACTIVITY SHOULD BE STRONGER AND MORE FREQUENT WITH SCATTERED BRAXTON-HICKS CONTRACTIONS. THE FETUS MAY BE SUCKING ITS THUMB BY NOW . . .' "

Gwen ignored Izzy's voice and set her mind to pulling the potpourri of clues together, adding her newest entry at the top of her mental list. That blessed *USA Today* which arrived every weekday morning with her breakfast and vitamins. Between the sports box and the banner, she'd noticed a tiny imprint in the upper left-hand corner of every edition.

Two letters: OL.

" '. . . HICCUP, CRY, AND RESPOND TO STIMULI INCLUDING PAIN, LIGHT, AND SOUND. YOUR VOLUME OF AMNIOTIC FLUID IS DIMINISHING AS THE—' "

"I'm tired," said Gwen. "Maybe we can finish this later?"

Izzy typed in the message.

"TOMORROW, THEN."

"Tomorrow."

"YOU WILL SLEEP TONIGHT?"

"I hope so," said Gwen. "The baby kicked fiercely last night."

"HE'S A FIGHTER, THAT BOY OF MINE."

"Good night, then."

"GOOD NIGHT, MY FLOWER. DREAM OF ME."

Yeah, right, asshole.

While Dr. Bertrand mopped the sticky jelly off her tummy, Starr kissed Gwen good night and left the room, Clem two steps behind. Izzy stood at the doorway, laptop under arm, waiting for Dr. Bertrand to finish. He pushed the ultrasound unit back into the corner and out of Gwen's reach.

"I feel as if my muscles are beginning to atrophy," said Gwen. "Tomorrow, I would like to start walking."

"Out of the question," said Izzy.

"She has a point," said Dr. Bertrand. "Exercise is good for the—"

"So what?" said Izzy. "Are you recommending we take the little mother into town for a stroll?"

"I'll pace the room if you'll let me," said Gwen. "Back and forth. You can watch if you like."

Izzy made sure she was addressing Dr. Bertrand. "Is it necessary?"

"It wouldn't hurt," said the old doctor.

"But would it help?" asked Izzy.

Dr. Bertrand looked to Gwen when he answered. "Yes. I think it might help."

"I'll ask Dean," said Izzy, gesturing for Dr. Bertrand to get a move on.

"If you don't ask him," said Gwen, "I will."

"Don't abuse the privilege of talking to a living god," said Izzy.

"I'm sorry," said Gwen, her tongue moving swifter than her brain. "I thought he was the father of *my* child."

"He is the father of us all!" said Izzy. "Now count your blessings and let's call it a night."

Izzy ushered Dr. Bertrand out of the room and shut the door behind them. Gwen counted. Fifteen seconds and the lights dimmed enough for sleep, but never enough that the camera in the upper corner couldn't get a video image.

She shut her eyes and concentrated on her latest clue, the *USA Today* and that tiny OL. Gwen knew the newspaper. In order to make its daily newsstand appearances, *USA Today* was printed regionally. From the full-color photographs, to the artwork, to the stories and headlines, *USA Today* was delivered from its New York office via satellite to any number of printing plants nationwide. Gwen hoped the OL might be a code for where her daily newspaper was printed.

If OL was a code, it could mean anything alphanumeric. But what if it was an abbreviation for a city or region? Once again, Gwen began running names of cities in her head which began with the letters *OL*. There had to be hundreds—though few large enough to support a printing plant for a national daily. *USA Today* was primarily an urban paper, read by city dwellers and hotel travelers.

"O-L," she whispered to herself.

Olcott, New York.

Olympia, Washington.

Old Forge, Pennsylvania.

Olney, Illinois.

More, she pleaded with her memory. Her brain was feeling like a sieve. There must be more. Geography had been a favorite grade-school subject. By fourth grade, she knew all the states and capitals and could recite them in singsongy, alphabetical order. She'd done it often for her father. He'd smile at her so proudly, then ask her to repeat them. This time backwards, he'd say. Gwen would try, sometimes succeeding. Others, missing a state and having to backtrack. It was a giggly game between a father and a daughter. When Gwen was a sophomore at Sarah Lawrence, she'd taken the train to Mass General to hold her dying father's hand. Moments away from losing his fight with lung cancer, he grinned through the oxygen mask and mumbled "States and capitals."

Gwen sobbed, then rallied to fulfill her father's last request, performing a letter-perfect reading of their favorite game. His eyes smiled at her, as if requesting that his little girl should give it a backwards go. Instead, he slipped into the coma from which he would never return.

Olcott, New York. No, thought Gwen. Small town. They'd driven for days, it seemed, after leaving Marblehead. That knocked out Old Forge in Pennsylvania and Olney, Illinois. Olympia, Washington, seemed the only logical answer to her riddle. If it *was* a riddle, Gwen reminded herself. OL could be alphanumeric code and nothing more. Not a city. Just a damn code. That, and she could hardly name every city in the country that might start with *OL.*

Olympia, Washington.

The city stuck in her mind, ringing some kind of internal bell. Could she have been driven some three thousand miles? Against her closed eyelids, she tried to picture the state. She could see Seattle and Tacoma in the west. The famed Space Needle poking through the cloudy skyline. Spokane to the east. Vancouver to the north. But where the hell was Olympia? It was the state capital, for God's sake!

Then the baby kicked.

HE'S A FIGHTER, THAT BOY OF MINE.

Gwen felt another jab. This one low, right above her groin.

HE'S A FIGHTER, THAT BOY OF MINE.

"Oh my God," said Gwen, her eyes snapping open. He'd told her. The son of a bitch had said it. A boy. He'd said it was a goddamned boy. Jesus God! Not a boy, she prayed. Not *his* boy. She wanted Will's boy inside of her, kicking and ready to come out fighting.

"Oh, Jesus," she cried, her concentration shattered to smithereens with that single wicked thought. She touched her belly. It was still sticky from the ultrasound jelly. He kicked again and again. A soft one-two punch, as if to say, *"I'm here, Mommy. I'm ready to come out and play."*

Gwen rolled to her side and, as she had on so many recent nights, cried herself into another fitful sleep. After which came the dreams. Those horrible visions of a faceless father and the beautiful baby that she was always forced to share.

10

Thousands of miles away, Vance Allatore slept in the cradle of another one of his repeating dreams. This particular three-walled one-act followed the same structure, but the location, cast, and extras shape-shifted as if by his own subconscious whim.

As usual, it starred the present-day version of himself, uncomfortably stuffed into his ten-year-old prosecutor's pinstripe, a pricey three-pieced number from Rick Pallack in Encino. During Allatore's heyday, Pallack had been the clothier to the stars. Game show hosts, mostly. And popular TV news anchors.

Allatore stood to address the jury, but they weren't seated in an L.A. courthouse jury box. They were seated in the hand-carved, wooden pews of an old, draft-plagued Irish church. The jurors, saints dressed in sackcloth and rope sashes. Some Allatore recognized. Others he was embarrassed not to know at all. Saint Jude and Saint Anthony were holding hands. The judge was Saint Vincent de Paul, the French ecclesiastic who'd founded the Congregation of the Mission in the early seventeenth century. A giant crucifix swung above his head.

In the front row of the massive church sat the defendant, Wesley Dean Theroux. In the killer's lap was a baby Rott-weiller—a seemingly happy little pup with its tongue slip-ping in and out as it panted. Theroux's left hand gently stroked the animal's silky neck.

"Ladies and gentlemen of the jury," Vance Allatore began. The monks laughed. As did the defendant. They all knew, of course, there were no ladies in the jury box. There were no women at all in the courtroom. "I'm sorry," said Vance Allatore. "It's been a while since I've done this."

"Carry on," said the judge, his voice whip-cracking the prosecutor's eardrums.

"Gentlemen of the jury," said Vance Allatore. "We've all had our little talks with God. And the facts he has placed in evidence are abundant and clear. Amongst us walk demons. Human in appearance, but underworldly in their practice. It is our sworn duty as servants of Christ to recognize these demons and, at our own personal risk, brave torment and even death in the name of their destruction. Are we agreed?"

At the moment Vance Allatore turned to face the accused, a cold breeze cut through the church. No longer was he wearing the slick Rick Pallack suit. It had been replaced by a burlap robe with billowy, unhemmed sleeves. The whole ensemble seemed to flap with every gust. Behind Theroux sat his family, one-hundred-fold and naked. Just as on the day they died. And when it came time for the prosecutor to close, the words would not release from his gullet. He was choking. He couldn't breathe. As if the gusts were taking away his own wind. The air was trapped inside him. Vance Allatore stared at Theroux, his focus wavering, then zoom-ing like a TV camera to that little baby Rottweiller. The killer was choking the poor animal, both hands around its neck and squeezing the innocent life from it.

"Open your eyes, you son of a bitch!" whispered the voice. "I want you to see me when you die."

Vance Allatore opened one eye; his focus was blurred and constricted to a tunnel-like vision. He saw patches of long hair, shadows of a face, and some kind of laminated card dangling from the intruder's neck. The meaty hand at the end of the outstretched arm appeared as rigid as a concrete pylon. It gripped Allatore's throat. He thought to scream, but his chest failed to expand due to the knee on his sternum.

"That's it," said the intruder. "You look at me! You look at me!"

To finish off his victim, the intruder lifted an old pillow. He was going to suffocate the former prosecutor. But that's when the first bullet struck, shredding the pillow in a burst of white stuffing. It passed through and shattered the intruder's right clavicle, spinning him ninety degrees to face the fury of five more bursts of copper-jacketed heat. The gunshots echoed off the tight walls of the basement, but were no louder than caps from a toy gun. Five pops from a flashing muzzle. The intruder slumped sideways as goose feathers dusted up the air.

A hand found the cord to the overhead pan-lamp, revealing Bill La Roy, his pant leg pulled up over his right boot, a shiny .380 automatic stuck in his outstretched hand . . .

. . . and a hardcover copy of Vance Allatore's crime tome in the other.

"I just came down to get your autograph," was all the shell-shocked La Roy could think to say. His eyes remained fixed on his uncalculated handiwork. A dead man lay only five feet away, the killing shot, a bullet wound, just below the intruder's left eye.

Vance Allatore caught his breath, sat up, then gave a good look at the dead man. "One of the twins, I think. Timothy or Jack."

"You sure?" asked La Roy. Suddenly he was spinning around, cursing that he hadn't purchased a second clip for the pistol. "You think the other one—"

"I'm sure he came alone," said Vance Allatore.

"Will!" said La Roy, speaking what he was thinking. Will must be next on the list. Or he could've been first. Already dead! But as La Roy started to race up the basement steps, Will was descending. Feathers were still floating. The first thing Will encountered was La Roy's shiny pistol.

"Where the hell'd you get that?" asked Will of the gun.

La Roy could only shrug. "What can I say? There's no such thing as a rumor in Washington."

Will pushed the gun away and slid past La Roy, certain his chief of staff had gone mad and shot Vance Allatore full of holes. Instead, he found the former prosecutor on his knees, whispering into the ear of a bloodied stranger.

"My God!" said Will. "What the hell's going on—?"

Allatore straightened. "I was having a dream. The demon was choking me to death."

"Is he dead?" asked Will.

"Thank God for it, yes," said Allatore. "Thank God for Wild Bill La Roy."

"Just wanted my book signed," said La Roy. "He, uh . . . He was, uh . . . He was about to stick a pillow over the head of Vance and, well, I just sorta . . . Well, you can see what I did."

Vance Allatore was on his feet, turning in place. "This basement is all concrete? Yes?"

"What does that have to do with anything?" asked Will.

"But you heard the shots from upstairs?" asked Vance Allatore.

"I was in the kitchen," said Will. "I was getting a late snack and—"

"Bill," said Allatore without a quiver of calamity in his voice. "I want you to go upstairs and see if there's any movement from the FBI. Don't cause an alarm. Don't turn on any lights. Just give it a look."

"Never thought I'd have to use it," said La Roy of his gun.

"Bill!" said Allatore. "Are you with me?"

"Check the FBI. No lights. I gotcha."

"And give me the gun," said Allatore, hand stuck out and waiting.

Without so much as an argument, La Roy handed Allatore the emptied .380 and headed up the stairs. Allatore pocketed the gun, then began searching the basement shelves. He found a box of Hefty garbage can liners and, with a penknife, began to split them into larger sheets.

"What in God's name are you doing?" asked Will.

"I want you to go upstairs," said Vance Allatore. "I want you to pack and leave for Washington with Bill La Roy."

"There's a fucking dead man in my basement!" said Will, his pitch demanding some sort of logical explanation.

"Now's not a time to think. It's time to move!" said Allatore, deviating only a moment from the task before him. He was cutting up garbage bags and laying them over the body. "You and Bill need to get out of here. You need to stick to the plan. Get on TV. Take your case to the people. If you get caught in your house with a mess like this—"

"That's right," said Will. "It's *my* house. So it's my mess. Who the hell is he, anyway?"

"One of Theroux's twins. Jack. Timothy. I don't know. I find it curious they came to kill me instead of you. Since you put my picture on TV, he knows I'm in the game. Fine. I must be viewed as a threat. You, on the other hand . . . Yes. *You* must be the designated patsy. While you play the role of public pariah, that explains Gwen's absence. If you were dead, then she'd have to make herself seen. Attend the funeral. Otherwise—"

"Otherwise, the FBI would be forced to look for her."

"Works for me," said Allatore, getting on with his chores. *Patsy? Or just a pat fucking answer?*

"Why is it you seem to know everything?" asked Will. The anger in his gut surged to burn the back of his throat. He was tired of being out of control. He wanted to cut the strings and strangle the puppeteer—whoever he was. Will wrenched Allatore back around to face Timothy. "And what the hell were you whispering to him?"

"That would be between me and the deceased, now wouldn't it?"

"Oh, so now you're keeping the secrets of the dead?" raged Will. "Who the fuck do you think you are?"

"I'm the one who's about to commit a handful of felonies," said an unblinking Allatore. He was ready to destroy evidence, dispose of a body, and clean up a crime scene. "I'm the one who's going to make certain he doesn't take us to hell with him. If you have a problem with that, fine. Call the police."

The shock in Will rose from his feet to his chest. He had a million more questions and not a single one seemed to find his tongue willing to move.

"You're still standing here?" asked Vance Allatore.

"I just can't believe what I'm seeing."

Vance Allatore wheeled, inches from Will's face. The words came out like a hot-lamped prosecutorial grilling. "This is it, Will. Time to believe or not believe. After all you've been through. After all you've seen. If you don't believe, you are lost. And so is Gwen. What's it gonna be, Will? Believe? Or not believe? And for God's sake, don't let a little thing like time get in your way!"

Face-to-face, Will and Vance Allatore. The shorter man squaring up to Will with Godzilla-like dimensions. Will's intellect was fighting his heart in a raging battle of wits versus worry. All while the sturdy fireplug stared him down with eyes that had seen far more than Will could ever imagine.

"FBI's not moving," said La Roy as he nearly stumbled down the steps.

"Good," said Allatore. "When you leave at this hour, let's hope they follow you. That should give me time to clean up here and take care of the body."

"Leave with Will?" asked La Roy. He didn't even hear the stuff about taking care of the body.

"The senator knows what to do," said Vance Allatore, returning his gaze to Will. "Doesn't he?"

Will was still on pause as he gave the scene a last once-over. The body. The gun. The scissored garbage bags. Goose feathers littering the basement like the last snow of the season.

"We're leaving," said Will.

"Leaving for where?"

"We're going back to Washington," said Will, his eyes and his heart locking in with Vance Allatore. "I've got work to do."

The automatic garage door quietly whined open, revealing the white reverse gear lights of Will's Thunderbird. Behind the wheel, Will backed the sedan all the way down the drive, twisted it onto the street, then pulled away. The FBI team logged the event at 2:51 A.M., then, as ordered, followed at a conspicuous distance.

All the way to Logan, Will and La Roy barely spoke a word. One, for fear there was a listening device planted in the car. And two, because each man was independently thinking the same scattered thoughts. Just how would Vance Allatore "clean up" the mess left in the basement? Could they trust him? If not, Will was seriously screwed.

They hadn't the faintest.

If only they could've seen the meticulous fashion in which the old prosecutor wrapped the body in plastic garbage bags, binding it with twine and rolling it into the corner. He then broke down the crime scene into a series of mental grids. The first order of business was finding all six shell casings. When that was accomplished, he unfolded his penknife and added an extra nick to each extractor mark so the casings could never be matched to the weapon. On the body, he'd counted four wounds with no exit points. That meant there were two more slugs to find. The first he found in the stuffing of the old couch. The other lodged in a near-empty can of paint. Under the weight of a hammer, the soft lead of the bullets easily flattened to silver-dollar-sized pancakes. More evidence destroyed.

Lastly, to avoid ballistic matches between slugs remaining in the dead body and La Roy's .380, Vance Allatore found a bore-sized file and ran it through the pistol's barrel. Afterwards, he wiped the gun clean of fingerprints, wrapped it in an oily rag, and pocketed it along with the six shell casings.

Allatore swabbed the blood from the basement floor with old newspapers, burning them in the furnace. Then he sucked up the dust and feathers with the Sullivans' brand-new Oreck vacuum cleaner.

The masterstroke, thought the former D.A., was the spilled orange juice. No matter how diligently one scrubbed human blood from a floor, there would always be microscopic traces left over. A simple squirt or two of the chemical luminol would easily highlight the trace evidence under the brilliant cast of a handheld black light. But the old prosecutor knew that something as simple as citric acid could sabotage the whole test. Essentially, luminol didn't know the difference between grapefruit juice and human blood. In the Sullivan's fridge, he found a half-gallon carton of Minute Maid. Before he switched out the basement light, he kicked over the carton of orange juice and ran a damp mop over the entire concrete floor.

Vance Allatore had survived the attack. The crime scene, he was happy to note, had not.

Boston's WBX's nighttime security guard, Hilton Jones, checked his desk clock. 4:02 A.M. It was time to switch off the burglar alarms and start the coffee machine. Two more hours and his shift would be over. The morning talent would arrive along with the skeleton crew that ran Channel 8's six to seven o'clock program. Bleary-eyed and hardly ready to read the morning news, anchor Kent Melville had forgotten his keys and needed to be buzzed in through the station's front entrance. He had his suit bag over his shoulder and was grumbling about how the weather was screwing up his golf plans—more rain expected through the weekend.

"Coffee up?" he asked.

"Should be about done," said Hilton with a preformed smile. Melville disappeared into the studio without so much as a good morning. But that was okay by Hilton. By the time Melville and the rest of the WBX Sunrise Team had grinned their way through *The Early Show,* wiped off their makeup, and begun writing the *News at Noon,* Hilton would be a history lesson, seated on his favorite Long Wharf outcropping, fishing pole in one hand, Budweiser in the other, alongside a tub full of stink bait.

From behind his security desk, Hilton reviewed the guest list for the morning's program. One for each half hour. The first, a "professional shopper" with tips for Mother's Day. The second, author of a cookbook.

"More stinkin' cookbooks," moaned Hilton. There were

always new cookbooks. Twice a week, by his count. Mostly written by women who, by his guess, did less cooking than jabbering.

The front door buzzed. Hilton checked his clock. 4:26 A.M. Too early for the guests, he concluded. None were scheduled to arrive until after five. Though once, he recalled, a fey movie critic, stumping some book of a zillion-and-one video titles, had shown up before three in the morning, hoping the station would have a couch where he could sleep off his encounter with a local transvestite and a bottle of Baileys. Hilton had obliged, offering the sofa in the green room. But when it came to airtime, the critic had locked himself in the bathroom with his arms wrapped around the toilet.

Hilton checked the security monitor. All he could make out from the grainy black-and-white image was two outstretched legs, as if somebody had seated himself on the top step with his back resting against the heavy steel door.

"Son of a bitch." He'd seen that same image a few times in his tenure at WBX. Some goddanged homeless person— a *bum* in Hilton's book—had rung the bell and parked himself on the stoop. Whoever it was had to be removed before the first morning guest showed.

Taking no chances, Hilton dialed the nearby precinct desk and politely asked the sergeant to roll over a unit to roust the vagrant. The security guard hadn't taken many risks in his career and wasn't about to start now. Who knew what the bum could be loaded on? Crack? PCP? And hell, the most Hilton was armed with was a five-pound, carbon-steel flashlight. For Christ's sake, the Boston PD wore 9-millimeter automatics on their belts.

"Forty-five minutes?" asked Hilton of the desk sergeant. "What is it, prime time for crime?"

"If you want," flipped the sergeant in a scrap-heavy Boston accent, "we can make it an hour. How'd you like them apples?"

"How would you like WBX to do a story on your slow-assed response time?" asked Hilton.

"PD's got more important things to do than sweepin' the

homeless offa your front doorstep," said the sergeant. "So do we send a car or no?"

"I'll let you know." Hilton slammed down the phone, thought for a moment, sucked back a deep breath, and unholstered his flashlight. As he stepped around from behind the security station, easing toward the reinforced door, an idea struck him. Holding the flashlight at the very end, he banged on the door and skipped back to the monitor to see if the vagrant had stirred. Not even a millimeter, by Hilton's calculation. *The SOB's probably dozed off.*

On Hilton's second approach, he raised the flashlight shoulder-high in preparation of a preemptive strike, threw back the bolt, then froze in sudden terror as the door swung open and a body slumped before him. Face up, eyes fixed, mouth agape in a twisted recognition of death. On the victim's bare chest was a note scrawled in fat felt-marker strokes:

MY NAME IS JACK OR TIMOTHY. THE FBI HAS MY FINGERPRINTS ON FILE. PLEASE REFER TO L.A. COUNTY D.A. CASE #5887336.

Hilton dropped the flashlight, retrieved it, then stepped away from the body, walking backwards until his butt hit the desk station first. His initial inclination was to punch the redial button on the phone and give that Boston PD desk sergeant a piece of his mind. His second inclination proved more potent. He punched up Kent Melville's extension.

"Yo, Mr. Melville. Hilton up here."

"All they got back here is decaf!" bitched the morning anchor. "You know anybody that's got some diesel stashed?"

"Listen to me, Mr. Melville," said the security guard. "I think I've got your new morning lead."

The two weeks' worth of not-yet-returned incoming calls had already been organized, categorized, and prioritized by the time Will and La Roy made their early morning return to the Russell Building. Under La Roy's expert direction, the skeleton team had a two-day jump on a telephone blitzkrieg to every major media source who'd requested an interview with the senator. First came the tease. The fallen senator was willing to talk. The question was, the chief of staff wondered, after a week living below the radar, was Will Sullivan still *the* story?

In a New York minute!

That's how Buddy Prince's supervising producer characterized Fox's late-night icon's personal response to La Roy's query. Over *Dateline, 20/20,* NBC's *Today Show, Rivera Live, Cochran & Company, Good Morning America, Charles Grodin,* and *Tom Snyder,* Team Sullivan had picked Buddy Prince as their leadoff interview for one reason alone. *Karma.* It had been on his show, when Buddy Prince was a fledgling post-midnight hopeful, that Will had chosen to come out of the alcoholic's closet. Buddy Prince was sure to give Will the respect and the soapbox from which to launch his newest campaign.

By three o'clock Monday, Will was delivered to the D.C. Fox affiliate, in makeup, plugged in, hooked up by satellite feed for the afternoon taping, and double-covered by another crew live on C-SPAN. Another La Roy coup. He'd succeeded in yanking the team off a dull Wildlife Federation news conference where President Addison was speaking, delivering the cable crew to cover Will's marathon no-punches-pulled interview.

With a Washington, D.C., nightscape as a backdrop, Will sat on a stool and faced the empty lens of a camera. His only link to Buddy Prince was the molded earpiece that coiled from his ear to a receiver pack clipped to the back of his pants. He prayed the gallon of sweat dammed up inside him wouldn't leak through his pancake and muddy the voices coming over the tiny speaker.

"Good evening, Senator," said Buddy.

"Good evening," said Will, trying to ignore his craving for a cigarette. Instead, he imagined Buddy's New York studio, a cozy little set with its small desk, two seats, and a twinkling model of a Manhattan skyline in the background.

"Let's get right to it, shall we?"

"Why not?" said Will. He focused on the red light on top of the TV camera. How many times had it lit his fuse? You son of a bitch, you *love* cameras, Will told himself. Relax. Don't be afraid to let it rip.

"*The* Washington Post *reported not one, but two new sources within the FBI that say they are investigating you for everything from filing a false missing persons report to campaign fraud.*"

"If there are charges, then bring 'em on. I invite the charges. Moreover, I'm here to invite the FBI to investigate the kidnapping of my wife instead of engaging in what is obviously petty politics. I'm here to throw down the gauntlet and challenge Attorney General Margaret Van Hough and the Department of Justice to make good on the promise they made to me and the American people."

"*So you're saying the FBI charges are false?*"

"Not charges, Buddy. *Allegations by 'unnamed sources'!*" reminded Will. "The FBI thinks it works for the government. I want to remind the FBI that they are charged with a *public* trust. Investigate the real crime! Find the kidnappers, bring them to justice, and bring my wife home safely."

"*Speaking of your wife . . . If she is indeed missing, why has she engaged a divorce attorney?*"

"I'm here to go on the record, Buddy," said Will directly to the camera. "My wife, Gwen Corbett-Sullivan, has *not* engaged a divorce attorney. Nor has she filed for divorce. These kidnappers are perpetrating a massive fraud and the media, along with weak members of this government, have taken the bait."

"*For argument's sake, let's say your wife has been kidnapped and—*"

"There's nothing to argue about. It's a fact. My wife *has* been kidnapped. And the FBI has the evidence which proves it."

In the green room, La Roy ping-ponged off the walls as he watched the taping over the monitor, punching at the air with each of Will's shots. "Thatta boy, homes. Stay on point. Don't get distracted."

"*Senator. If your wife has been kidnapped, what is the political agenda of her kidnappers?*"

"Spin, baby, spin," said La Roy to the monitor.

Will kept his gaze to the camera direct, ignoring the perspiration welling in his palms. "For matters concerning the investigation, I can only speculate. And I think it would be irresponsible to pollute the airwaves with conjecture. What is not conjecture is the crime—the kidnapping—the need for an FBI investigation—and the fact that my wife is *not* divorcing me. She is pregnant and is in grave personal danger."

"Ooh," said Buddy. *"Those are some strong words."*

"To a point," said Will. "That's why I'm going public with this. I need your help, Buddy. And the FBI needs a mandate."

Will withdrew three four-by-six photographs from his pocket, holding them in the direction of the camera lens. "This is a photograph of my wife. If anyone has seen or heard from her, I would like them to please contact the FBI. They have a toll-free number for missing persons. 1-999-657-8944. Now, here's another picture. This is a woman known to me and my wife as Izzy. She was our housekeeper. She and the other woman pictured here were at our home at the time of the kidnapping. They, too, are missing. And we believe they are part of the plot. Once again, if you recognize these people, please call the FBI at—"

"Maybe we can put the number up on the screen for the senator," said Buddy. *"In the meantime, let's move on. Are you still an alcoholic?"*

"Once you're an alcoholic, you're always an alcoholic," said Will.

"There've been reports that you've fallen off the wagon. For example, a drunk driving incident, cover-up—"

Right there, before the camera, Will knuckled down. If the TV camera was a bullshit detector, he would surely lose the viewers if his answer wasn't direct and from his center.

"Buddy, I struggle with temptation daily. That is the cross all alcoholics must bear for the rest of their lives. I accept it, just as millions of my alcoholic brothers and sisters successfully do every day. But now I have a new struggle. A winnable struggle that, with the help of your viewers and the FBI, I can solve. I want to save the life of my wife and the child she carries! She's out there!" said Will, voice crumbling as if on perfect cue. "And maybe she's watching. Or her captors. Or someone, God willing, who's spotted one of these three people!"

Once again, Will held up the photos, this time including the old picture of Clem. "I beg your audience to pick up the phone and dial the FBI."

"Okay," relented Buddy. *"Let's put that number on the screen again."*

The hour blew past and, by the end of the program, Will had spun Buddy Prince into plugging the FBI number four more times. Next was *World News Tonight,* where Peter Jennings asked the question:

"There is talk that you or members of your staff had a recent blood alcohol test destroyed."

"I did no such thing," said Will. "Nor did any member of my staff. I was drugged by these kidnappers. And the evidence will prove as much. The question I pose to you in the media is, will you help me get my wife back? Or will you get in the way? What's it gonna be, Peter?"

As was his style, Larry King tossed softballs:

"What can we in America do to help, Will?"

"You can show these pictures," said Will. "You can show these pictures and put up the eight hundred number. Send a message to the FBI. Something is bound to break. Some information that could lead to the rescue of my wife and child!"

Stoked, Will plowed through each of the programs, knocking back interviews like tequila shooters. But it was when he appeared on *Rivera Live* that he not only faced the usual coterie of cynical lawyers, but a live linkup with Boston divorce attorney Sherman Stratford.

God bless Geraldo. He cut Will loose to attack the deceitful prick. "I ask you, sir, have you *ever* actually met my wife?"

"Some time ago," said the attorney.

"But not since you took on her supposed case?" asked Will. "Am I correct?"

"We communicate by telephone and fax."

"So you cannot say for certain that you have actually spoken to my wife or an impostor?" pressed Will. "Were you engaged by personal check or cashier's check?"

"That's privileged information," said the smug attorney. *"But I have her signature on a fax."*

"Is a fax easily forged?"

"I'm not an expert in that, Senator. I'm a divorce attorney."

"You have *no* authenticated signature of engagement? You have *no* personal check you're willing to disclose? And you don't know whether it's my wife you've spoken with over the phone or not?" asked Will. "I submit, sir, that you are a conspirator in a massive fraud! You are protecting criminals! And if it wasn't for the shield of attorney-client privilege, you could be prosecuted as an accessory to a capital crime!"

So rattled was he by the fierce attack, Stratford could only retreat. *"Senator, I have no comment on that."*

The only stumbling block in Will's daylong TV siege proved to be Forrest Sawyer, sitting in for Ted Koppel on *Nightline*. The program producers had Will electronically pitted against Sally Crudup, a representative from the Sisters Against Abuse Foundation. She attacked Will with nothing but angry rhetoric:

"How do you answer the question, Senator Sullivan, that in the United States, three out of ten women are physically abused within marriage?"

"It's a sad figure—" answered Will, interrupted before he could return the spin.

"And over seventy percent of those abuse cases involve drugs or alcohol," blasted Sally Crudup. *"And you're here to tell the American people that you are the exception rather than the rule?"*

Will stood tall. "I'm here to tell the American people that my wife is not abused, she is not divorcing me, and that she is missing. Kidnapped. In need of your and my help."

"Denial, denial, denial, Senator Sullivan," attacked Crudup. *"It is the crutch of most alcoholics."*

Win most and lose gracefully when the game is stacked

against you. That's the advice La Roy had proffered before
the blitz. Will had scored strongly in his Monday assault.
They retired for the night to La Roy's apartment, ordered
pepperoni and Pepsi from Domino's, and prepped for the
big news conference Tuesday morning. In the press release,
Will had promised to stand before all comers, answering
each and every question until the vipers were satisfied,
bored, or simply cooked on the subject. Counter-volleys
were expected from the FBI. Before falling asleep, La Roy
hoped the toll-free lines at Justice were clogged with as
many pranks and cranks as his paranoid countrymen could
muster. The plot was in play. Muscle the FBI into prioritiz-
ing their investigation away from Will and back onto Gwen.
Sure, they'd think Will was playing his own game of politics. But the entire Department of Justice was nothing more
than a political tapestry. All Team Sullivan needed was to
find the right piece of thread and pull. Then the unraveling
would begin.

YOU ARE ALL FAMOUS. YOUR PICTURES
ARE ON TELEVISION. TOMORROW THEY
WILL BE IN PRINT. EVERYWHERE.
     we saw. and we are afraid. you never
     spoke of this.
IT IS FROM FEAR THAT MAN CREATED
GOD. SAFETY IS TO NEVER
LEAVE MY SHADOW. AM I UNDERSTOOD?
     yes, my love.
YOU MUST FOLLOW MY INSTRUCTIONS
TO THE LETTER.
     we are ready.

Tuesday morning.

On barely three hours' sleep, Will put in quick stints on
Good Morning America and the *Today Show,* priming himself for the all-media press conference. Every facet of the
media would be there with their crosshairs aimed at the
young senator from Massachusetts. A sure-to-be petulant
crew from print and electronic news, pumped up for a dog-

fight. They'd be certain to resent Monday night's blitz, reasoning that the Sullivan camp had left the *real journalists* out of the mix in an attempt to define the public platform.

In La Roy's words to the skeleton staff, "We gonna get the rattlesnakes to come outta their holes and into our net."

And what a big net it was. Originally scheduled to take place in the Capitol Rotunda, it was moved across the street at the last minute to the Dirksen Building where Will had held his FDA hearings. Cameras were mounted on risers. A local fire marshall was engaged to keep the room from spilling over its limit of four hundred.

At 10:08 EST, Will Sullivan took to the dais under the fireworks of flashing cameras, briefly staring down the attendees before reading a succinct statement.

"I'm here to set the record straight," he began. "And to answer *all* questions until you, the media, are satisfied. There will be no limits on time or subject matter. I only ask for the sake of others, you try not to repeat yourselves. I'll take your first question."

With that said, the entire room seemed to launch to their feet, screaming over one another to get a question off. For a brief moment, at least from La Roy's perspective, the scene looked strangely presidential.

"You, sir," said Will, pointing to an elderly print writer.

"Thank you, Senator. Most of your office and committee staff members have quit since the abuse allegations surfaced. And the White House has officially dropped you from its shortlist of vice presidential candidates—"

"Do you have a question?" asked Will.

"Without charges filed, how does all this fuss make you feel?"

Will was direct. "That loyalty has its price."

"Is that a shot at the president?" asked the elderly writer.

"If the shot fits . . ." said Will. "Next question." He pointed to an AP reporter he recognized. He couldn't recall the jowly fellow's name.

"The Associated Press this morning reported a source inside the Justice Department that says you're at odds with the FBI. They think your kidnapping story is a hoax. You say their campaign fraud investigation is a hoax. Which hoax should the American people believe?"

"Are you married?" asked Will.

"I don't see what that has to—"

"If it was your wife? Pregnant? Taken from your home to God knows where? Would you want to engage in public word games of what's a hoax and what is not?" Then as if cued, Will spun off his most quotable passage, hoping to hell they'd take the bait and run it up their flagpoles. "You all look at me and see a politician. But I'm a husband and a father first. And this husband and father is standing at the edge of an abyss that could very well end tragically without assistance from the American public. Now, you in the media can help . . . Or as I said last night, you can get out of the way. Next question, please."

"Have you ever beaten your wife?" asked Gary Modetti, arm raised but simply shouting over the rest of the press.

Will locked onto Modetti, wishing he could reach out and snap the weasel's neck. "Categorically, no, never, ever, and absolutely not. I only pray that soon she'll have the opportunity to look you square in the eye and answer that same ugly question."

Will aimed an index finger at another man, a squat, fifty-something White House reporter.

"Senator Sullivan," said the reporter. "Women's groups are outraged at the mere thought that you might've abused your wife. Do you have a message for them?"

"Yes," Will said. "They have a reason and a cause. But I am not their poster boy for action, nor is my wife the Rosa Parks of spousal abuse. I stand before you, answering all your questions in exchange for one thing. If I help you with your stories, I pray you in the press corps will assist me in exerting pressure on the FBI!"

Like a charge of adrenaline, he could feel the veins bulge in his brain. Blood surged as he waved his hand over the corps in search of another comer. "Next question!"

"Vanessa Curran," announced the reporter, as if nobody had ever heard of her. She'd elbowed her way to the front row. "A confidential source inside the FBI told me you suspect your wife's kidnappers to be the former members of the W. D. Theroux cult. If this is true, might this coincide with the disappearance of your wife's fertility specialist, Dr. Harvey Bertrand? Or even more strange, the reemergence of Theroux's prosecutor, Vance Allatore?"

Was it one question or five? Will gazed at the towering blonde and his conviction deepened. At that very moment, even if he'd tried, he couldn't think back far enough to recall the brief affair. Or even the familiar smell of her perfume. He wanted but one thing: his answer to sound articulate, without giving away too much.

"I can say only this," said Will. "Politics makes for strange bedfellows. As public figures we court dangers about which private citizens have little knowledge or understanding."

"Is this a confirmation of my question?" asked Vanessa.

"You find Dr. Harvey Bertrand?" said Will. "It's my instinct that you'll find my wife. Next question."

For more than two hours, Will stood square before the press, wearing the only armor a politician can afford. A blue suit and his wits. Without so much as a glass of water, Will Sullivan took all barbs, potshots, challenges to his character, redundant questions, foolish queries, and even taunts from a women's group who crashed the event, shouting insults from the rear of the hall. All the while, he stayed on the same damn point, defining a simple platform.

If you have any information regarding the whereabouts of my wife, dial 1-999-FB-FUCKING-I!

The questions finally dried up. Will thanked them for coming and stepped from the dais into La Roy's outstretched arms. If nothing else, at least he'd earned their respect. No politician had the guts to go fifteen rounds with a rapacious press. It was always so controlled. Tell them little and leave them wanting more.

Will hoped he'd left them wanting to know the truth.

SULLIVAN FIGHTS BACK!
FBI Reports Telephone Tie-up

Gwen wanted to scream when she read the *USA Today* headline. The front-page story was accompanied by a full-color image of her husband in a take-no-prisoners posture at the news conference. She'd reread the story so many times that by the time she decided to eat her morning waffles and sausage, the breakfast had turned cold.

"Fight 'em, Will," she'd said to herself. "Fight for me!"

The baby kicked her and she wrapped her arms around her stomach, imagining, praying that it was Will's and the nightmare would soon conclude. "Fight for us!"

The vault door clanked, swung open, revealing Izzy with the laptop under her arm and Clem with the videocamera.

"He wants to talk to you," said Izzy. "Now!"

11

"I want to talk to him alone," demanded Gwen, her arms crossed and defiant. She would be unyielding.

"That's *not* how it works!" said Izzy. "You know that."

"Ask him!"

"He'll say no!"

"Tell him I want to speak in private with the father of my child," said Gwen. "I'd like a little intimacy."

Izzy's jealousy raged, her mind reeling back to the days when the family was strong, but by no accounts equal. She herself had demanded more attention from Dean. Private attention for which she was scorned. Dean had sweetly told her to ignore the bickering. The others were merely jealous that he'd plucked himself a favorite flower.

"You're afraid, aren't you?" said Gwen. "You're afraid to ask him."

After a cold stare, Izzy pressed her lips together and typed in the request, tapping her fingernails while waiting for Theroux's response. He didn't take much time with his answer.

As Izzy handed over the laptop, she hissed, "Break my computer again and I swear I'll break your fuckin' face."

Izzy pulled Clem along with her. "Me too?" he asked.

"You too," she said. "He wants to be left alone with her."

Gwen waited for the vault door to close before swiveling the computer so the screen faced her. She half-expected to see Theroux's face staring back at her. As it turned out, there was nothing of the sort. Just a standard chat setup. A blank slate with a blinking cursor. She collected her thoughts and typed:

      Hello.
HELLO, MY FLOWER. ALONE AT LAST.
      Yes. Alone.
YOU HAVE QUESTIONS FOR ME? OR JUST
THE NEED FOR PRIVACY?
      I waanted to taalk.
RELAX, MY LOVELY FLOWER. IT IS JUST
YOU AND I.
      Forgve mee, but myy tuping stinks.
BREATHE EASY. IT IS JUST YOU AND I.

Taking the advice, she pulled back some of the stale air and tried to calm her mind. There was a point to this private communication. Gwen hoped to hell she could pull it off.

      Why do youu keep mee in tthis dark
      and awfl place/?
ARE THE ACCOMMODATIONS NOT TO
YOUR LIKING?
      I feel ass if Im undrgrround. Or in
      a deeep Dark Dungeon.
DEEP, YES. DARK, NO. THERE IS
LIGHT. I HAVE SEEN PICTURES.
      But hve you beeen here/? It is horrrible.
      The air feeels unhelthy.
OH, BUT I HAVE BEEN THERE. A LONG
TIME AGO. YOU MUST IMAGINE THE
TALL TREES THAT GROW ABOVE YOU. THE
GREEN HILLS.
      I would liike a window.

IT WOULD NOT BE SAFE FOR YOU.
 I neeed sunligt.
THE BABY LIVES IN THE DARK AND
SO SHALL THE MOTHER. SOON, WE
WILL GAZE AT THE SUN TOGETHER.
 I wnat to seeeyou i Want to knoww
 whhat you loook likee.
WHEN YOU LOOK INTO THE FACE OF
OUR CHILD, THEN YOU WILL SEE
ME AND GOD IN ONE.

Chilled to her agnostic marrow, Gwen found herself frozen at the keyboard. Her thoughts unconsciously shifted to Will. It was his face she hoped to see in the child. His and hers. A mixture—

YOU ARE THINKING OF HIM?

Christ Almighty! Could he read her thoughts through the computer? Gwen had to catch her breath.

YOU WONDER IF HE'S TRYING TO SAVE
YOU? OR HIS CAREER? OR BOTH, MAYBE?
 I was just pausing.
HE WILL FAIL.
 He is my husband and I love—
I SEE YOUR TYPING HAS IMPROVED.

Shit!
Had she blown it! The lousy typing was all part of a Hail Mary plot. A downfield pass into a million possible arms. Gwen cursed herself for knowing so little about cyberspace. She'd always left that to Yvonne. When her computer crashed, all she needed was to point to the screen and say, "I broke it. Please fix."

ARE YOU THERE?
 I was madd. And when I gET mmmad, it
 kills my nervs.

AND NERVES MAKE FOR YOUR BAD TYPING?
    i rpomise to get betterr.
WE WILL TALK EVERY DAY, FROM NOW
UNTIL THE BABY COMES. I WILL READ
TO YOU. I WILL RECITE TO YOU POETRY
SO BEAUTIFUL YOU WILL FORGET THE
TIES THAT TEMPORARILY BIND YOU.
    bUT can yooou make this end"?
HIS BIRTH WILL BE A NEW BEGINNING
FOR US BOTH. A FRESH START IN THE
UNIVERSE OF SOULS.

12

America's number-two cop was so agitated she looked as if she needed her tight Victorian collar resized to a forty-one. As she knifed into Will and La Roy, the duo couldn't help but wonder if that much-ballyhooed cameo she wore around her neck might pop right out of its precious setting.

"Let's see where we stand," Lois Freehold badgered, framed by the American and FBI flags. She glanced over to her deputy, Perry Ingalls, and counted off on her fat fingers. "I got a former D.A. turned renegade fanatic, running around God knows where doing God knows what. I got some dead guy named Timothy or Jack, delivered to a TV station in *your* backyard, Senator. A message on his chest addressed to me, no less. And I've got an eight hundred number reserved for regular citizens that's so tied up that Ma Bell gave me an ultimatum. Add new switches or lose the account altogether."

Seated in a stiff chair across from her, Will challenged, "I don't see what any of those things have to do with me."

"Don't play games with me, mister!" warned the FBI director. "I'm this close to tightening the noose around your neck."

"You talking indictments?" asked Will.

"The A.G.'s got a grand jury seated and itching to hear what I have to say."

"Then what's stopping you?"

"Questions with no answers."

"Such as?"

"Where's Vance Allatore?"

"Not a clue."

"What knowledge do you have about this dead body that showed up at WBX in Boston?"

La Roy let loose a smug little smile, crossing his legs. The distinct body language revealed an obvious, personal knowledge of the crime. But he wasn't talking.

Will answered, "I don't know. Was it big news up there?"

"The man was murdered," she pointed out. "If there's any way I can connect you—"

"I've got a question. Why don't you want to help me?"

"We both know why."

"Is playing politics that important to you?"

"Coming from you, I'll take that as a compliment," she returned.

"Release the file, Lois," urged Will.

"And help you with your little PR campaign?" The FBI director's mouth bore the hints of an upturned smile. "I've got you on everything from destruction of physical evidence to accepting illegal campaign donations."

"You summoned me here for this?" asked Will. "Or do you want to make a deal?"

The FBI director eventually sat, palms down on her polished desk, her fingers splayed to reveal perfectly red acrylic nails. Like the ubiquitous cameo and the brightly colored suits, it seemed another vain attempt to look feminine. "You stop the press. Stop hammering my office. The toll-free number. The whole charade."

"In exchange for . . ." prompted Will.

"We won't indict," she said.

"I want the file."

She shrugged and looked over at Perry Ingalls. "As far as the FBI's concerned, there's no file and there's no Theroux cult."

La Roy was on his feet, looking ready to slam his fist right through her tabletop. "You're a fuckin' bitch!"

"Put a collar on him," said an unmoved Lois Freehold.

"Fuck you!" said La Roy. "I'm my own man and, I swear to God, when this is over, I'm gonna brand you the Wicked Witch of the East to anyone who'll give a listen! There's gonna be a tattoo on your ass with the imprint of my snake-skin boot."

"That's the deal." She totally ignored La Roy and turned to Will. "Take it or shove off."

La Roy roared on. "When this is over you're not gonna be qualified to police the toilets at Union Station!"

"Does he amuse you?" asked Lois to Will. "He must. Or else you woulda fired his black ass a long time ago."

Perry piped in. "La Roy's the senator's *sponsor.*"

"Oh, that's right," she said. "Senator Willy's an alcoholic. And don't think we believe this sobriety shit. We know all about your little bender at the Watergate."

Will was already standing, brushing the creases from his slacks and politely returning his chair to its rightful place. "So help me, Lois. If anything happens to my wife that you could've prevented . . ."

Before they could exit, the director left them with a final nugget. "Oh, and Senator, if you're looking for any more help from Special Agent Salinas? You can find him back at his old desk in Oklahoma City."

The air outside the FBI headquarters was unusually warm and breezy. Will chose to send LBJ back to the garage while he and La Roy made the trek back to the Russell Building on foot, fouling each step with a trail of smoke from his fil-tered Camel. The senator and his chief of staff hadn't made it through the crosswalk at Pennsylvania and Constitution when Will's cell phone trilled. The sound sent a quick shock through his system. And hope swelled for the split second before he answered, thinking it might be good news about Gwen.

"Please hold for the president of the United States," said the voice.

They kept walking along Constitution Avenue while Will waited for Addison to pick up the line. Some passersby recognized Will, acknowledging the senator with either a nod or conspirator's whisper to a friend. All the while, La Roy urged Will to hang up. Turn off the phone and hurl it into the Capitol reflecting pool.

Will hung on.

"Whooeee," said the president with the snap of a phone line. "I swear, the way I hear it, you got Lois Freehold's tit in the ringer and she's squealing like a stuck piggy."

"Afternoon, sir," said Will, cold but respectful. "Is there something I can do for you?"

"I'm proud of you, son," said the president. "Do you realize you are the first man who's stood up to that cunt since the rumor surfaced that she was J. Edgar's love child?"

"She got a file on you, too?"

"Hell hath no fury like a scorned FBI director."

"Again, sir," said Will, "to what do I owe the pleasure?"

"No pleasure in this, Will. No pleasure in any of it. I was just wondering how you were holding up under all the irrelevant hooey?"

"Frankly, sir, I didn't know you gave a damn."

"But I do," said Addison. "I'm your friend *and* a politician. That means, while I'm kissing the baby, I'm also dipping into his college savings to pay off the Social Security debt. It's a lousy job, Will. Sure you still want it?"

"Why the hell won't you help me?" asked Will, the respect in his voice vanishing with every shortened syllable. "And if not me, Gwen."

"Because I can't, son," said Addison. "I'm not in a position—"

"Gotta keep your options open?"

"Part of the job of keeping policy on track. Sure woulda been fun having you-all on the ticket. Hell, I was even gonna cave on the La Roy issue. Thought he might bring a little color to the campaign, if you know what I mean."

"I'll be sure to tell him that," said Will.

"Aw, do him a favor," said the president. "And keep that one between us."

As the president hung up, Will stopped, La Roy right there alongside him. He closed his eyes from frustration and took a deep breath, purging the anger with the longest exhale of his life. He opened his eyes, only to find a wad of warm spit spattering his face. A squat woman with fierce eyes stood in his path. Fifty-five years old, in pigtails, black leggings, and an extra-large T-shirt with words blazing: STOP THE VIOLENCE. NOW, TODAY, AND FOREVER!

"ABUSER!" she shouted, finishing off her ambush with a shove and a quick look around as if half-expecting a cop to arrest her, making the protest official.

But when no cop appeared, Will asked her, "Is that the best you can do?"

As La Roy defensively moved in between Will and the woman, she suddenly found her legs and fled at a dead run, screaming her way down D Street.

Fishing for a handkerchief, La Roy erased the phlegm from his boss's face. Will couldn't help but laugh ironically. "And to think I once found the job dignified."

"Next time, we'll take the Metro," said La Roy.

The hotel room in Boston's seedy Combat Zone was dark, noisy as hell, and paid for in cash. A third-floor flophouse in a decrepit building deemed livable by an assortment of transients and heroin-addicted hookers. The walls were either splattered and stained or bubbled by the new paint. Navajo white, figured the former prosecutor. So quick was the job that the painter hadn't thought to mask the Rust-Oleum gray shag. The paint had dripped everywhere, coagulating in the carpet fibers like blood from a week-old corpse. Life on the front.

For three days, Vance Allatore had sat in the hotel room in a metal folding chair, feet up on the double bed, waiting for somebody to come. Or the phone to ring. Somebody should be trying to communicate with the dead twin. He still wasn't certain which one had come to kill him. And he'd found no clues since finding the perpetrator's camera bag after scouring the Marblehead property. It had been stashed inside the plywood pool equipment housing. Inside the camera bag he found a telephoto lens, a Nikon, a receipt showing the camera had been paid for in cash, a Snickers bar, and a hotel room key with a return address stamped on the attached plastic paddle.

When Allatore walked through the hotel's doors and marched up the steep stairs, nobody gave a lick of notice, or questioned the thick little man when he entered the building, let alone the killer's room. After an initial search that turned up nothing more than an old duffel bag stuffed with T-shirts and torn Levi's, Allatore walked around the corner to a local market, bought bottled water, bananas, a *TV Guide,* and enough granola bars to last a week. He then settled in with that forged press credential around his neck, his rosary bundled tightly in one fist, and La Roy's newly loaded .380 auto in his lap.

Nobody came, called, or sent so much as a telegram.

So piece by piece, Vance Allatore tore the room apart, pulling up heating grates, dismantling the radiator, pulling back the carpet and lifting up loose floorboards. He searched anywhere Timothy or Jack might've hidden a personal phone book, a wallet, or notes. Anything that might lead him to the other twin, Theroux, or, most importantly, Gwen.

He came up with nothing.

By Tuesday morning, the old prosecutor's patience was worn, he was sick of granola bars, and he had resigned himself to watching brain-dead reruns of game shows like *Pictionary* and *The Price Is Right.* All the answers were dumbed-down for the lowbrow audience, but still teasing enough to keep him awake. And heck if he could guess the price of one of Bob Barker's cars. Higher or lower? Who cared? Here and there Allatore had also caught a few of Will's TV interviews and excerpts from the press conference. He was proud, thinking he'd seen a spark of character in the young politician. A good sign for a soul in desperate need of salvation.

The picture on the TV was annoyingly skewed. A constant fun-house mirror image, warping with each and every change in picture. Allatore marveled that after watching the lousy TV for so long, his brain had actually started to compensate, straightening the lines and cleaning up the shabby audio. After the ensuing headache, he took to trying to fix the TV. He discovered the screws which connected the plastic back to the frame had all been removed but for one. With his penknife, Allatore removed the last screw, then pulled off the back of the TV set.

"Holy Mary, Mother of Jesus," exclaimed the born-again Catholic, as he gently reached inside the guts of the set and removed a small black box with TOSHIBA printed on the top. No broader than a Gideon's Bible and no thicker than a videocassette. Vance Allatore opened the lid of a new, state-of-the-art pocketbook computer, complete with a four-inch color screen and a retractable modem connector.

"And let's not forget the Hallelujah," Allatore whispered to himself.

Will was getting tired of the leash. Just the thought of one more night with La Roy watching out for his well-being, suggesting hot steam baths and mixing disgusting herbal teas, felt like a ligature tightening slowly around his already taxed psyche. He needed to breathe. He needed to think. The only company he craved was his Gwen's. And with every day that passed, he felt her essence was slipping through his fingers.

Working on overtime, LBJ circled the Georgetown block once to make sure there were no vipers lurking, then let Will out at the side gate. The senator climbed the steps, turning the corner to his front door, only to find young Allison seated on top of three crates of files, videotapes, and books. In a micro-second, she was on her feet, pert and forcing a confident smile. But her magnified glasses betrayed red-streaked eyeballs, dead tired from slaving over her research.

"You know, we have couriers for deliveries," said Will, slipping by her and shoving a key into the lock.

"I thought you might want a verbal download," she said, following Will and hauling the first crate inside.

"Verbal download?" Will pushed the door open.

"You know, instead of going through all the research yourself." Allison slid the second box inside the door. Will helped with the third. "You can ask me questions, I can answer based on all that I've seen or read—"

Will deadpanned, "La Roy sent you over here to check up on me."

"Oh, no!" said Allison, a bit too quickly, totally giving away how bad a liar she was. It was a gift.

"Go ahead," said Will. "Do a sweep. He told you to look in all the cupboards and the fridge and let's not forget the dishwasher. Senator Earnest might have a bottle stashed in the dishwasher."

Will switched on the lights, his nostrils flared. The lingering fine fingerprint dust was still in the air.

"Maybe I should just go," she said, hanging near the door.

"Good idea," said Will, regretting his tone while wishing she would just disappear. The only voice he wanted to hear belonged to his wife. And if he couldn't have her . . .

"I'm just trying to help!" said Allison, her bubble bursting along with a cloudburst of tears. She'd gone better than forty-eight hours without a crumb of sleep, gorging herself on Oreos and Diet Cokes. All for *him*.

Will squeezed his eyes shut with instant penitence.

You're a real shit, Earnest.

Easing in behind her, Will turned Allison about-face, pulled her close, and let her unfold in his arms. She sobbed like a lost toddler finally found, unleashing a hellfire of pent-up hurt and frustration, and a rage of unappreciation. And damn it if right now Allison didn't miss her mother!

For a moment, Will closed his eyes and imagined she was Gwen. Tears pooled in his own eyes. He could've cried himself. He could've let loose. Somehow, he kept it all within his skin.

"I'm very sorry," said Will.

"No, sir," said Allison. "I'm sorry. I shouldn't be crying."

"You don't need an excuse. I was short. And I'm truly sorry."

As quickly as the sobs had begun, the moment became

distinctly uncomfortable. While it was utterly nonsexual, they were close enough for second-guessing. Allison stepped back and began pointing to the crates. "It's really pretty simple. This box is a Nexus search on Theroux, the cult, yada yada yada. From trial to present." Allison recomposed with a deep breath. "Okay. This box over here has all the books written on the same subject. I tabbed the important passages in case you want to just browse. And this carton is—"

"Videotape," prompted Will.

"Yes, sir. The most recent piece is a CNBC interview with Theroux. There's some background and it investigates the present state of his appeal."

"Well done," said Will.

"Thank you, sir," said Allison, wrinkling her nose like a teenager. "I think I'll be going now."

"Get some sleep."

"You'll find your wife, Senator," she said. "I just know you will."

Will nodded his thanks and she was gone. He locked the door behind her, his mind flashing through the thousand crisper apologies he could've made. Allison was young, sweet, and loyal to a fault. All for him.

Asshole.

"Gawd," said a familiar voice. "I thought the little cookie would *never* leave."

Will spun in time to catch a glimpse of those ridiculously long legs, descending from the darkness of the stairwell in a black crepe Gucci suit.

"How did you get in here?"

"Would you believe the building super let me in?"

"No," said Will. "I don't believe that for a minute."

Vanessa held up a house key for Will to view. "Can't believe you haven't changed your locks in the last five years."

"I don't remember giving you a key."

She stopped on the last step. "Best I can recall we were at the Ritz. Both of us, drunk off our asses. And the sex, I don't think, was that stellar. Not your fault. I'm a notoriously lousy lay when I'm potted."

"That doesn't explain the key."

"I coulda stole it. Or, during a moment of weakness, you might've given it to me. I really don't remember," she said, holding it out for Will. "All the same, here it is."

Will accepted the key, but was looking at her heavy bag.

"Oh, don't worry, lover. No more hidden cameras. I'm only here to help you."

"Well, you can help yourself out of my home," said Will. He sidestepped the cartons left by Allison, tossed the spare key into an ashtray, and gestured toward the door.

"I'm serious," she said. "You asked the media for help. In turn, I took your plea to my bosses. They agreed."

"To help me?" said Will, cynical and distrusting her so, he was not the least bit curious about her angle. He was looking for a cigarette.

"Looks like it's true you picked up *one* of the old habits." From her oversized alligator Kelly bag, Vanessa pulled out a fresh carton of Camels and tossed it at Will. "I'm here to offer you all the resources of my network in helping you find your wife."

Will opened the carton and peeled the cellophane from a fresh pack. "In exchange for?"

"Unlimited access," she said. "Cameras on *you*. Twenty-four hours a day. We're glued to you until the story breaks." Then she lowered the boom. "One way or the other."

"Dead or alive," confirmed Will.

"Or divorced," she added, reaching out and offering Will a flame from an engraved silver butane lighter. "Half the brass still thinks you're a goddamned wife abuser trying to spin yourself out of some negative numbers."

"And what do you think?"

Vanessa lit her own cigarette. "What does it matter what I think? I'm in the driver's seat."

"You're trespassing. Thanks for returning the key."

"What if I were to get my hands on a certain FBI file you've been having some difficulty—"

"I've seen my file. Thanks."

"I'm talking about the Theroux file."

She'd never seen such a hard look from a man before.

Will's eyes were unblinking spotlights, trying to cut through her thick skin to see some kind of truth. "Don't fuck with me."

"I'm asking a simple transactional question. If I were to get you the file, would you agree to the terms?"

"The complete file?"

"I hear it's got pictures and everything."

Will noticed her right shoulder was sagging under the weight of her bag. The satchel suddenly looked less than stylish and uncomfortably heavy. As if she were toting a telephone book. Two quick steps and he'd stripped it from her.

"Hey! You can't—"

"I just did." He turned the bag over and dumped the contents on the sofa. A stack of five-hundred-plus Xeroxed pages, bound with thick crisscrossing rubber bands, spilled forth with a thud.

Vanessa tried to step in and retrieve her property, but Will simply shoved her away, leaving her holding the empty bag.

"Shit!" said Vanessa.

"I think we're even," said Will. He was madly sorting through the papers, scanning odd pages, and all but ignoring his uninvited guest.

"Do you know what I had to do to get that?" she screeched.

"The door's to your left."

"I need the story, Will."

"It's not a STORY!" Will exploded, wheeling back at her. "It's my fucking LIFE!"

Vanessa watched him for a moment longer, searching her right brain for some kind of creative solution. He was back on his knees, hunched over the piles of paper, separating Xeroxed photos from text.

After a frustrated minute, she sighed and headed for the door. "You can keep the cigarettes. I've actually quit." She didn't bother to shut the door behind her.

Will called after her. "Vanessa!" He could hear her heels clicking down the stairwell, stop, turn, then, one by one, return to the threshold.

"Yes?" she said.

"Have your crew in my office at eight," he said. "We'll work out the details."

So charged was Vanessa, she wanted to race back inside and kiss him. But Will looked almost pathetic, knelt over the file as if within the papers he'd find his soul. With a sudden respect for his privacy, Vanessa reached inside and swung the door until the latch locked.

Alone at last, Will thumbed to the section containing photographs. One by one he laid them out on the floor in a panorama of images. First, the very same, early photos of Izzy, Starr, and Clem. Then some fuzzy bank robbery photos culled from a security camera, with drawn-in arrows pointing at two suspects, male, the same height, labeled in the corner TWINS?

More photos. Theroux as a boy. Mug shots of Theroux as a pimp. Even some of the killer as a wannabe movie star, complete with two professional eight-by-ten head shots. One serious. One smiling. There was even a resume indexing Theroux's made-up theater credits, workshops, and teachers.

There were the crime scene photos of those ten-year-old murders which followed the trial. Photos of the eighty-eight suicides/victims. Photos of case detectives, coroners at work, and then a much younger, cocksure deputy D.A., Vance Allatore—hardly the man Will now knew him to be.

But the last three photo sets were enough to make Will's heart do a double flip. The first set was coroner's photos of Timothy, nearly naked and scrubbed clean of blood, bullet wounds intact. There were pictures of the dead man, leaning against a door with those scribbled words on his chest.

MY NAME IS JACK OR TIMOTHY . . .

The second set, nine-month-old pictures of a bloody scene of utter butchery in a North Carolina motel room. The victim, a reporter named Charles Hunt, alleged to have been working on a book about Theroux. The attached report was marked INVESTIGATION INCOMPLETE.

And finally, a series of black-and-white video stills taken from an Arkansas trooper's fiber-optic camera. It catalogued framed images of a blonde in a short skirt and skimpy top, teasing the officer into a moment of weakness, disarming him, then murdering him with his own weapon. After the deed, as the temptress stepped closer to the hidden camera, you could see a tattoo just underneath her naval. A sword piercing her navel ring.

"Izzy," Will found himself hissing as he drew his gaze up from the distorted image of the former housekeeper. On paper, her eyes appeared as dark, pixilated recesses. Will wanted to reach into the picture and rip her heart out—if she had a heart at all.

13

To: FatherFigure@Allentown.net
From: TwinTowers@mobius.com

SUBJECT: MY BROTHER

Dear Father,

I've seen privileged communications from inside the government mainframe. They have found a body they are calling "Jack or Timothy." I am worried.

Jack

To: TwinTowers@mobius.com
From: FatherFigure@Allentown.net

SUBJECT: EYE ON THE PRIZE

My son,

Worry not of your brother. Worry
only for my child. For he is the future.
It is time for you to finally
rejoin your family. Leave today
and do not look back.

Dad

14

With eyes red-stained from another sleepless night, the young senator had spent the last fifteen hours poring over articles, videotapes, and that all-important FBI file. Once everything was organized into an ad hoc presentation, Will had repaired to his Russell Building office at dawn, turning his formerly ornate and stately space into a massive bulletin board. There, he pinned, stapled, and Scotch-taped papers to the hundred-year-old mahogany paneling without a pinch of regard for either the building's history, the men who'd occupied the space before him, or those who'd move in when he moved on. Will was at war and this was his war room.

When La Roy had arrived with Benny Yao, who'd returned early from his vacation, Will had dispensed with any greeting and torn into a caffeinated, hyper-driven tour of evidence.

"There!" He'd stabbed at the pictures of Clem and Starr and Izzy's tattoo, matching his official descriptions.

"And listen here!" he had pled, reading transcripts of Theroux's telephone conversations with lawyers and media personalities.

"And look over here . . ." He'd switched on the TV and VCR, showing them a cued tape of Harve Langer's recent CNBC story and interview with Theroux. Will paused on the inserted image of Theroux at his IBM ThinkPad, legally downloading information from his appeals attorneys. That's when Will had drawn La Roy and Yao's attention to the pages of text the FBI had illegally gleaned from Theroux's official downloads.

"I've read through them," Will said. "Nothing incriminating. Legal musings, mostly. But . . ." And Will was off again, jumping from one document to the next, spinning a web that at once both dazzled and troubled his captive audience.

"Earnest. This is all really impressive," La Roy said. "But all it proves is that the FBI had a file. That and you're preachin' to the church choir."

"Theroux's communicating with his family!" Will snapped. "Remember, Bill? Allatore said that after the trial, he figured out the finger tapping. The Morse code. I wonder if somewhere, *inside* the communiqués with his outside attorneys, he's sending messages."

Benny Yao was making notes. "I could sub it out to an encryption specialist. It's more money, Will."

Will answered flatly, "So bill me."

Gesturing a time-out, La Roy offered a news bulletin. "This might be a good time to bring this up," he said. "And don't ask me how this started. But as of yesterday, we've been getting checks addressed to the *Will Sullivan Defense Fund.*"

"The *what*?" asked Will.

La Roy shrugged. "Beats the hell outta me. But it's clear that, for one, you still have support out there. And two, if the cash falls within the FEC guidelines, why not open an account? That way we can fund Benny's team and—"

"No!" said Will. "I'll pay my own damn bills. Return the checks with a letter—"

Myriam slipped into the room. She carried a FedEx package, red-tagged as having been "examined for suspicious materials" and cleared by the Capitol Police Force. At the Central Mail Office, the box had been weighed, audio-scanned, thermal-photographed, and X-rayed for the possi-

bility of explosive content before being delivered to Myriam by the interoffice messenger.

"I think you should look at this."

The package bore no return address. Nor any note. Only a
tiny Toshiba computer, wrapped in the torn cover of a Gideon's
Bible. When the lid was opened, Will discovered a single
folded page from a Bible. The last chapter of 1st Timothy. All
the text had been lined through with a fine-tipped blue pen,
with the exception of a certain few words in the last paragraph.

> **Timothy,** *guard what has been **entrusted** to your care.*
> *Turn away from **godless chatter** and the **opposing**
> **ideas** of what is falsely called **knowledge,** which some*
> *have professed and in so doing have **wandered from**
> **the faith.***
> **Grace be with you.**

"It's from Allatore," said Will, delicately holding the
page up for La Roy and Benny Yao to see. "He's saying this
computer belonged to Timothy."

Waving the tiny Toshiba in the air like a Bible in the hand
of a tent-show evangelist, Will stuck an index finger at the
TV and the frozen image of Theroux at his own computer.
He was trying to make a connection. "How do you think he
was talking to his flock?"

"I'm on it," said Yao.

"You're not on it," drilled La Roy. "You *own* it!"

Outside Will's inner sanctum, Vanessa Curran was on a
high burn. She and her usual two-man crew, Kruger and
Wallace, had shown up a half hour early, at 7:30 in the
morning. Only to be placed in a four-hour-plus holding pattern. It was past noon and all she'd seen of Will was a typed
letter that Myriam had asked her to sign.

"It says," paraphrased Myriam, "that you or your network
will not disseminate or air any information, video, or audio
regarding the senator, his wife, the pending investigations,
or his office, either until permission is granted by the senator or until July first of this year. Whichever comes first."

"And you expect me to sign this?" asked Vanessa.

"You *and* the members of your camera crew," insisted Myriam.

"Then I want my own letter—signed by Will—that guarantees me and my network unlimited and exclusive access during the agreed-upon time period."

La Roy appeared in the doorway, grin intact. "Sounds good enough to me. You ready to roll some tape?"

A practiced camera-commando, Kruger was on his feet, sun-gun blazing from the top of his BetaCam 3. Vanessa had a compact out, checking her makeup, when La Roy leaned in close. "Never mind the touch-up, missy. Your star is Will Sullivan, and right now, he's waiting for you."

Both doors to Will's office were flung wide open in a clear invitation. There, standing before his desk, was the weary U.S. senator, in chinos, a wrinkled dress shirt, and zero makeup. Under the camera's sudden glare, his eyes were dark, unblinking sockets.

"Good afternoon," said Will, his throat like gravel. "We'll start with an *update* of what we know, followed by a *summation* of what we think. Let's begin . . ."

GOOD MORNING, MY FLOWER.
    Good mrning.
SLEEP WELL, DID YOU?
    I was awaake aloot. i wish they
    wouuld let mee sleep witht the
    lights offf.
THE BETTER FOR ME TO SEE YOU,
MY FLOWER.
    Yoou wattch me sleep?
WHEN I AM LUCKY. MY TIME IS SHORT.
BUT EVERY DAY, WE GROW CLOSER TO
THE BLESSED EVENT.

Gwen drew a heavy breath. Her rib cage ached from the fetus pushing against her sternum. Dr. Bertrand explained it as nothing short of normal, prescribing some flexibility exercises. Starr was dispatched to go into town and return with a book he recommended called *Yoga for the Expectant Mother.* After their first joint session, Starr proved as limber as a twelve-year-old gymnast. And Gwen just felt worse.

She typed:

> I knoww its a boy.
> AS DO I. TELL ME, WAS IT INSTINCT?
> A motherr kkNows.

Gwen had been awake most of the night, planning each mistaken keystroke she was about to make. When she awoke she'd continued scheming. Another deep breath and she typed some more. First, giving away what she'd gleaned from her daily dose of *USA Today*. In that space between the sports box and the day's headline, that tiny OL.

> I rread in USA TODAY that your
> most rrecent appeOL was rejected?
> MY SURVIVAL IS NOT PART OF THE
> GRAND SCHEME.
> I AM parrt of your scHEme to . . .? i'm
> SoRry. i don't knoww whatevEr?
> YOU ARE PART OF NO SCHEME. YOU ARE
> THE PRICELESS MOTHER OF HEAVEN'S
> FUTURE.

Next, Gwen moved to the highway-cone-colored, plastic milk crates upon which her TV had been propped. The crates were stenciled with the logo from Sunnyside Dairy.

> I findd my dark thoughts changginG to
> The SUNNYSide of things.
> SUCH AS WHAT, MY FLOWER?
> Silly, reallly. I wonder iff my MILK
> will coMe in?
> IT WILL. AND WHEN OUR SON FEASTS FROM
> YOUR BREAST, HE WILL GROW STRONGER THAN
> ATLAS.

Gwen's final clue. The serial numbers etched into the bed frame and the ultrasound unit. SMS439 and SMS1558. She'd spent countless hours calculating how to fit one number or the other into her badly typed Internet conversation without it being obvious. A code with the million-to-one chance that someone, somehow might read her painfully plotted SOS. If she let reason take hold, the plan seemed lame. Who else would possibly read the remains of her daily chats with Theroux? And then see that it was code? The odds were so long that if she thought about it enough, her brain would just give up and hope would die.

So she returned to the few bread crumbs she had left. And dropped them into those preposterously typed phrases.

> I dreamed Of you last night.
>
> TELL ME MORE.
>
> We werre spooning. Do youu know what sppooning is?
>
> I DO.
>
> You weere behind me. Left hands on MY BrEasts. but i Didn't knoww what you looked liike.
>
> AND THEN?
>
> I wantedd to turnn over but youu said no.
>
> YOU THINK I DON'T WANT YOU TO SEE MY FACE?
>
> Theree's more. You took MY hand and wroote your phone numbeer. I remember SMS1558. Dooes that mean anythingg to youu?
>
> LORD BRYON SAID, *"SLEEP HATH ITS OWN WORLD, AND A WIDE REALM OF WILD REALITY, AND DREAMS IN THEIR DEVELOPMENT HAVE BREATH, AND TORCHERS, AND THE TOUCH OF JOY."*
>
> I'm nott as well rread as yOU might thinkk.

HAVE YOU READ THE BIBLE?
     no.
*"WHOSO REGARDETH DREAMS IS LIKE HIM THAT
CATCHETH AT A SHADOW, AND FOLLOWETH AFTER
THE WIND."*
     I'm so lost witth all this.
ECCLESIASTICS 34:2 . . . AND LOST YOU ARE NOT
WHEN IT IS I WHO HAS FOUND YOU.

*Found me? Fuck you! If you were here I'd cut out your
heart and—*
Gwen had seized, momentarily frozen at the keyboard.
The juice in her stomach had boiled up to her throat in a
mouthful of hot spit. Another deep breath, another pain at
her rib cage. The heartburn was horrible. And she damn
well needed to keep her bearings. She was still online with
him. The cursor was blinking, awaiting her reply. She decided to recycle the clues. Back to front this time.

          i keep tHinking about thE dreamL andd
          if it means somrething about me Personaly
          or if it has greater MEaning.
THE MAKING OF THE DREAM IS ONE THING. THE
MEANING YOU GIV—

The usually fluid typing of Theroux stopped abruptly, as
if the connection had been terminated. He was hardly
searching for a thought. It was obvious to Gwen that he only
needed to finish—

I MUST GO. GOOD NIGHT, MY FLOWER.
KISS KISS.

A box appeared on Gwen's screen: CONNECTION
TERMINATED.
Gwen reread her words, praying her phrasing hadn't been
too obvious. Praying that someone other than Theroux was
reading. She closed the computer and gave a look up to the
camera mounted in the corner. She knew somebody was

watching. Probably Izzy. The door would open at any moment, Izzy would enter, retrieve the laptop, and part with a remark designed to sting like a snapping wet towel.

But the mother-to-be was wrong. It was Clem who entered, his hair looking as if he'd conditioned it with dirty motor oil.

"Ya had a good talk with him?" asked Clem.

"He had to go," said Gwen.

"Had his reasons, I'm sure."

"I need to go to the bathroom," said Gwen.

"Izzy should be back in about half an hour."

"I need to go now. I'm carrying a lot of pressure here." Gwen pointed to her swollen stomach.

"You're not supposed to go to the bathroom without girlie supervision," said Clem, repeating the policy laid down by Izzy and Theroux. Every time Gwen had to relieve herself, either Starr or Izzy would blindfold her and lead her some forty-two paces. Two left turns and a right. Then while she went about her business, one or the other would stand and watch. It was unnerving enough to have a woman watching. A man would be an even greater complication. Gwen even kicked Will out of the bathroom when she had to go.

"I don't mind if you watch," fudged Gwen, feigning need and embarrassment in the subtle flashing of her eyes.

"Izzy wouldn't have it," said Clem. "She'd deep-fry my balls and feed 'em to the cat."

The cat? That was news to Gwen.

"Please," she begged. "If I don't go I swear I'll wet the damn mattress."

Clem exhaled, looking back out the door as if he half-expected Izzy to walk through, even though he was sure she'd be gone for at least another thirty minutes.

"You won't tell, I won't tell. How's that?" he asked.

"As long as I empty my bladder, your secret's safe with me."

"Lemme get the blindfold," said Clem.

"Do you have to?" asked Gwen, hoping to stretch an inch into a yard.

Clem turned suspicious. "You have to pee or not?"

"I have to," said Gwen. "I really do."

"Then wait." Clem left the room and returned with the blindfold. She didn't resist as he placed it over her face, snapped the elastic behind her head, unbound her wrists and ankles, then helped her from the bed.

Forty-two steps, give or take a stumble. You're making inroads, Gwen. Be patient. And pray for a savior.

15

"Quit what you're doin'. Seven weeks till D day and Missus Governor wants to make sure you're in good enough shape to kill."

While the guard laughed at his own joke, Theroux quietly finished off his "kiss kiss" good-bye to Gwen and, before turning off his ThinkPad, copied his Internet conversation with Gwen to the computer's hard drive. He would study it later. Something about it had troubled him. Something that glitched in his photographic mind. An emotional attachment? Possibly. He already had such strong feelings for her and the unborn child. Could his empathic sensibilities possibly be overriding his photographic talent? He didn't know.

"Hep to it," said Charlie. "Bet you can't remember the last time you had a full physical."

"Yours was last week," deadpanned Theroux, first shelving his computer, then clearing the wrinkles from his jumpsuit. He stepped up to the mesh door and gave Charlie a stare that cut to the bone. "You barely passed. A question of too much bad cholesterol and the diet-killing beginnings of adult-onset diabetes."

"Who the hell is tellin' you this shit? Jeezus Chriiist!"

"You are, Charles," said Theroux with an earnest smile. "You tell me everything I need to know."

"Fuck you and gimme your wrists," spat Charlie, totally unnerved by Theroux's idea of parlor games. In retaliation, when the con slid his hands through the slot in the cell door, the guard notched the handcuffs so tight they bit into the killer's skin.

"You think that hurts me?" asked Theroux. His eyes practically melted the steel mesh.

"I don't care if it hurts and I don't care if it don't hurt," said Charlie. "The only thing I care about is who's in charge."

"And that would be you?" confirmed Theroux.

"Fuckin' A."

"You're a slave, Charles."

"Shut up and gimme a slow three-sixty," ordered Charlie. While Theroux slowly turned clockwise, the guard threaded the waist chain to the cuffs. "Okay. Feet."

Same drill, only this time Charlie had to get on his knees and reach through a lower slot to affix the ankle chains.

Looking down upon the guard, Theroux recited in a voice a full octave lower, " 'The slave is doomed to worship time and fate and death, because they are greater than anything he finds in himself, and because all his thoughts are of things which they devour.' "

"Sounds smart," said Charlie, aching as he returned to his feet. "You think that up all by yourself?"

Theroux grinned broadly. "That's for me to know and you to most likely never, ever find out."

Charlie ignored the freak and barked into his walkie-talkie. "Open twenty-four."

The rollers cued and the thick mesh between the convict and guard electronically slid away. Theroux took a step closer. "You believe in life after death, Charlie?"

"How's this," said the guard. "I pray to God every night that he kills you dead and sends you straight to fuckin' Hades."

"Just me?"

"You and every other son of a bitch waiting for his turn on the table."

Theroux pictured Charlie's list. It was long and choked with killers, kidnappers, rapists, wife beaters, the infamous, and the forgettable. Thousands living on America's death row. All waiting on an appeals process that was paced somewhere between a crawl and a winter grass. It was an elite club. A few even traded correspondence. During Theroux's stay, he'd received fan mail from some of them. They all wanted him to write back.

Humans, he thought.

"Let's get a move on," said Charlie.

"Yes," said Theroux. "Let's."

The staff offices of Will Sullivan's suite, once populated by overeager analysts and legislative aides, had been converted overnight to an ersatz crisis center. As Benny Yao's muscled assistants had removed most of the Civil War collection from Will's condo as collateral, the private investigator had a substantial team of investigators move into Will's near-vacant office to man phones and coordinate the private search effort. In Yao's practice, no police agency or sheriff's department in the continental U.S. was too big or too small to canvas, fax, interrogate, and cajole for potential information on Gwen's whereabouts.

Against La Roy's better judgment, Will had clipped on a wireless microphone and was personally guiding Vanessa Curran and her camera crew through the maze of telephone and fax wires.

"And you're not afraid of using government property for this obviously private effort?"

"Because of all the innuendo and hearsay, my office had effectively been shut down," said Will. "In my opinion, that's a waste of government space. The sooner I rescue my wife, the sooner the taxpayers get what they paid for."

Vanessa directed Kruger to swing the camera around to capture a behemoth of a woman riveted to a large computer screen. Yao moved in to offer an explanation. "This investigator is operating a database that profiles kidnappers, their intent, their actions to date, then compares them to the FBI model—"

"Senator!" shouted Myriam.

Reflexively, Kruger swung the camera a full one-eighty, nearly cracking Vanessa in the skull with the lens, only to find his viewfinder crowded with FBI agents storming the room.

Without warning, the crew had served Myriam with a warrant and right-turned their way toward the back offices. Myriam chased after them, shouting, "SENATOR SULLI-VAN!"

Undaunted by the blaze of the camera's light, the special agent in charge held his arms up high as if to gather the attention of the room. "We have grand jury authority to confiscate all files and documents pertaining to the issued warrant. If you would please stop what you're doing and exit in an orderly fashion— "

"SENATOR!" Myriam was still shouting. "MR. LA ROY!"

There were times when Vanessa Curran's height had been a disadvantage. In high school, mostly. She'd been thin, gangly, and towered over most insecure boys. Her six feet finally become an asset when she'd turned into a news reporter. Her size and long reach got her into spaces where the mostly male reporters would crowd out their smaller peers. In a packed room, she could usually spot her target—in the present case, Will Sullivan. One moment he was next to her, doing a running commentary, the next he'd up and vanished.

"Where is he?" Vanessa asked Kruger. The cameraman simply shrugged her off and kept shooting the raid.

"I can still hear him," said Wally, tapping the wireless audio transmitter with one finger while holding the headset against his right ear. "It sounds like he's running."

"Running where?" asked Vanessa, still searching over the scattered heads of the FBI.

Wally cupped the headphones tighter over his ears. "Sounds like he's running down stairs."

"Can you track him?" whispered Vanessa.

"Do I look like a bloodhound?" pitched Wally. "He's wireless and running out of range."

"Did he say anything?"

"All I heard was something about 'Gideon.'"

"Gideon?" mouthed Vanessa, who was instantly cursing her dumb self for signing the stupid-assed letter. Already she had footage enough that could not only lead on the *CBS Evening News*, but would certainly make the network pricks sit up and beg for mercy as she renegotiated her contract.

To: TwinTowers@mobius.com
From: FatherFigure@Allentown.net

SUBJECT: A PICTURE OF HEALTH

My children,

Your father has passed his physical exam. I am now ready to depart this earthly shell and leave the rest of the great work to all of you. As the weeks will soon count down to days, I breathlessly anticipate the birth of my son. To see his face. And in it, God himself.

Now, to the work of raising our child. After much deliberation, I have decided that for the safety of my son, he should be raised inside a conventional marriage. Therefore, after his birth you must go forth and marry. Starr to Jack. Izzy to Clem. Church services. But when you speak of God, you will think of me.

Starr and Jack shall be the primary parents, while Izzy and Clem the boy's Godparents and protectors. Only remember this. He is not yours. But mine. And I will always be watching.

Dad

Izzy's fuse had first been lit when Theroux had denied her the privilege of bearing his child. And now, reading the e-mail, the charge inside her had turned nuclear. How dare he give the primary care of his child to Starr and Jack! They were but two secondary family members, so lucky to have been resurrected that Izzy had often wondered if there'd been an error in their Jell-O cocktails. In her opinion, there had been sisters and brothers far more deserving of life after death—smarter, more clever, and dedicated to Dean in ways Starr or Jack could never comprehend.

Damn him!

Dean had given Izzy life and a new soul, only to shun her womb and plant his seed in another. Now he was asking her to marry the one man she'd vowed never to fuck, and give up the only child she might ever know.

From inside the vault, Gwen could hear the screaming, wailing, and crying. It was so muffled, for a while she was certain the hysterics were from Starr. A complication with her own pregnancy? A mystery that had still eluded Gwen. Who was the father of *Starr's* unborn? Gwen knew only that it wasn't Theroux. Izzy had made that much clear.

Gwen heard the voice. Izzy's voice, shouting. *"The day I marry you, motherfucker, is the day I kill you and then myself."*

Calmer voices prevailed. A man's. Clem? She wondered. A woman's. Okay, that was Starr. Then a new voice. Higher in pitch, male, but without the sweet swing of Dr. Bertrand's Southern inflections. Gwen heard the crash of an object thrown against her door. Then Clem's voice rose over the muffle. *"Clean it up, bitch!"*

Izzy screamed back, *"I'll marry you because Dean says I have to. But you try and fuck me, I swear I'll cut your dick off and stuff it down your throat until you choke!"*

The baby kicked. A heel shot into Gwen's kidneys. It practically doubled her with pain. Another kick. A fisted little bull's-eye into the same sore target. Gwen moaned from the pain, spiking the audio feed in the next room. Silence overcame the underground cells, followed by the clanging of the vault door unlocking. Izzy was first over the threshold. Then Clem. Their patient was fetal and howling in pain.

"Get Dr. Bert!" ordered Izzy.

"Shit!" said Clem. "I think he just fixed!"

"There's adrenaline in the fridge!" said Izzy. "Stick him with it and get his fat ass in here now!"

Izzy hung over Gwen. She put her hand to her stomach and asked where she hurt.

Gwen put a palm to her backside, then convulsed, shrieking with a pain she'd never imagined. The baby wasn't kicking. Something was wrong. Very wrong. "Oh, God," said Gwen between rushes of pain. "I'm gonna die."

"You're not gonna die and neither is the baby," said Izzy, her voice as collected as that of a veteran nurse.

Dr. Bertrand stumbled into the doorway, his eyes at a narcotic half-mast. He had one hand on the jamb, the rest of him was leaning on Clem.

"I said to stick him," growled Izzy.

"Not necessary," said the old doctor, attempting to stand on his own and catch his shortened breath. "Plus there's a risk of sudden tachycardia. That could leave me dead and your patient without a doctor. Hmmm?"

"She's hurting bad." Izzy pointed to Gwen's lower back.

Clem eased Dr. Bertrand over to the bed, dropping him into a chair.

"Began like a bad kick, didn't it?" the O.B. asked.

Gwen nodded just as another torturous wave took over. Her teeth bit into the bedcovers as she screamed.

"Most likely a kidney stone," said Dr. Bertrand, slurring over the patient's muffled tirade. "Can't tell without a picture. Should be able to pick it up on the sonogram. Won't pick it up if it's in the ureter. Otherwise, we'll need an X ray—"

"We don't have an X ray!" blasted Izzy. "And the hospital is not an option. That's why you're here!"

"Just roll the machine over here and let's have a go," said the doctor. Nuked as he was, Dr. Bertrand was quick. With Gwen pitched to her side, he was quick to pick up the kidney stone on the monitor. By his estimate, it was no larger than the head of a pin. Enough, though, to cause pain worse than labor.

"For starters," said Dr. Bertrand, "I'm going to need water . . . and a strainer from the kitchen . . . and maybe a six-pack of Budweiser."

"You're not drinkin', old man!" said Clem.

"Not for me," said the doctor. "For the patient."

"Won't it harm the baby?"

"Not this once," said Dr. Bertrand. "But the alcohol will cleanse the kidney and, with some luck, push the stone through."

"And what if the stone doesn't move?" asked Izzy, expecting the worst.

Dr. Bertrand might have been whacked on smack, but he still had a lifetime of experience at his disposal. He knew the implications of what he was about to say. "The stone doesn't move? She goes to the nearest emergency room."

With her eyes squeezed shut from the pain, the words passed over Gwen like fuzzy helium balloons, batted back and forth with badminton raquets.

"She's not leaving the bunker!"

"A large stone could be lethal if not cared—"

"She's seven weeks out. We could induce her."

"Not with an active stone. Her body might refuse the medication. The complications—"

"Then a C-section! We take the baby now!"

"We both know that without proper facilities, we take the baby, we lose the mother, and still risk the life of the child. No. You do as I say and we cross our fingers the stone passes!"

Eventually the pain overtook Gwen and she passed out, her face pressed into the wet spot where her teeth had clenched the bedcover. When she awoke, on her back with her head propped up, she was wearing a fresh pair of tartan flannel pajamas. The pain had diminished, but was not entirely gone. Starr was seated next to her, applying a cold compress to her forehead.

"Some hour, huh?"

"I was hearing voices," croaked Gwen.

"Bad dreams, I bet. Ever since I hit the eighth month, it's been one tommyknocker after another."

A twinge of pain reared in Gwen's left kidney. She gently bucked, then heard the distinctive carbonated hiss of a beer can popping open. Her nose curled as Starr served up the bubbling Budweiser. "Doctor's orders," she said.

Gwen didn't argue, though she hesitated a beat as she read the warning on the red, white, and blue can:

WARNING:
CONSUMPTION OF ALCOHOL DURING PREGNANCY CAN CAUSE SERIOUS BIRTH DEFECTS.

"Dr. Bert says it'll help move the stone," said Starr.

Gwen nodded slowly, then washed back the first gulp. The fizz stung the back of her throat. She never was much of a soda drinker, let alone beer from a can. And when Will had entered AA, she pretty much stopped drinking altogether. But she finished the beverage anyway, then forced down another twelve ounces between belches. By the time she'd killed off the second can, a pleasant buzz had settled between her ears.

In that one moment, she worried that Will really might have fallen off the wagon. He'd been kicked so badly by the media and Washington establishment, he might have found his only refuge in alcohol. Gwen remembered her words to him should he ever take another sip.

I will leave you. I will never talk to you again. And I will tell the world that my husband is a twisted drunk who cares about himself above his position, his constituents, and his country.

A bitch of a threat. Gwen wished to God she could take it all back. Every angry word in exchange for stroking his face just one more time.

I love you, Will. And I forgive everything.

Mo Gaffney had been in a bad mood ever since he'd been handed the federal subpoena back in November while urinating in the restroom of a roadside Friendly's. Mo thought the server was looking for an autograph. After all, Mo *was* "world famous" in New England. During the following months, he'd developed an ulcer and complained of migraines and itching feet. All from the daily stress that came with waiting for his big day in front of Will's FDA committee. And for what? Following instructions from his Providence connections? Mo had simply leased a few Lexus sedans to some anonymous names on a list faxed to his main headquarters. He didn't know they were FDA executives. He didn't know the mob was kicking back the interest payments on the vehicles. And most importantly, he didn't know the boys from Rhode Island were heavy into pharmaceutical ventures.

Mo just sold cars.

And that's exactly what he told Will's FDA committee. Two days' worth of unnecessary obfuscation, covering the microphone with his pudgy fist and exchanging whispers with his three-hundred-dollar-an-hour attorney. The Providence mob had recommended he fess up and tell the truth—tell the committee anything they wanted to hear, only forget the mob names. Otherwise, Mo would be dead. They reminded Mo that he was nothing more than a witness. A car dealer who was absent of any wrongdoing. The FDA execs had all but resigned under the threat of indictment. The game was up. Tell the truth and let's get on with business, they'd plainly told him.

But oh no. Mo played like he was a character in the McCarthy hearings, citing Will's investigation as government harassment and the irresponsible scapegoating of solid citizen Mo Gaffney. He demanded a public apology. And, of course, none came.

For Will's TV audience, though, it had certainly been entertaining.

From a rear booth at a Westbrook diner, Mo Gaffney nervously hammered out a tune with his knuckles. Today's hit was an eight-track flashback by Supertramp. Most of the words escaped him, but the melody and rhythm had hung with him all morning along with a hook that stuck like cheap aftershave.

Take the long way home.
Take the long way home.

The cartoon centerpiece of Will's FDA hearings was quietly grinding while he waited for a sit-down with the politically crippled Will Sullivan. The old railroad Amtrak car was parked on concrete blocks at the end of the Stop and Shop's parking lot. Called Arnie's, the joint boasted the best chili dogs and fries in the whole wide world. In Westbrook, maybe, thought Mo. The diner was a mile down the highway from one of Mo's first dealerships. He had picked the joint because, for one thing, he knew that at three o'clock on a Monday afternoon, the railroad car would be practically empty. He also knew that between himself and the road-ruined senator, he'd be the most likely to be recognized.

Standing guard near the front door was Big Mickey, a welder from Mo's Cadillac body shop. And posted near the pay phone at the rear was more muscle in the guise of a mechanic named Duff. Not that Mo expected trouble. He just thought, for look's sake, it gave him an air of fortitude.

From the bathroom, Sully nudged past Duff without so much as an "Excuse me" and returned to Mo's booth.

"Your Willy-boy's late," said Mo, smacking his lips at the idea of the shoe being on the other guy's foot. He couldn't help but twist the knife into Sully's pride. "Hey. You know that grand jury subpoena the papers keep talking about? Maybe it finally caught up with your little wonder boy."

"Like that would make the two of you even?" Sully withdrew a pillbox from his coat pocket, popping two B-12s and a green Cozaar pill. He washed all three back with a Coke.

"That shit give you headaches?"

"The B-12?"

"The heart pill," said Mo. "My old man used to take that shit and it'd hit him like a cold Slurpee."

"No headaches," said Sully, checking his watch, then casting a hopeful look out the window. It killed him to be in any form of concert with Mo Gaffney and inside, Sully was slowly dying from the public drubbing his son was enduring. Will was, after all, his only child. And a father's love was turning out to be deeper than any ego-driven ambition.

"He should be here soon," said Sully.

Pounding out more beats of the Supertramp song, Mo wondered what kind of stupid hair had been up his fat ass when he'd agreed to the rendezvous. He should've followed his initial instinct and had the young senator whacked for embarrassing him on national TV. His business had taken an initial eleven percent dip. Mo'd even gone as far as speaking to some of his associates in Providence, who'd advised the vengeful car dealer that it was a lousy business decision. Stupid, even. And if Mo were to make a *move* on a U.S. senator without permission, there would be serious repercussions.

Next came the surprise call from Sully. Will Sullivan had a deal he wanted to throw back at Mo Gaffney. Mo's terms. Mo's backyard. Will would come to Mo. Only would Mo listen?

"I'm waiting five more minutes," said Mo.

"You'll wait as long as it takes," said Sully, unafraid of the car dealer. Mo's rep was all bark and no bite. That, and if curiosity had a face, Mo wore it like a latex Halloween mask.

Sully marked the time on his watch anyway, then took another gander out the window in time to see a rented Chrysler cross the A&P lot and stop next to Mo's Lincoln Mark IV. From his seat, Mo recognized a black man behind the wheel. Bill La Roy. Will stepped out of the passenger side wearing chinos and a chambray shirt, his hair unshapen and wind-tossed. He climbed the wooden steps to the diner, stalling only when Big Mickey blocked his path. Mo gave his best Don Corleone nod and Will was passed through.

"Them boys up in Providence must really be amused by you," said Sully.

"Shut the fuck up." Mo didn't stand for Will, who slid in right next to his dad.

"Thanks for setting this up, Pop," said Will. "And Mo? I wanna say thanks for meeting with me."

"You know I didn't have to," said Mo, fingers tapping the table and his chin up in the air.

Will ignored the car dealer's body language and looked straight across at him, realizing the closest he'd ever been to the character before was under the killer TV lights of the FDA hearings. Back then there'd been twenty feet between them. Desks, microphones, and a megaton of political bullshit. At close range, Mo looked like somebody's funny uncle. Only the funny uncle wasn't acting very funny.

"You think I'm an asshole," began Will.

"I *know* you're an asshole," laughed Mo.

"And what if I heard that you thought I was such an asshole that you wanted me cut down?" asked Will. "I mean, you're the big connected guy. Am I right?"

"Have some respect," reminded Sully. "Mo didn't have to meet you."

"Yeah," said Mo. "Listen to your old man."

But Will pressed on. He had his own agenda and wanted to see if Mo would bite. "You haven't answered my question."

"There's time yet," bullshitted Mo. "And lately? With your run of luck? Maybe I figured to let you sizzle for a while in the old fryin' pan, if you know what I mean."

Will leaned closer. "You didn't have me killed because either you didn't have the balls or the backup. Which was it?"

"Fuck you," said Mo, his chest puffing like a cock robin's. "You think you're untouchable? I can get to you anytime I damn well please. Hell, I can get to *anybody*."

Will appeared satisfied with the answer. "Good." He leaned back in the booth and gave a confident wink to his father. "I think we can do business."

"Meeting's done," said Mo. He moved to stand.

"I'm prepared to apologize," said Will. "I will publicly apologize for what I did to you on TV."

"Like it matters anymore," said Mo. "Business is back up. And you aren't no kinda sterling endorsement no more. You apologize to me, my business is likely to take another dip. Nope. I don't think so. You're just a bag a shit waiting for the garbage man to throw you on the truck."

Unfazed, Will pressed on. "You like the horses, Mo?"

"Every so often I like to—"

"So if Mo Gaffney was a horse running for office, what kind of odds would you give him?"

Mo steamed. Because of Will and his FDA hearings, Mo's chances at office were a history lesson. He shoved a pudgy index finger into Will's face. "Cuzza you, Mo Gaffney's the long shot from hell."

"Well now, so am I," said Will, trying to give Mo a sense of common ground. "But I'm here to say that *this* long shot's got legs. To bet against me is a loser's bet. I'm gonna find my wife and I'm gonna beat this."

"Still tryin' to sell that apology, Senator?" asked Mo.

"I'm selling you the next open seat in the statehouse."

Mo laughed. "Like you got that in your back pocket."

"Not today," said Will. "But when I'm back on top of it?" He gave a shrug. "Who knows. I could back a world-famous car dealer."

Sully agreed. "We could make it happen, Mo."

Teased, Mo's brain grinded. "Like I said, it's a fuckin' long shot."

Will leaned in with a politician's confidence. "But if that long shot's the only shot you got?"

Mo finally got it. It took him a moment. He was slow, but savvy enough to see the carrot dangling from the stick. "Okay. So what do I got that you want?"

"Just now, you said you could get to anybody—*anytime.*"

"And I could," boasted Mo. "And that includes you if you fuck me again!"

Will dropped the rest of it on the table. "I'm looking to get to a guy in prison. You could do that?"

Sure, Mo could do that. The deal was struck. Mo went his way, Will and Sully theirs. And this time, when father and son parted, there was an unrehearsed embrace. Son to father with seemingly nothing in between. No ambition or politics or competitive expectation. They must have held each other for a full half a minute before letting go.

Washington, D.C.

With the Sullivan Senate office all but raided, ransacked, and practically shut down by the FBI, gun-for-hire Benny Yao volunteered to save Will a couple of bucks and a few headaches by moving his operation into the Georgetown condo. That included making up new keys, adding extra phone and fax lines, and procuring precious parking. The headaches piled up anyway. It turned out to be against the condo association's rules to run any kind of business out of the building. The association president, Walter F. Wang, seemed to have nothing better to do than complain, going so far as to inform WWDC, who aired the association's grievances on their six and eleven o'clock news.

"Never mind about Wang," said Will, talking over a dying cell phone from a speeding rental car. La Roy was behind the wheel, keeping the FBI tail in his rearview's sights. They were heading toward Marblehead when Myriam hooked him up with Benny Yao. "What do you got?"

"Look, I pulled a coupla solids over at the DEA," said Yao. "Since they're sharing that billion-dollar database with Justice, I was able to grab a good chunk of the FBI call-ins and stick it into our own search engines."

"You gotta get to the good part," said Will. "My phone's about to run out of juice."

Yao, wearing his wireless headset, was standing centered in what was once Will's living room, now cleared of Civil War junk with the furniture pushed up against the walls to make room for portable desks, phone lines, and computers. "We were up all last night loading the FBI data into the Profiler. And I think we've come up with some interesting cross-matchings."

The silence at the other end of the line was either Will's phone gone dead or the senator waiting for some actual information. "You there?" asked Yao.

"I'm waiting," pressed Will.

"Sightings from Bangor to Guam," said Yao. "I guess your Larry King interview ran on CNN International."

Christ, thought Will, could he just get to it? His phone was beginning to double-beep, signaling his cell-life was shortening with every second.

"The model catalogues IDs, dates of the IDs, then rates the sources from a credible five to a none-credible zero. After which, it tries to look for patterns, connecting the dots along some kind of time line that might fit a natural pattern of travel. Get where I'm going?"

"Yeah, yeah," pushed Will.

"And according to the Profiler, the largest concentration of credible IDs are coming from the Southwest. Texas, New Mexico, Arizona, California. You follow?"

"Why don't I call you back from a pay phone?" said Will.

The investigator droned on, hunched over a twenty-inch computer screen, running his finger along a map of the U.S., tracking points between Texas and Southern California. "What I'm trying to say is that the program is giving us a road map. Picking up a credible four in San Antonio. That would be a Clem. Moving west, we got a three in Midland—an Izzy—a four in Roswell—if you can believe anything credible in Roswell—also an Izzy—"

"Benny, I swear—"

"A five in Albuquerque—Clem again—a four in Winslow, two threes in Flagstaff—Izzy *and* Starr. I got a Clem again in Needles, I got him in Barstow, then it stops with a sighting of—now don't get your hopes up—but someone claims they saw Gwen in Lone Pine, California."

Gwen?

A heat flash bloomed over Will's face, followed by a nasty sweat that chilled him in the blast of the car's air-conditioning.

"Myriam?" asked Will, collecting himself. "Are you still on?"

"I'm here, Senator," said Myriam.

"Wait. Where am I and what time is it?" Will was looking at his watch, road signs, calculating how long it would take to get to the airport. "Okay. I want to fly out of Logan at seven, arriving LAX ASAP. Two seats. Me and La Roy."

Yao broke back in. "Will? You still got that FBI tail?"

"Yeah." Out the side-view mirror Will glimpsed the front end of the Ford Taurus.

Benny Yao's monotone turned dour. "You can get on a commercial airline at Logan, but I can almost guarantee you, by the time you touch down in L.A. there'll be a grand jury subpoena waiting for you when you get off. Just to yank your chain."

Scrambling to keep focused, Will shifted angles. "Fine.

Myriam? I want a private jet delivered to Logan. Totally at my disposal."

Hearing the surge of hope in Will's voice, La Roy began looking for an off-ramp in order to turn back south. "Question is, Earnest, who's gonna loan *you* an aircraft?"

Ignoring him, Will put Myriam to the task. "Pull any kind of coup you can muster. Anybody who owes me a favor. Anybody who's wanted next to me. Call CEOs. Lobbyists. Foreign governments. I don't care about impropriety. I just want my—"

"Will!" interrupted Yao. "You don't *need* to go. Stay outta sight. I've already got a team—"

"Goddammit, I'm going! Send your people, but I'm going. Myriam?"

"Yes, Senator?"

"I want Benny's ID list waiting for me on the plane. Names, addresses. I want rental cars waiting and a flight plan filed to the nearest airport to—where was the last sighting?"

"Lone Pine," said Yao.

"I got it," said Myriam, adding, "Do you want me on the plane?"

"Thanks," said Will. "But I need you there."

While La Roy returned the Chrysler to Hertz, Will sweated over a pay phone inside the small charter terminal, a site resembling a plush, leather-sofa'd club more than a waiting platform for transcontinental flights. Will was hooked up again with Myriam in Washington, trying to fend off the desperate interference and track down an aircraft. Any aircraft. Two months prior, it would've sickened Will to accept or solicit the use of a private jet. For the senator, the offer was always there, dangling like a carrot on a stick. The temptation of a free ride. Every damn day of the week there was some foreign government, corporation, or lawyers' lobby offering Will use of its private jet. The constant and consistent availability, let alone impropriety of it all, made it seem that there were more private jets flying in and out of Dulles Airport than commercial airliners.

And though Will had always said a cautious no to the of-fers, now he couldn't get a single devil's soul to say yes to his urgent request. Myriam attempted to patch Will through to corporate officers, various board directors of Fortune 500 companies, mega-billion-dollar lobby groups, diplomats, agency heads, even one of the joint chiefs. Most said they'd get back to him. And those who he got through to either sat on the fence or apologized that the timing was all wrong. With the FBI investigation, pending indictments, and grand jury subpoenas in the hands of federal servers, Will Sullivan was just too hot for anybody to touch. They all wished him luck, then, after hanging up their telephones, wished he'd never called in the first place.

After two hours of watching Will work the pay phone, La Roy got into the act, producing a packet of commercial air-line tickets purchased under assumed names. Low-budget items that would, after five layovers and three plane changes, deliver the two of them to the small Ontario Air-port in Southern California's Inland Empire. La Roy's shell game flew in the face of the FBI and dared them to follow.

"It's not optimum speed, but they get us to California by eight tomorrow morning. From there, we can rent a car, go to this Lone Pine place, and work our way backwards."

Will was eager to get moving at any price. He nodded his agreement. "When do we board?"

"Forty-minutes," answered La Roy, his eyes slipping off Will to the approaching charter attendant. La Roy's type. A pouty little blonde in a gray uniform with matching pumps.

"Senator?" asked the attendant. "I believe we have an air-craft waiting for you."

"You *believe* there's an aircraft waiting for him?" asked La Roy. "Or do you *know* this to be a fact?"

With a screw-you smile that clearly said, *I'm used to working with demanding customers,* the young number ig-nored La Roy and addressed Will. "Do you have luggage?"

A Gulfstream IV was waiting on the tarmac. Will climbed aboard first, stepping into the large, comfy, air-cooled cabin. The mystery was solved with the first whiff of her perfume.

"Unlimited access," said Vanessa Curran. She was curled into a swiveling captain's chair. No seat belt. Her camera crew was scattered about the rear. "Unlimited access in exchange for full—"

"For full cooperation from your network and its resources," finished Will, reminded of the agreement. It was making sense.

"I showed my bosses the footage we got of the FBI raid." Vanessa gestured to their plush surroundings. "As you might figure, they're kinda hooked on the Will Sullivan story."

"We're going to Lone Pine to find my wife."

"Buckle up," said Vanessa, motioning for Will to sit next to her. "And who's for champagne?"

"Coffee," said La Roy, strapping himself into the nearest seat.

As Will fit the buckle around himself, Vanessa swiveled closer and tongued a whispered warning. "Ditch me again, asshole, and our agreement's terminated."

"What do we have to do to get this bucket moving?" asked Will.

Vanessa snapped her fingers.

Six hours later, Will and his entourage were in Lone Pine, California.

Despite the lateness of the hour, La Roy had browbeaten the local newspaper into opening their doors in order to place a full-page ad in the next day's edition, complete with pictures of Izzy, Starr, Clem, and, most importantly, Gwen. In the meantime, with Vanessa Curran and her camera crew in tow, Will tracked down the solitary person who'd sighted Gwen and reported it to the FBI. Benny Yao's Profiler program had categorized the sighting as a three. Neither great nor bad. But anything was worth a look.

That was until the source turned out to be a ten-year-old boy, holed up at home with a blazing case of chicken pox. It was approximately 1:12 A.M. when U.S. Senator Will Sullivan knocked on the door of the single-family stucco home. When the light over the porch switched on, Kruger fired up the molten-hot blaze of the camera's sun-gun, only to near-mortally shock the boy's mother into verbal apoplexy.

The sleepy boy explained. "I'm sorry, Mr. Senator. But I was visitin' my mom at the hospital . . . she's a nurse? I saw you talkin' on the TV about your Mrs. Senator? The one who got kidnapped? Anyway, I sees this pregnant lady comin' in from the ambulance who looked a lot like the picture they showed on the TV. So's I called the number and, like, said I was my mom. Cuzza only hospital folks are supposed to be usin' the phone . . ."

A simple call to the Lone Pine Hospital pinpointed the day and hour of the boy's sighting. The pregnant woman was identified as a local hairdresser who'd gone into early labor. Shortly thereafter, she'd delivered a healthy seven-pound baby girl. Will thanked the family, hustled the camera crew off the poor people's property, then met up with La Roy at a nearby motel for a mere three hours of sleep.

Stopping at nothing, Will worked the Profiler-generated map backwards. Barstow, Needles, Flagstaff, Albuquerque, Roswell, Midland, finishing off in San Antonio. It was an eight-day campaign with four flights, three rental vans, and a maximum of twenty hours' sleep. The expanding crew now included La Roy, Allison, and three of Yao's investigators. They would hit a town fast and hard, interview the source of the sighting, drop in on the local newspapers, summon law enforcement participation, and exploit Will's star power on local TV. Myriam would call ahead and Allison would provide advance footwork. A call went out to local campaign volunteers recruited from computerized lists procured from the DNC. Sometimes fifty showed. Sometimes, only five. Brightly colored copies of the newspaper ads were distributed as flyers, slipped into mailboxes, stuck on car windshields, under doormats, taped inside retail store windows, and stapled to telephone poles.

And every waking step of Will's quest to find Gwen was covered by the CBS cameras. Even when Will took on the cameras of the local TV stations, Vanessa and her crew captured the TV stations covering Will.

"My wife has been kidnapped," he would repeat over and

over again. *"And I'm here following what my investigators have categorized as 'qualified leads.' But I can't do this alone. I need help. Anybody's help. We need good folks to distribute these flyers, talk to their friends, sort through any recent photos or videotapes that might reveal strangers. Mostly, please be on the lookout for these people."*

Will would always flash the colorful flyer to the cameras. Then take on the cynical questions:

"Excuse me, but are you really looking for your wife, or are you trying to elude a grand jury subpoena?"

"Senator? How does all this jibe with the recent accusations of drunk driving and spousal abuse?"

"Please, Senator Sullivan. How do you respond to this? Some are calling your campaign to find your wife a cynical effort to restore your credibility with the public."

Meanwhile, Will moved on.

Barstow. The man identified as Clem turned out to be a vagrant living in an abandoned copper mine.

Needles. The Izzy sighting was a woman in a dark blue Land Cruiser, driving east with two malamutes. The partial Nevada license plate turned up positive on the owner, a cocktail waitress working at the Mirage Hotel in Las Vegas.

Flagstaff. Another Clem sighting. Source not found.

Albuquerque. Clem again. Actually ID'd as a biker named Walter working as a manager of a local donut shop.

Roswell. Izzy and Starr. Both seen driving a red Dodge Ram. The partial license plate matched no known vehicles. The lead ran out.

Midland. Clem. A truck stop sighting. Dead end.

San Antonio. Clem. Source not found.

As the plea for help expanded, so did the calls to the twenty-four-hour, round-the-clock hot line. And Benny Yao's Profiler program began drawing new maps. A two-hundred-mile stretch across North Dakota through Montana. A five-hundred-plus-mile swath running from West Virginia through Tennessee and Kentucky. And an eight-hundred-mile stretch following Route 1 up the California coast, cutting across Oregon, the state of Washington, and finally dying off in the resort town of Sandpoint, Idaho.

Tirelessly, and expending thousands of gallons of CBS's jet fuel, Will ran down every possibility. Each and every substantial sighting. Talking until he was hoarse. Shaving with dull razors. Sleeping only when his body demanded. And finally losing a battle against a flu virus and a balance-hindering ear infection.

And as illness caught up with him, so did the grand jury subpoenas. All three were served: Will, La Roy, and Allison Flannery. Handed the subpoenas at the precise moment the anguished senator was doing a live shot from one of Sandpoint, Idaho's more spectacular lakeview vistas. He was there to make his hundredth or so plea for information on the whereabouts of his wife, her kidnappers, or any clue that might lead to Gwen's rescue.

FEDERAL GRAND JURY
EASTERN DISTRICT
CIRCUIT 110c
155 54TH STREET
WASHINGTON, DISTRICT OF COLUMBIA

SUBPOENA

SERVED UPON: WILLIAM DANIEL SULLIVAN
ACTION: FED. CODE 91-88, 904.7, 944.44-F

Under penalty of prosecution, WILLIAM DANIEL SULLIVAN is commanded to appear before the above-referenced grand jury, therein to answer and give testimony in the aforementioned pending actions . . .

16

The watering system for the Rancho Seco Country Club sprang to life at sunrise, sending staccato geysers of reclaimed water over the freshly mown turf. The early morning golfers paid bargain rates to play the championship layout. Old men in polyester Sansabelt slacks and worn paisley shirts sped their golf carts past the empty fairway lots. Each eighth-of-an-acre parcel was READY TO BUILD, complete with county sewer and water lines stubbed in. But so tall grew the weeds and star thistle that the PRICED TO SELL signs were dwarfed and difficult to read—a dismal reminder of the development's grim neighbor, the triple field of razor wire, guard towers, and the four gray domes which made up the Rancho Seco Maximum Security Men's Facility.

Theroux had never seen the golf course. Though he'd read about it and the surrounding community on the Internet. The developer was so desperate to stave off his impending bankruptcy, he'd paid for his own Web page in order to increase awareness and advertising. The pixilated photos on the Rancho Seco Country Club Web page were green to shining green. Lushly landscaped. A sight for sore golfers, thought the killer. Golf was a game he didn't care to understand. It looked damn silly. Especially when they used the little white carts. In Theroux's opinion, the game was on par with the likes of shuffleboard and lawn bowling.

Yet each morning when he woke, he imagined the golf course spreading out beyond the concrete walls and razor fence, dying on the vine as if the cancerous growth of inmates had spread beyond the boundaries of the prison.

Before breakfast arrived—even before the first bustle of new guards as the graveyard crew switched out with the day crew—Theroux's internal clock would wake him. After a brief series of stretches, one hundred push-ups, and some Tai Chi, he would light up his ThinkPad, activate the secret cell phone linkup, hook into one of the five Internet service providers he subscribed to, and begin a morning of composing and sending e-mail. First, a wake-up call to Izzy, Starr, Clem, and Jack. They were no longer so spread out that he had to write daily instructions to each.

After ten scattered years, the surviving resurrected were together again, all in the service of the father, Gwen, and her unborn. But Sheila. *Where the fuck was Sheila?* Was she just late to the party? Still tidying things up in Dallas? Maybe she was dead. Or maybe she got busted. Theroux's comfort was in his conviction that she would *never* give him up.

Next, Theroux composed queries to his appeals team, saving those to his hard drive for the routine afternoon download. Those e-mails were usually laced with lacerating sermons, indicting everyone from society, to the system, to the president of the United States. All of it was feigned anger and outrage, specially fitted for those who were *not* supposed to be reading, including prison officials, the FBI, and the L.A. County district attorney's office. His diatribes named names just for the sake of putting in a scare.

It was Theroux's way of saying "Boo!" to those who feared him as long as he was still alive.

After that, he put pen to paper and answered the previous day's mail. Most were interview requests from news agencies and graduate criminology students. During a lonely spate some four years earlier, he had the grad students send pictures along with their requests for interviews. He gave audiences only to the women whom he deemed young, attractive, and potential candidates for his personal process of motherly selection. That was where his plot to father a child had first gone from seed to seedling. His faith in appeals dashed long ago, the killer had gone to bed one frozen prison night with the psyche of an injured boy—and woken at daylight filled with an unearthly sense of purpose. Had he summoned God or a demon? He couldn't tell or touch it. The killer in him was simply imbued with a renewed sense of purpose. A whisper to his sickly nerve center.

You shall have a son!

Progeny was the only hope he had of resurrecting himself. He would live on through a child! Only those visiting graduate girls had proved too bookish, prudish, or infertile in their posture. Each was missing that most important *something* that only Theroux, the boy, could remember.

Daddy, please don't hurt my mommy! Please don't . . .

Theroux not only needed someone fertile, but someone who *wanted* to be pregnant. Was desperate to carry a child for nine months. And, again, someone who fit his distinct criteria for intelligence and beauty, and who had a certain, indescribable quality usually seen only in movie stars.

Someone not unlike himself.

The breakfast tray arrived between eight and eight-fifteen. Knowing him to be a persnickety eater, the cooks took twisted pride in serving Theroux meals that came back half-eaten. On that particular Tuesday, he used his plastic fork and knife to trim the fat off the bacon strips, separate the egg whites from the hardened yolks, and pick the raisins out of the spackling paste the prison called oatmeal. Theroux drank the lowfat milk in a breathless chugalug. He placed the breakfast tray in the return by eight-thirty, allowing a crisp half hour to nap before yard time. The killer meditated, dreamed, and plotted. Time was getting shorter by the minute. He needed to use every moment of it wisely.

"Yard time," said the guard, a short, round-faced fellow

with a name tag reading F. REDDING. He wore thick-framed glasses with an elastic safety strap to keep them snug to his face. Redding shoved the half-eaten breakfast tray away with his foot, leaving it for the cleanup crew of inmate trustees. Then he placidly went about the task of attaching ankle and waist chains to the prisoner.

"You're new," said Theroux, doing his long-practiced three-sixty.

Redding had heard all he'd needed to about Theroux. Heard that he mind-fucked guards just for the hell of it. So Redding had his own little game to play. He called it "Shut Up and Walk."

"Show me your mouth," ordered Redding, an officious procedure guards more comfortable with Theroux chose to ignore. Theroux obliged, showing the guard his teeth while Redding shined a flashlight inside. No objects. Redding spoke into his walkie-talkie. "Twenty-four to the yard." The doors slid open and Theroux walked.

"Pleased to meet you," said the killer, offering up a cordial smile.

"No, you're not," answered the guard. "Now shut up and walk."

Yard time.

Or an hour in the round, thought Theroux. He could sit, walk, or stare up at the sun. The only scenery was the sky, the three surrounding domes, and the guard towers. Inside the space were bleachers, a grass baseball field, and a cyclone-fenced weight-lifting pavilion, all encompassed by a circular dirt running track for those unshackled inmates who needed to sweat their time.

Theroux shared his precious yard time with twenty-five other death-row cons, shuttled in and out in five-minute increments. When Theroux hit the yard at five past nine, another con finishing his hour was being escorted back to C block. And though conversation between inmates was encouraged by prison counselors, fewer than half engaged in any public dialogue. Most kept to their own sick selves.

The killer liked to shuffle through his hour, starting on the track near his home dome and walking it counterclockwise. His newest wrinkle was the cigarettes. Camels. A recently acquired taste that contradicted his otherwise healthy regimen. Late one night, he'd been ego-surfing Web-link after Web-link for anything having to do with himself and his favorite U.S. senator. One of those links took him to an antismoking page, picturing celebrities and public figures with their habits exposed in bold, ugly color. The newest celebrity smoker was none other than Senator Willy. He was pictured paparazzi-style, cigarette in mouth, hustling through the streets of Washington, D.C., with his infamous chief of staff alongside. Theroux recalled his research on the subject, remembering that Will was an ex-drinker *and* ex-smoker. Camels were the senator's brand. The next dawn, he'd placed his order with a trustee. By afternoon, Theroux had received a carton. Like a kid who'd stolen from his mother's stash, he couldn't wait to blaze up.

"Hurry the hell up!" said Charlie, standing guard at the open door of Theroux's cell. This while another guard, nicknamed Wiz due to his supposed prowess with just about anything electronic, tried in vain to download the contents of Theroux's ThinkPad to a 500-megabyte zip-drive. The unit, about the size of a Sony Discman, was easily overnighted from Providence, driven, handed off, then smuggled into the prison by Charlie himself, who was charging the visiting "rehabilitation consultant" from Rhode Island a cozy grand to heist Theroux's hard drive.

"The computer's asking for a goddamn password!" said Wiz. "You didn't tell me I'd have to hack the thing."

"You said you know computers!"

"I know the *hardware*. That and some of the operating system's language. But Jesus, Chuck. I haven't seen nothin' like this. I don't know where the fuck to start."

Charlie checked his watch. 9:55. They had ten minutes to download before Theroux was returned to his cell. "It wants passwords, then start typing passwords."

"It could be a million—"

Charlie started spitting a stream of free-associated words.

"Start with *killer*. Uh, *murder*. Or *mind reader* . . . or *asshole*."

"Nothin'," said Wiz.

"Type anything!"

"We got what? Five minutes? I say we give it up and come back."

"He'll know we were here," said Charlie. "That and I ain't turnin' my back on a thousand bucks."

"You know, I talked to Spillman and—"

"You talked to Spillman?" asked Charlie, sounding more incredulous and nervous by the split second. "About the thing here? About us doing this thing?"

"He won't say shit."

"That's not the point."

"Well, I talked to him," said Wiz. "And he said that the contents of this here computer is privileged. You know? Lawyer stuff. And that if Asshole can prove his computer's been tampered with, that it might be grounds for his appeal. He could get himself a stay of execution."

"Screw Spillman and screw you," said Charlie. "If I could, I'd shove this computer so far up W.D.'s ass he'd be shitting microchips for a week."

Wiz turned back to the computer, hammering the space bar, doing double- and triple-key combinations to unlock the damn unit. "It's not happening, pard."

Charlie, who hadn't budged from his post at the open door, looked in at Wiz, his lips pressed so tightly together that they formed a perfectly flat, horizontal line underneath his nose.

Wiz asked again. "Whatcha wanna do, pard?"

10:05 A.M. After fifteen cycles around the track and four Camels, Theroux's yard time was over. Before Redding could call the killer's name, Theroux was at the gate, pulling a final drag from the cigarette and stubbing it out with his shoe.

"I'm punctual," smiled Theroux. "Always have been." As if that was the answer to Redding's mental question.

Theroux was escorted back inside, up the crisscrossing

metal stairs to C block's third tier and down the gangway to his cell. Three doors away, the killer sensed his world was out of kilter. Was it the looks from the other inmates? Was it an odd smell? From behind him, Redding barked into the walkie-talkie. "Number twenty-four, back to cell."

Theroux's door slid open. The killer could feel the gangway vibrate underfoot. He tried to quicken his steps. But the ankle chains were rated to keep prisoners under speeds of two miles per hour.

Sweat stung Theroux's forehead. He sensed violation. A mental rape. As if some holy entity had reached into his soul and slashed at it with a new razor.

Arriving at his cell door, Theroux turned a hard right, scanned quickly, then drew his eyes to the short shelf above his desk.

The scream was heard all the way into Central Command. A bellowing from a prisoner so guttural, so deep, and so deathly, they could only guess that it welled from the nether regions south of the human surface. The scream bounded off the concrete walls of the dome, sending chills and gooseflesh rippling from cell to cell. The devil had spoken. And he was pissed off.

PART | THREE

1

Spokane, Washington.
　Fifty-one miles from Sandpoint, Idaho.
　A '66 Chevy half-ton pickup. Scratched metallic green. Original wheels. License plate, 1GHF598. Three forward gears plus a granny. Straight six underneath the hood. Smog-approved, street-legal, and registered to Señor Alec Guzzman, caretaker of the one-hundred-acre Farthmore Estate in an area known as Deer Park. Only Alec Guzzman wasn't driving his prized fixer. It was Izzy behind the wheel, edging up past the fifty-mile-an-hour speed limit and somewhat confident in her newest guise as a bald-headed, jack-booted lesbian. Dean's instructions were true perfection. And she feared neither a Spokane cop nor a county sheriff passing by, or even some nosy local who didn't recognize the woman driving Alec's Chevy.
　Hell, she'd already been pulled over once. All she'd had to do was wait for the cop to call the main station, where they'd informed him that while Mr. and Mrs. Guzzman were visiting their native Guatemala for four months, Sally Anne Mercer and her brother Jim were occupying the care-

taker's house on the old Farthmore Estate. They would have access to both the Guzzman's pickup and Plymouth Astro van, plus keys to the main house and instructions for general maintenance.

The good Guzzmans had sent polite letters saying as much to the Spokane PD, the Spokane County Sheriff's Department, the local utilities, the Farthmore Estate trustee, and the Deer Park Homeowners Association.

Poor Alec Guzzman had signed the letters under considerable duress. Clem had put Alec's Ruger .22 to Mrs. Guzzman's head while Izzy dictated the letter. The letters were mailed. A local travel agent issued two tickets to Guatemala. Then Izzy drove Mr. Guzzman to the First Bank of Spokane, where he withdrew ten thousand dollars in American Express traveler's checks. They returned to the estate in time to find a grave dug ten paces from the Little Spokane River. Mrs. Guzzman was already dead and waiting for her husband to join her. Alec Guzzman wailed briefly over his wife's body, crossed himself, mumbled a Hail Mary, then accepted the twenty-two slug in the back of the head without any protest.

Clem buried the Guzzmans while Izzy moved in.

The Farthmore Estate, long vacant and lying in petrified state until the absentee landlord returned from an indefinite vacation, sported two entrances. Both of them gated. The first, a right-hand turn off Highway 2 through a massive pair of wrought-iron gates onto a fieldstone drive. The second entrance, a mere quarter-mile up the highway, was easy to miss be it day or night. It was on the inside of a hairpin turn, tucked between two towering live oaks and guarded by a single swinging cyclone gate with a rusted NO TRESPASSING sign purchased from Mike's Hardware.

Izzy shoved the old pickup into neutral, set the parking brake, and jumped from the cab. Her anguish-earned hundred and ten pounds hit the dirt at a light trot. After months as a heavyweight matron and yielding to the daily temptations of junk food, she was back to her fighting weight, shorn of all her hair and looking naturally tan, earthy, and healthy in her Wolverine boots. The only hitch was the green contact lenses. They itched. She swiftly dialed the padlock's combination, swung the gate open, rolled the pickup through, and reversed the sequence. In a matter of seconds, she was back in the truck, swerving up the winding dirt track to the caretaker's cottage, a modest two-story ranch house set back amongst a thick clump of long-needled pine and quaking aspen.

The morning mist had eventually given way to bright sunshine, clear mountain air, and a mean temperature of seventy-four degrees. Perfect. Izzy tried not to think of the day when she'd have to leave behind such a pastoral place.

She parked the truck and began carting boxes of groceries and supplies through the front door of the cottage. Thirty-two steps each way. In the living room she found Dr. Bertrand in his usual afternoon pose. His body was sunk into a large easy chair—his eyes closed, the *Spokane Register* on his lap. On the reading table next to him were his works. A hypodermic needle, cotton balls, alcohol swabs, a spoon, and a Zippo lighter for cooking the powder.

Opposite Dr. B. were three TVs turned down to a mere whisper of volume. The bank of thrift shop sets was permanently tuned to CNN, CNBC, and MSNBC, VCRs constantly running. Just in case Dean appeared to send them a message. It'd been weeks since they'd lost contact.

Izzy ignored the old man and lugged the four boxes one by one into the country kitchen. The cost of the groceries rang in her head. Two hundred and eleven dollars, eighty-five cents. Izzy'd tabulated the total, including tax, long before the checker had finished scanning the last dozen eggs.

Starr, her hair permed and bleached to Oklahoma platinum, was seated in the sunny breakfast nook, doing a daily crossword puzzle torn from Dr. Bertrand's paper and practically ignoring the small, black-and-white TV monitor spying on Gwen. But as was her habit each and every time she walked through the kitchen, Izzy checked both the picture and sound. The mother-to-be was fetal and napping. When the volume was turned up, Izzy could hear her snoring.

"Where's Clem?" she asked.

"Getting fly-fishing lessons from Jack," said Starr without even looking up. "They keep talking about going down to the river and catching us dinner."

The river and its buggy shore. A five-minute walk down the gravel path to the rear of the buttoned-up main house. Izzy had been down there when she was scouting the property. She'd practically been eaten alive by the grossly over-populated swarm.

She leaned over Starr and checked outside the window. In a grassy clearing to the rear, Jack was indeed giving Clem a fishing lesson, casting Alec Guzzman's favorite rod back and forth, back and forth, then slinging the handmade fly toward a sky-blue wading pool. Both men were transformed versions of their shaggy selves. Jack had gone from blond to a conservatively cut brown. And Clem had simply gone native again. His beard was heavy and his eyes were browned by disposable contact lenses. The coup de grace in Dean's scenario of transformations was Clem's nose. The father figure had ordered it permanently disfigured. Pummeled to the point where he'd probably never regain his olfactory senses. Izzy was glad to have performed the operation with her two fists.

"Lunch for the queen bitch?" asked Izzy.

"On the stove and in the oven," said Starr, rubbing her tummy and adding, "You know, I think I'll be early."

"Just as long as you're not late," warned Izzy. "Or Dr. Bert's gonna induce you."

Lunch was a specialty of Starr's. It was always comfort food. Today's menu called for captain's pockets. A wonderfully gooey mixture of spinach and ricotta cheese sandwiched inside a flaky pastry. The once-hefty Izzy had slowly come to abhor mealtime at Farthmore. The smells of buttery breads and juicy, fresh-barbecued burgers made her despise Gwen all the more. The sooner Gwen was dead, the sooner her temptation to eat everything in sight would be vanquished.

"I asked the social worker if I could see pictures of the parents," said Starr. "She said I couldn't. Don't you think that's unfair?"

"They got their rules and we've got ours."

Three days earlier, Jack and Starr had posed as expectant parents, indigent and unable to support the child Starr was bearing. They filled out all the necessary paperwork. A painfully short form, barely one-tenth the length of the form for adoptive parents. All the state of Washington bothered about was whether the parents were drug addicts or HIV positive. That, and they had to call the caseworker when the mother went into labor. As described by Social Services, Starr would keep the infant for twenty-four hours, then hand it over to the social worker.

Starr usually ended up sobbing when conversation surfaced about giving up her child. Izzy said she wouldn't put up with the crybaby act, telling her to buck up and keep her eye on the prize. Dean's unborn child.

Izzy sucked back a can of Sprite, ate two plain slices of whole-wheat bread, then held her stomach to a mild roar as she prepared to deliver Gwen's lunch. An afternoon prescription of prenatal vitamins was already dosed and waiting in a Dixie cup. Izzy picked up the tray, walked through the pantry to a second door, pushed it open with her foot, and descended sixteen dark steps. When her feet hit the concrete, she automatically flicked on the overhead light switch with an elbow, turned a hard left, then walked the low-ceilinged, slightly sloped, seventy-five-foot passage that dug deep into the mountain. She came upon another door, larger and painted army green. She had to set down the tray to throw the three bolts. The hinges squeaked and the bottom of the door scraped the concrete.

A second light switch ignited the central bunker cell. Like Gwen's room, the cell was a corrugated half-arch. Twelve feet at the top, striped with power cables, air ducts, and water pipes. The cell had four vaultlike doors. Two forward, two aft.

The door to her immediate right was also army green and stenciled white with O.R.

The second door on the right was labeled POST OP.

The first door on the left, SUPPLIES.

And the last door, BUNKHOUSE.

In chalk, BUNKHOUSE had been crossed out and replaced

with three words written in Dean's own hand: YOU ARE
HERE!

The walls of the central cell were pasted with faded military instruction banners with dark warnings, the likes of:

WHAT TO DO TO AVOID NUCLEAR FALLOUT

And . . .

TEN MOST SIGNIFICANT SIGNS OF RADIATION SICKNESS

From the first day she'd set foot in the bunker, Izzy had
paid little mind to the forty-year-old warnings. The dungeonlike bomb shelter had been just as Dean had described it. And the age-old threat of a survivable nuclear
attack was insignificant in comparison to what Dean
planned for the end of the world. The *real* end of the
world.

"I've had three incredibly precious days stolen from me,"
Will had said to the press. "And now I'm going home." His
one-sentence sound bite referred to his three-day internment in front of the federal grand jury, where accusations
were slung from four federal prosecutors. The baseless
charges were cannonballed at Will, and ranged from the
gray area of receiving gifts in exchange for legislative support to the difficult-to-interpret allegations of campaign financing fraud and an outlandish obstruction of justice
charge. The prosecutors tried to convince the grand jury that
the senator had overstepped his public service boundaries
with his media-hyped fraud-in-the-FDA hearings, and in
doing so, had single-handedly demolished a two-year, $4
million DOJ investigation.

The beleaguered senator denied all charges, defended
himself without an attorney present, and whenever he could
muster the energy, tried reminding the grand jury that his
wife was in imminent peril, the FBI was not helping, and
that every moment he spent on the witness stand kept him
from his duties as a husband and a father.

That stone-faced grand jury, twenty-four strong, remained impassive. Will calculated that, during the last year alone, they must have heard testimony from so many political hacks, one more member of government pleading for his life must have sounded akin to the fox asking for one more unguarded tour of the chicken coop.

After the three-day duel with a federal grand jury, the nation's suspicion that Will was just another self-aggrandizing, credulity-lacking baby-kisser was fast on the rise.

ABC, NBC, and CNN pollsters found the country split:

Do you think Will Sullivan is a criminal and spousal abuser?

Yes	42%
No	50%
Don't know	8%

Do you believe Will Sullivan's claim that he is a victim of an overzealous Justice Department?

Yes	41%
No	42%
Don't know	17%

Do you believe Will Sullivan's wife, Gwen Corbett-Sullivan, has been kidnapped or is simply in hiding?

Kidnapped	26%
In hiding	29%
Don't know	45%

Afterwards came the migraines and the depression. Will couldn't recall which came first. And cigarettes didn't seem to help anymore. Neither did caffeine or those double doses of extra-strength Tylenol. All that was left was either booze or home. Will picked the latter, returning to a house that brought him little sanctuary, bad memories, and consistent nightmares.

Crossing from the front step into the manor, Will busted out in a cold sweat while La Roy seemed positively giddy with the anticipation of getting a look at the basement. He wondered just how Allatore had cleaned up the crime scene. Since that deadly night, La Roy's reckless imagination had crept around the basement, looking for possible clues. Mistakes were always made. That was the rule of forensic science. What had Allatore, an experienced former prosecutor, forgotten to cover up?

"Nobody's stopping you from going down there," said Will. "Just don't expect me to reenact the night in question with you."

"I'm just gonna peek," said La Roy.

Will dared to light up a cigarette. Gwen would never have allowed him to smoke in the new house. He wondered if it was an act of disrespect or simply a craving he couldn't deny.

"I'm going to find the Advil and check in with Benny," said Will, breaking away from La Roy and heading for Gwen's desk in the den. The house was cast in the ethereal half-light of early evening. The high, steeply pitched ceilings reminded Will of a church. He stopped, cursed himself for not praying that day—praying for Gwen's safe return—then asked forgiveness for the cursing. It all seemed so damned contradictory. Curse. Pray. Curse again. Guilt. Shame. Pray again.

If you are God and you can hear me, give me strength enough to believe and remove this drowning fear.

The battle with depression was almost overwhelming. He'd spend the day fighting off the black beast, then after sleep brought a brief respite, he'd wake up feeling as if buried in a grave. Six feet under with a thousand pounds of dirt to crawl through just to get out of bed.

She's dead, Will. You know she's dead.

With a glass of month-old water from the fridge, Will knocked back four Advil, then a shot of Pepto-Bismol to keep the double dose from burning a hole in his gut.

In the den, he reached for the telephone to call Benny Yao for the morning update of bad news. Next to the phone he found a notepad pilfered from the bedside of the EconoView Motel in Scituate. On it was a brief scribbling in Vance Allatore's hand. It read:

"Be courageous and strong, for that is the Will of God."

Joshua 1:9

Will must have stared at the notepad for a full two minutes, counting back the more than three weeks since he'd seen the former prosecutor. Can't be that long, he tried convincing himself. Lost for a reference point, he turned across Gwen's desk and picked up her personal calendar and flipped through the month of May. Will counted twenty-two days since he'd last seen Allatore, two weeks since he'd received the FedEx. Where the hell was he? Had Theroux finally gotten to him?

Slapping back through the calendar pages, Will found himself searching for what he feared would be a terrifying watershed number. Gwen always checked her calendar before bed, slashing across the day that had been with a red marker. Will flagged back fifteen more pages until he came upon her signature slash. Fifty-three days since she'd been stolen from him. Fifty-three days would make her nine months . . .

Jesus, no!

Will flagged ahead in the calendar, nearly tearing the pages as he madly turned them until he landed on a date marked in a pink and blue happy face. Gwen's due date. June 28. Less than three weeks hence. The very day Theroux was sentenced to die.

The phone rang. Will jumped and picked it up on the first half-ring, but didn't identify himself. He waited for the caller to speak first.

"Will?" asked the voice.

He recognized Yao's nasal inflections. "I was just about to call you. Whatcha got for me, Ben?"

"You're a hard guy to track down," said Yao.

"It's not me you're supposed to be looking for," snapped Will.

"We're trying," said Yao, preparing to go into what La Roy called *the Ben Zone.* That monotone drone, the ultimate antidote for sleeplessness.

Out of his left ear, Will was hearing voices coming up from the basement stairs. Familiar. La Roy's and some other . . .

"Are you with me, Senator?" asked Yao.

"I'm gonna have to call you back," said Will.

"One more thing," Yao continued. "I've got this Vanessa Curran problem—"

Will hung up and craned his neck, straining to hear the second voice. La Roy's was nowhere to be heard. But the woman's? At first, he thought it was Vanessa Curran, caught up with him once again. But that was before he felt the skin on the back of his neck pull as if it were being stretched by a legion of tiny weevils.

It's Gwen!

The chair toppled over as Will bolted from the room. He gripped the door frame and spun himself into a hard right turn, down the hallway, and stared into the black hole which was the basement. Gwen's voice carried up the steps into his ears, caressing him with hope. His knees went wobbly at the first step. He found the banister and worked his way down.

She's here. I can hear her. Please, Jesus. Let it be my wife . . .

2

The dedication for CBS's new Washington bureau took the form of a laid-back, tie-in-the-briefcase, pre-weekend office bash. Michelob, a major advertiser during football season, sponsored the event by rolling in kegs of brew, twelve cases of California Chardonnay, and enough hard liquor to ignite five city blocks were someone at a rival network to throw a match.

The four-story, Potomac-view factory had been turned into a high-tech cable, wood beam, and Sheetrock marvel with floor-to-ceiling windows and enough white paint to stripe a million miles of highway. A sharp contrast to the dark New York suits who'd shuttled south for the event. Herbert Gluckman, vice president of News, shook hands, kissed all the bureau darlings on the cheek, and schmoozed the denim and button-down oxford-clad segment producers.

After an hour of chitchat, Gluckman ducked into a quickie meeting with his prize diva Vanessa Curran, executive producer Dennis Forlani, and senior producer Mitch Hubbard.

"It's coming to an end," said Gluckman, the deep sonics

of his voice as thick as juice from a Georgia peach. "And it's coming to an end right now." At the request of the overextended producing staff whose job it was to provide oversight for Vanessa Curran's Will Sullivan "epic," Gluckman was, in effect, lowering the boom.

Seated on a charcoal-gray chenille sofa, coolly poised as if she was ready to take dictation from the New York suit who'd made her, Vanessa feigned taking notes.

"You spent a lot of network dough for what?" asked Gluckman rhetorically. "Thirty, forty hours of tape? More?"

"Sixty-six," said Mitch Hubbard.

"All on a story you say has no finish?" said Gluckman.

"Not yet, Herb," said Vanessa. "But what we've got so far is pretty much—"

"Crap!" finished Gluckman, gesticulating downward. "You got a U.S. senator on his way into the toilet. Sad, sad story. Everybody's covering it. And what do we have? Some up-close-and-personal bullshit and a signed letter saying that we won't air a lick of it until he says otherwise?"

"Or August 1st," corrected Vanessa.

"June 28," said Gluckman.

"Actually," said Vanessa, "I'm quite sure it's the first of—"

"June 28, sweetie. That's the day this Theroux character gets his ticket punched, am I right?" asked Gluckman.

"Yes. I believe so," said Vanessa. She was looking to both her producers for a little backup. Instead, she was framed by two men whose arms were crossed, their mouths firmly shut.

"I mean, that's what this quest is all about," continued Gluckman. "Sullivan thinks his wife has been kidnapped by this so-called cult. We got him goin' from town to town to town, spreadin' this leaky sack of shitty gossip like spoiled molasses. Which we all know is steer manure because he's a self-deluded drunk and a wife beater. By the way. I have it on good authority the soon-to-be-ex Mrs. Sullivan is hiding out at a friend's in the Hamptons until her hubby's ship is finally sunk. She's no dummy. She's got a career in this business. If he goes down, he's goin' down alone. You follow me?"

Vanessa followed just fine. She didn't exactly agree. But the sermon was influential. So she spun it. "What I have is the story of a famous man on a tragic trek. It's got politics, lost love, an FBI conspiracy, a cult leader, and—"

"Your story has no fuckin' finish!" said Gluckman. "So listen to me. 'Cuz I'm about to give it to you. Kiss off the sulking-senator crap and get me some stuff on this Theroux. We wrap Sullivan's tragic political demise around the end of this cult messiah, and air the full one hour, *prime time,* on the night the bad boy bites the big one."

"Sullivan's still got his fans out there," reminded Vanessa. "Some people actually believe in him."

"Some people actually believe in the Tooth Fairy. But that don't mean he's a homo," said Gluckman with a wink to producers Forlani and Hubbard. "This week. If we can time this right, we'll get an indictment on Sullivan precisely the day we go to air."

"You know something I don't know?" Vanessa's radar was on suspect mode. "I mean, I'm pretty hooked into the FBI and I haven't heard—"

"We've both been around, Vanessa," said Gluckman, his eyebrows arching incestuously. "I know you and Sullivan go back a ways. Had some kinda wild thing, the two of you? Yeah?"

Vanessa's sex life was hardly a secret. But so far, she thought her brief bout of drunken sport-fucking with the Massachusetts senator was about as confidential as nuclear codes.

"We had a little *something,*" she stiffly admitted.

"Well, I had a little *something* with Margie Van Hough when she was just a Sigma Kae Little Sister back at Penn. And you know what? We still talk once a week. You on my wavelength?" Gluckman checked his watch and swung on his jacket, ready to return to the party downstairs. "The indictment's comin' down. It's just a matter of relationships and good timing. For you, for the network, and for Margie Van Hough. A thousand bucks says the indictment lands on June 28. And I want your cameras there to cover it."

* * *

"To tell you the truth, I don't think Vance ever left," said La Roy. "While we were out busting the dust, ol' Allatore was watching a lot of TV. He even installed himself a mini-satellite dish."

La Roy was giving his shocked-to-the-socks boss a quick tour of the redecorated basement. Not only had the room been swept of all crime scene evidence, it was now cluttered with TV monitors and professional video decks. VHS and three-quarter-inch videotapes were scattered amongst legal pads covered in Allatore's incoherent scribblings.

As for the voice which had pulled Will to the basement, La Roy could only wag his head in apology. "What can I say, Earnest? It was in the deck. All I did was press PLAY."

"Play it again," demanded Will.

"Bad idea. I think you—"

Will didn't wait for La Roy. He stepped up to the deck marked B and pressed the large PLAY button. A twenty-three-inch color monitor flashed color bars, then a PBS logo appeared. A four-year-old *Frontline* documentary un-spooled. Titled *The Campaign Game,* its principle subject was spin-mistress and siren of the DNC, Gwen Corbett-Sullivan.

"You want to torture yourself?" asked La Roy. "Fine by me. As long as I don't have to watch."

"I want to be alone with her."

It crushed La Roy to hear it, see it. Will stood a mere five feet from the screen, eyes unblinking. It was a sad and pa-thetic request, met by La Roy's compliance and under-standing. He left the remote on the sofa and quietly crept out of the basement.

Will never heard La Roy leave. He only heard what his ears craved. Her voice. He imagined Gwen was talking to him, instead of some faceless interviewer.

"I never planned to be in this business, really. I began as a junior marketing consultant for Meyers and Librande in Boston . . ."

The temptation to reach out and touch the screen was monumental. Gwen looked devastating. Medium-length hair. Perfect skin. Nary a hint of makeup. She wore a white, high-necked suit with a split collar. Her gray eyes were radiantly photographed in close-up. Yet Will knew the static touch of his fingertips to the TV screen would only break the spell. So he closed his eyes and turned down the volume until the buzz in the twin speakers vanished. There, he said. She was there, next to him, whispering.

"My husband was my first real candidate. We met shortly before his first run for the House. I guess you could say he had all the right things to say in public and in private . . ."

"Where the hell are you?" Will bitched, kicking over a box with such force that he ruptured the cardboard. Slogging through the darkness of the guest bedroom, he ignored the burned-out bulb, making do with the faint light from the corridor. "C'mon, asshole. Show me your face!"

"You okay, Earnest?" shouted out La Roy from the bottom of the stairs. He'd been disturbed while eating his dinner of cold cereal and canned apple juice, reading the ingredients listed on the side of the box: sugar, defatted wheat germ, wheat starch, trisodium phospate, mixed tocopherols.

Tocopherols?

La Roy remembered reading someplace that tocopherols were highly addictive substances the cereal companies used to bewitch little children. "Will? You all right up there?"

Will ignored him, pushing over one box and starting on another. He knew precisely what he was looking for. A little more digging and he'd surely come up with it. And in a box that felt like a crate full of old office supplies, his hand found a round porcelain figurine, eleven inches tall, holding a guitar.

There you are, you son of a bitch!

The figurine in hand, Will made a quick left into the corridor and escaped down the rear staircase.

Out the back door, the sun was gone and all that was left of the day was the faint reflection of the harbor lights against a starless sky. Will could smell the rain coming. Soon it would be pelting the landscape. Despite the threat, he didn't have sense enough to run for cover. He simply dragged a deck chair around to the far side of the swimming pool, turned his back to the house, and slid onto the damp cushion without an earthly care.

Just Senator Willy and Elvis.

The porcelain figure was just as he'd remembered it. Even in the quasi-light, it glistened with rich blues and blacks. A flame-red acoustic guitar was slung around the icon's shoulder. God only knew what tune he was wailing. For all the years the decanter had sat upon the top shelf of his home office, he'd never so much as wondered. It had been a gift from a constituent, illegal in receipt, but too kitschy to turn away. It was eleven inches tall of promise, reputedly containing some of the finest single-malt whisky ever bottled in the republic of Ireland.

The missing tax stamp was a sure sign that Elvis had been smuggled through airport customs. And when Will twisted Elvis's head ever-so-slowly, the cork underneath sqeaked out an alcoholic's tune. Will's nostrils were filled with the perfume of good liquor. His lizard brain was in control—the beast yanking at the chain with each turn of the cork.

"Are you lonesome tonight? Do you miss me tonight?"

Will froze at the husky notes, timbered to sound like Elvis, but nothing close to Las Vegas quality. This voice was something more akin to a Miami Beach drag queen's act. The warbling was slightly off-key and coming from his immediate right.

"Are you sorry we drifted apart?"

The bald head of Vance Allatore broke through the darkness before the rest of him surfaced. He was camouflaged in dark green garbage bags from head to toe and carrying a fishing rod in one hand and a catch of rock cod in the other. Each fish was hooked by its own bungee cord.

"Glad you could make the party," groused Will, partially relieved it wasn't La Roy there to hack him to death with a sponsor's hellfire.

"Hope you saved some for me," said Allatore, leaving the rod and the fish on the deck while kneeling to rinse his hands in the pool water.

"Haven't started yet," said Will, sure that he was going to knock back the whole decanter without any help.

"You know, I'm surprised," said Allatore, sitting on the end of the lounger. "Old La Roy struck me as a pretty good watchdog. How'd you get Elvis there past him?"

"The King has his ways," Will answered flippantly.

"You know, I once saw Elvis," continued Allatore. "I musta been eighteen or so. Lake Tahoe. Me and some cronies were pretty tripped on acid, but I swear this happened. Elvis was on stage, doin' the pose, you know? Like this." Allatore stood and struck a classic Elvis-like karate stance, imaginary microphone to his lips, finger raised toward the heavens.

"He was singing 'How Great Thou Art.' " Allatore held the pose. "And right in the middle of the song, some drunk ups and yells, 'Play Hound Dog!' Elvis stops singin', but doesn't move a muscle and says, right in the middle of this great hymn, 'Shut up and listen to the goddamn hymn!' "

Allatore collapsed back onto the lounger, laughing and shaking his head in disbelief. "That was some weekend."

"She's dead," said Will, his voice dim and flat. But the words were like armor-piercing bullets fired from a soul nearly emptied of ammunition. "She'd dead and she's not coming back."

"Funny thing, hope," said Allatore. "It exists only in that fragile little space between cynicism and faith."

"Please, no philosophy lessons."

"Hardly," said Allatore. "It's three-card monte. You ever play it?"

Will answered by turning Elvis's head another half-twist. It squeaked, then popped. That scent again. The beast was ready to pounce.

"Three-card monte. Three cards. One cynicism card, one faith card, and the hope card's the queen of hearts. The dealer says, 'Follow the queen, find the queen.' He makes the cards dance. You point to one. And it's the faith card. So you lay down another bet, he does the dance, you point. This time, it's the cynicism card. Round and round you go, each deal, looking for the hope card—the little queenie. But it always comes up either the faith card or the cynicism card."

"You got a point to this?" asked Will.

"It's a three-card game," said Allatore. "None of the cards matter without the other. Without faith you have abject cynicism. Without cynicism, you have no faith. And between the two is this fragile thing called hope that seems to elude us when we really need it."

"I'm past looking for hope," said Will. "At this point I'm looking for a sign from God."

"You want a sign?"

"I want my wife back."

"You're not going to find her in ol' Elvis there."

"I don't want to find her," said Will. "I want to forget her. Just for an hour."

"Got a question," said Allatore. "When was your last confession?"

"Hell if I know," said Will.

"Tell you what," said Allatore. "Make your confession to me. Right here. Confess about your plans to drink it up with ol' Elvis and I'll be bound by a covenant with God not to tell La Roy that you fell off the wagon."

"One problem," said Will. "You gotta be a priest."

"Actually," said Allatore, "that's exactly what I am."

There was leg-pulling and then there was kneecapping for the sake of a joke. Will gave Allatore a sideways smirk, waiting to see the old prosecutor give up a smile. Will found none. Vance Allatore was dead serious. There were no signs of any leg-pulling.

"Vance Allatore a priest?" said Will. "There's a crock if I ever heard one."

"That's what my ex-wife said," recalled Allatore. "Of course, that was until she brought my little girl across the pond to see me perform my first Mass. And wouldn't you know it? I almost made it through without crying."

Will caught a steely look from the former prosecutor. Unblinking and deathly serious.

"Where do you think I've been for the last ten years?"

"La Roy's bet was an institution."

Vance Allatore unfolded the story of a busted man, the marriage he destroyed and the painful divorce which followed, the book, the nerve-splitting breakdown, and a soul-searching trek that led him to a tiny seminary in the Ballinskelligs. A pastoral outcropping of cascading green slopes and craggy rocks on the southwestern coast of Ireland. "I thought God had called me over there to play out my retirement years on all the great old golf courses." Allatore shrugged.

"So why'd you come back?" mocked Will.

"I told you," said Allatore. "God told me to finish what I'd begun."

"And you didn't think to tell me you were a priest?"

"Is that what you needed to hear to believe me? That I'd come back ordained?" asked Allatore. "That's a pretty shallow opinion of your own God-given bullshit detector."

"Well, here's to ya, Father Vance." Will held up the headless decanter in a toast and readied himself to let the whisky flow. "My bullshit detector is officially on the fritz. So why don't you leave me to finish what I've begun."

"Question. What do you have to lose by confessing your sins?" asked Allatore. "Unless you're afraid to find out the King ain't really dead?"

Will found himself without a snappy remark, the glib retorts drying up like his empty tear ducts.

"Will it get you off of my back?"

"Let me put it this way. If you don't confess, I'll feel compelled to tell La Roy about the premeditated little bender on which you're about to embark."

"A compelling argument, Counselor."

Allatore took it as a compliment. "Yup. I still got it."

And so came Will's confession. If anything, it was just to get rid of the little bugger so he could get on with the whisky. The confession began as a patronizing little speech in tacit exchange for the priest's confidence. A deal was a deal. Vance Allatore would not snitch to La Roy about Will and Elvis.

Then came an emotional landslide which shocked the depressed senator.

After some careful, kind questioning from the priest, Will admitted his long-past infidelities, counting them off from a fling he'd had during his engagement and ending with Vanessa Curran. He confessed to the consistent lies and petty disputes over pride and power that came with holding high office. He confessed to the sins of vanity and his love for TV cameras. That his drive to chair the FDA hearings was a well-veiled PR campaign for his own future career plans: to occupy the White House. To be the leader of the free world. The most powerful man on the planet.

It was like a snowball gathering fiery momentum. Will was gushing like an open wound. He confessed to knowing of campaign finance law violations. Not those the FBI was investigating. But ones he'd gotten away with. He confessed to accepting gifts from lobbyists, free vacations disguised as party symposiums, lavish meals picked up at the expense of special interest groups.

And lastly, Will confessed to his longtime lie that his home was free of liquor. When all along he knew the silly-assed Elvis decanter, placed on the highest shelf of his office, was full up with Irish whisky. Out of reach? Yes. But never out of the sub-cortex of his alcoholic's brain. He'd convinced himself that Elvis was his own personal reminder of the evils of drugs and booze. The truth was, it was Will's only little test of pride. That contrary to the Alcoholics Anonymous credo, he was *not* powerless over alcohol. That alcohol was powerless over him. That he could sometimes stare at the decanter and spit on his addiction. Hah! I beat you!

"It was a stupid lie," Will testified.

As his shame spilled, Will's eyes squeezed shut as he felt the bottom start to slip out from underneath his entire emotional being. He was falling at a dizzying speed with no hand to catch his, no rope to grab on to.

Bad things happen to good people.

Oh my God, thought Will. What a crock. He *was* one of the bad guys. And he deserved nothing better than God's angry wrath.

"You're a good man, Will Sullivan."

Will heard words. A garble of sound as if water had been injected in his ear canal. Was it Father Vance Allatore who'd spoken? He heard a rattling of Latin. A blessing? Or was he handing Will his penance?

When Will opened his eyes, Allatore had his fishing rod in one hand and his catch in the other. "I said, 'You're a good man.' I better get these fellahs in the fryer before your chief of staff decides to make a meal of my last box of Cocoa Puffs."

Allatore left Will with the porcelain Elvis and a startling sense of consciousness. He was no longer careening into a void, but was simply seated on a cushioned chaise longue next to the swimming pool at his Marblehead home. In one hand was the open decanter and, in the other, the cork. And without so much as a second thought, Will tipped the flask to dump the whisky onto the grass. Only none poured out. The decanter was empty, save for a tiny, marble-sized cedar ball which rolled gently onto the turf. Picking up the ball and holding it high overhead, he tried to catch a crust of light from the house. In his fingertips, he gently rolled it until the words scribbled upon it became clear:

I LOVE YOU WILL

He gripped the cedar ball in his fist as he wondered just how long ago Gwen had flushed out the whisky and left him the message. He hadn't the faintest. But hope swelled in his heart and a fire started in his belly.

She's alive, he thought. *Dammit, Will. She's got to be alive.*

3

"The decks and TVs are rentals," said Allatore, giving a quick tour of the Victorian's redecorated basement. "Believe it or not, I still got a little room left on my credit cards. The dish? Well, it was easy enough to put that on your phone bill. And the rest of it? I had it shipped out from a storage lockup I've had rented in L.A. for the last ten years. Got transcripts and video of the entire trial." Allatore scratched his beard and shook his head. "Sweet Jesus, I haven't watched this much TV since I was seventeen and *Star Trek* was on channel four at ten o'clock."

Using one of his legal pads for reference, the prosecutor-turned-priest sorted through the piles of videotapes, slammed a cartridge into a deck, and fast-forwarded it to the correct time code.

"Right," said Allatore. "Now remember what I was telling you about the Morse code?"

There it was—the state of California versus W. D. Theroux. The single camera was focused on the witness stand, where a forensic pathologist was giving testimony under direct examination from Vance Allatore.

"Nice suit, Father Vance," said La Roy. "Wouldn't have known you were such a snappy dresser."

"Would you look at me?" said Allatore. "I was so damn wrapped up with my own image that I cut a deal with this men's store in Encino. Rick Pallack. Rick made sure I had a new suit for every day I was on TV." Allatore pointed to the monitor. "Now watch as the camera makes a move to the left here."

As described, the camera slowly panned left, leaving the witness and Vance Allatore, focusing its lens on a smartly attired W. D. Theroux, appearing as at ease as the presiding judge.

"Looks like he's listening to the testimony, right?" asked Allatore, who got nods of agreement from both La Roy and from Will, who was seated on the sofa, his arms splayed wide across the back. "Pay close attention to his hands. His left hand especially. See his ring finger. It's tapping the tabletop. Looks like a nervous twitch."

On the monitor, Theroux's left finger was indeed tap-tapping away during the forensic pathologist's testimony. But in irregular beats.

"Son of a gun," said La Roy. "It was right there for every-one to see."

"But not that easy to decipher," said the priest, flipping through the pages of his legal pad for the decoded tran-script. "If you were to read what he's tapping out, it's nothin' but a buncha gibberish. An *M*, then *N*, then *F*, then *G*, then another *G*, then a *T*, and an *H*, and a *W*." Mockingly, Allatore threw up his hands. "Ten years ago, this stuff drove us nuts. No words. Just letters. No vowels. All consonants. Then we bring this FBI analyst in, see?"

"What's he doing with his right hand?" asked Will.

The priest pointed an index finger and triple-tapped his nose as if he were playing charades. "Good for you, Will. You found the primer!"

Putting his finger on the screen, Allatore drew a circle around Theroux's right hand. Very slowly, almost imper-ceptibly so, Theroux was curling and unfurling his fingers. Anywhere from one to five of them.

"The right fingers are the vowels," said Allatore. "One finger is *A*. Two is *E*. You get the picture. All five is the letter *U*."

Gooseflesh broke out on Bill La Roy's neck. With a grin as wide as a face could manage, he stepped closer and closer to the monitor as if being drawn into a real-life conspiracy. "So what's he saying?"

"Nothing of substance," said Allatore, reaching for a binder filled with old text. "After all our work, we were only deciphering Theroux's simple, day-to-day instructions to the survivors. Like this one here:

"Jack. If the police find you and question you, pretend you are partially deaf in one ear. Ask them to please speak up, then answer as if you hadn't heard the question clearly. Policemen have little patience. They will tire of you and move on.

"And two days later," continued Allatore, "when I was doing my direct of the chief medical examiner:

"Izzy. I'm suspicious of this new chemical called aspartame. It's a sugar substitute that might cause imbalances in the brain. All of you, stay away from products containing this aspartame."

"He sounds like my momma," said La Roy.

"He acts the role of the parent," said Will. "He was giving life lessons."

"Every day of the trial," said Allatore. "All day long. Even when he was on the stand in his own defense, he's running the same code, giving more advice than orders. Micromanaging his family from the courtroom." Allatore fanned a stack of legal pads. "We got volumes of the crap. It drove us nuts. While we were looking for a smoking gun. An admission of guilt. An order to kill someone. Some big piece of the puzzle. We get W. D. Theroux giving personal tips on everything from oral hygiene, to what books they should read, to the technique to make a deal on a car—"

"So he's a control freak," said Will, prowling around the TV, trying to catch Theroux's videotaped gaze. It was as if he'd been injected with a sudden understanding of the killer. "The son of a bitch couldn't bear a moment where his children were out of contact. Out of his personal touch."

"Then you see where I'm going?" asked the priest.

"He's still talking to them," said Will.

The priest snapped his fingers. "Exactly. Now, what about the computer I sent you? It belonged to Timothy—"

"Oh, we got it, okay," said La Roy, trading looks with Will. "You think maybe we should tell the good father about *Theroux's* computer?"

"Theroux has access to a computer?" asked Allatore.

"Not anymore," said Will.

June had begun with a low-pressure pocket hanging over New England, inviting what seemed like a chain gang of thundershowers and cloudbursts. Massachusetts was wet from the Berkshires to the Cape. And after a winter's worth of bad weather, windshield wipers were at a premium. Preparing for such catastrophes was part of Mo Gaffney's off-market trade. At his formidable request, shipments of wiper blades were held up on the docks of Portland, Providence, and Boston until the demand reached a price nearly double the suggested retail. At that point, Mo called the docks, the wiper blades were finally shipped, the backorders filled, and everybody got their cut.

That was why Mo loved to watch the rain. It was dumping heavy at Arnie's. The huge drops sounded like a thousand rubber mallets pounding on the diner's rusted roof.

The cast was all there. Mo Gaffney, Big Mickey, and Duff. La Roy and Sully flanked Will. The FBI tail was parked near the Stop and Shop, no doubt firing off a roll of Fujicolor with the aid of a telephoto lens.

"Did you get it?" asked Will.

Duff handed a large padded envelope to Mo, who let it lie between himself and Will.

"Bet you didn't think I'd be able to do the thing, did you?" asked Mo.

"On the contrary," said Will. "I had loads of faith in you."

As he reached for the envelope, Mo Gaffney snatched Will's wrist and squeezed it hard. "Ain't nothin' on that machine that says squat about your missus!"

"You already looked at it?" asked Will.

"Sure I did," said Mo. "You didn't expect me just to give it to you and take your word for it?"

Will wrenched himself away. "Okay. So what did you find?"

"Not what I was lookin' for," said Mo, chin thrust forward. "And I can tell you, not what you was lookin' for, either."

"Fuck this shit," said La Roy. He snatched the envelope, ripped open the flap, and slid the computer onto the table. Theroux's ThinkPad was in two pieces, the screen separated from the body. The CD-ROM drive had been removed and there was a crack across the bottom all the way from the modem port to the battery backup.

Mo turned sheepish. "Goddamn shipping foul-up—"

Will's face skewed into a blitzkrieg of sudden rage. "Bullshit!" His fist was balled and wanting desperately to flatten Mo's nose until it bled. "You asshole! You messed with it, didn't you?"

"So what if I did," snapped Mo. "I put up the risk, I should get the first reward." He waved his hands over the busted computer. "So what if I had one of my guys give it a little look-see."

"A mechanic, I'll bet?" asked Sully.

"No, dickwad," said Mo. "His name's Ali. He's a computer turd I got working in my shop. He was gonna take it home and give it a once-around-the-block. Except he left the package with a buncha other stuff in the back of his Seville." Mo was appearing more embarrassed with every word that came out of his mouth. "Anyway, those Seville's got motors for everything. Door locks, seats, you know? Anyway, he was giving Big Mickey over there a lift home and what can I say. Big Mickey's, you know . . . big. Needs legroom. When he rolled the passenger seat back too far?"

A gesture to the computer said the rest. It had been crushed by the Caddy's reversing passenger seat.

"I WANT THEIR HEADS!" screamed Theroux.

The prisoner sat shackled in the crowded office of the warden. His angry words formed a guttural wail that shook all present. The warden, Mark Restovich, his deputy warden, Phil Grolch, and senior counsel for the California state prisons, Callie Weisbauer. They were flanked by four guards. Opposite them were Theroux and his mega-team of attorneys. Six in all. Some paid for, others joining the party in their own political enterprise of forestalling an execution at any legal cost.

Theroux's chief attorney, a genteel African émigré named Daniela Sowheto, tried to act as the calmer head. "We're all in agreement that my client's civil rights have been infringed upon."

"Somebody stole his computer," agreed Restovich.

"Not somebody," growled Theroux. "It was Whitney, Jones, and Muldoon!"

"You don't have any proof—"

"I KNOW WHO DID IT!" snarled Theroux with such commanding wrath that most present were inclined to informally agree.

All but Warden Restovich. He was sixty-four years old, less than a year from mandatory retirement, and hardly about to hand over control of *his* prison or *his* office to a death-row killer.

"We're investigating," said Restovich. "And in the meantime, we've ordered you a new computer."

"That doesn't satisfy the clear invasion of attorney-client privilege," pressed Sowheto.

"If you'll allow me," said Callie Weisbauer. "That assumes that the computer was stolen to obtain said privileged information. It might've been stolen for parts, as a lark, for a pawn-shop sale, even for a kid. We don't know—"

"I *know* why," said Theroux, his volume modulated to a mere grumble. "They took it because they want inside my head."

"Who is they?" asked the warden.

Theroux cast a cagey glance around the room, trying to meet the look of each and every guard. They knew. And he knew their thoughts. Only he himself could not give up the truth. None present—the lawyers, the prison officials—were players in his private breeding game.

Weisbauer spoke up. "Once again, there's no proof—"

Sowheto interrupted, "We've informed the Ninth Circuit of this violation. And we expect a stay of execution until this matter is resolved in a court of law."

"We expected such," returned Weisbauer. "And that is your client's right. But that fight's with the state's attorney general and the L.A. County D.A.'s office. We can only offer restitution for what Mr. Theroux lost."

"What was *stolen*," pissed Theroux. "I want the guilty parties identified."

"So what?" asked the warden. "So you can have them killed like you did the judge and jury that sent you here? Well, I got two words for you, mister. *Good* and *luck*."

Theroux was still picking up vibes from the guards when the warden fired his toothy salvo. Theroux let his eyes meander back to Restovich before the rest of his head swiveled into place. His nostrils flared. "Luck has *nothing* to do with it, Warden. When God throws the dice they're always loaded."

The office turned so cold that when Theroux and his team were ushered out, Warden Restovich barked at his secretary, "You wanna get somebody in here to fix that damn thermostat?"

The next two hours bored Theroux so silly his mind seemed to wander uncontrollably. To Gwen. To Will. To Vance Allatore. All the while, his fingers were doing silent gymnastics as his legal team occupied a private soundproofed chamber reserved for consultations. The attorneys took painstaking turns to impress their client with their continued assaults on the appeals process and brilliantly tendered writs of habeus corpus. But Theroux knew the odds of a stay were a thousand to one. He'd studied all the case law, read all the recent decisions, and counted the bodies while the determined decimation of America's death-row population continued. The system was a killing machine. Theroux was about to fulfill his destiny as its next lamb.

Lawyers were fools, he thought. He didn't want to *forestall* his execution. Hardly. He was looking forward to the day his name would be immortalized in the annals of human suffering.

What Theroux wanted was his damn computer back.

He wanted to talk to his family, touch them, see them, direct them down the road to their own destiny and, in return, feel their unconditional love. The rage sealed inside the shackled killer boiled without his lawyers ever noticing. They babbled and joked and gave uplifting little sermonettes. All while the client graced them with obligatory smiles, guffaws, and appreciative platitudes of thanks.

Just before Theroux returned to his cell, an associate of Daniela Sowheto's had one final piece of business to go over with him. As June 28 neared, the requests for media interviews increased. Theroux checked the list. Most of the names were the same cast of characters. Repeat offenders, he called them. He instantly nixed any print interviews. Those would do him no good at all. If he was ever to communicate again with his family, he would need TV. Theroux needed someone willing to give him as much airtime as he'd want to impart his final instructions.

Vanessa Curran of CBS News.

"I want *her*," ordered Theroux. "Set it up as soon as humanly possible."

"What about the others?" asked the lawyer.

"They can get in line behind the blonde," said Theroux as he was led back inside the facility. "TV. That's all I care about. Maximum exposure. And soon. You do that for me and I'll buy you a Mercedes."

The attorney grinned, promised, and even gave a Scout's honor gesture before crossing out all the print and radio requests and highlighting Vanessa Curran's name as his first call to return. TV it would be. And the sooner it happened, the happier the client would be.

4

The screaming lasted for nine hours. Wrenching howls from the other side of the heavy door. From Izzy and Dr. Bertrand Gwen could hear little more than muted voices. The only sounds which seemed to make it through the concrete were the shrieks of pain that would ebb and flow like crashing waves. All the while Gwen teetered on the brink of terror, excitement, and a strange embarrassment at having cried out while trying to pass a mere kidney stone.

Then came the eerie moments of silence. Gwen found herself either drifting back to sleep or bursting out in a cold sweat. She was soaked through her nightgown. And when the air-conditioning kicked in, she'd get chilled and have to pull up the covers. Only to have the screaming start all over, build like an orchestral movement, crescendo, and then fade back into the damp quiet.

Four hours later, it stopped for good.

Gwen lay fetal, staring at the concrete wall, wondering . . . wishing that she'd hear something. A voice. Another scream. A baby's cry. Instead, by her count, she got miles of silence.

Then at what she figured was dawn, the door clanked and swung open. Clem, sleep-racked and eyes dilated from the handful of amphetamines he'd been chewing, delivered the dull breakfast tray of cereal and toast. For the third day in a row, there was no newspaper. No *USA Today*. Gwen was beginning to be afraid she'd lose track of time.

"How's Starr?" she asked hopefully.

"Don't know," said Clem. "They took her to the hospital around five. Somethin' about an upside-down baby. Izzy drove 'em. Dr. B. Jack. Just you and me till they come back."

"But is Starr okay?"

Clem shrugged and looked as if he was going to leave.

"I didn't get my newspaper," said Gwen. "Three days now."

"So what?" said Clem.

"I miss it," said Gwen.

"I'll hook up the TV," said Clem. "If that'll get you off my back."

Gwen swept the hair from her eyes and tried to keep the interchange going. "I haven't talked to Dean in days."

"Join the club, sister," said Clem.

"Did something happen to him?"

"I don't know what I don't know."

"So you've lost touch, too?"

"The man's in prison! They gonna kill him in a couple weeks! So who knows what kinda shit they put him through?"

Gwen braved a question. "Why do you do this for him?"

"You wouldn't understand—"

"Try me," said Gwen. "It's just you here. And big ol' me with nothin' to do."

Clem hung on the edge of the door, swinging it in, then out. His busted nose pointing east and west with the shifting of the shadows. It was as if he was at the edge of pond, deciding whether or not to jump in with all his clothes on.

"I miss talking," pleaded Gwen.

"Talkin' ain't all it's cracked up to be, sister."

"You know a better way to communicate?"

A twisted smile appeared on Clem's face. Half juvenile, the other half delinquent. "If you weren't so knocked up . . ." Clem stopped himself before he overstepped the obvious boundary.

"You'd want to make love to me?" asked Gwen.

"I seen pictures of when you weren't . . . you know. With the baby." Clem was nodding. "Yeah. I can see what Dean saw in you."

"Saw what?"

"Somethin' special," said Clem. "Clean, maybe. Not like Izzy or Starr or any of them other bitches."

"They were prostitutes, weren't they?" asked Gwen.

"Oh, yeah. Me and Dean used to run 'em down in Hollywood. Of course, that was before we all got, you know, *the message* and turned to the family way. It was pretty wild. Inside this one week. The one where Dean had the vision? He got me switched from collectin' from the bitches to handing out leaflets at Hollywood and Vine. And you know what? I didn't care one way or the other. The money was just as good and the pussy was still for free."

"But why me?" begged Gwen. "Why not Izzy or Starr?"

"Oh, he never touched Izzy or Starr. Not never. He never touched the girls. Or the guys, either. 'Cuz some of them, you know, wanted him, too. They all wanted to fuck him. But Dean was like, you know . . . We were like his little children. That would be, you know . . . Ingenuous."

"Incestuous," corrected Gwen.

Clem snapped and pointed his finger. "Just like that."

Gwen lowered her eyes, took in a vast breath, exhaled, and prayed her rehearsed speech wouldn't make him slam the door shut on her or the conversation.

"It doesn't have to be this way," said Gwen. "You could let me go. You could leave the door open and I could walk out of here. I wouldn't press charges. I would just walk. I wouldn't so much as look back. I would forget all of it. I'd say I was gone, I'd reconciled with my husband, and it would end the whole episode—"

Gwen's nerves had her so zeroed in on her practiced speech, she hadn't heard Clem laughing. He was in the full throes of a narcotic hysteria by the time she stopped herself and waited for him to catch his breath.

"Nice try, sister."

"Why are you doing this to me?"

"Because he took my life and gave it back to me!" seethed Clem, the smile receding behind bared teeth. He was snapping his fingers again and again and again. "Just like that!" Snap-snap-snap. "One second I'm dead. The next I'm alive and lookin' at a burnin' bush. Only the bush was Dean. Resurrected. A god amongst men. Destined to die for me! That, sister, is a kind of love you'll *never, ever* know!"

The door slammed shut and was bolted. Not to be opened again until lunchtime, when Clem silently served up an ugly meal of canned soup, a tuna sandwich on whole wheat, and the prenatal vitamins he'd forgotten to give Gwen with breakfast. Gwen asked about Starr but got no response at all. The same was repeated at dinner. More soup, more tuna, and no words from an increasingly fatigued Clem. Though he didn't respond, Gwen suggested that he might be able to use some sleep.

Slam. Clank.

"Good night, sister."

"For example. And I'm using your definition. What could be more cultlike than, say, the Republican or Democratic parties? You vote their party. Believe in their party. And once you're in the party you rarely leave. What better definition would one have for a cult?"

"Is that Webster's *definition of a cult?"*

In a room choked with cigarette smoke, Will froze the MSNBC tape, the most recent filmed interview with Theroux. He studied the frame, looking for anything that might remotely look like some sort of code. Message. Was Theroux signaling?

Twisting the wheel on the remote control to the left, the image sped backward. Over the speakers came the high-pitched squeal of tape running backwards at high speed. Will pressed PLAY and watched the interview section again.

"... *And I'm using your definition. What could be more cultlike than, say, the Republican or Democratic parties? You vote their party. Believe in their party. And once you're in the party you rarely leave. What better definition could you have for a cult?*"

Freezing the frame again, Will glanced over his shoulder to Allatore. The priest was stretched out on the sofa. "Like I was telling you," explained Allatore. "I've gone over this piece a hundred times. He doesn't gesture, sign, twitch a finger, or pick his nose. Clearly, he's not communicating with anybody other than the TV audience. The interview was obviously done long after he had access to other forms of communication."

But Will rewound it again, playing the tape forward, then back. Analyzing every pixilated frame. Repeating the interview until Allatore had nodded off and was snoring so loudly that Will had to double the volume. And when he hit the reverse button, the high-pitched squeal of the rewind just added to Will's splitting headache. He popped three Tylenols and lit up another cigarette.

Upstairs, La Roy manned a new three-line telephone system.

The Sullivans' private telephone number had appeared anonymously on the *Women Against Men* bulletin board on the World Wide Web. What began as a nuisance had quickly escalated into a full-scale nightmare. As the phone rang and rang with hateful calls from women's groups, local lines were clogged and the utility wanted to change the number. Threatening to sue, Will insisted that they not. Gwen might yet call. If she somehow broke free from wherever she was held captive, she might only have time to dial one number. Will wanted that number to be open, operating, and manned at all times. Three lines were added just to handle the occasional overload. And, courtesy of Benny Yao, an antibugging filter was jacked in merely to annoy the FBI with ear-gouging HF noise.

La Roy, Allatore, and Will all took turns at the makeshift switchboard. La Roy wore a RadioShack headset with a three-line remote switch so he could stand, stretch his legs, pour coffee, and, if need be, take a leak.

The Internet, surmised La Roy, had become the world's biggest damn bathroom wall.

"Hello?" answered the chief of staff, who'd settled into a fat chair with a fresh cup of caffeine.

"Will Sullivan, please?"

"Speaking," lied La Roy.

"She should've cut your dick off, you prick—"

La Roy switched off, sipped from his coffee cup, then added a hatch mark to the column marked HOSTILE.

"Hello?"

"I'd like to speak to Senator Sullivan."

"Speaking," said La Roy. "What can I do for you?"

"Star 69," said the voice. *"I can't afford the long distance."*

The line double-clicked as the caller hung up. La Roy checked the caller ID box. It read UNKNOWN CALLER.

Another sip of coffee, then another hash mark. This one in the column marked NEGATIVE THREAT.

"Bill La Roy's a dumb nigger!"

La Roy whirled around, thinking he'd heard the voice shouting from the hallway. He listened to the silence, then heard strains of the MSNBC interview rising from the basement. He wondered if he'd heard right.

The telephone rang. One ring and La Roy answered, "Hello?"

"Is this Senator Will Sullivan?"

"Speaking," lied La Roy.

"Star 69! I can't pay for this call. Hit star, then the numbers six and nine!"

Click-clack-click. The line died again.

"Star 69 yourself, pal," said La Roy, putting a mark into a new column he labeled REPEAT ASSHOLES.

"Bill La Roy's a dumb nigger!"

Once again, La Roy swiveled in his seat. Oh, he'd heard it that time. He rose to his feet and he walked toward the basement, lending one ear to the sounds from below, the other to the next call.

"Hello?" answered La Roy.

"It's Benny Yao," said the investigator.

"It's Bill," said La Roy. "Got anything?"

"Maybe I should talk to Will," said Yao, the downturn in his voice signaling more bad news.

"You got lousy news?" asked La Roy. "From now on it gets filtered through me."

"Fine," said Yao without a fight. Then began the droning reportage. "Since we're close to the due date, I've added staff and that means expense. We've expanded the search and spread the resources, focusing primarily on hospitals, maternity wards, outpatient delivery services, i.e., registered midwives. Sites we can't get a man to, we're using faxes."

"You using the doctor's picture?"

"Along with the usual suspects," said Yao. "Now for the bad news. This busted-up computer you sent me?"

"Bill La Roy's a dumb nigger!"

This time, La Roy was standing at the threshold of the basement stairs. The voice boomed upward, enveloped in an echoing garble.

"That computer," droned Yao, "the ThinkPad? When we yanked the hard drive and hooked it up to a new source, the damn thing nearly cannibalized itself."

"What?" La Roy was half-listening as he ever-so-carefully descended the basement stairs. The telephone signal was beginning to crackle. The farther he lowered into the basement, the more La Roy was getting out of range.

"There was a computer virus," said Yao. "Turned on, we think, by the new power source. Whoever set up the computer must've added it as a safety precaution against theft."

"It's wiped out?" asked La Roy. "Everything?"

"My guy fed the unit some antivirus software," said Yao. "There's a buncha corrupted text files. But it's sorta like pickin' though the ashes of a forest fire with a pair of chopsticks."

"Well, if there ever was a man for the job—"

"What?" asked Yao. "You're breaking up."

La Roy backed up a step. "I'll pass it on to Will. Any more bad news?"

"I can think of some."

"Later," said La Roy, switching off and descending fully into the basement. Will was seated cross-legged in the middle of the concrete floor. Allatore, twisted sideways on the sofa, was fast asleep with his face burrowed into the cushions.

"Bill La Roy's a dumb nigger?" asked the suspicious chief of staff.

Will glanced briefly over his shoulder, then turned back to the TV and the MSNBC interview. "What did you ask me?"

"I heard 'Bill La Roy's a dumb'—" La Roy stopped as part of the MSNBC interview rolled.

"I think Sullivan's a good choice. I think he's the president's choice. But the other day, I saw his chief of staff on some talk show. Crossfire, *maybe. And I'd venture to say that he's two eggs short of a true omelet."*

Under Will's control, the tape froze. "Is this what you came down to see?"

"Is that all there is?" asked La Roy. "I mean, the only part where he talks about me?"

"As far as I can tell," said Will.

"I swear I heard him say, 'Bill La Roy's a dumb nigger.' "

Will continued with his work. "Who was on the phone?"

"I said I *heard* 'Bill La Roy's a dumb nigger.' "

"Not from here you didn't."

"You sayin' I didn't hear it?"

"Who knows what kinda crap you pick up over that . . ." Will twirled a finger around his ear, miming La Roy's radio headset, and once again rewound the tape.

"I heard it three—"

"Bill La Roy's a dumb nigger!"

"There it is!"

This time Will heard it, too. Intermingled amongst the garble from the rewinding tape, he distinctly heard something which *sounded* like *"Bill La Roy's a dumb nigger!"*

"Yeah, okay. So it sounded like *Bill La Roy's a* you-know-what."

"A nigger," said La Roy. "Play it again."

Pressing the PLAY button, Will and La Roy watched the

brief segment again. Will froze the tape and twisted the server into the rewind position.

"Bill La Roy's a dumb nigger!"

"Reverse speech!" said La Roy.

"Reverse what?" asked Will.

"Reverse speech. That's what it's called," said La Roy, a tremor of sudden excitability in his voice. "I know. You've never heard of it. But it's not new. And I swear it's real."

"Reverse what?" asked Allatore from the couch, awake with one eye open.

"Reverse speech," confirmed La Roy. "What do you think Nixon's tapes were for? So Tricky Dick could archive his alleged paranoia? No. He'd tape his meetings. Play it back at just the right speed and the lie is turned to truth. Nixon called it his divining rod into the subconscious."

"So what's on the eighteen-minute gap?" asked Allatore.

"Anybody's call. Vietnam. JFK. J. Edgar's dress size."

Will turned dismissive. "Do I hear the phone ringing?"

La Roy jumped to his feet. "I know this sounds like typical Bill La Roy pseudo-psycho-kinda-science shit. But don't believe me. Believe your own ears!"

"It sounded something like *something,*" conceded Will. "So what? What's it prove?"

Vance Allatore bolted upright on the sofa. "Play another section," he demanded. Was he sleepwalking? Or did waking come that easy to the priest? "Play the part where he talks about you being the favorite for the vice presidency."

"This is ridiculous," said Will. "We don't have time—"

"What could it hurt?" asked the priest. "We either hear something or we don't. Play the section. Please?"

"Play it," demanded La Roy.

Looking at the time-coded transcriptions, Will stopped the tape, did a speed rewind, then stopped at the appropriate mark. He pressed the PLAY button.

"A true believer is one kind of man. Living your beliefs is another . . . So what do you think of all this gossip about Will Sullivan of Massachusetts replacing James Harper on the next presidential ticket?"

"Okay," said Allatore. "Now rewind. Same speed as before." With their ears turned to the speakers, all three men listened for the words laced amidst the garble:

"Nonbeliever . . . He won't make it to the Atlanta convention."

Vance Allatore slapped his hands together. La Roy, on the other hand, was shaking his finger at Will. "And you don't believe me."

"I *still* don't."

"Then play it again!"

Will was stumped. He'd heard what he'd heard. As had La Roy and Vance Allatore. Was it some kind of odd phenomenon? A coincidence? An error on the audio track?

"Right now, I'd buy real estate in the Bermuda Triangle if it got my wife back."

"You can't afford real estate in the Bermuda Triangle," said La Roy. His ears suddenly pricked up. "Do you hear the phone ringing?" In an instant, La Roy was charging back up the basement stairs.

Will looked to Allatore. "What do you think?"

"I think God works in weird ways that we're not meant to understand."

"So now it's God talking to me from the TV?"

"Could be," said Allatore, scratching his beard and rubbing the sleep from his eyes. "I was dreaming about the child. Cute little bugger. A boy."

"What of it?"

"Do you give much thought to it?" asked the priest. "You might very well rescue your wife. And with her, a child that isn't yours."

Will turned to the TV and that frozen image of Theroux. "He's evil. I know that much."

"So you wonder if the father's evil, so would be the child?"

"Something like that."

"Understandable," said the priest. "Freud had a few interesting things to say. Once he said that man was born with a God-shaped hole in his heart."

"And we fill the hole however we choose," added Will. "Yeah, I heard that, too."

"Know what I say?" asked Allatore. "I say God made

man with a God-shaped hole in his heart. And gave man free will to fill that hole with whatever he decides."

"In conclusion?" pressed Will.

"I say whoever fathers a child—any child—has an awesome responsibility. Be it yours?" Allatore gave a nod to the screen and the image of W. D. Theroux. "Or his."

It was a crushing question. When the possibility of adoption came up, Will had wondered if he could father another man's child. But the child of a Theroux? Will asked his heart for an answer and received nothing in response.

When La Roy had reached the top of the basement stairs, his phone set was still ringing.

"Hello," said La Roy, puffing for air.

"Will Sullivan, please?" asked the woman.

"Speaking," lied La Roy, still puffing.

"Bullshit," said the woman. "This is Vanessa Curran. And I need to talk to Will. Is this Bill La Roy?"

"You're thrilled, aren't you?" said La Roy "Tell me you're thrilled it's me."

"Put . . . Will . . . on . . . NOW!"

The negotiations for the CBS interview with W. D. Theroux were bordering on anarchy. Warden Restovich, Theroux's chief counsel, Daniela Sowheto, and Vanessa Curran were all at odds. Vanessa was backed up by independent TV producer Zach Schumwat, who was moonlighting from his gig at MSNBC in order to coordinate the Theroux interview in her one-hour news special set to air the night of the execution. He was brought on because he knew the players and the territory, having secured the last successful TV interview with the notorious killer. For the bucks and a chance to work his way back up to broadcast-level news, Schumwat would've returned to a foxhole in Iraq.

The conflict was over where the interview would be held. Restovich, holding the proxy of the Department of Corrections, insisted Vanessa meet with Theroux in the same holding room where all the other interviews had been taped. It was secure and controllable, but in Vanessa Curran's opinion, not sexy enough for prime time. With the help of a guard, Schumwat had found a keen spot on the emergency helipad. It was within the compound, but outdoors with a backdrop that included trees, rolling hills, and a few green patches of the nearby golf course. They argued that in order to increase production value, they'd planned to bring in two extra cameras to record the interview *à la* Barbara Walters. And with two extra crew members to handle the lighting and hang a butterfly scrim to diffuse and soften the sunlight on the blonde star, the holding room was just too small.

The pretty pitch made Restovich want to puke. The last thing he wanted was *his* death-row killer to look *good* on TV.

A further complication was Daniela Sowheto, who so desperately wanted to be included in the prime-time story that she was withholding her vote of support in the matter until Vanessa Curran and Zach Schumwat agreed to *her* terms.

Easy enough, decided Vanessa. Tape was cheap. They'd shoot the lawyer bitch and get on with business, knowing full well that they wouldn't use an inch of the interview unless Daniela Sowheto said something newsworthy, noteworthy, or of absolute necessity to the strange story the network had ordered:

The Senator vs. The Killer:
A Date with Destiny, Divorce, or Death?

A compromise was eventually reached and the interview was scheduled for 7 P.M. in the B dome's fifth-tier rec room. With the Ping-Pong tables folded up, the space would be large enough to accommodate three cameras, all the lawyers, guards, corrections personnel, and the TV crew. That, and the western-facing crash-proof window would deliver an hour's worth of ultra-warm key light—*magic hour*—to those behind the camera.

Fitting, thought the killer. If they only knew the magic he'd planned for the interview.

Theroux was seated directly opposite Vanessa Curran. He

wore his prison-issue orange jumpsuit, chains, and the life-giving Natural Beige pancake. His smile was engaging, his eyes flirting with the six-foot Amazon-babe CBS had sent to conduct the interview. He worked her up and down, dismissing the usual lusty stares of a death-row inmate in exchange for a more appreciative pose. Theroux feigned *respect* for women and wanted Vanessa to get the mental message. In doing so, it would surely open her up for a psychic revival unlike anything she'd ever experienced—even the psychedelic mushroom adventure she'd taken on her senior spring break in Guadalajara.

"Some ground rules," said Theroux in a tone so quiet, only Vanessa could hear.

"Fire away." Vanessa spoke, knowing full well once tape rolled, rules were left for referees and grade school principals.

"How do I know that when you leave here the interview will make it to air?"

"You don't," she said smugly. "It all depends on the powers that be. Network, you know? And whether or not you give good interview."

"Oh, I plan to," said Theroux. "I give *great* interview."

"Then you have nothing to worry about," teased Vanessa, behaving far less like the journalist and more like a fifteen-year-old girl held for detention by the school's cutest math teacher.

"We're hot," said Kruger. "Cameras A, B, and C up."

As nods came from the other two operators, Schumwat leaned in and whispered in Vanessa's ear, "Remember, honey. He loves to leave the script."

Vanessa shooed the producer away. His job was done. He'd gotten them in, set the team up, and prepped her on the job. As far as she was concerned now, Schumwat could catch the early flight back to MSNBC and the single-digit share of cable television. It was her show and she was going to run it the way she damn well wanted.

"Two weeks," began Vanessa.

"Two weeks, yes," said Theroux with a go-ahead tip of his head.

"Time is short, so I won't try and waste it. There've been

stories, one of which we've been covering, about a certain United States senator and his assertion that his wife has been abducted by surviving members of your cult."

"You're referring to Senator Will Sullivan and his wife, Gwen," confirmed Theroux with manners so polite a viewer might mistake the interviewee as a head of state, if only it weren't for that highway-cone-colored jumpsuit.

"Yes," said Vanessa. "How do you respond to his insistence that you are behind such a plot?"

"It's ludicrous," said Theroux. "And sad. For both of us, I think. He's clearly grasping at straws in an attempt to put a public face on his marital discord."

"And how is it sad for you?"

"I am set to die in two weeks. And my efforts for a stay of execution are made worse by this constant demonizing. I don't know this senator. I have never met him or his wife. I am not a political person."

"Yet," Vanessa jumped in, "in a previous interview, we've seen outtakes of you talking about politics, a subject you claimed to have great interest in, even mentioning the senator by name."

"I said I've never met the senator or his wife. I never said I hadn't spoken of him. No different than when I've spoken of the president, or the governor of this state, or even you, Ms. Curran." Theroux leaned forward, his head twisting an incisive twenty degrees as if to get a better look at her. "For example," asked Theroux, "is your interest in this assignment merely professional? Or did you . . . Yes. I'm sorry. You did. You and the senator had an affair sometime back."

Eyebrows in the room arched in surprise. But Vanessa barely fidgeted, steeling her pose and feeling powerful in the knowledge that she was the ultimate magician in the room. Anything she or her bosses didn't care for would be cut out, never to see the public airwaves.

"So, Mr. Theroux," continued Vanessa, "there is no kidnapping plot that involves members of your alleged family—"

"What family?" asked Theroux. "When I die, I will die alone. The Department of Corrections has received no requests for visitation by anyone related to me. The only requests are from journalists who want to bleed from me one last story before I'm dead and forgotten. And believe me when I say, Ms. Curran, I *will* be forgotten."

"Oh, I doubt that very much—"

A cell phone rang. Zach Schumwat dumped his headphones and barked, "Stop tape!"

The operators for cameras B and C switched their units to pause. Kruger, though, kept his camera running, feigning the shutdown and leaving the lens squarely framed on Theroux's questioning visage.

"Okay, who's got a cell phone?" asked Schumwat. "I wish you'd please leave the room or shut the damn thing off."

The phone trilled once more, with Vanessa Curran proving the villain by reaching into her coat pocket and pulling out her StarTac. She coolly flipped it open and answered. "This is Vanessa Curran."

And Theroux knew. The picture in his head said it all. Before she'd so much as handed the phone to him. Even before she'd said, "Mr. Theroux. This call is for you." Theroux knew he'd been set up. He knew the conspirators involved. And he knew the man who'd plotted the surprise attack. Deeper than his ears, the killer's sensitized skull picked up the vibrations from Kruger's Ikegami as it transcribed his reaction on magnetic videotape.

Turning his shackled palms up, Theroux gestured for help with the phone. The guards tensed as Vanessa stood, took two short steps across to Theroux, and gently held the StarTac to the killer's left ear.

"Hello?" said Theroux.

"This is Will Sullivan."

"Yes, it is. Good evening, Senator," said Theroux, his gaze bouncing around the room as if to make sure every single pair of eyes was on him. "Your ears must have been itching because we were just talking about you."

"Where is my wife, you son of a bitch?"

"Last I read, Senator, was that your wife was hiding from you."

"I'm begging you to let her go!"

"I, sir, am the one in chains."

"Goddammit where is she?"

"You astonish me, Senator. After all, this is national TV. You must not believe your popularity ratings could get any lower."

"You will die and you will go to hell!"

"Oh, but I'm going to live forever. It's you who's going to . . ." Theroux trembled, his eyelids fluttered closed, and, against the thin membrane, he could see the words of Alexander Pope flicker along with images of a pale, silver-faced man in anguish.

" 'We think our father's fools, so wise we grow,' " quoted Theroux ever-so-slowly. " 'Our wiser sons, no doubt will think us so.' " Theroux's eyes opened and fixed on Kruger's camera as if he was looking directly at Will. "Now that he's gone, William, is that how you'll remember *your* father?"

"My father's not gone. He's still very much alive."

"No?" asked Theroux, his head cocked sideways.

And in the brief, mesmerizing moment, the guards proved a step too sluggish with their feet. The killer rocked back in his chair until it tipped, twisted his entire body ninety degrees, and swung his legs overhead. The chains that bound his ankles roped neatly around Vanessa's swan-like neck. As Theroux crashed to the floor, he brought her with him, swiveling his hips and pitching her like a six-foot mannequin. Her flailing legs swept the B camera off its tripod. A soaring, spiked heel grazed Daniela Sowheto's ear. And the StarTac cell phone Vanessa was holding tumbled antenna over receiver, crunching against the floor at the precise moment Vanessa's neck snapped at the finish of her deadly somersault.

It killed her instantly.

While the crew and lawyers stood motionless in sudden horror, guards jumped in, untangling the killer from the convulsing reporter. Vanessa was dead and twitching, eyes fixed and staring at Kruger as if telling him to kick the camera off the tripod, aim it at Theroux, and record the moment. Don't lose it. Get it on tape. All of it.

Theroux thrashed against the guards, trying to get his

face into Kruger's wobbly camera. His mouth foamed as he tommy-gunned an earful of Latin. *"Vas animus totus suffocare ex sanguis ex scortum!"*

That's it, thought the killer. *That's it. Get it on tape. Shoot me close and I'll be on every news program from California to Tobago. Hear my words and so will my family. Tonight. Tomorrow. Soon. Not when Vanessa Curran or her network wanted to run it. But now. When they need to hear from me. When they need my instruction. And then they will know what to do.*

Theroux shouted. "BLOOD FLOWS AND FATHER KNOWS, WHEN IT IS MY TIME TO GO!"

With those words spat nearly twelve inches from Kruger's lens, a gag was slipped into Theroux's mouth while a baton crashed against his shoulder blades. The killer dropped out of frame. And there was the end of the interview.

The line had gone dead when Vanessa's cell phone hit the floor. From his station in the Marblehead den, Will quickly got a new tone and hit the redial button. Instead of a staticky pause followed by an electronic ring, Will got the cell provider's standard recording:

"I'm sorry, but the mobile customer you are calling . . ."

He tried five more times with the same result.

"That was some kinda exchange," said La Roy as he appeared from the kitchen with a smile so broad Will wondered how it got through the door. La Roy had listened in on the call. "I got goose bumps on my goose bumps, if you know what I mean."

"Is it the caffeine that gives you that cat-that-ate-the-canary grin?" griped Will. "Or the fact that my life has turned into one of your true-crime conspiracy games?"

"I wonder what all that shit was about your old man—"

The phone rang. Will had it to his ear on the half-ring. It was Vanessa, he thought, and the interview was about to continue.

"This is Will," he said.

"Senator Sullivan," said the voice. "My name is Richard

Levinthal of the Boston Police Department. I'm the sergeant on call at Mass General—"

"This is about my father," said Will, his instinct catching on quicker than his conscious self.

"I'm afraid so, sir," said the cop. "Your father had a heart attack."

"Is he okay?" asked Will. "Is he alive?"

The cop stalled at the other end of the phone. This was part of his job description. He must have done it ten or more times a day, delivering bad news to the decedent's nearest of kin. But this one hurt more than usual. He was delivering more bad news to the embattled senator. "I'm sorry, Senator Sullivan."

5

To hear the coroner tell it, the seventy-five-year-old Sully suffered from classic congestive heart failure. It began with a prolonged day's worth of weakness, edema, and shortness of breath caused by his heart's inability to maintain adequate circulation to the lungs. But to hear Shell Malone, the Pintail Pub's chief of the bar, the lousier the old councilman felt of late, the more he'd plowed into the private stock of Black Bushmills. The excess drinking had created a volatility in Sully that some of the more vocal Pintail patrons had liked to exploit. Of late, Sully's biggest button carried the label THE WOES OF YOUNG WILLY.

A proud, defensive father, and backed by that rogues' gallery of famous pols, Sully invited all comers upstairs to his office to debate the merits of his son's tenure in Congress and deny the improprieties and infidelities rumored in the daily press.

Daniel "Sully" Sullivan died in Joe Kennedy's leather desk chair. The attack came at the end of a fifth of whisky and a shouting match over his daughter-in-law's pregnancy. The newest rumor was that the child wasn't Will's, but one of Gwen's West Coast colleagues with whom she'd been hiding at a private estate on the island of Maui.

When Will informed his mother of his father's death, she didn't seem to understand at first. So he told her twice more. Her tapping finger told him enough. She'd gotten it the first time. And that she understood well enough to be left alone to her own grieving. There were no tears. This had been coming for a while. Sully had been living on borrowed time, flying too high on wings that should've been buried with old Joe.

Shell-shocked and nearly broken, Will forged through the funeral arrangements with La Roy, his one and only public shoulder to lean on. Fortunately, there was plenty of help to be found at city hall. The city's Office of Operations willingly handled most of the chores. The mayor and city council picked up the tab, planning a public processional followed by an open casket memorial at Southy's Saint Catherine's Church.

Taking up the rear in the long line of anecdote-laced eulogies, Will took to the pulpit without a single note card or thought about what he might say in front of the assembly of peers, constituents, distant family, FBI agents, and TV cameras.

"I wasn't prepared to lose my father," said Will, choking back his emotions. "I find myself wondering why it is that death brings such immense regret . . . I regret not telling my father I loved him. I regret not saying, 'Thank you, Dad, for a lifetime of support.' " Blankly, Will stared back at the collected mourners as if his eyes were reaching deep into a void.

"But I'm not prepared to regret losing my wife," said Will. "So if you'll excuse me."

With a half-nod of approval from his decrepit mother, Will left the pulpit to Bishop Moynihan. He left the church through a side door where Bill La Roy was waiting.

As for Vanessa Curran, her funeral was scheduled for the very same Wednesday. Only hers took place in her native De Kalb, Illinois, attended by her parents and a plethora of network and local news crews. Vanessa's star had risen and peaked with her Theroux interview. The video aired in various pieces for three nights from coast to coast. Dan Rather had even eulogized the blonde bombshell of a reporter, devoting the final two minutes of his newscast to her. Critics later complained that he'd practically nominated her into some kind of Journalists' Hall of Fame alongside the likes of Ed Murrow and Charles Kuralt.

"It makes me sick to watch it," said White House senior strategist Sean McCallister of the overplayed tape of Vanessa Curran's murder. In the grandeur of his West Wing office, he was seated on the corner of his desk, shirtsleeves rolled up and barely stomaching a series of videos prepared for him by the Communications Office. Also attending were both Slammer Sisters, Attorney General Margaret Van Hough and FBI Director Lois Freehold.

"Okay," said McCallister to his assistant. "Now show us the Sullivan funeral."

The tapes compiled from local news coverage of Sully's funeral were jacked into the VCR. There were images of the processional down Southy's Dorchester Street. A variety of local and national politicians, their wives and children, all black-clad and trailing a slow-driving hearse. Fire trucks pulled up the rear. Also taped were the mourners entering and exiting the cathedral. The same crowd, mostly. Not a one was smiling.

"What are we looking for?" asked Margaret, somewhat clueless about why she had been summoned to the White House.

"At White House request, the Press Office ran these tapes up and back again," said McCallister. "And for the life of me, them, and a lot of other White House staff, nobody can see hide nor hair of Mrs. Will Sullivan."

"You mean Gwen Sullivan?" asked Margaret.

"Gwen," confirmed McCallister. "Now, for the longest time, we must admit the story our young senator has been spinning stretches all credulity. But Mrs. Sullivan—Gwen—being so callous as to not show up at the funeral of her own father-in-law? I'm afraid the White House has a problem."

"The White House has lots of problems," said Lois Freehold. She didn't need to elaborate. Will Sullivan wasn't the only story on the front pages. The presidency was suffering one domestic policy defeat after the next. The opposition was hammering hard and the press wasn't lying down for Addison.

Margaret Van Hough brought the point back home. "The White House has a problem? Or President Addison?"

"The White House *is* President Addison," answered McCallister.

"It's a matter of investigative fact," said Director Freehold, "that Gwen Corbett-Sullivan did not care much for, let alone like, her father-in-law. The same fact goes for Daniel Sullivan's former feelings for his daughter-in-law Gwen."

McCallister was shaking his head. "I know Gwen. She's tough. But she's no bitch."

"Unlike your present company?" asked the FBI director.

"I didn't say that," said McCallister. "The White House *respects* its top cops."

"Then respect our domain and our investigation," said Freehold. "We have the president's proxy to run things—"

"Hold on a minute, Lois," interrupted Margaret. "So what are you saying, Sean?"

"I'm saying that if Gwen Corbett-Sullivan shows up dead or if there's a shred of proof to Will Sullivan's very public allegations . . . This cult thing? The divorce or the abuse stuff being some kind of fraud—"

"Fraud?" Lois Freehold leaped to her feet with a scorching finger aimed at McCallister. If she'd have been a man, McCallister would've taken the sudden movement as a threat. "Will Sullivan is a wife beater and a drunk. He's mixed money with campaign fraud—"

"Sit the fuck down!" said McCallister. "This is my office and—"

"You don't run the White House," spat Freehold. "And you sure as hell don't run Justice—"

"And Lois? Neither do you!" said Margaret, her tone nearly as terse as McCallister's. The FBI director didn't sit. Instead, she put the chair between herself and McCallister and paced, arms crossed, fuming.

"You're right," said McCallister. "I don't run the White House. I run the committee to reelect your commander in chief. And the word is this. You want to keep up this pissing contest with Sullivan, it's my job to make sure the White House doesn't get wet."

"Sean," said Margaret. "Are you aware that we've got a grand jury ready to indict—"

"He's circling the drain," admitted McCallister. "And by no means does the White House intend to vindicate Will Sullivan." Wanting to put a fine point on the White House's position, the strategist crossed and sat in Lois Freehold's chair, turned it to face the attorney general, and bent forward in his most diplomatic pose. As if he was about to impart a great secret on the attorney general. "But should Senator William Sullivan somehow—and I mean *somehow*—vindicate himself in the eyes of the American public? I think it's only fair that the White House *appear* to have assisted him in his time of need."

"He wants us to split the goddamn baby!" said Freehold.

"I want," said McCallister, ignoring the FBI director, keeping his eyes focused on Margaret, "for *our* president to have his cake and eat it, too."

Margaret smiled, as if coming to a mutual understanding. "You guys are working off polling data."

"And if I was?"

"What's it say?"

"That despite your considerable efforts to make him your next scalp, the threat of a very public divorce, those godawful *Time* and *Newsweek* covers, and enough negative media to sink a fucking aircraft carrier?" McCallister let the moment hang before finishing. "Thirty-one percent of likely voters believe the son of a bitch when he looks into the camera and says that all he wants is to see his wife and little baby safe and bloody sound."

"What are his negatives?" asked Freehold. "What percent believes he beat his wife?"

"Republicans or Democrats?"

"Does it matter?"

"In an election year?" McCallister gestured to the funeral images on the TV with his prominent chin. The pictures showed another image from the funeral procession. Will Sullivan pushing his mother in a wheelchair. "You want to put a number on public sympathy?"

"I understand." The attorney general nodded.

"You make a move?" warned McCallister. "You damn well better make sure it's the right move."

At the Marblehead Queen Anne, amongst the fifty-plus bouquets and wreaths left to wilt at the front gate was a UPS overnight package addressed to Will from CBS News in New York. Will didn't bother to gather the flowers. He was through the front door of the house, ripping the envelope open while making two lefts into the service hallway before charging down the steps to the basement. He held the video-tape high. "Father Vance! I think we've—"

With every expectation that a greeting would be forth-coming from the priest, Will was stunned to find the base-ment empty. The few remnants of Allatore—his jacket, hat, shoulder bag, and backpack—all gone. A note was taped to the VCR. All it said was, *Play.*

La Roy reached past Will and pressed the PLAY button. Two seconds passed before Vance Allatore appeared on the TV screen, having videotaped himself in that very room.

"Sorry to leave without so much as a handshake or a Hail Mary. But God called while you were out. He said the road has forked. And it seems he wants me to take another path. When I think about it, there's not much more I can do for you. You know what needs to be done. I pray you won't feel abandoned. That you'll stay the course and do what must be done. He is with us both. He is talking to you. Don't turn a deaf ear.

"Once again, I'm sorry about your father. I know what he really meant to you. And one day, so will you. Godspeed. And so long for now."

Vance Allatore blessed the camera lens with the sign of the cross before crawling out of frame and turning off the camera.

"One question," said La Roy. "If Father Vance hadn't been here to take God's call, you think God would've left a message on the voice mail?"

Will didn't think to try and answer. He all but canned his feel-ings of betrayal, popped the Allatore tape out, and sent it tum-bling to the floor. He replaced it with the tape from CBS. Color bars and a time code box appeared on the monitor. Will dialed the remote into fast-forward. The numbers in the time code box blurred until the image of Wesley Dean Theroux popped up. Will twisted the volume up until he could hear Vanessa's voice clearly on track one. Theroux was on track two.

"Monitor the volume and take notes," said Will. He tossed La Roy one of Allatore's legal pads and kicked a pen across the floor.

"I want to warn you, Will," said La Roy, finding a comfortable seat on the old sofa. "This might not work. It might just be what it is. An interview that ends tragically. And between you and me, I could do without seeing Vanessa Curran's neck snapped in two for the ninety-ninth time."

"Just write down what I hear," said Will, his voice full of command. He switched the tape from pause to play. And so began the interview:

"We're hot," said Kruger. "Cameras A, B, and C up."

"Two weeks," said Vanessa.

"Two weeks, yes," repeated Theroux.

"Time is short, so I won't try and waste it. There've been stories, one of which we've been covering, about a certain United States senator and his assertion that his wife has been abducted by surviving members of your cult."

"You're referring to Senator Will Sullivan and his wife, Gwen," answered Theroux.

Will stopped the tape, dialed the rewind knob to quarter-speed, shut his eyes, and listened for the answer. Amid the garble, he heard the words *"Gree-tings, my chi-ldren."*

"Greetings, my children," repeated Will.

"Oh, I heard it," said La Roy, the prickly hairs on his forearms standing straight on end.

Will dialed up Vanessa's next question, where she asked about his allegations that Theroux was behind the plot.

"It's ludicrous. And sad. For both of us, I think. He's clearly grasping at straws in an attempt to put a public face on his marital discord."

Pause, quarter-speed reverse, then go. Once again, Will closed his eyes to listen. He repeated to La Roy the words as he heard them.

"My last communication before I join the rest of your brothers and sisters."

While La Roy wrote feverishly, Will skipped past Vanessa's next question straight to Theroux's answer.

"I am set to die in two weeks. And my efforts for a stay of execution are made worse by this constant demonizing. I don't know this senator. I have never met him or his wife. I am not a political person."

And in reverse, Will listened intently to every answer, speaking aloud as if the words of Theroux were coming through his own mouth.

"Burn, furthermore change your names in the way that I've taught you. Move. Then change them again.

"Don't ever leave America. For the ultimate freedom it provides will offer my child the ultimate sanctuary in which to thrive.

"Raise the child as a boy. But when he turns a man, treat him as a god, for it is he who will usher in the final apocalypse."

"Jesus," said La Roy. "Does he really think that—"

"Did he say it was a boy?" interrupted Will.

La Roy had to look back down at his notepad. *"You* said boy."

"Gwen is having a boy," said Will, forgetting about paternity for that one moment and trying to put a meaning on the strange glow he felt inside his own hollowed shell.

"Here's the part when you called," said La Roy with a gesture toward the screen.

And there it was. The cell phone ringing. The producer calling to kill the cameras. And Vanessa Curran standing, stretching her long legs past Kruger's camera and offering the cell phone to Theroux's ear.

"This is Will Sullivan," repeated Will, recalling the moment he first spoke to Theroux.

"Yes, it is. Good evening, Senator," said Theroux on tape. *"Your ears must have been itching because we were just talking about you."*

Will froze the tape, quarter-dialed the rewind function, and prayed Theroux's subconscious would betray him. La Roy could only hear the rewinding garble of words played backwards. But Will heard and repeated for La Roy's pen:

"You are as foolish as your father."

Pause, fast-forward, next question.

"Where is my wife, you son of a bitch?"

"Last I read, Senator, was that your wife was hiding from you."

On rewind, Will heard another answer spit from Theroux's sub-brain:

"She is buried, but not yet dead."

"I'm begging you to let her go!"

"Death will be her release."

"Goddammit where is she?"

"And furthermore, you will be left to suffer her death."

"You will die and you will go to hell!"

"And there I will sit at the left hand of my uncle!"

"No way!" said La Roy. He threw the legal pad across the room. "I will not go *believing* this son of a bitch is Beelzebub's great-great-nephew!"

Will picked up the notes, reading them back. "She is buried, but not yet dead . . . Furthermore, you will be left to suffer her death."

La Roy put a hand under his baseball hat and rubbed his fuzzy head. "Forget it, Earnest. He didn't give away shit."

"She's buried but not yet dead. Furthermore," repeated Will, turning back to Theroux's frozen image on the monitor. "Furthermore *what*?"

Upstairs, the phone had been ringing. Good news for La Roy, because he needed to get the hell out of that room. Breathe some air. Make some coffee. When he left, Will was starting over from square one, replaying the tape from the opening color bars.

The only way young Isaac knew to retrieve cannibalized files from a virus-plagued computer was to yank out the hard drive and feed it into a spanking-new system loaded with the TRW-developed software Rescue Now! The risk was great—it could destroy the new computer and, at the same moment in time, consume the original disk. All files would be DOA. The key to success was hooking the jury-rigged setup to the fastest printer available, ordering the computer to randomly print anything it could determine was a text or graphic-interface file, and hope to hell that the ad hoc system didn't eat itself before precious documents could be plucked from cyberspace and turned into hard copies.

Eight hundred and forty-three pages later, Theroux's hard disk was reduced to magneto-silicon goo. A new computer would be expensed against Will Sullivan's account, and Benny Yao would be hanging onto the phone until somebody picked up at Marblehead. What Isaac delivered was too important to keep. Benny'd made a resolution that if nobody answered within the next twenty rings, he would shuttle himself up to Marblehead to deliver the goods in person.

"Hello," answered La Roy.

Yao could hear La Roy rattling around the Marblehead kitchen. "It's Benny."

"We're not in the mood for bad news, Benny."

"I think we got something down here."

"If it's got anything to do with ghosts or goblins, you might have to wait for my curly hair to come back." La Roy still had the chills. He wanted hot coffee and a long steaming shower.

"You got something I should know about?" asked Yao.

"You first."

"You know that computer that I said was all but done for?" asked Yao rhetorically. "We pulled somethin' off it. Eight hundred and some pages. Mostly computer gibberish. A lotta nothin'."

"But there's somethin'?"

"I'd say so," said Yao. Absent was his usual drone. Benny Yao actually sounded excited. "We're faxing it to you as we speak. Twenty-five pages. And are you sitting down?"

"Hit me," said La Roy.

"Some of the images are video stills of Gwen in captivity."

La Roy wheeled, lowered the phone, and shouted, "EARNEST! GET YOUR ASS UP HERE!"

The OfficeJet was churning out the fax, sliding grainy halftones into Will's hands. There, oddly printed in frames the size of playing cards, were still pictures of Gwen. Very pregnant, seated upright in a bed, bound at the ankles and wrists. The room was nondescript, the light falling away at the edges into black laser ink. But there was no doubt it was Gwen. Alive. And staring back at the camera as if someone was speaking to her.

La Roy had the cordless phone to his ear with Yao at the other end. "Did you get the document files yet?" asked Yao.

"They're coming through now," said La Roy.

"They are clearly text tracings of conversations between Gwen and Theroux," said Yao. "What's odd is her typing. I mean, there's a lotta mistakes. Misspells. I can't tell if it's Gwen's actual typing or someone, say, one of the family, typing for her."

Will had scanned the page in hand, but hadn't yet read a word. "Can't be," he said. "Gwen's an ace typist. This can't be her . . ."

As Will's eyes frantically flew back and forth, practically inhaling the contents of the document, La Roy translated to Yao. "Will says that Gwen is an ace—"

Forgve mee, but myy tuping stinks.

"It's her!" said Will with a swell of sudden ebullience. She'd written Theroux back in the first person. "It's *her*. She wrote this. It was *her* at the keyboard."

"So how do you explain the typing?" asked La Roy. "Drugs?"

"Could be," said Will. "I just know it's her. That's all."

Yao overheard Will. "Good. Then when she says that she feels like she's in a dungeon—"

"Buried, but not dead," said La Roy, remembering the transcription of Theroux's reverse-talk.

Will was reading on. Theroux's words:

YOU MUST IMAGINE THE TALL TREES THAT GROW ABOVE YOU.

"There's another page coming," said Yao. "And because this page showed up a couple hundred pages later, we're thinking it's from another session."

Yanking page number two from the machine, Will bent over and put it under the white flood of Gwen's desk lamp.

What he read made him want to puke. The intimate prose made it look as if Gwen was talking through a computer keyboard directly to a lover:

GOOD MORNING, MY FLOWER.
    Good mrning.
SLEEP WELL, DID YOU?
    I was awaake aloot. i wish they
    would let mee sleep witht the
    lights offf.
THE BETTER FOR ME TO SEE YOU,
MY FLOWER.

"Did you read the *USA Today* reference?" asked Yao. "They're letting her read—"

"*USA Today*," repeated La Roy to Will.

"I'm there," said Will. His gut churned and his brain squeaked.

Something's wrong, Will. Something's wrong with . . .

"It's the typing again," said Will. "It's wrong. It's not *her*."

"It could be nerves," explained La Roy.

Will grabbed a yellow highlighter and began crossing off every misspelled word. But nearly every word was misspelled, typo'd, or butchered. He came up with nothing but yellow streaks.

"Now on page three," said Yao. "I think there's something in this number. SMS1558."

"Here," said La Roy, pulling the third page of text out of the fax machine.

"Wait!" said Will, shoving the page away. He was still on page two, dispensing with the highlighter and trying something else. He took a pen and darkened each capitalized letter that Gwen had typed into her conversation:

    I rread in **USA TODAY** that your
    most rrecent appe**OL** was rejected?

And after Theroux's response:

> **I AM** parrt of your scHEme to . . . ? i'm
> soRry. I don't knoww whatevEr?

Will strung the capped letters together, etching them into the margin.

USA TODAY OL I AM HERE

La Roy couldn't believe what he was reading. "Holy Sister of Swami . . ."

"She was talking to us," said Will. "She's trying to tell us where she is."

La Roy ordered Yao to hang on while Will continued, finishing off page two and going onto page three.

> **I** findd my dark thoughts changginG to
> The **SUNNYS**ide of things.
> SUCH AS WHAT, MY FLOWER?
> **S**illy, reallly. **I** wonder iff my **MILK**
> will coMe in?

Into the margin Will wrote again, line by line. Gwen's message took form in the hand of her husband:

IG SUNNYS MILK M

> **Y**ou weere behind me. **L**eft hands on **MY**
> BrEasts. but i **D**idn't knoww what you
> looked liike.
> AND THEN?
> **I** wantedd to turnn over but youu said
> no.
> YOU THINK I DON'T WANT YOU TO SEE MY
> FACE?
> **T**heree's more. **Y**ou took **MY** hand and
> wrootte your phone number. I remember
> **SMS1558.** Dooes that mean anythingg
> to youu?

YL MY BED
I Y MY SMS1558

i keep tHinking about thE dreamL andd
if it means someething about me Personaly
or if it has greater MEaning.

HELP ME

La Roy gasped in a sudden wheeze, drawing enough cof-fee into his lungs that he was bent over hacking.

Yao was at the other end of the phone, shouting, "BILL? BILL! IS EVERYTHING OKAY?"

Will snatched the cordless from La Roy. "I'm sending you back a fax right now."

"If it's the translation of the Theroux tape—"

"No," said Will. "It's a note from my wife."

"From Gwen?"

From Gwen. Yes.

All day, Gwen had smelled the gasoline. At first, it had floated in the stale air in small waves. But when it began to sting inside her nostrils, she complained. Clem answered her call, appearing so greasy and drug-weary, he seemed to have gone a week without sleep or a bath. And he brought the stink in with him. He was soaked in gasoline. So much so that Izzy yanked him by the back of the collar and sent him out of the room with a boot.

"Take a fuckin' shower!"

"I'm not done yet," said Clem.

"You are for today," said Izzy.

Izzy had been gone for five days. During which the food had turned from poor to downright lousy. It was hard for Gwen to eat. And now the smell of gasoline worried her that the air might be poisoned.

"It's nothing to worry about," bullshitted Izzy. "He's working on the old generator."

"I want to talk to Dean!" demanded Gwen.

"Dean's done with talking," she said spitefully. "We have

his final words. He's said good-bye to us all. So I suggest you move on with your petty life and get over him. Just like I had to."

"What happened to my newspaper?" Five days without the *USA Today* had left Gwen lost and afraid for her mind. She needed a handhold.

"I'll have Starr bring you a book when she gives you a bath."

Starr?

"Is she back?" asked Gwen. "Is she okay? What happened to the baby?"

The door was shut. Clank. Over and out. Izzy was gone. The stone-coldness of Izzy left Gwen wrapping herself in a blanket, curling around the sphere that was her stomach. How could she *ever* have trusted, let alone liked, this woman? She'd always considered herself a good judge of character.

Her thoughts returned to the baby. It felt different. He had dropped and was kicking her twice every half hour. Pounding. He wanted out. He wanted to breathe the air and suckle his mother. He wanted life and, despite the evidence of his paternity, Gwen wanted life for him. It was the only instinct she had left. Not to have *it* out. But to have *him* in her arms. Once there, she felt, she could keep him safe from *them*. Izzy and Clem and Jack and . . .

"Hi there," said Starr. Her smile was pained and traced on. Transparent as hell. She carried a bucket of soapy water, a bottle of Lotus Blossom body lotion, and a dog-eared paperback with yellowed pages. Gwen, though, was glad to see her. She waited for the door to close.

"How are you?" asked Gwen. "Is the baby okay?"

"I hope so," said Starr. "She's with her new family now."

"Your baby girl?"

A genuine smile broke out on Starr's face, shining briefly, then receding behind a pained facade. "She's not mine anymore."

"Adopted?"

Starr nodded, left the bucket on the floor, and loosened the Velcro restraints on Gwen's ankles and wrists. Then as she had every other day for two months, she unbuttoned Gwen's nightgown and began the sponge bath, beginning at Gwen's feet and proceeding northward.

"I can't raise a baby. I have no husband. I have no means of support. She's better off."

"Better off without her mother?" pressed Gwen, always wanting to keep the conversation afloat in hope of a glimmer of information.

"Better off with her new family," she said, damming any emotional outbreak with a face so frozen she could have been on display at Madame Tussaud's. "You know, I met them. They were like you and your senator. Professionals, you know? Lots of money. From Boise. I asked them and they said they'd already hired a nanny. But I reminded them that a nanny was no replacement for a mommy. A real family, you know?"

The wash water was a few degrees south of lukewarm. Cool to the skin and scented with a chemical designed to smell like a florist shop. Gwen would sometimes close her eyes and imagine it was Will working the washcloth over her thighs. Instead, as Starr moved from Gwen's pubis, working the damp cloth over her stretched tummy, Gwen couldn't help but notice Starr's breasts. A week before, they'd seemed naturally enlarged by her pregnancy. A cup size larger with maybe an extra inch added to the strap. But hardly the engorged pair that Starr now carried. She was huge. Her T-shirt was ill-fitting, tight, and stained with leaking milk.

Starr was lactating . . . yet she wasn't nursing?

"How soon did you have to give up the baby?" asked Gwen.

"What do you mean?"

"After you had her," said Gwen. "How soon before you had to give her up to the new parents?"

"Oh, no time at all," said Starr. "I had her for a day. I don't remember much. I barely got to see her eyes open before the woman from Social Services came in and *whaddayouknow*. My baby was gone forever."

It'd been five days since Starr had been driven to the hospital. Clem had said the labor was long and painful, but shorter than twenty-four hours.

Gwen quizzed herself. During the fifth month of her pregnancy, she must have read four separate books on lactation. She questioned how long, if at all, she should breastfeed. One month? Two? Six? And would she pump? Being a professional woman, she'd probably have to . . .

That's it! Gwen suddenly realized. Starr was pumping. Her breasts had become engorged. But why? When she'd given her baby up for adoption so soon? Was she providing the new parents with pints of her breast milk? It was possible. Shipping it all the way to Boise? From where? Gwen asked herself. Was Boise nearby? Or a thousand, two thousand miles away?

Starr began to scrub Gwen's breasts, soaping the nipples with a sudden lack of regard for their sensitivity. She scrubbed away as if Gwen's breasts were just another heel or kneecap—without the reverent delicacy one would expect for Baby Dean's future milk source . . .

"You're the wet nurse," said Gwen, her mouth tripping over her hard-charging mind.

Starr froze, squeezing the washcloth into a tight fist, trickling a stream of soapsuds into Gwen's armpit.

"I don't know what you mean," said Starr, her eyes on full avoidance.

"Your breasts," said Gwen, committed to her theory. "You're lactating."

"What can I say," said Starr as she worked over Gwen's shoulders. "My tits are like a stuck valve. Can't seem to turn 'em off if I wanted to."

"You're going to kill me." Gwen's words undulated with a heart-stopping fear. It had been an obvious question in her mind for months, but her feral necessity to stay optimistic had straight-armed the issue.

"Naw," said Starr. "You're the queen bee. We're here for you."

"Look at me and tell me I'm lying," said Gwen, her voice thickening with anger, every word bolder than the last. "I'm going to have the baby. You're going take it, kill me, and feed him yourself. With your milk. That's what Dean wants. That's why I'm here. That's why you were pregnant in the first—"

"Starr?" asked Izzy. She was standing in the doorway, elbows bent, hands on her hips. "You about done in here?"

"Just have to dry her off," said Starr, working faster.

"Dr. Bert wants to do another sonogram," said Izzy. "If the baby's healthy, he thinks he might want to induce labor."

"When?" asked Gwen.

"Was I talking to you?" shot back Izzy.

Dr. Bertrand ambled through the door, then wheeled the ultrasound unit to the bed like some old drunk pushing a pretzel cart. His eyes looked barely focused, at three-quarters mast and hidden behind blue-tinted prescription glasses.

"How's my patient?" His lips were pinkish, pale. His teeth, yellow. Gwen wondered if he even recognized her. Robotically, as if on remote control, he went about his business. He groped inside her to gauge the baby's position, then jellied Gwen up in preparation for the sonogram.

Theroux's family assembled in the underground room to see the monitor. Izzy, Clem, Starr, and Jack. Gwen watched their usually opaque faces squish with delight at the green and black tracings of Theroux's child. They giggled when the baby moved. Pointed. Squeaked like little children staring into their first fishbowl.

Dr. Bertrand whispered to Izzy. She nodded and gestured for the others to leave. With a couple of dry knuckles, Dr. Bertrand gently touched Gwen's cheek. "I'm sorry," he said.

"Sorry for what?" asked Gwen.

Dr. Bertrand merely shook his head and left the room.

"SORRY FOR WHAT?"

Izzy stayed behind to impart the good and bad news. "The baby's not in the right position to induce. So we'll wait a while to see if it turns."

Scared shitless, Gwen pressed, "So why is he sorry?"

"For the safety of the baby . . ." Izzy checked the restraints, making sure they were intact. Then left the room with Gwen bound to the bed. She closed the door on Gwen's screaming.

6

"Eastern Washington," said Yao over the telephone. "In or around Spokane."

That's all Will needed to hear. He'd get the rest on the way to the airport. La Roy had the bags ready to go. Nothing fancy. Just sweats, jeans, T-shirts, and underwear. Will had picked up the conversation with Yao on his cellular on the way to Logan Airport. Behind the wheel of the Thunderbird, La Roy checked the rearview mirror to make certain the FBI tail was within range to pick up the conversation.

"Okay," began Yao. "The first message, *'USA TODAY OL I AM HERE.'* "

"Yes?" said Will.

"*USA Today* publishes regionally. On every front page there's a tiny code that lets the retailers know from where the newspaper was shipped. The letters *'OL'* are code for Olympia, Washington."

"But that's western Washington. Near Seattle," said Will.

"Gwen gets us closer with two more clues," said Yao. "The second message, *'IG SUNNYS MILK M.'* We found a

Sunnyside Dairy in the town of Merrion just outside Spokane."

Will's pulse surged with the information. He found himself holding his breath as Benny Yao dealt the last card.

"The third part is our bull's-eye. Where she says in her dream, *'MY BED, MY SMS1558'?* We got a positive product number on a hospital bed rented in late April from Spokane Medical Supply. I've got investigators on the phone. We'll find the renters and start our track from there."

"We're already on our way," said Will.

"At this time of day, the best we could do was route you through DFW, San Francisco, then Seattle. I've arranged a charter that should put you down in Spokane around four in the morning."

"You coming?" asked Will.

"Wouldn't miss this for all the oil in Kuwait," said Yao. "I'll meet you on the tarmac. From there, we've got rooms booked at the Quality Inn Valley Suites, right off I-90."

"What's the date today?" asked Will.

"June fifteenth," said La Roy.

"Thirteen days until—"

"She might be early," warned Yao.

"And she might be late!" shouted La Roy.

Staring straight ahead at the trail of stacked taillights leading into the Hub, Will's mind began to drift. From the unknown whereabouts of Allatore to the backward words of Wesley Dean Theroux.

She is buried, but not yet dead.

"Where are you, Vance?" Will muttered to himself before closing his eyes to pray.

Elk Grove, California.

Seventeen miles south of Sacramento and bordering a soil-rich delta, it was a dry, flat gathering of peach and almond orchards, two-lane drags, a street called Main, a drugstore known amongst the locals as Doc's, and fast food galore where the town edged State Highway 99.

Father Victor Guerrero had been the parish priest of St. Augustine's for twenty-nine years, ministering full-time to a mostly illegal immigrant population that came and went with the harvests. In his spare time, he reffed boys' basketball and umpired girls' softball at the local high school, tied flies so ugly the dumbest striped bass in the Sacramento River wouldn't rise to them, and when he could get whole leaf tobacco, he rolled his own cigars in the shoddiest of Cuban traditions. But hell if he didn't smoke them anyway, proud that he'd made the effort of his forefathers before him.

And lately, every so many months, the good Father Guerrero would be called on to perform the one rite for which he could be called an expert, a rare task for which few priests were trained.

"My name is Allatore," the road-worn priest introduced himself. He was rumpled, entirely unkempt, and reeked of Greyhound diesel fumes. "Did you get the letter?"

"The DHL, yes," said Father Guerrero, who invited Allatore out of the heat and into the dark coolness of the rectory. A volunteer secretary sat in the corner of the cramped space. Working at a donated Macintosh in the corner, she laid out Sunday's liturgy for printing. "Mrs. Calvin? Could you please get us a couple of glasses of water?"

A beetle-sized fly, halfway tied with banana-yellow thread, lay on Father Guerrero's desk. "You catch fish with that?" asked Allatore.

"Oh, no," said the older priest. "I just do my best to scare the buggers into deeper water. Now, where'd I put that envelope?"

Allatore helped, pointing to the white and red shipping sleeve on the shelf near the older priest's head. From it Father Guerrero removed a yellow envelope. And from that he withdrew a letter.

"It says you're on leave from Kerry, Ireland?"

"The Ballinskelligs," said Allatore.

"But you sound so American," observed Father Guerrero. "And your name is faintly familiar."

"Let's just say I'm late to the priesthood, Father."

"Better late than not at all, yes?"

The secretary returned carrying two glasses. With her

Parkinson's in semi-check from medication, she handed off the water without spilling much, then nodded her good-bye. She closed the door to leave the two priests alone.

Father Guerrero shook the letter. "Your bishop must think well of you to send such a letter. But all the way from Ireland?"

"The bishop is aware of my calling."

"Which is?" asked the older priest.

Allatore settled into an old swivel chair. It creaked when he turned to gaze out the window. Across the brown and baking expanse, he could make out the distant twin towers of the Rancho Seco nuclear power plant.

"I've come a long way to finish the Lord's work. Maybe we could start with a prayer?"

"For whom?" asked Father Guerrero.

"A man, his wife, and the baby she carries."

Under a blanket of cloud-covered darkness, the chartered prop-jet touched down at Spokane International Airport at 4:45 A.M. PST, where it made a sharp left turn off runway 8 and taxied away from the terminals. It parked in between the FedEx and UPS hangars. When the engines stalled, Will stepped out onto a rain-slicked stairway, ignored the drizzle, and greeted Benny Yao. La Roy was two steps behind, covering his head with a three-month-old issue of *George* magazine.

Yao led the way between the hangars to the open door of a nondescript warehouse painted a drab flesh tone. "Get any sleep, Senator?"

"You gotta be kidding," deadpanned Will.

"Dumb question, huh?" asked a smiling Benny Yao.

"There are dumber questions," piped up La Roy. "Like, who picked up the tab on the charter?"

"You're about to see," said Yao, pointing toward a pair of double-swinging cargo doors.

Will was first, shoving through the doors, only to stop dead at the sight of twenty-odd federal agents. FBI. They were bunched together in a corridor of cardboard cartons. Some of the agents were standing, others were seated on boxes, sharing cigarettes and small talk until the senator's arrival. They fell into silence at Will Sullivan's entrance.

Deflated, Will sarcastically asked, "It takes this many agents to serve an arrest warrant?"

Ralph Bedletter, the FBI kidnapping profiler, pushed to the front with Steve Salinas a step behind him. Bedletter said, "It takes this many agents to find your wife, Senator."

"You're a little late to the party, aren't you?" asked La Roy.

"Better late than never," said Steve Salinas, whose outstretched hand reached toward Will. "Good to see you, Will."

" 'My assassin will appear in the face of my closest friend,' " quoted La Roy.

"Julius Caesar?" asked Bedletter, arms crossed and unimpressed.

"Lucky Luciano," corrected La Roy.

Will turned to Benny Yao for an answer, having yet to accept Salinas's hand. "What's going on, Benny?"

"The evidence was just too damn compelling." Yao shrugged. "I took a chance and made a phone call to Ralph here. And he called the director."

"The FBI's come back around to your side," said Steve Salinas. "We're here to help."

"Does Lois Freehold know that?" asked Will.

"You can ask her yourself," said Bedletter. "She'll be here tonight."

Will took a moment to size up the bunch of Feds. They appeared as tired as himself. God knows from which faraway office they'd been culled for this last-minute rescue effort. Could he trust them? Or were they there on the director's orders just to save enough face while pounding the final nail in Gwen's coffin?

"Sorry about Sully," volunteered Salinas. He felt like shit, still offering up that hand which Will had yet to accept.

But Will reached forward and gave Steve's shoulder a gentle squeeze. "We'll talk later." Then he turned to Ralph Bedletter. "So let's go find my wife."

"Whoa, cowboy," said Bedletter. "Not so fast. *We'll* go find your wife. The FBI."

Will clenched a fist. He felt like socking the arrogant SOB. "Then you can leave on the same bus you rode in on," he said.

Benny Yao moved in. "Senator. We're close now. Real close. And you are way too *high* profile. All we need is the wrong person to get a good look at you or Mr. Bill here?" Yao was shaking his head. "It could get Gwen killed."

"I haven't come this far—"

"You're here now," said Bedletter. "And when we find your wife, I'll make sure you're right there at the moment we secure her release. But for now, it's a hotel room for you. Drapes pulled. Waiting for us to call."

Will put the heels of his hands to his eyeballs. His head felt like it was swelling to an extreme. A migraine was on the rise. He was so close. So damn close.

"We'll find her," assured Bedletter. "Just let us do our job. By sundown, my guess is—"

"No promises!" barked La Roy, protective as a pit bull.

Bedletter's hands went up in mock surrender. "Fine. No promises. Just let us get to work."

Will nodded, then followed Benny Yao to an idling rental car. After that, a hotel room with a mini-bar would be waiting. Will's impulse to raid it the second he walked through the door was as strong as he could ever recall. Could he resist the temptation just one more time?

Dressed in civilian rags, the FBI contingent joined Benny Yao's squadron. In two-man teams, they quietly cut up the Spokane County landscape, flashing FBI-generated picture packets to hospital staffs, paramedics, pharmacies, real estate agents, medical subcontractors, filling station attendants, grocery store clerks. In the meantime . . .

Nobody at Sunnyside Dairy in Merrion remembered delivering a single carton of milk to anybody in the photo directory.

Nobody at Spokane Medical Supply recognized anyone in the photos, either. The invoices for the rental showed the initial deposit had been paid for with a stolen credit card in the name of Dr. Elliot Barnett, who had also rented an ultrasound monitor. Not a single payment had been made since. The equipment had been catalogued as stolen.

And by twelve noon, no hospital or emergency worker had been able to identify the likes of Izzy, Clem, Jack, Starr, Dr. Bertrand, or Gwen Corbett-Sullivan. Investigative teams were slated to return when the shifts changed.

A commercial real estate agent turned in the first eyewitness clue. Her name was Harriet Oglethorpe, a part-time agent, part-time substitute grade school teacher. And to one of Yao's investigators, she positively identified the photo of Harvey Bertrand as Dr. Elliot Barnett for whom she'd brokered a lease on a closet-sized space in the Fayette Medical Building in southern Spokane. The address matched the Spokane Medical Supply Company's records. But when the FBI broke down the door to Dr. Elliot's sixth-floor office, all they found was an empty medical suite and a pile of junk mail and unpaid bills inside the threshold.

The search continued with investigators surreptitiously flashing the photo-pack to each and every tenant. The pile of junk mail was quickly returned to command center at the Quality Inn Valley Suites. There, forensic investigators were especially interested in the unpaid bills, faxing copies back to the Bureau in Washington for instant analysis and address checks.

Four o'clock. Zilch.

The curtains were drawn while La Roy slept and Will kicked around the suite, damning the frozen telephone with every glance. He willed it to ring with news of his wife. He had tried settling in for some TV to distract his mind, turning it on and off and on again until La Roy barked at him from his bed to "make a freakin' decision!"

"I want out! Just put me in a car and I'll drive. I mean, I'm one more pair of eyes, right? I might see something, somebody. I could recognize Izzy or Clem or Dr. Bertrand or Starr—"

"Or somebody might recognize *you*," said La Roy. Naptime was over. He sat up on the bed, jammed a pillow behind his neck, and wished to hell that someone at the hotel knew how to brew a decent cup of coffee. "We're close, Earnest. Let the G-men do their jobs."

"Since when are you on their side?"

"Look," said La Roy. "When I saw all them feds, I felt as sandbagged as you. Thought we were on our way to the poky. Since then, though, I've been running it up and down the La Roy flagpole, and I don't see any downside to the FBI joining in the chase. Sure, they're late to the party. But we invited 'em, remember? On national TV, no less."

Will flipped through the cable channels. He knew them all by memory. Two was hotel information. Three was *Spectravision Preview*. Four was MTV. Five VH1. Six CNN. Seven PBS. Eight ESPN. Nine USA. When the channels hit double digits, the local network affiliates were lined up at numbers eleven, twelve, and thirteen. At five o'clock straight up, each channel launched into its own newscast. Will quickly surfed back and forth, settling on ABC's channel 4 and an image which took him one second to recognize, but another ten to process. It was a live helicopter image of the Spokane Quality Inn Valley Suites.

La Roy heard a rumble overhead and said, "Turn it up."

On the screen they saw a live shot outside the hotel's entrance: a pixieish local reporter doing her stand-up.

"*. . . unconfirmed sources say that Massachusetts Senator Will Sullivan and an FBI hostage negotiation team are holed up inside the Quality Inn Valley Suites, poring over possible leads to the whereabouts of his missing wife, Gwen . . .*"

La Roy threw the curtains open, only to see two more TV trucks angling for front-door parking. "They're onto us! Jesus Christ! Who the hell leaked—"

"Shut up!" said Will, picking up the phone and dialing the command room's extension.

Salinas picked up on the half-ring. "Steve Salinas."

"We're on TV," said Will. "Or haven't you guys noticed?"

"It's Gary Modetti," said Salinas. "About two hours ago, he posted a live interview with an FBI source on his Web site. Whoever it was, spilled it."

Gary Modetti, having lost his secret pen pal, feeling spurned by Vanessa Curran, and then left out of the game by just about anybody inside the Will Sullivan camp, had burrowed deep into his well of sources, coming up with a mole in the FBI. When Modetti heard that the Bureau had secretly joined forces with Will in Spokane, the trash talker took the interview straight to the Internet, personally transcribing his questions and the mole's answers live for anybody who logged on.

The Washington wire services, who'd come to monitor *A La Mode* for breaking dirt, simply reported the "report." From that point, it took barely ten minutes for Spokane news directors to jump on the story, yanking their respective electronic field crews off a high school hot dog swilling competition and putting a hefty focus on the breaking story at the Spokane hotel.

"This could get Gwen killed!" said Will.

"I know!" said Salinas. "Here. Benny wants to talk."

"It's good news and bad news, Will," said Benny Yao, trying his best to put on a positive spin. "Since we're out of the bag, we've engaged the local PD and sheriffs in a priority-one APB. We're releasing pictures to the local press—"

In an angry tug, Will snapped the cord and tossed the phone across the room.

7

At the purchase counter of a Deer Park hardware store, Izzy stood slack-jawed, watching the TV shelved between the Swiss Army knives and the Blue-Blocker sunglasses display. The volume was low. Yet between the snapping gums of the dentured clerk and his fumbling to make change, Izzy'd heard enough. The FBI were close. As was the Mister. He was shacked up in a north Spokane hotel.

Well, thank you, Mr. and Mrs. Fourth Estate.

She snatched her paper bag full of kerosene lantern wicks and bolted before the clerk could hand her the dollar thirty-one in change. He shuffled after her, only to get a mouthful of dust as she roared off in the '66 Chevy pickup.

He's here! With the FBI! What did they know that would bring them so close?

It burned her to keep the truck under the speed limit. But if there ever was a moment that required restraint, a trained mind, and nerves like gunmetal, Izzy was straddling it as if it were a bucking bull. As the sun rested at the top of the treeline to her left, she listened to her numbers. Four point three miles until the turnoff. Her hands rested on the steering wheel at the ten and two o'clock positions. She kept the speedometer at forty-eight miles an hour. And under her seat was a .40-caliber Smith & Wesson with a sixteen-shot clip. Just in case.

No cars followed. And no cars passing gave her a second glance. Izzy pulled off just shy of the hairpin turn, leaving the engine idling while she opened and closed the gate behind the truck. She then powered down the winding dirt stretch to the caretaker's cottage.

"WE'RE GONNA INDUCE HER!" she shouted as she burst through the front door. The living room was vacant. As was the kitchen. Izzy stopped to look at the monitor. Gwen was restless, but alone. Izzy called out, "JACK! CLEM!"

"They're in with Dr. Bert," said Starr, her voice tinny and small. She was behind Izzy, leaning her face against the doorjamb.

"In where?" demanded Izzy.

"In his bedroom," said Starr. "Poor Dr. Bert."

"Well, tell him to get his fat ass up!" said Izzy, turning to the refrigerator and sliding the produce drawer open. In it were all the prescription medications they'd stolen for Dr. Bertrand. The serum to induce was marked PITOCIN. Izzy wanted it ready for when—

"He's dead, Izzy," said Starr.

"Who's dead?"

"Dr. Bert," said Starr. "He overdosed while you were in—"

"THE FUCK HE'S DEAD!"

Izzy blew past Starr and marched down the tight corridor to the small bedroom where Dr. Bertrand spent most of his time when not knocked out in front of the TV. He'd stacked up piles of paperback novels. To steady herself, Izzy counted them. Forty-six. The lace curtains were drawn and limp. Clem and Jack stood helplessly over the sagging twin bed. Both were drawn and ragged from pained efforts to revive the old doctor. Izzy noted eighteen desperate sighs. Twelve from Jack. Six from Clem. As for Dr. Bertrand himself, he was bleach-white from his chin to his knee-high socks, and otherwise naked except for a pair of marine-blue boxer shorts. An inch above his right knee was a blood pressure cuff he'd inflated in order to bring up the veins behind the joint. The practiced addict had used a compact mirror to guide his needle.

"What was the dose?" asked Izzy.

"I don't know. You think maybe too fuckin' much?" asked Clem sarcastically.

Izzy picked the disposable hypodermic off the nightstand, quickly flicked at it with her fingernail, then held the barrel up against the setting sunlight. The fine deposits from the mixture left a milky indication of Dr. Bertrand's personally prescribed dosage.

"The motherFUCKER!" said Izzy.

"Did he kill himself on purpose?" asked Starr from the doorway.

"Old junkies don't die by accident," said Clem.

Izzy reloaded the dirty hypodermic with the Pitocin.

"What's that?" asked Jack.

"We're gonna induce the queen mother," said a maddened Izzy. "It's baby time!"

And when Izzy knew she had all their attention, she informed them of the sudden FBI presence in Spokane. The Mister was only eleven miles away at the Quality Inn Valley Suites. It was time, she told them. Time to fulfill Dean's destiny with a perfect child.

Time had been all but lost for Gwen. Lately, the lights in her room seemed never to dim. With no newspaper to hang on by, she was forced to rely on her reduced meal service. Breakfast cereal was her eight o'clock. Her first soup and sandwich was her twelve noon lunch. Her granola bar snack was her three in the afternoon. Her second soup and sandwich, six-thirty. But if she let her subconscious latch onto a different time line, her day would begin to spin out of control. For as far as she knew, breakfast was served at noon. Dinner at midnight. The paleness of her captors quizzed her at every glimpse. Except for Izzy, she wondered if they'd ever seen the sun at all. As if Dean's clan were little more than modern-day vampires, spending their days in that dungeon, waiting for the day when they could suck the life from her baby.

She awoke to the prick of an IV needle being stuck in her arm, Starr was to one side. Jack at the foot of the bed. And Izzy on her left with that syringe full of Pitocin.

"Do you have the right dose?" asked Jack, the urgency in him startling Gwen to further consciousness.

"If it's not enough," said Izzy, "we'll stick her again."

The Pitocin seeped into the IV, draining into Gwen's bloodstream as fast as her veins would allow.

"What are you doing?" asked Gwen. "Where's Dr. Bertrand?"

"Napping," said Izzy. "And *we're* having a baby. Care to come?"

"What?" said Gwen. Was she dreaming? Confusion abounded.

"No," said Izzy. "You're not dreaming. You're having your baby now."

"Without Dr. Bert—"

"We women had babies for a million years without no doctors," said Izzy, her voice oddly singsong. "So I don't see any reason why you can't."

With a nod from Izzy, Jack kicked out the wheel blocks and pulled on the bed. It began to roll, Gwen with it. Starr made the IV stand heel as Izzy and Jack pushed Gwen through the door. A pain surged in her abdomen. Sharp, searing, forming a cresting wave that receded as quick as it came. She howled.

"She's already having contractions!" said Starr. "I think it's too fast."

"Put a watch on it," said Izzy. She was at the head of the bed, turning it toward the "O.R."

Pitch darkness enveloped Gwen as the next pain swelled. The baby kicked, its feet fluttering as if it were a swimmer trying to make the turn. She screamed again. She heard Starr at her ear, saying something like "Breathe . . . quick breaths . . . breathe . . . quick breaths . . ."

Lamaze, thought Gwen. *Fucking Lamaze. She hadn't had a single lesson in fucking Lamaze . . .*

The room turned from black to an assault of blazing white photo floods bracketed to the pipe-striped ceiling. Gwen's eyes adjusted. The room was whitewashed. She was next door. In a makeshift operating room. Yes. This was where Starr was in labor. Next door to her dungeon. This was where Starr had her baby—

"JESUS!" screamed Gwen in another rush of pain.

"Two minutes apart!" said Starr. "That's too fast. You gave her too much of that shit!"

"Fast, my ass," said Izzy, forcing Gwen's legs into the stirrups. "Gwenny's havin' our baby."

Starr leaned into Gwen. "Reach down, sweetie. Touch yourself. You know how you're supposed to feel down there. Tell us if you're dilating."

Not by order, but on impulse, Gwen stuck a hand down between her legs in time to feel a rush of warm fluid.

"Looks like your water just broke," said Izzy. "Should be no time at all now."

No time at all? The pain waved in again, crested, and crashed. Again. Izzy was shouting for Gwen to push while Starr was at her ear. "Breathe, honey. Breathe little short ones, then when the pain gets bad, push hard!"

Jack appeared with the fetal monitor. Starr strapped it to Gwen and twisted up the volume. A speedy beeping filled the room. The baby's heart was racing. Too fast? wondered Gwen. She couldn't hear very well. With every push, her ears plugged with her own screaming.

"Breathe," said Starr.

"Push," said Izzy.

"WAIT!" shouted Gwen. Her arm stretched past Starr to point at the fetal monitor. "Please . . . listen."

The speedy beeping had been cut in half, slowing to a mere sixty beats per second. As the pain of the contraction receded, the fetal heartbeat returned again. North of one hundred.

"There," said Izzy. "Everything's fine. Now get ready to push."

Another contraction arrived, this one without the usual build. It hit Gwen like a knee to the kidneys. She howled, biting down on the wet washcloth Starr had been using to wipe her brow. Then she heard it again. As the pain reversed with the undertow, the fetal monitor showed that the baby's heart was beating slowly and irregularly.

Oh my God, I'm killing it!

"I don't think she should push anymore," said Starr.

"Fuck that," said Izzy. "I can just about see the head."

Starr pressed up next to Izzy. "I think the cord's wrapped around the baby's neck."

"And how would you know?" asked Izzy.

"I read about it," said Starr. "And all pushing does is restrict the air to the baby's lungs."

Izzy's teeth were gritted so tight that she snapped a crown. She suddenly found herself spitting pieces of enamel and saliva streaked with blood.

"So help me, if you kill my baby . . ." said Gwen.

"What are you gonna do?" asked Izzy. "What the fuck are *you* gonna do to *me*?"

"It's not what I'll do," said Gwen between puffs of breath. "It's what *he'll* do."

More contractions. Gwen arched her back in a spasm of pain. Once again, the fetal heart rate plummeted.

"STOP PUSHING!" screeched Izzy, about to blow a brain-circuit.

"She's not pushing!" said Starr. "It's the drugs! You stupid bitch! You're gonna kill the baby!"

Anger grabbed hold of Starr. She lashed out with a fistful of sharp fingernails, three of which scored Izzy's cheek. But before Starr could ball her fist to strike again, Izzy had stripped the protective paper from a scalpel and backhanded it deep into Starr's heart. Starr wheezed, looking down at the impaled instrument more in surprise than horror. Then her knees gave and she buckled to the floor. Shock took over. Within ten seconds she was dead.

Izzy felt Jack behind her. She wheeled with another disposable scalpel. This one still in the packaging. But every bit as lethal.

Jack's arms went up in a sign of surrender. "C'mon, Iz. Get a grip!"

"We're gonna cut it out," said Izzy. "Get on some gloves." She flipped a handful of surgical gloves into Jack's face.

"And then what?" he asked. "You just killed the fuckin' nursemaid."

"I was a formula baby," said Izzy. "And that's how I'll raise our son."

"MY SON!" growled Gwen, her voice an octave below a whisper.

"Tie her feet and arms," ordered Izzy, her eyes fixed on a five-inch stretch of skin just a notch above Gwen's pubic hair. Izzy'd seen the scars before. On other women. Caesareans.

Gwen flailed miserably as Jack attempted to tie her down. But with another contraction, her back arched and, with the wash of pain, her limbs momentarily lost all strength. The Velcro straps were easily secured. Gwen was bound. All she could do to prevent Izzy from slicing her open was summon the demon who'd fathered her child.

"HARM MY SON AND YOU WILL FOREVER TWIST ON THE SPIT OF MY ANGER!"

Izzy froze to look at Gwen. Her victim's eyes were rolled back into her head, lids fluttering. The voice was strangely *un*-Gwen. Guttural and hoarse. The scalpel hovered. Izzy was ready to make the incision.

Kill the mother. Save the child.

"Listen!" said Jack.

"I heard her!" snapped Izzy, refusing to believe the words were Gwen's . . . but Dean's voice *through* her.

"No," said Jack. "The heart rate. The baby's heart!"

Sure enough. Gwen was in the middle of another contraction, but the baby's heart rate had returned to over a hundred. Staccato, but normal. At least by Izzy's ears. The extent of her medical knowledge was in her hand. A scalpel that was inexplicably shaking.

"What do we do now?" asked Jack.

Izzy, always quick with an answer, was momentarily stumped. A case of the shakes overwhelmed her. She dumped the tool into a sterilized dish, ran a sleeve across her face, then backed off.

What to do now, Izzy?

The rage inside Izzy erupted into an explosion of uncontrollable shuddering and tears. Gwen heard the sobs. She caught snippets of sound as Jack attempted to calm her in a quiet voice. All the while Gwen felt as if she were balanced on the point of a giant saber. One slip and she'd be impaled. Dead, just like Starr. She couldn't recall where the voice had come from. The one that threatened to burn Izzy on a spit. Imagination? Or from someplace deeper . . . or farther off? Wherever, the worm had turned along with the baby. His heart rate was strong and swift. And the drug-induced contractions were beginning to subside.

"What do I do?" cried Izzy. "Where are you, Dean? I need you."

"Help me," croaked Gwen. "Help my baby."

"I'M NOT TALKING TO YOU!" screamed Izzy.

"Yes," whispered Gwen. "You *are* talking to me." She forced a dry swallow as another shallow contraction reared. "Please. Save my baby. I'll tell you what to do."

8

A hard black darkness rolled over Spokane. The high clouds offered no reflection and left a pale mist that was best described as falling fog. The inclement weather deterred neither the FBI nor the gathering media. News crews were steadfastly planted in front of the Quality Inn, ready at a moment's notice to blaze up the hotel's exterior at the mere mention of Senator Will Sullivan.

"You sure you want to do this?" asked Benny Yao.

Will was in the FBI command suite with La Roy, Ralph Bedletter, Steve Salinas, and eleven other agents and investigators who were banging their heads against the walls, hoping like hell for a decent lead. There'd been nothing returned in the last two hours. Time was thin. And Will was taking point.

"We've unzipped and exposed ourselves," returned Will. "No sense in acting like we're not here."

"What are you gonna say?" asked Salinas.

Will snapped, "What I've always said!"

"Maybe we should wait until Lois shows," said Bedletter.

"It's not a photo op," pounced La Roy.

Salinas stripped off his sport coat and offered it to his old roomie. "At least wear a jacket, Will. You're still a U.S. senator."

As expected, the news crews torched up the Quality Inn the moment they saw Will coming. Five paces in front of La Roy and Steve Salinas, he wore white Reeboks, faded jeans, a white polo shirt, the borrowed navy blue jacket, and the worn look of a man who'd rather face a firing squad than another damned TV camera. The distance between the front entrance and the waiting rattlesnakes was thirty slick yards of cobblestone-formed concrete. He kept his eyes turned down, on the path and away from the glare of the klieg lights. Fifteen more steps and he'd be squaring off with an ill-rehearsed statement.

Ladies and gentlemen. I have furnished the FBI with information that leads us to believe that my beloved wife, Gwen, is being held captive nearby—

"WILL!" shouted Benny Yao, chasing up the path behind him. Ralph Bedletter was at his heels. Will stopped and turned back. "We just got a call," said Yao. "A hospital—outside of town—called . . ."

"Park Memorial," said Bedletter. "They got a walk-in Jane Doe. In labor. Nobody pressed her for a name because they didn't want to spook—"

"Where's the hospital?" demanded Will.

"Four, five miles tops," said Benny.

Turning their backs to the salivating horde, the ad hoc group huddled around Will and hustled him back inside the hotel. They ran straight through the lobby and into the rear parking lot. When a spotter caught a glimpse of a fast-moving caravan of rental cars peeling away from the hotel, the news crews scrambled. A traffic helicopter picked up the chase and relayed that the route was a straight track to Park Memorial Hospital. The rumor that Gwen Sullivan was giving birth was already doing the rounds. En route, camera teams checked their battery packs, reporters fixed their hair and makeup, and overeager news drivers tried not to pile up when running northern Spokane's red lights.

*   *   *

Park Memorial Hospital.

Will wanted to be first through the door. He wanted Gwen to see his face beaming when the FBI stormed the hospital. But as the caravan slowed to let the Spokane Police Department's tactics team by, Ralph Bedletter leaned over the backseat and turned reality up a few notches.

"Now, they don't know we're coming," he warned. "We don't know who or what we'll find there. So until the situation is stable, we need you to sit tight, Senator. In the car. When your wife is secure, we'll bring you in. Am I clear on this?"

Before Will could think to put up a protest, the radio squawked with news that Lois Freehold's aircraft was two minutes from touching down at Spokane International. A police helicopter was waiting to deliver her to the hospital. It would be one hell of a photo op.

Will looked down to find his fists so tight that his overgrown fingernails had cut into his palms. La Roy gave him a handkerchief and a loving pat on the back. "Almost home, Earnest. Almost home."

They stopped eighty yards short of Park Memorial's entrance. The thousand-watt red and white banner screamed EMERGENCY over a canopy large enough to protect three ambulances. The tactics van was already parked across the lot and emptied. Some fifteen Spokane PD squad cars were dispatched around the hospital, jamming the exits with whirling lights and uniformed cops.

Will watched from the car, catching what glimpses he could through the slow-turning wiper blades. He could see Bedletter under the awning with Benny Yao. Yao was gesturing wildly while Bedletter seemed far too at ease with a walkie-talkie to his ear.

"She's not there," said Will.

"No news is no news," said Steve Salinas.

"She's not fucking in there!"

La Roy put an arm around Will. "I think we should wait—"

Will kicked open the door, stepping out into the mist. Behind him were the arriving TV trucks, held back by a police line drawn by the Spokane PD. Bedletter was walking toward Will. Yao in tow.

"She's not in there, is she?" Will shouted. He knew. He didn't know how he knew, but hell if he didn't *know*.

"Tactics is going floor by floor," said a defensive Bedletter.

"The Jane Doe who was in labor?" pressed Will. "It wasn't Gwen. Yes?"

Bedletter looked momentarily beaten. It was Benny Yao who gave up an answer. "She's a transient. Her face was covered in dirt. She was brought in by two men. One who vaguely fit the description of Clem."

Bedletter sighed. "She doesn't even speak English."

Will's knees felt as if they were going to give. His stomach was ready to heave. La Roy offered him his arm, worried about the cameras. "Let's get Will inside, okay?"

Once again, the TV cameras got little more than Will Sullivan being ushered inside another building. FBI Director Lois Freehold, after a briefing from Ralph Bedletter, handled the duty of addressing the assembled cameras.

"On the record, the FBI is here to assist Senator Will Sullivan," she read to the TV audience, the local feeds uplinked to a live CNN broadcast. "The FBI has in its possession ample evidence that has led us to this place and this time. We are prayerful that the senator's wife, Gwen Sullivan, will soon be reunited with her husband. Thank you."

Serving a desperate longing to be alone, Will excused himself from the grossly enlarged powwow that included La Roy, Benny Yao and his investigators, Lois Freehold, Ralph Bedletter, and other FBI agents. Not to mention the Spokane County sheriff and chief of emergency services. Will feigned a need to go to the bathroom, then slipped upstairs to an empty corridor in the hospital's north wing. He found an empty bench near a pay phone and sat down, staring vacantly at the opposite wall.

He wanted to cry, but he couldn't. He wanted to scream, but thought better of it. There were patients and nurses about. A shout would bring somebody running. And he needed to be alone. Left with feelings that twisted his being into a single raw nerve, he opted for stillness. Quiet.

To save electricity, the corridor was half-lit. Only every other fluorescent panel was illuminated. The rest were cool gray boxes inset in an acoustic-tiled ceiling. The walls were painted a peachy-white with heavy black rubber base-boards. Both originals and prints—from oils to watercolors to kindergarten collages—were staggered between brass plaques inscribed with a special thanks to a charitable few who'd aided in the construction of the hospital's wing.

Will's synapses flashed, recalling the hundred brass plaques which had adorned his father's personal study. A thank you from the Rotary Club. One from the South Boston Boys' Club, thanking Councilman Daniel Sullivan for his generous support. Politics was plagued with brass plaques. If they could get away with it, special interest groups would forego the use of brass plaques or pen sets and simply etch their personal thanks right on your fore-head.

As a brief distraction, Will found himself skimming the donors' names. Those rich enough to give something back to their community or seek a tax deduction.

MR. & MRS. PAUL SVINGALLA
IN MEMORY OF
JANE ALEX BEGALLA

RICHARD KIPLINGER
IN MEMORY OF HIS LOVING WIFE
DARLA

IN MEMORY OF
DREW ALAN FARTHMORE
THE FARTHMORE FOUNDATION

The third plaque. Will found himself reading it back-wards and forwards and without a clue as to why. The name tugged at his aching left hemisphere. *FARTHMORE.* A con-tributor, maybe? A handshake? He'd met too many people in his career. An unhealthy number. Yet the name nagged at Will. He read on to other plaques, hoping to clear his mind, but kept returning to the two-by-four-inch monument glued to the wall directly across from him.

FARTHMORE.

Will rubbed his eyes with the heels of his palms, then moved the massage to his temples. His ears buzzed. He was hearing words, snippets of sentences, sound bites, and the tube of an overhead fluorescent about to extinguish itself.

"Burn, furthermore change . . . I've taught you . . . Move . . . Then change . . ."

His eyes snapped open and focused on the black-and-white linoleum tile. The sickening backwards speech of W. D. Theroux had somehow made a quick dash from his memory to his inner eardrum. He tilted his head, once again gazing at the plaque.

IN MEMORY OF DREW ALAN FARTHMORE.

"Burn, furthermore . . ." said Will aloud.

THE FARTHMORE FOUNDATION.

Will's mind was playing tricks on him. It was brain fatigue intermingled with random associations. Bloody subconscious word games. Yes. Word games. He heard echoes approaching from the opposite wing. He recognized La Roy's booming baritone. And Benny Yao's flat pitch. Nearing. They were looking for him. It was time to dust the senator off and start over again.

"Burn furthermore."

Inching closer to the plaque, Will bent at the waist to get a closer look at some fine etching he hadn't noticed before. A quote:

> *"To live once, a happy man.*
> *To live twice, now there's a plan."*
> *Luc Alain Theroux, 1765*

The tremor rose from his feet and crashed against his skull in a blinding shock of white pain.

Luc Alain *Theroux?*

Snatching the handset from the pay phone, Will dialed

zero, his D.C. office number, and then his calling card number. He checked his watch. It was 11 P.M. in Washington. What the hell was he thinking? He was ready to hang up when Allison answered.

"Senator Sullivan's office."

"Allison!"

What followed was a brief pause. "I'm sorry, Senator," she said. "I saw it on CNN."

"Just listen to me," said Will. "I want you to find a copy of the transcript I made with La Roy. The backwards stuff."

"Reverse speech," corrected Allison, owning the task the moment he'd asked. "Hang on, sir. It's somewhere . . ."

Will heard Allison drop the telephone. In the meantime, he could hear La Roy getting closer. Yao along with him. He thought he heard Bedletter's voice, then Lois Freehold's. Any moment they'd be rounding the corner.

"Got it," Allison said, back on the phone.

"Furthermore something," said Will. "Burn, then furthermore blah blah—"

Allison was on the passage in a heartbeat. *"Burn, furthermore change your names in the way that I've taught you. Move. Then change them again."*

Will swung around and looked at that damned plaque. "Burn farthmore."

"Furthermore," corrected Allison.

"Next page," said Will, his eyes still fixed on the name on the hospital wall. *Drew Alan Farthmore.* "And read down to the part where I ask Theroux where my wife is."

"Okay, I got it," she said. "You asked, *'Goddammit, where is she?'* You heard Theroux say in reverse speech, *'And furthermore, you will be left to suffer her death.'* "

"At Farthmore," Will said.

Again she corrected, " *'Further-more.'* "

But, Will questioned himself, was that what he'd *heard?* Amid the twisted garble of the backwards videotape? *Furthermore or Farthmore?* His gut turned. He wanted to pound the handset against the pay phone until an answer came.

"Senator?" asked Allison.

"Gotta go, Allison," Will said. He hung up, turning one last time to read the plaque. *"Burn Farthmore,"* Will whispered to himself.

Goddammit where is she?

"At Farthmore . . . you will be left to suffer her death."

Lifting the white pages, Will flipped to the Fs, his index finger tracking downward in search of a *"Farthmore."* None were listed as residences. Only businesses, highlighted in bold ink:

FARTHMORE TIMBER, Spokane, WA
FARTHMORE FINANCIAL, Spokane, WA

Will's subconscious screamed at him to run.

Sure, Earnest. Tell the FBI what you suspect about "Farthmore" and you'll be back at the Quality Inn, or stuck in the back of a van, waiting to hear that the Bureau is running down the flimsy fucking lead. Meanwhile, Earnest, your wife is dead. Hear me? She's dead. D-E-A-D!

Will heard Bedletter's tumult of a voice. For some reason, they'd stopped moving. Stalled at a water fountain. Or the restrooms. Will was still alone, unseen, with one ear listening for footsteps, the other, struggling with his subconscious.

Just drop the phone book and run. Run to Gwen. Save her.

Hope, thought Will. Where was his hope?

Fool! It's the queen of hearts in a game of three-card monte.

Where was Vance Allatore? Where was his father when he wanted to be little Willy and just cry? And where, God, was Gwen?

Where was Gwen? Farthmore, dummy!

La Roy rounded the corner to the north wing's corridor. Accompanying him were Benny Yao, Steve Salinas, Bedletter, and Lois Freehold. La Roy, though, stopped at the intersection, staring as if he'd seen a ghost. Yes, the corridor was empty, but the phone book underneath the pay phone was swinging and he could have sworn he'd caught a glimpse of the stairwell door slowly swinging shut.

"Earnest?"

"Let's check the chapel," said Benny Yao.

La Roy finally broke away. "Sure," he said. "Why the hell not? Maybe he's down there with Father Vance cookin' weenies."

"Don't push yet!" shouted Izzy.

"Not so loud," moaned Gwen. "I can hear you just fine."

Opposites were suddenly attracting in a twelve-by-fourteen-foot space called common ground. Gwen was giving birth to Theroux's child. And from somewhere within herself she'd found the calm center to control the room. At first, she'd coolly asked Jack to remove Starr's body. She also asked if, within the old bunker, there were any emergency medical books. She'd sent Jack on a search for birthing tips while she and Izzy got things straight.

"Neither of us want to harm the baby," she'd said. *"Am I right? Neither of us—"*

"Want to harm the baby," confirmed Izzy. *"Yes."*

"So we can do this," said Gwen. *"You and me. We can have Dean's boy if we work together. Are we understood?"*

Jack had reappeared waving a dusty copy of an old fall-out survivors' manual. Within it, the most basic instructions for birthing a child without a doctor's presence.

The Pitocin had long since worn off, leaving Gwen with more options. She couldn't control the contractions. But she could push or not push at her own discretion. Focusing on the wave and pressing down from the crest of the pain.

"We should get the video," Jack said.

"You're not getting anything," said Izzy. "Keep your nose in the book."

Jack was the designated reader. Seated on a stool next to Gwen, he'd read the instructions and flash her the diagrams. Gwen lay with legs bent, gripping her knees. It wasn't Lamaze. It was an epidural-free, medieval exercise in childbirth. All pain with everything to gain. A baby in her arms. Her child.

"How many fingers?" asked Gwen.

"Three," said Izzy. "Wait. Four. I think I've got four."

"Four fingers and we're at ten centimeters," said Gwen. "Ten centimeters and I can push."

The baby's heart rate was steady. In a miraculous bit of fetal gymnastics, he had wormed into a somersault and freed himself from the umbilical cord's deadly noose.

Izzy looked up from between Gwen's legs. Her eyes were bright and her smile strangely genuine. "I think you can push at the next contraction."

Gwen nodded, took five quick breaths, held her breath, and waited for the contraction, following it with a mighty push.

"Yes!" squealed Izzy. "Yes, yes, yes!"

Another sharp contraction and Gwen bore down again, molar to molar, teeth locked and jaw set. The pain was something she'd never imagined. Her spine felt as if it would snap at her coccyx if she pushed down any harder.

"There's the head again," said Izzy. "I can see the head."

"Read!" demanded Gwen.

"Oh yeah," said Jack. "Both your index fingers, Izzy. One high, one low. 'Gently slide them inside as the mother pushes . . .' "

"You there?" asked Gwen.

"Got it," said Izzy. "Now push again!"

Wave. Crest. Push. The cycle continued. Millimeter by millimeter. Gwen and Izzy in a bizarre harmony. Captive and captor. Birth mother and substitute midwife. The baby was inching his way into a very real world. If only Gwen had the time to plot her next move. What to do after the child was born? She would obviously protect the child with her life. The instinct was overwhelming. But for God's sake, how, when her life was worthless the moment the umbilical was cut? Gwen gripped her knees and bore down again, the capillaries in her face ready to burst.

The ambulance driver didn't care much for the inside of hospitals. His brother had died in a hospital when he was only eleven. Ever since, stepping through the doors of an emergency room gave him goat chills. Eddie was more than happy to sit out the excitement at the end of a run in the comfort of his driver's seat. Radio tuned to nighttime talk.

"Eddie," said Will after he'd hopped through the passenger door and offered a hand. "My name's Will. Will Sullivan."

After his initial start, Eddie recognized the senator and tentatively stuck out a hand as one would when sneak-attacked by a famous politician. "How'd you know my name?"

Will tapped a finger to his chest. "Name tag says Eddie DuPre. EMT."

Eddie felt stupid. Of course he was wearing a name tag. He'd forgotten anybody ever read the stupid plastic rectangle pinned to his blue jumpsuit.

"I need to find a place," said Will. "You can do that for me, can't you, Eddie?"

"Hey," said Eddie. "Like, I'm supposed to stay with the truck."

"But you can find places," said Will. "That's *why* you're the driver."

"It's the dispatcher," said Eddie. "She's the one who knows. She tells me where to go. Man, I just drive."

"Okay," said Will, eerily resolved to have his way. "Let's call the dispatcher. I'm looking for a residence. A place called Farthmore."

"Aw, heck," said Eddie. "I know where that place is. Can't be more than five miles from here. It's like an old ghost house—"

"Ghost house. Good. So let's go look at it, then. You and me."

Eddie was looking around, over his shoulder, out the window, into the back of the ambulance. "I can't . . . I mean, I gotta wait for my crew, ya know?"

"Do you know who I am?" asked Will.

"Sure, man. You're that senator."

"Then you know why I'm here?"

"Sure, man. To find your missus."

"And you don't want to help?"

"Oh, no, sir," said Eddie. "It's like, well, you know I want to help. But it's like, my job—"

"I need to get someplace fast," pressed Will, his charm

turned up to what little wattage he could muster, his words playing like quick notes on a fiddle. "And it seems, Eddie, you can get me there fast. Now, I need to know if you're the guy who can do that. Are you that guy, Eddie? Are you that guy?"

"I . . . I could lose my job."

"You could lose your job. Yes. But I could lose my wife. Are you married, Eddie?"

"I'm engaged." Eddie grinned. "We're getting married in April—"

"Then you understand. That's good." Will reached across the switch-covered console and twisted the ignition key. The big V-8 roared. "Five miles, Eddie. I bet you could be there and back in a . . ." Will snapped his fingers and gave a nod.

Something in Eddie made him drop the ambulance into gear. As if by rote, he reminded Will to put on his seat belt. The Christmas tree lights lit up in full display and the siren screamed at the darkness.

Wesley Dean Theroux could feel it. He could feel a barometric change in his inner atmosphere. That place from which he could smell another man's soul. The shrinks had written about it, calling the phenomenon "possibly paranormal, but most likely an acute sense or instinct about subjects in which he has a profound interest."

Assholes!

The baby was coming. *His* baby. And it wasn't supposed to happen like this. Clem was supposed to have run a live video feed to the bootlegged cell connection in Theroux's computer. Only the computer was gone. Sure, the Department of Corrections had replaced the unit with a spanking-new ThinkPad. The next model up from his original. It had more memory, a quicker modem, and a brighter screen. It just didn't have what the other computer had. A cell-chip that was his link to the outside. His link to his family.

Like a caged mother lion, Theroux paced his tiny cell. He pressed his hands to the walls, picked up random books and gripped them as if hoping to get some kind of psychic signal. Nothing. All he had to go on was that shift of his inner barometer. That twist in his gut that told him the game was on and he'd been left at home to watch the flickering highlights on the eleven o'clock news.

Thirteen days.

Thirteen days and he'd be a dead man. The executioners would jack him up with a deadly dose of . . . whatever. It didn't matter. As long as the mixture did the trick. His work was done. A boy was to be born. A boy who would one day turn into a man who'd carry on his father's plan. To bring it all down. To bring the world to an ugly, catastrophic end.

"I want a newspaper," he'd demanded. The closer he was to death, the more the prison officials catered to him.

Which one? the warden had returned in a written note.

The Spokane Spokesman Review.

If there'd been a birth, there would be a burn. A big, big fire. His instructions would be followed and the estate would be torched. The newspaper would surely cover it.

And then he'd know if he had a son.

"Okay," said Eddie. "This is as far as I go. Any further and I'm trespassing."

"What do you know about this place?" asked Will, his eyes resting on the property before him.

"Just the same old rumors an' stuff. Been around since I can remember."

"What kind of rumors?"

"Old man Farthmore killed his wife. Some say it was an accident that turned into a murder. They, like, had this little boy who may have seen it happen and ran off. Some thought the old man killed him, too. Drowned him in the river before he shot himself. Poor little boy? My old man said they dragged the river for a month. But the boy never turned up."

The tuning fork that was Will's instinct sang with a high note. Gwen was there. Somewhere nearby. Will said his thanks and stepped out of the ambulance. He didn't want to keep the young driver any longer. The radio had been squawking. The dispatcher was looking for the missing ambulance and spreading the FBI report that Senator Sullivan had gone missing.

"They're looking for you, sir," said Eddie.

"You can tell them I'm here," said Will.

"Hey. Why don't you take this with you?" Eddie withdrew a long, carbon-steel flashlight from underneath his seat. "Looks like it's dark where you're goin'."

Will thanked Eddie with a nod, then closed the passenger door. Eddie watched for a moment while Will climbed the Farthmore Estate's huge wrought-iron gate, dropping to the other side and switching on the flashlight. The beam briefly swept over the ambulance, then turned toward the winding drive that led to the main house. It appeared to Eddie as if the senator was running, for the flashlight beam narrowed and disappeared about as quickly as Will Sullivan had said hello.

"Dispatch? This is forty-four," said Eddie into the radio.

"Forty-four?" said the dispatcher. "Where the hell are you?"

The Farthmore Estate.

A twenty-three-room brick chateau rested upon a gentle knoll at the end of the red clay motor court. The black-windowed home backed up to the river while the front door faced a curtain of timber that abutted the mountain beyond. The gardens and surrounding lawns were three months overgrown. And the exterior lights seemed as if they'd been extinguished in an all-encompassing electrical dropout. The house appeared dead. Inside and out. Lifeless.

Will's heart sank with the feeling that he'd up and sprinted down a dead-end road on a ridiculous hunch. He was an ocean away from his comfort zone. And now his ego-driven paranoia had gone and convinced his better self that the vacant estate of Drew Farthmore was the end of the rainbow.

She will die and you will suffer her death.

Then Will's nose caught a drift of gasoline.

A cool breeze rolled off the river, carrying with it the distinct smell of fuel. At first, Will swiveled with the flashlight. Looking for a car. Tread marks leading to a vehicle with a leak. But the ground under his feet was dry and crusty. No tracks. Just leaves on clay. The smell of gas vanished, then wafted back in with the return of another mild gust. Something in Will made him switch off the flashlight—a prickly fear that made him stand stone-still and turn his nose toward the smell. He was facing the house. Could this be where it ended? Was Gwen nearby? He asked the twisted knot in his stomach for an answer but got nothing in return. Just those black windows staring back at him. And the reflection of a tiny beam from a pen-sized flashlight . . . At first he thought it was his reflection through a large bay window, but then remembered his flashlight was switched off. The light appeared to dance, as if clenched in the teeth of a running man.

Instinct warned Will to turn and sprint toward the house, away from the man, who had moved from right to left. Will would go to the right. He sprinted toward the corner of the four-car garage. His heart pulsed in his throat as he gasped for air.

Instinct, hell. Call 911!

Will peered back down the drive. If the ambulance was still there, he'd never be able to see it. The gate was a good quarter-mile away and the ambulance was probably long gone. Eddie was surely having a good laugh with the dispatcher over the nutcase senator's dumb-assed idea to leave the FBI in the dust. And for what? A flashlight and a sudden case of the heebie-jeebies? All on a knee-jerk hunch?

You're an idiot, Will!

The telephone cable joined the house near the garage. While Will stared up at the heavens in search of his next groovy idea, he somehow picked out the wires against the black sky. And where there were phone lines, there would certainly be an actual telephone. Okay, he coached himself. One step at a time. Eye on the prize. Get a grip, get inside, pick up the nearest phone, and dial 911. Then find the basement. If Gwen was there, she was underground. A basement. It was a big house. If the basement was anywhere near the size of the chateau's footprint . . .

Will tested all four garage doors. Each was padlocked. A

flashlight aimed through the dusty portals revealed two cars under blue tarpaulins. Once he'd made it around the south corner, he could hear the river. The stink of gasoline was gone in the breeze and a patch of sky had opened up through the clouds. Moonlight speared its way through, putting a glimmer on the slow-moving river. It was strangely enchanting. Peaceful, even. Will caught his breath, crouched down, and crept up painted white steps to a magnificent wooden deck. Maybe two thousand square feet. Inset was a covered pool surrounded by lonely chaise longues.

A row of eight French doors faced the river. The last was an invitation. It yawned to the night. The smell of gas came again, thick and nauseating. He tried to hold his nose, but found it nearly impossible because he was shaking so. His body rippled at the thought of walking into the dark house, uninvited, and running into his fellow intruder. A prayer came to him. Part of a psalm.

Yea though I shall walk through the valley . . .

Flashlight held high and ready to strike, Will slid through the door and knelt behind a sheet-draped couch. He switched on his flashlight, running the beam along the baseboard until he found a thick, yellowed telephone wire. He let the beam follow it to a round mahogany pedestal. On top was a rotary phone. Basic black, yet dusted to a grayish brown.

Will stood, switched off the light, and was about to ease around the sofa when the smell of gas hit him so hard his eyes turned to water. They burned like hell. He could taste the stuff at the back of his throat. Suddenly his feet were off the floor. Suspended. And arms were about him in a bear hug that sent his head snapping backward. His skull hit flesh. He heard cartilage break and a voice.

"Motherfucker!"

He didn't know if he'd swung the flashlight before his feet hit the floor—or after. He only knew that, without so much as a preordained thought, he'd gripped it like a Louisville Slugger, turned, and struck pay dirt. The carbon steel made solid contact over Clem's left ear, fracturing his skull and shattering the flashlight's lens. Once he'd found his target, Will kept swinging. One pelting blow after another. Clem howled, brought his arms up over his head, only to have his wrist shattered, fingers crushed, and his forearm snapped clean through. All the rage in Will uncoiled in a flurry of blood-spattering blows. Clem went down, his legs giving out and his chest caving under Will's bent knee.

"Where is she, you son of a bitch?" cried Will, his voice a shrill squeak of manhood.

The penlight, once held in Clem's mouth and now forever wedged between his cracked molars and his swelling cheek, switched on with the aid of Clem's last working muscle—his tongue. In the narrow beam he saw Will. The senator's face was speckled with Clem's blood, the carbon-steel flashlight raised and ready for the final blow.

"Mubberfugger," croaked Clem. Then he started hacking uncontrollably.

"Where is she?"

"Fuggin' kill me," said Clem. "Pleebe. Fuggin' kill me. I wam him oub up my dweams!"

"I want my wife, you piece of shit!"

"You wibe?" asked Clem. "She'b deb alweady. An so ab I. An so arb you, mistuh."

Clem's fingers flinched. In them, Will heard the distinct double-click every smoker knows as the perfect pitch of a Zippo lighter.

The gas!

Will sprang back in barely enough time to miss the spark. The etched flint gave way to the lighter's wick, which barely caught fire before the flame was rushing up Clem's petrol-soaked pant leg. He was ablaze in an instant without so much as a whimper. Death was Clem's release. And he welcomed it.

The sofa was next. The flames leaped to the curtains and a nearby love seat, encircling Will. The walls caught fire. The whole room was soaked in gas. The telephone pedestal was roaring across the rug.

Burn Farthmore!

"GWEN!" Will's voice tried to rise above the fire's roar.

Smoke stacked against the ceiling, lowering every deadly second. Soon the room would be choked.

"GWEN!"

Will dropped under the smoke, on his knees and holding a sleeve over his mouth. The heat blistered his skin. And just when his body was telling him to cover and rush for the open door, his eye caught sight of a Mission-style tabouret cluttered in silver picture frames. In a surreal moment split between certain death and escape, he thought he saw her. Gwen. Was it her pictured in a faded family snapshot? She appeared to be holding a happy toddler in her lap—a boy.

The Farthmore living room reached its flash point a mere five seconds after Will crashed through the French doors to the outer deck. The room behind him turned white. Every pane shattered from the sudden shock. The entire mansion was afire. The upstairs windows began to snap and rain eighty-year-old glass. Will stumbled from the deck to the overgrown grass to avoid the burning debris. A voice inside him demanded to survive. Even though he was certain there were no more reasons left in the world to live. Gwen was surely lost in the fire. It was over. And he'd probably killed her.

Clouds had closed the hole in the sky. Darkness reigned, save for the firelight. Will waited for sirens that never came. When he turned to curse the house for not burning bright enough, a glimmer caught his attention. The house was ablaze from the four-car garage to the attached servants' quarters. But stretching from the house was a trail of fire that turned at the river and twisted into the woods. A series of gasoline-fired ringlets. Had the gas been stored in the woods? Will recalled that he'd seen no parked cars other than the dusty models entombed in the garage.

It all felt like an alcoholic's dream. A magnet was pulling him down the trail, picking up his feet until he was jogging and then running. The path of fire first turned toward the river, then back uphill, over a rise and through a meadow. For the fuel to burn, it had to be fresh. Will cared little for logic. He was following a lit fuse without a clue where it would lead him.

9

June 15. 9:26 P.M.

Jack marked the time and date of the birth by his watch. The infant was born screaming and covered in blood and a purplish film of amniotic goo. As per the instructions in the survivors' manual, the cord was clamped at two ends and scissored in the middle, then swaddled by Izzy in a sterile cloth.

"He's beautiful," Izzy said in tearful admiration. "And he looks like his father."

"May I?" asked Gwen, at once relieved the episode was over while anguished by what was to come. The pain of death seemed like little more than a pimple compared to the loss of her child. He was as much Gwen's as Theroux's. She needed to hold him. "Please. Let me hold him. Just once."

Izzy's head snapped toward her. "Why should I?"

"Not for me," said Gwen. "For him."

The baby was still crying. His tiny voice rebounding off the walls in an ear-splitting screech. Izzy paid no mind to it. She was in love with his red face. And the baby was hers.

"He needs to feed," said Gwen between heavy breaths.

"On my milk . . . Just for a moment . . . It will make him strong."

"You'd say anything to hold him!"

Gwen sobbed and nodded. The truth had leaked through. She would say anything. She would do anything. Pray to anything if just for a minute she could cradle the child and touch her nose to his.

"What's the harm?" volunteered Jack.

"She's nothing but an empty womb," snorted Izzy. "She's dead. Put her down." Izzy tossed Jack a prepackaged heavy-gauge needle and hypodermic. Jack obediently tore open the packaging, affixing the needle to the barrel.

Izzy took her index finger and dug it under Gwen's chin. So deep into where her carotid artery was that she left a red mark for Jack's easy reference. "Right there," said Izzy. "Ten cc's of this shitty air oughta do her just fine."

"Please!" begged Gwen. "Before I die!"

"C'mon, Iz," said Jack. "It's her baby, too."

"It's Dean's baby!" said Izzy. "And mine!"

Then with a screech so loud Izzy thought her eardrums would burst, the baby wailed.

"Maybe it's hungry!" said Jack.

"Starr's breast milk is in the freezer," said Izzy, thrilled, panic-stricken, and confused at the same moment. "Upstairs." Like handing off a football, she passed the newborn to Jack. "I'll be right back."

Izzy was gone at a dead run. Leaving Jack with the wailing baby. He pocketed the needle as casually as he would a ballpoint pen. Then began looking lost—like a ten-year-old holding a screaming little cousin. What to do with a screaming child? All Jack saw was a red-faced, six-pound mouth, tiny-tongued, opened wide, making more noise than a fire truck.

"What do I do?" he demanded of Gwen.

"Shoulder him," she said. "Hold him close. Talk softly."

"I've never . . ."

"I know," said Gwen, her understanding turned up to a maximum. "I can show you," she said.

Jack was instantly tempted. He was holding the screaming infant away from him. Like it was a nuclear bomb with a hair trigger.

"Undo my hands only," said Gwen. "I'll show you how. Then I'll give him back."

Jack looked toward the door. "But Izzy—"

"I'm his mother!" said Gwen. "This is for him, god-dammit. And he needs me! Understand?"

It was all the shove Jack needed. He released the Velcro straps which had turned Gwen's wrists raw. She sat up quickly, light-headed, but holding her arms out for her child. Jack was happy to give up the crying infant. The baby settled into the warmth of his mother, easing his lungs and lowering the amplitude of his screeching. He was six pounds of pure instinct. Home. Where an infant belongs. Cradled by the pure and protective love of his mommy.

When the baby's cries turned to a very natural whine, Gwen whispered softly. "It's okay, little man. Mommy's here. And mommy's going to show Uncle Jack how to hold you, see."

With a go-ahead nod from Gwen, Jack drew closer.

"Don't be afraid," said Gwen. "He's just a little bitty baby who wants to be loved. Come close and see."

Jack eased nearer, a wide unabashed smile of wonder spreading across his face.

"Now, gently stroke his head," said Gwen. "Very, very gently."

With unwavering focus, Jack reached out to the infant. His fingers so close to stroking the black, newborn hair. Dean's perfect progeny appeared to be staring up at Jack with cloudy blue eyes. It was mesmerizing. So much so that Jack didn't flinch when Gwen's free hand slid the hypoder-mic out of his breast pocket and plunged it into *his* carotid artery. The target was clear. Gwen had even seen blood pulsing through the artery as he'd leaned forward to touch the baby. Holding tight to her baby the whole time, Gwen had executed the killing as per Izzy's instructions to Jack.

Jack never touched the infant's hair. He took two steps back before his heart sucked the embolism into its left ven-tricle. The muscle gasped, losing its prime, then failed in an explosion of pain. Jack convulsed, reached out for something to grab, then flung himself against the wall. He was dead in mere seconds. Time enough for Gwen to undo the restraints around her ankles.

"C'mon, little man. Your mommy's gonna take you home."

The sprint couldn't have taken more than three minutes. But despite the youthful appearance that attracted so many cameras, Will was sorely out of condition. Tack on the three months of sleepless hell, it was a wonder he could walk, let alone chase fire. His lungs ached for relief.

The fire-scorched path broke the trees near a shed which was already in flames. The tree limbs hanging above it crackled as sap turned the smoke black. What was left of Clem's gas had already gone up. Soon the entire woods would be engulfed, the caretaker's cottage with it.

Will took a bead on the front door of the cottage. Locked or not, he imagined a television entrance. Like Mannix or Baretta. Shoulder down, busting through. All surprise. But Will didn't take the three wooden steps leading up to the door into account. Or that his legs were more akin to rubber than the steel of his imagined TV heroes. When his foot hit the first step, he wobbled. His second foot missed entirely and his left knee hit the top of the third. He felt a crunch, then howled as his shoulder dug into the unvarnished redwood. Wood splinters jacked into his arm, from his shoulder socket to elbow.

When his eyes opened, he fully expected to see Izzy standing over him, shovel in hand, ready to chop off his head with a single stroke. Instead, he only saw the firelight licking the sky. Trees were going up one after another. Sparks shot into the night. Someone would have to see it. Someone would have to come help.

The door was unlocked and the lights were on. Will reeled on his one leg, looking for a weapon. Something to swing with. Like the flashlight he'd used to fend off Clem. He found a sooty fire poker in the wood basket. But instead of his best Ted Williams pose, he found the poker made a handy cane. No sooner did he swerve into the tight hallway than he caught a glimpse of a near-naked dead man spread out on a twin bed. Dr. Bertrand's face was pasty-white with death. His mouth, a hideous roach hole.

All doubt vanished at the sight of that single, agonizing visage. Wherever he was, Gwen was. Dead or alive, the cast was assembled at Farthmore. And per Theroux's instructions, the estate was burning.

There was a pot of boiling water in the kitchen and an open freezer full of frozen breast milk. Pumped, dated, and stacked like ammo in Playtex cartridges. The basement door was ajar and the light below was flickering. Will entered carefully, one hand on the rail, the other spearing the intermittent darkness with the poker. Had he lingered another five seconds, he might have caught a glimpse of the monitor. Gwen was pictured in black and white, huddled in a corner, a newborn bundle held tightly to her chest.

Will had also missed the wicked coffee tins in every corner of the cottage. Carefully packed by Clem, each contained a lethal mixture of fertilizer and fuel oil. Ready for his Zippo and a quick exit that would never come.

Izzy stood at the door to the bunker's O.R., warmed bottle of breast milk in one fist and sheer anger in the other. Jack was dead at her feet. Gwen was missing, but hardly far. Probably in her room, tucked in tight with the baby. That dumb-fucking Jack. Now he'd put the baby in danger. Who knew what Gwen would do in exchange for her own life? Hold the infant hostage? And where the hell was Clem, anyway? Izzy squeezed the bottle of milk until it exploded in her hand.

Motherfucker!

Peeling the wrapper off a new scalpel, Izzy flicked away the protective cover with her fingernail. Then she let the blade bite into her right thumb until it bled. If the pain was there, then so were her nerves. She began to count her steps out of the O.R. and into the heart of the bunker. One, two, three, four, five, six. She estimated it was four steps to the storage locker across the way. Seven steps to the latrine and the chemical toilets. And eight more to Gwen's gray-green room.

Had she counted the infant's fingers and toes? Were all the digits there?

Fantasy carried Izzy to the storage locker. While she was checking for Gwen, she was planning her future. She and Clem would marry. And though she'd never let him touch her, they'd play the perfect partners, raising a perfect boy child. San Diego, she thought. Or Mission Viejo. The California promise. Where life for little Dean would always be sunny and in the seventies.

Passing the storage locker, Izzy pushed open the door to the chemical toilets. They were empty. Meaning Gwen was right where she should be. In her room, with the infant. Izzy wasn't the least bit worried. She knew Gwen well enough. She wouldn't hurt her own child. She might make a threat. She was cunning enough. She just wasn't a killer.

Izzy was the killer.

In the five steps to the last door, Izzy pictured a California blue sky, the sun in her face, and little Dean on a warm beach. Two yeas old, maybe. She'd teach him to dig for sand crabs. At night, she'd tell him stories of his father. Eventually, the boy would know his destiny. Dean had prophesied as such. Yet she wondered if he'd been looking so far ahead that he hadn't seen the immediate future.

Dr. Bertrand. Dead.

Starr. Dead.

Jack. Dead.

God must have been looking out for Izzy, too. She knew her fate was to mother Dean's child. She'd felt it in her gut from the beginning. Now her task was to finish it. Cut Gwen to pieces, gather up Clem's lazy ass, and burn Farthmore. Izzy palmed the scalpel and reached for the vault door to Gwen's bunker. Her fingers slipped around the lever. Whatever Gwen had to offer, Izzy would negotiate until the child was hers and Gwen was dead.

"GWEN!" roared Will. He was hoarse and on the brink of nervous exhaustion. He shouldered his way through the portal, freezing mid-limp at the threshold when he found himself twenty paces opposite the bald beast. He'd never felt or seen anything so primal in his life. She was a stalking animal and he'd just made the mistake of crossing her path.

The lights flickered. The generator wires were on fire. The palmed scalpel slid into Izzy's fingers, twirled in her fingers, and ended in a fist. She knew just how she was going to kill him. Her chin lowered, her gaze was unwavering.

And then she charged, screeching out a banshee wail that could frighten the most stalwart of men.

Then the power failed. The bunker plunged into blackness.

10

When Lois Freehold's FBI Lear jet had hit the tarmac at Spokane, she'd fully expected news. Not necessarily good or bad. Just news. As she was helicoptered to Park Memorial Hospital, she'd suddenly foreseen a resolution to the media mess. And per her instructions from Justice, she was tailoring a prepared statement that would reflect the FBI's unity with Will Sullivan.

The last thing Lois Freehold had expected to hear was that Senator Sullivan had up and vanished from the hospital. That some willing EMT had given him a lift to some abandoned estate which, by current reports, was consumed in flames.

"Was he drinking?" she asked, standing at the precipice of a snit. "He had to be drinking. What else could've come over the SOB?"

The team was assembled at the hospital's closed-off south entrance, waiting for the caravan of rented cars to pull around. Bedletter, Yao, Salinas, La Roy, six senior FBI agents, and America's number-two cop, Lois Freehold.

"I can't say if he was drinking, ma'am," said Bedletter.

"If Will Sullivan was drinking," said La Roy, "then I'm Barry Goldwater's love child!"

"Is that supposed to be an answer?" asked Lois Freehold.

"He wasn't drinking," said Benny Yao. Steve Salinas added his nod. "What we know is that he was on the phone to staff in D.C., getting a readback from some transcripts."

"Ten'll getcha twenty that Will found himself a clue and followed it," said La Roy.

"Without the FBI?" asked Bedletter, trying to sell the question as incredulity, disguising the rank embarrassment he felt for losing the U.S. senator.

La Roy returned a smug grin. "Don't suppose he likes being told to wait in the car," he said. "You know, with his wife and all being in such mortal danger."

The arguing continued as they piled into their respective cars for the five-mile drive. Meanwhile, the U.S. Forest Service was air-dropping water and chemical retardants on the fire in Deer Park. Ground crews held the flames at the highway while sheriff's officers cordoned off the mounting press at the half-mile marker. The department claimed it was for safety. But they'd also received orders from the FBI to keep rabid photographers from sneaking through to document the potentially grisly aftermath.

By 1 A.M., two swooping C-130s and a hard-charging team of firemen had pushed the blaze into the river. Eighty acres had been lost. Plus two homes. Naturally, the emergency and forensic crews worked over the mansion first. Its stone walls stood as a shell of what had once been a grand piece of French-inspired architecture. Under diesel-generated klieg lights, they pored over the torched manse. At 3 A.M. a single body was discovered, burned beyond recognition. Word quickly passed that the body was expected to be identified as that of Senator William Daniel Sullivan. The story went on the wires as quick as the average cell phone connection. Nationwide, newspapers churned the story into newsprint.

At dawn, attention was finally paid to the caretaker's cottage. Signs of life were neither expected nor found. Fire crews cleared the charred rubble, looking for Mr. and Mrs.

Alec Guzzman. What they found in the rubble was one more body, also burned beyond recognition . . .

. . . and a kitchen opening that led to a basement. The wooden steps had been turned to charcoal. A truck ladder was used for three firemen to descend in full oxygenating regalia. The cellar was smoke-filled and heat-dried. But the search for life continued.

The FBI clan stood within telephoto range of the media. There too were Benny Yao and La Roy—all so silently waiting for any news of Gwen. Even if it was the worst. It would be information enough to bring some kind of closure. They crowded around the Spokane fire chief and listened to the squawking over his radio.

"Bigger than it looks down here," said the investigating fireman. His oxygen mask made his voice sound as if he was broadcasting from inside a toilet bowl. *"There's an open door. Lemme see if I can get a light through it. . . . Well, would ya look at that. Looks like we got some kinda secret passage down here. If I got my bearings right, the bugger slants toward the mountains. 'Bout six feet of clearance."*

"Underground," mumbled La Roy, remembering the words of Theroux.

"All concrete," continued the fireman. *"Eighty feet. Okay, now we got another door. This one's steel, half-open. I'm stepping through . . . Yup. What I thought it was. Looks like ol' man Farthmore build himself a nuclear survival bunker. God knows when—wait. I got me a DB at nine o'clock."*

"Dead body," said Steve Salinas, in case anyone within the group didn't know. It was all so morbid, so cold and sad.

"We got confirmation that the fire came all the way down here. I got a dead white female with a hundred percent flash burn. Wait. Phil's got somethin' in one of the rooms down here. I see four doors. Goin' through one marked S-U-P-P-L-I-E-S . . . Aw, hell. 'Nother woman. White female. Bleached blonde—"

"Starr?" questioned La Roy. "Then the other one's Izzy!"

"Not so fast," said Salinas. "We got no IDs. We don't even know about—"

"The body in the big house," said La Roy, not one to give up on hope. "That could just as easily be Clem and *not* Will."

"Shhh," said Lois, her ear turned closer to the fire chief's radio.

"Last door," said the investigating fireman. *"Got a chalk mark on the door that spells . . . lemme read this . . . G-W-E-N."*

A unifying chill ripped through the FBI and Sullivan camp. They were there. Ground bloody zero. Only too late.

"Pushing open the door. Tryin' to get a light inside—"

The radio turned to static before screeching with frightening overmodulation.

"HOLY MARY, MOTHER OF GOD!"

11

It was a CNN live event with every TV station in North America foregoing its usual programming in exchange for the satellite feed from Spokane, Washington. Not since the rescue of Baby Jessica had the spotlight of a nation been so acutely tuned to a live-as-it-happens rescue. An FBI-culled pool of TV camera and print photographers was on the scene, standing in the bed of a scorched '66 half-ton pickup, lenses aimed at the caretaker's cottage, waiting for the moment of the decade.

It was 7 A.M. June 16.

Gwen was the first to appear to a small tumult of applause and clicking camera shutters. She was strapped to a stretcher, wrapped in yellow blankets, and vertically lifted into a pack of beaming firefighters. The oxygen mask strapped across her face couldn't hide the smile. Her eyes squinted into a sun which she hadn't seen in months. The relief was apparent. Her ordeal was over.

With a hand from a firefighter, Will was next. Gingerly, he made it to the top of the ladder. More applause followed, as every shutter snapped on every camera. His every movement was captured. Will turned his back to the observers and knelt to receive a bundle from below. The infant was passed into his arms. A glassy-eyed baby who cried at the first blitz of sunlight. Tears flowed from fireman to sheriff's deputy. There was even more applause, louder and growing, as Will Sullivan, cradling the infant in his arms, limped out of the rubble under his own power.

Camera lenses zoomed. Will's face was lacerated with two diagonal cuts. One from his right eye down along his cheek. The other split his lower lip and gouged his chin. His arms were cut. As were his hands, having already been bandaged by a paramedic.

As he moved toward the waiting ambulance, Will heard calls from the press, begging for a statement. Any kind of quote. Holding the baby close, he stopped a mere five feet from the ambulance, turned three-quarters toward all the lenses, and said in a voice so choked some even wondered if he'd said it at all:

"It's over."

Will rode the ambulance to Park Memorial, holding the infant in one arm and gripping Gwen's hand with the other. They didn't need to talk. Everything had already been said during those black hours before dawn. Apologies. Prayers. And tears of joy and redemption.

"The FBI is proud of its effort in the rescue of Gwen Sullivan and her child," said Lois Freehold to a press crowd so clamorous, they had to empty the hospital's west-facing parking lot simply to accommodate all the warm bodies. *"More importantly, and I'm sure I speak for all of Justice, we humbly admire the courage and determination of one of our nation's elected. A hero. Senator William Daniel Sullivan."*

"Couldn't have said it better if I'd written it myself," said La Roy, a grin on his face, hot coffee in one hand and TV remote control in the other. "Actually, I *did* write it!"

The guffaws from the attending agents were loud and loose. The team, including Benny Yao and Steve Salinas, was ensconced in a hospital waiting room while inside a private room across the hall, Will Sullivan was downloading the events of the previous evening to Ralph Bedletter and his kidnapping investigators.

It was a small room. One bed. Chairs had been brought in, but nobody was sitting. Will, uncomfortable on the hospital bed, with a young resident removing the splinters in his shoulder one by one, let his words come in gut feelings as images careened through his head. He was trying to string everything together. He had no clue as to whether or not he was making any sense.

"I think that's when the lights went out. I remember her screaming . . ."

Izzy appeared to have covered those twenty paces in the blink of an eye. She was upon him, scalpel cocked and ready to puncture his right ear. The bunker went black. He could feel the breeze as she missed him with the first swing, but then she cut him with the second. A backhanded downward slice that stung like lemon juice on an asphalt tattoo. Will ducked, trying to bring the fire poker down on top of his assailant, but all he caught was air. It was dark. He remembered it as dark. But in his mind, he could still see her face. Screeching. Upon him. The blade was slicing him. He rolled to his left, found a wall and his feet. He could hear her slashing at the air with the blade, lunging. His lip was cut. He screamed, batted the scalpel from her hand, only to find her teeth attached to one of his fingers. He balled his other fist and cocked her in the side of the head. Once, twice, three times. She wouldn't let go. She'd moved up to his arm. Another bite, working toward his shoulder, and then his jugular. He twisted left, put her head in some kind of lock, then dropped himself to the floor. Her head cracked on the floor. Oh, he remembered that. The dull thud, followed by her heavy grunt.

"I think I called her a bitch," said Will, breaking up the room without so much as trying. He was on recall. Piecing it together. "Then came this sound. I hadn't heard anything like it before. I don't think she had, either."

It was subsonic. The bunker vibrated. Then it was as if all the air was being sucked out.

"I heard Gwen. She called out to me," said Will.

As he crawled toward her voice, he'd felt a shock of heat. The room began to glow. Gwen was kneeling in the doorway of her room, hand outstretched to Will. Her mouth was moving. Her lips begging him to move.

"There was this scream. I don't know if it was Izzy . . . or the fire itself."

The fire arrived as a disemboweling roar, feeding on nothing but oxygen and forty-year-old paint. As Gwen dragged him inside and shut the door, Will thought he saw the flames swallow Izzy.

"Or maybe that's what I wanted to see. I don't remember much after that." Will stared into the void that was his memory. He shook his head. "There wasn't any light. We wondered if there was any air. So we decided not to talk. We just laid there. On the bed. Gwen, the baby, and me. No words. Just . . . peace. Yeah. We were all at peace. We could've died and that would have been okay."

After a silent moment that would later be transcribed as a full minute of dead tape, Ralph Bedletter gently prodded Will. "Next thing you remember was the firemen."

Will nodded slowly. He was looking nowhere. At nobody at all. Just into space.

"I'd like to go back there," said Will.

"To where?" said Bedletter.

"To that moment," said Will.

Without a knock, Lois Freehold entered. All the agents seemed to snap to at her appearance. The FBI director had the oddest smile on her face. Becoming, thought Will. Or no? Maybe he'd just never seen her smile.

"I just saw the baby," said Lois. "He's absolutely gorgeous."

"Thanks," said Will, the politician returning. Lois had no idea of the baby's paternity. Neither did anybody else in Justice. If the right agreement could be struck, they were willing to put a lid on the whole putrid matter. Those with knowledge were either dead or . . .

Vance Allatore, thought Will.

Instantly, Will had free-associated to pictures of the

priest. Where had he gone? And why? What a monumental part he'd played in the endgame, and he wasn't even there for a handshake or a hug.

"Can we have a moment alone?" said Lois. It was as unrhetorical as a question could get. A demand for her troops to hit the door without further instructions. They filed out. After which, it was just the FBI director and the senator.

"If you're here to make a deal—"

"I'm here to make an apology," said Lois. "The Bureau mishandled this. Between you and me, I admit it. But you could see, without a ransom demand this kidnapping appeared—"

"To be a cover for my own unethical foibles?"

"Why'd they take her, Senator?"

"You looking for the truth or something to feed the press?" asked Will.

"You could bury me with our mishandling of this."

"I have no intention of doing so—"

"Then I owe you one." The FBI director pulled up one of the empty chairs. "Let's begin with a bit of odd news. The president is sending *Air Force Two* to assist you and your family in a safe return to the east." And there it was again. That crooked smile from a woman unaccustomed to showing her teeth.

Will was wrecked, ragged, and looking about as politicianlike as a derelict dirt farmer. Yet his instincts were intact. He *was* a politician. And at that moment, as much as he'd have liked to drop a nuclear bomb on Washington, D.C., he couldn't help but look dead in the face of opportunity and pull the trigger.

"I want to know about Gavelgate," he asked quietly. "I want to know what Del knew. I want to know about the files he ordered on members of Congress."

June 28.

The warden had met the killer's request with unspoken relish. During Theroux's final days, the *Spokane Spokesman Review* was delivered daily, neatly folded alongside Wesley Dean Theroux's breakfast. The first edition Theroux got a peek at bore the same front-page photo that days later graced the covers of *Time, Newsweek, U.S. News & World Report,* and *People.* It was a crisp, clean, full-color close-up of Senator Will Sullivan, battered and slashed across the face, exhumed from the underground crypt that had killed so many of Theroux's family, cradling his infant in his arms. The senator as hero father. The most famous American on the planet.

Theroux had burned the newspaper in protest. After a terse reprimand, Theroux proceeded to burn his books. His cell was ransacked for matches and then the death-row con was used as an example. He was forced to endure a humiliating strip and cavity search in front of the entire third-tier population. Suffering the catcalls and howls usually reserved for sleazy strip bars, Theroux gave every prisoner with a view a firsthand look at his porcelain-white skin and the tattoo that stretched along his torso.

In the meantime, accounts of the demise of Theroux's forgotten few flourished in all forms of media, each story drawing on the same misleading information spoon-fed hourly from the FBI and the emboldened Sullivan camp. The kidnapping had been, from day one, a silent attempt by the cult leader to secure a stay of execution and a new trial. Not a soul in the media even considered musing about the infant's paternity. And though most death-row cons are granted press interviews during their last week of life, an appeals judge ruled that a gag order be placed on the killer for all his remaining days. The judge had cited the murder of Vanessa Curran as just cause.

It would be irresponsible, wrote the judge, *for the state to sanction any interviews that might put some thrill-seeking journalist in danger.*

At night, Theroux seethed, bucked in his cot, and tried desperately to unbutton his magic. All he got in return were ugly pictures. Clem was dead. Starr was dead. Jack and Timothy were dead. And Izzy. Beautiful, obedient Izzy. His broken little flower. He'd glued her petals back on in the form of wings just to show her she could fly.

Is there another out there? Is someone listening? Sheila?

Theroux's head was filled with static and his gut with the bleeding ulcer of a mortal. On the day of his date with death, he was moved to a large, comfortable holding cell where he kept a two-hour silent vigil with his attorneys. Since he'd made no requests for a last meal, the prison served a cold pasta salad with leeks and sun-dried tomatoes. Theroux wouldn't touch it.

With four hours left before the execution, the clergy was summoned. Fifteen years earlier, the California high courts had demanded that the state provide a dying man his request for spiritual counsel. A noble idea that soon turned into an exercise in state-sanctioned prostitution. A killer could claim his religion was some obscure form of sexual paganism. Therefore, prisons were sometimes required to usher hookers in for an inmate's final spiritual counseling.

In recent years, the California legislature had done away with that idea. Therefore, in cases where clergy was not requested, the state provided a priest just in case. Theroux's legs and arms were shaved and a vein in each tapped as he was prepped for the needle. For propriety's sake, he was swaddled in an adult diaper, then chained to a chair while the assigned clergyman would offer the final goblet of redemption.

The priest entered the prison, robed, at peace, and prepared for a long walk to the death chamber. He'd identified himself to the escorting guards as Father Victor Guerrero of Elk Grove. His name was on the shortlist marked as: WITNESS TO THE EXECUTION.

Theroux spat, sounding as street as he did the day he stepped onto Hollywood Boulevard, "Don't want no priest to share my last bit of oxygen!"

The warden sounded only slightly understanding. "You can hear the prayer or not. Your choice, Dean. Just do us all a favor, be polite and wait till it's over."

" *'I neglect God and his Angels, for the noise of a fly, for the rattling of a coach, for the whining of a door!'* "

Unless the killer's quote had been from a memorable movie, the warden wouldn't have been very impressed. He gestured for the priest to enter. And as much as the name tag hanging from the priest's neck might have been stamped with the name of Father Victor Guerrero, Theroux looked up to recognize another man. An enemy.

The priest was Vance Allatore. Robed, rosaried, and ready to give absolution.

Theroux's pupils constricted as if he'd unblinkingly found himself staring into a blaze of light. His teeth bared in a semi-grin, semi-snarl. If allowed, he'd have leaped from his chair and buried his jaws in Vance Allatore's throat.

"Father?" cued the warden.

"He's no priest," said the killer. "He's an enemy of the state. He's here to kill me."

"Father, please?" pressed the warden. "Ignore him. Let's have the prayer."

As a serene Vance Allatore raised a hand to give the sign of the cross, Theroux began to rant in a mixture of languages. Greek, Latin, French, Spanish, Yiddish, Gaelic, Swahili. It spewed like vomit. All while the priest administered the special rite.

"The Lord, my God, has commanded me to offer you his hand. Your soul can be redeemed in the Father—"

" 'But he that hides a dark soul and foul thoughts. Benighted walks under the mid-day sun—' "

" 'Eternal rest give to them, O Lord; and let perpetual light shine upon them—"

" 'One short sleep past, we wake eternally, and Death shall be no more. Death, thou shalt die!' "

Over Theroux's protestations, the priest boomed the absolution in a commanding voice reminiscent of his infamous jury summations. " 'ENTER NOT INTO JUDGMENT WITH THY SERVANT O LORD; FOR, UNLESS THOU GRANT HIM FORGIVENESS—' "

Theroux whispered at Vance Allatore—if you could call it that. His lips moved to a hissing sound just before he worked his body sideways, strong to the left and tipping the chair, rocking it up onto two legs. And before a guard could close on him to right the chair, Theroux threw his weight to his right. The chair toppled. But Theroux hardly braced for the fall. Instead, he tucked his chin behind his shoulder and let the impact do the rest. His spinal cord severed and cut his motors in a micro-second.

The killer was dead. Not from a lethal injection. But by his own mortal doing. The state would have no satisfaction. Nor would the Corrections Department's approved witnesses. Death came to Theroux forty-one minutes early. The paramedics who were rushed to the scene could not revive a man who was due to die in under an hour.

Vance Allatore closed his black Mass book along with his eyes in a brief prayer. The warden kindly thanked the priest and showed him the door.

The following evening, CBS ran a prime-time, one-hour news special on the Sullivans' three-month ordeal. Mostly from Will's point of view, it was hardly investigative journalism. The producers liberally used most of Vanessa Curran's footage and dangled no unanswered questions in exchange for a tidy ending. Theroux's role was merely a footnote in the story of a young statesman's heroics in his dogged quest to rescue his beautiful and popular wife. The piece veered, ever-so-briefly, into the media's role in the spectacle, but overall, it came across as if the network had stuck to the high ground in its eternal belief in Will Sullivan.

The news special won the night, garnering a forty-four share of the TV-watching households.

Other stories followed. Networks, cable organizations, and radio chat shows, in some desperate need for redemption, continued to cover Will Sullivan. The nation couldn't seem to get enough of it. It sorely needed a hero and Will Sullivan was it.

12

August 15. Atlanta.

Daniel Vance Sullivan turned two months. His parents, Senator Will Sullivan and his wife, Gwen, celebrated the big day with a lemon tart from room service, two lit candles, and a Beanie Baby lion cub purchased from the Omni Hotel's gift shop.

"Is he sleeping?" asked Will, turning the last loop of a red tie and soothing the creases in a brand-new navy Brooks Brothers suit.

Gwen quietly closed the bedroom door and turned up the volume on the Fisher-Price monitor. She wore slippers, a heather chenille robe, circles under her eyes, and a smile only a new mother would understand. She crossed her fingers. "Pray he sleeps three hours."

"I can't believe you're not coming with me," said Will.

"You're lucky I'm in Atlanta," she said, then gestured to the hotel couch. "Anyway, I've got the best seat in America."

"If you're lucky, you'll sleep through it."

Gwen straightened Will's lapels and checked his hair. "Just remember to leave them wanting more of you," she reminded.

"Tell me I'm doing the right thing," he said, revealing a rare insecurity.

"It doesn't matter," she said. "No matter what the result, you've got me and Danny."

"That I do," said Will. "That I do."

They kissed and he left her to retire to the couch with the remote control and a carton of chocolate milk. She was nursing the baby in three-to-four-hour rotations, and still hadn't had a full night's sleep since the ordeal ended. Despite her schedule, she'd found time to hand off her last few campaigns to other consultants, take an official leave of absence from her Boston office, and put the Marblehead house and the bad memories that came with the property on the market. If Gwen was lucky, she'd fall asleep before Will made the short walk across the street to the convention center.

But first, Will had to put things right with the president. Outside the hotel suite, he was surgically swept into the arms of the Secret Service. Six escort agents, four men and two women, walked the still limping senator to the elevator and delivered him three stops upwards to an entire floor reserved for the president and his staff. On the way to the president's expansive suite, Will was chatted up by various campaign courtiers, speech doctors with notes, press liaisons, and communications personnel. He pressed fifty hands on his way to Del Addison. And when he'd finally been let into the president's quarters, he found himself strangely alone. A quiver of déjà vu crept through him.

"Read the speech?" blurted Addison, appearing from the bedroom and crossing the largely Baroque living room in lengthy strides. "I hope they told you it was okay to fiddle with it. Make it your own. I mean, we're not talkin' a total rewrite. Just a tweak or two to put it in your own words."

"It read just fine, sir," said Will, managing to keep his disrespect in check. He was, after all, addressing the leader of the free world.

"Well, that's just swell," said Addison, who'd stopped at the bar. Will could hear the ice in the tumblers, the splashing of liquor. Then the president turned, offering a double shot of golden bourbon on the rocks. "Care to join me in a toast?"

The prick, thought Will. Was it another test? Or just a schoolyard rat-fuck from the big bully? "I don't drink," was all Will said.

"That's right. I'm sorry," said the president. "Diet Coke's your stew. Fine. Got some in the little fridge back there. So where's my Gwen?"

My Gwen, asshole. My Gwen.

"Downstairs," said Will. "With the baby."

"And how's the little man doing?"

"He's doing fine, sir."

"Loosen up, William," said the president, loading himself into a big easy chair with feather pillows. "You look like you're on your way to see the hangman."

"I was wondering," said Will. "Am I?"

"Are you what?"

"On my way to the hangman?"

The president gave Will one of his patented stares. One of the same he'd reserved for out-of-line cabinet members or pushy denizens of the White House press corps. "I getcha. You wanna know if you're climbing aboard the *Titanic.*"

"It crossed my mind."

The attorney general and the FBI had turned a special prosecutor loose on White House involvement in Gavelgate, the scandal that wouldn't die.

"I shoulda fired those two lesbians when they tried to bury you and your missus," said the president. "But hell. You beat 'em. So will we. The two of us will kick their asses, both houses, the Supreme Court—even the *New York Fuckin' Times* if we want."

In the last month, the *New York Times* had taken on the White House and all its alleged abuses with an unrelenting vigor. Front page, every day.

"I've come to face the fact," said Will, carefully, "that maybe you like my numbers more than you like me."

Addison's approval ratings had hit a new low. Barely thirty-three percent. Where Will Sullivan's were astronomical. Over eighty. Nothing like a little public redemption to up a politician's profile.

Will retrieved a Diet Coke from the mini-fridge, barely

stopping to inspect the various liquors that just so happened to encircle the single can of Diet Coke. He found a seat opposite the president. The coffee table that was between them could've been a mile wide.

"Your *numbers,*" griped the president. "You know, Will, when I kicked you off the ticket last April, it was for good. At least, that's what I figured. Sure, it was politics. You were circling the drain. I had to cut you loose. For the sake of the party, for the sake of keeping in sync with Congress. Not to mention my presidency. If there's anybody who'd understand a practical, political choice, I'd expect it would be you, son."

Son? Will regretted the times he'd looked to Del Addison as a father figure. All the while he'd had his very own flesh-and-blood father who was loyal and loving till his untimely death. It made him boil. But he wouldn't dare show it. Not yet. That day would come.

"And I was willing to stick by my decision," continued Addison. "Until, of course, a couple of months back when everybody and his mother's brother practically threatened to impeach my Southern ass if I didn't put you on the ticket. Christ, son. I'm proud of you. You've got a nationwide constituency of true believers. I got polls that say you're more popular than Cheerios. Of course I had to have you back. But that's the game. You understand. I understand. This is the business we've chosen."

"It is," confirmed Will with a slight tone of malignancy. He popped the Coke can. It hissed back at him.

"And that's why you're here," said the president. "Because like your Uncle Del here, you know the smell of opportunity. And that's why you'll make a damn fine vice president. And after that, well, we both know how the story ends."

A knock at the door was followed by the entry of a White House communications officer. "Sorry, gentlemen. But it's time for the senator."

Will checked his watch. "It looks like I'm on. You'll be watching me?"

The president grinned meanly. "Wouldn't miss it for all the hooch in Panama."

Will rose and shook the hand of a man who wouldn't so much as stand to wish him luck.

* * *

The Georgia Dome in Atlanta was rocking, the delegates well-oiled with booze and hopes for four more years of party rule on the Hill. And though it was supposed to be President Addison's *Reinvention Convention,* it was, without a doubt, Will Sullivan's night. He was the featured speaker who, with his tacit acceptance of the number-two spot on the ticket, could focus the light of his newly minted star onto a dying party. The popular opinion was that Will Sullivan could personally save the presidency from a scandal-ridden slump.

But first, as a matter of procedure, Will had been chosen to take the dais and officially nominate Del Addison for a second term.

At 10 P.M., prime time from coast to coast, Will used a donated red, white, and blue cane to walk the final steps onto the red-, white-, and blue-striped stage. A brass band played from the pit below. And ten thousand screaming delegates rose in a standing ovation hardly seen at a Democratic National Convention since FDR was nominated for a third term. It lasted more than eight minutes. During which Will withdrew a step from the lectern and humbly accepted the tumult of blind acceptance. He was the phoenix. Ascended from a career in ashes to a position of ultimate respectability.

The timing of the ovation was perfect. Just long enough for a brilliant, La Roy-engineered assault on the fifty delegate leaders scattered throughout the arena. La Roy's minions, backed by a groundswell of antiadministration whispers, deployed with a military precision and a perfectly pitched message from the DNC leaders.

At the end of the stirring fanfare, Will stepped up to the microphone, ignored the TelePrompTer-cued speech waiting for him, and imagined himself in front of a roomful of recovering alcoholics. It was tent-revival time. And Will was prepared to shake up the souls of the faithful.

He began speaking with an unconscious ease about the events of the past year—his ordeal, the human lessons learned, the life which had been returned to him, and, of course, the new life which had been born to him. He made no allusion to the true nature of Gwen's abduction and the certainty of the last few months that their child was the bastard son of Wesley Dean Theroux.

In patching their life back together, Will and Gwen had left the tender subject unsaid and unresolved. But when Danny's blood was drawn for a precautionary lead test, curiosity had gotten the better of Will, and with Gwen's blessing, he'd discreetly asked for a paternity evaluation. As if the answer, however foul that it was certain to be, would bring some peace and closure to the war-torn couple.

The DNA test took every minute of five weeks—a tortured period of time which Will survived only by gifting the child with his heart and soul. And in return, the boy had given Will his very first smile. All gums. But genuine. Proving that the damned test mattered nary a lick in the long run.

But the results of the test were confounding and oh-so-ironic. With a five-billion-to-one chance of error, the lab verified that Will was indeed Danny's birth father.

Had the whole thing been some kind of twisted joke? Had Theroux been betrayed? Or was it an old-fashioned supernatural occurrence? Will had spent many a sleepless night tumbling over all the strange details, trying to make sense out of something that just never made any sense.

Gazing out over the vast Democratic assembly, Will regained focus and shifted tone, speaking gravely and candidly about the crippled presidency, Gavelgate, and the Department of Justice's investigations into the White House. From there he segued into more positive themes, spinning hope for the America in which his son, Daniel, would grow.

In the fifteen-minute speech, not once did Will mention Del Addison by name. Or the prospect of the vice presidency. Or so much as link himself to the presidential ticket. At the end, as an even greater fanfare followed, Will stood flush in the face of it, and reflected on the moment. Before him were ten thousand pairs of hands applauding *him.* Twenty million households watching on television. And for what? Surviving a killer's twisted plot to father a child through his wife? Sure, he'd rescued his wife and child from the clutches of evil. But wasn't Gwen the real hero? Still, his subconscious cried, why me?

Why did this happen to me?

And then as if Vance Allatore were standing next to him, he heard a whisper in his ear.

"Because bad things happen to good people."

Will nodded, said his good night, accepted the tumult of the ovation which followed, then abandoned the podium.

As was predicted an hour earlier by none other than Gary F. Modetti, the convention was about to be brokered for the first time in more than sixty years. Del Addison would fail to garner enough first-round votes to clinch the second-term nomination. On the second round of voting, Will Sullivan's name would be tossed into the hat by Congresswoman Lane Allejandro.

If only Will's father could've been there to see him come out the winner.

January. Port Magee, County Kerry, Ireland.

It was the forty-ninth straight day of rain. Despite the permanent drizzle, pubbers kicked the mud off their boots and bellied up to the seaside bar for their daily pints of Murphy's and Guinness. Amongst the woolly men was a single anomaly. A gray-suited stranger in a raincoat. He was thin, platinum-haired, and distinctly American. The pub-keeper kindly directed him to a corner booth where he waited for nearly three hours before his host finally arrived.

Father Vance Allatore appeared no different than the locals. Rubber boots, lamb's-wool vest, wax-coated rain jacket. A plaid cap covered the father's bald head.

"Vance Allatore," greeted the priest, seating himself across from the lawyer. "You must be Mr. Kellogg. Please forgive my tardiness. My daughter's visiting me and, well, we've had a lot of catching up to do."

After a polite five minutes of small talk about the weather, how green the country was, and the occasional Gaelic street sign, the lawyer got down to business.

"I heard a rumor that you were the last to speak with the man known as Wesley Dean Theroux."

"I was," said Allatore, waiting for the other shoe to hit the floor.

"I thought you might be of some help, then," said Kellogg. "You see, I'm the chief officer from the Farthmore Trust. Have you heard of it?"

Vance Allatore conveyed that he'd heard the Farthmore name connected with the heroic rescue of Gwen Sullivan and her child. But to the lawyer, he remained pretty mum. He revealed only a sketchy knowledge.

"After some rather painstaking investigation, it has come to our attention at the foundation—embarrassingly so—that Wesley Dean Theroux was merely a sad pseudonym for our own Drew Farthmore III. Mind you, none of us knew about his escapades or were more surprised than I. I was his father's last lawyer. All we knew was that Trip—that's what we called young Drew—was abroad. We sent his checks to an offshore account for tax purposes. He cashed them. That's how we knew he was alive . . ." Kellogg stopped himself. He was cold, nervous, and rambling.

"You have a question to ask me?" asked Vance Allatore.

"There's a substantial sum of money at stake here," said Kellogg. "We need to know if there was an heir. Any children Trip . . . Theroux might've fathered?"

The old prosecutor sat back in his seat, his eyes casting left and out the window toward the wafting diesel smoke of a passing tour bus. Oh, there was most likely an heir. A true child of Theroux's. Allatore had no proof beyond the chilling vision, repeated nightly for more than a week. The cure proved to be a pint of Guinness before bed.

"All of that, you know, 'family' are confirmed dead, yes?" asked Kellogg. "The last of them in the fire."

"All but one," said the priest. "Sheila. Last anybody could remember, she was acting as a nurse at a fertility clinic in Dallas. She disappeared. No one's seen her since."

In Allatore's repeating dream, Sheila was in a Mexico City hospital, nine months pregnant and laboring to give birth to the true child of the demon. As per Theroux's personal prophecy, he had been betrayed. But not by Marcus as he'd thought. The real Judas was Sheila. She'd saved Theroux's seed for her own purposes, impregnating herself before crossing the border. She would be mother and lover to the child, raising it in Dean's perfect image.

But was it just a dream? Or was God revealing something to him? Father Vance would need more information before he answered the call. Until then . . .

"I think you've come a long way for very little help," said Allatore.

"So his last words gave away nothing?" asked Kellogg.

"I didn't say that," said Allatore, who smiled smugly and ordered up a couple of pints. "Let's toast your foundation and the good works it will do with all the unclaimed money."

"I'm afraid the cash will remain in trust and earning interest until an heir comes to claim it."

"How much money are we talking about?" asked Allatore.

"One hundred and sixty million and growing."

Ouch, thought the priest. The good works that could be performed—

"I'm told you know the Sullivans," segued Kellogg.

"I'm acquainted with them," said Allatore.

"Remarkable," said Kellogg.

"They're good people," said Allatore.

"That's not what I meant," said Kellogg. "I was just thinking about the resemblance between the late Mrs. Farthmore, Trip's mother, and Mrs. Sullivan. Uncanny, really."

"Five billion faces on the planet," said Allatore. "Some should look alike."

Kellogg was shaking his head, as if making an excuse for Theroux's horrible reign. "The poor boy was barely six when he watched his mother die."

"It's over now."

"It is. Yes. Then as one American to another, let's have a toast."

Why not? Allatore agreed, holding forth his pint. Glasses clinked. "To President and Mrs. Sullivan."

"To the First Family," answered Kellogg. "I'm told they named their son after you."

"That so?" grinned the knowing priest. "That so?"